T0088019

BREATH
OF
GODS

BOOKS BY TINA LeCOUNT MYERS

The Legacy of the Heavens
The Song of All
Dreams of the Dark Sky

THE LEGACY OF THE HEAVENS
BOOK THREE

BREATH
OF
GODS

TINA LeCOUNT MYERS

Night Shade Books
New York

Copyright © 2020 by Tina LeCount Myers

All Rights Reserved. No part of this book may be reproduced in any manner without the express written consent of the publisher, except in the case of brief excerpts in critical reviews or articles. All inquiries should be addressed to Night Shade Books, 307 West 36th Street, 11th Floor, New York, NY 10018.

Night Shade books may be purchased in bulk at special discounts for sales promotion, corporate gifts, fund-raising, or educational purposes. Special editions can also be created to specifications. For details, contact the Special Sales Department, Night Shade Books, 307 West 36th Street, 11th Floor, New York, NY 10018 or info@skyhorsepublishing.com.

Night Shade Books® is a registered trademark of Skyhorse Publishing, Inc.®, a Delaware corporation.

Visit our website at www.nightshadebooks.com.

10 9 8 7 6 5 4 3 2 1

Library of Congress Cataloging-in-Publication Data is available on file.

HC ISBN: 978-1-949102-36-9
PB ISBN: 978-1-949102-35-2

Jacket/cover artwork by Jeff Chapman
Jacket/cover design by Shawn King and Mona Lin

Printed in the United States of America

For my father.

A cast of characters and three glossaries—one for English, one for Jápmemeahttun, and one for Southern Lands terms—and a map can be found in the back of this book.

We return to our Origin.
We return to begin anew.
One life to begin.
One life to change.
One life to end.

—Jápmemeahttun Song of Return

The last battle between humans and Immortals shattered the fragile peace of Davvieana. To the south, the human Olmmoš celebrated their victory. The Jápmemeahttun, called Immortals, defeated and decimated, lived on in the Northlands, veiled by the Song of All. Gifted by the gods with a life lived in two parts— the first as female and the second as male—the Jápmemeahttun had once restored harmony to their world when their numbers overwhelmed the land. After the war with the humans, the Immortals were left with more females than males. With their closed life-cycle, where one soul left the world as another gave birth, the Immortals would never again regain their numbers.

Dárja, the guide child of the legendary immortal hunter Irjan, had pledged to fight and die as an immortal warrior. She survived the last battle only to be taken prisoner by the humans. In the human prison, she encountered Marnej, Irjan's son. Raised by the Brethren of Hunters, Marnej had become an immortal hunter, like his father. But unlike Irjan, Marnej wanted to prove his loyalty to the Brethren. Marnej's curiosity about his father compelled him to seek out Dárja, the one person who could tell him the truth about Irjan. Lives shrouded in secrets and lies made Dárja and Marnej wary and resentful of each other. When the Brethren of Hunters paraded Dárja before the High Priest of the Order of Believers, a contest of wills between Believers and Hunters revealed that Dávgon, the Brethren leader, knew a dark secret: both Irjan and Marnej shared immortal blood with their human blood. Betrayed by his Brethren leader, Marnej freed Dárja, and together they fought their way out of the Stronghold of Believers to seek refuge within the Song of All.

Bávvál, High Priest of the Order of Believers, sought to consolidate power among the human Olmmoš by eliminating the Brethren of Hunters. Those Hunters not killed by his soldiers were imprisoned, including Dávgon, the leader of the Brethren. However, a small band of Brethren survived the betrayal and swore an oath to avenge themselves against the High Priest. Managing to keep one step ahead of the High Priest's soldiers, the leader of the remaining Hunters, Válde, was forced to contend with the morale of his beleaguered men, while facing a challenge to his power from within.

Tasked with bringing an end to the Brethren of Hunters, Niilán, once a common foot soldier, had been raised, against his will, to the rank of commander in the High Priest's personal regiment. Niilán harbored no ill will against the Brethren, but he followed orders to bolster the ranks of Believers in far-flung garrisons while searching for the elusive Hunters.

Dárja and Marnej remained at loggerheads as they continued their trek north. Fueled by jealousy over Irjan and stymied by injury, the age-old prejudice between humans and Immortals flared. Marnej had been raised to hate his father as a traitor to the Brethren of Hunters, yet he secretly yearned for Irjan's love. Dárja, raised by Irjan among the Immortals, resented his loyalty to his biological son.

Dárja and Marnej arrived in the immortal homeland to learn that Irjan had been killed in the battle. Dárja blamed herself, believing her last argument with Irjan prompted him to take up arms. Marnej, abandoned by Dárja and left to his own devices, struggled to find his place among the Immortals.

Although grateful for Dárja's return and accepting of Marnej's presence, the community of Immortals struggled with their own survival. There were no longer enough males to share the burden of work, nor would there ever be. The females had to balance the pressure to give birth with the fear that the Song of All could no longer protect them. Dárja, having at last found a friend and ally in Marnej, convinced him that they could protect the life bringers. Unsettled by his feelings for Dárja, Marnej reluctantly supported her plan, which could finally provide a role for them within the community and a path forward for the Immortals. With the cautious blessing of the Elders, Dárja and Marnej left with the life bringers, Okta and Úlla, carrying the last hope for the Immortals to give birth safely.

To the south, Niilán, along with what remained of his regiment of Believers, continued to track the Brethren, who had stolen horses, killed soldiers, and set fire to garrisons and temples. To avoid capture, the Brethren of Hunters split their forces, with the main group hiding above the Great Valley, while Válde rode south, drawing away the soldiers. Backtracking into the Great Valley, Válde came upon a mêlée, involving his men, soldiers, and two souls he never thought he would see again—Dárja and Marnej.

Grateful for Dárja's escort in the disorienting world outside the Song of All, the life bringer Úlla inadvertently revealed that Marnej had shared Dárja's long-held secret that she would never give birth. When reunited with Okta and Marnej at the birthplace, Dárja's rage erupted. However, chastened by Okta, Dárja's tirade ended with the arrival of soldiers in the Great Valley. Dárja left Úlla and Okta to continue the birthing, following Marnej out to confront the riders.

Dárja had little time to wonder why humans were battling each other before Marnej begged her to leave. She fought until a soldier plucked her out of the skirmish. Struggling to free herself, Dárja looked back to see Marnej fall upon the snow. Dárja and her would-be savior rode through the northern divide, where she escaped to hide out until the soldiers had passed. Making her way back to the valley, Dárja heard Úlla's scream, then watched from her hiding place as soldiers swarmed over Úlla and Okta's birthplace. With no weapon, there was nothing she could do. Dárja retreated back into the woods. Marnej had fallen and she had failed to protect Úlla. Dárja could never return to the homeland of the Immortals.

PROLOGUE

THERE IS NOTHING YOU or I can do for them," Okta said, holding Úlla back. The ancient healer gently guided the nieddaš deeper into the snow-laden trees. "What is important is you prepare for the birth and ready yourself for the changes to come."

Pointing to a gap in a dense thicket, he said, "Go. Hide now. Cover yourself and remain hidden. No matter what happens."

The nieddaš shook her head as if lost in a nightmare.

"You must do this, Úlla," said Okta. "The binna are tethered beyond those trees. When it is safe, ride to the Pohjola. Keep to the forests."

Úlla hesitated, her eyes pleading.

The ancient healer enveloped her in an embrace. "Go," he whispered. Releasing her, Okta felt a stab of pain and believed it was his heart breaking until it reached his core and he knew his end had come.

"Go," he said again, gasping.

Úlla drew her dagger, her teeth chattering as she disappeared into the thicket.

Okta offered a silent prayer to the gods. He unsheathed his blade, turning to face the snow-covered valley. A fresh wave of pain racked his weakened body. He sagged, leaning on his sword.

"Okta," Úlla called, her voice thin and wavering.

"Stay where you are, Úlla. Remember what I said."

The healer straightened. He looked out across the expanse. In the fading light of the short day, he could see the advancing soldiers. Before the last battle with the Olmmoš, he had tried to honor the possibility of peace between their two kinds. *At what cost?*

Okta threw off his furs. He would not need them when he was done. He regarded the miehkki in his gnarled hand. The heft of the blade and the familiar feel of its hilt reassured him. As a young warrior, they had been together through many battles and together had slain more Olmmoš than he cared to remember. Today, it seemed a few more lives would be cut short by its honed edge. He took an unsteady step forward, then another.

Standing out in the open, Okta greeted the first of the mounted soldiers with his blade ready. He parried a blow meant to cleave him in half. He staggered back into a soft snowbank, then recovered to slice through the soldier's leg as he made another pass. The satisfying scream of the Olmmoš rider suffused the ancient healer with the thrill of his warrior days so long ago. The first soldier gave way to another and another, until Okta's senses reeled with the sights and sounds of men and horses intent on killing him. His body burned with pain and fury.

From deep inside him, the voice of agony welled up. He fought against it as he swung his blade. He could not stop it, just as he could not stop the Olmmoš soldiers who overran him. Okta begged the gods for more time. The voice within his soul was too powerful to be ignored. It consumed his consciousness.

I return to my Origin to share my life force.
My life ends so that a new life begins and another transforms.
I leave as I entered, and the whole is unchanged.

The chorus exploded from him. The chant rose to meet the sky, to meet the waiting gods. Okta fell to his knees, his arms outstretched. Úlla's screams echoed in his last moment of awareness before he succumbed to the light within him.

Part One

ONE LIFE To BEGIN

CHAPTER ONE

WHATEVER THOUGHTS OF REWARD Niilán had entertained disappeared the moment he saw the half-naked Jápmea female and her bloody newborn huddled in the snow. He turned from her stricken face toward his beaming soldiers. Disgust welled within him. "I asked you to bring me the heads of the last of the Brethren of Hunters. Instead, you bring me a helpless female and her offspring!"

"Sir, she's one of them Jápmea—an Immortal," a soldier said, his accent thick and coarse.

Niilán turned his cold fury on the man. "I can see she is Jápmea. I also see that we are no closer to fulfilling the High Priest's orders. One Immortal will not save our hides from a painful end. If we do not bring back the heads of the remaining Brethren to the Vijns, our lives will be forfeit." Before any could protest, Niilán spoke decisively. "We will make camp here for the night and await the return of the others." The cowed and sullen men moved uneasily. Finally, they shuffled off, their mutterings low and unsettling.

Niilán looked to the fissured rock that marked the northernmost boundary of the Great Valley. Above the snow-topped granite ridge, the waning moon promised to shine upon a clear, cold night. Beyond, the remaining Brethren of Hunters had likely slipped out of his grasp. Frustration vied with apprehension as Niilán reviewed his actions. The thrill of the chase and the prospect of success had been as heady as a strong cup of juhka or a woman's lust-filled kiss. *I finally had a fresh trail to follow,* he thought bitterly. He had ridden the length of this valley as if chased by demons. His every sense had been intent on the backs of the mounted riders fleeing north. They had been within his reach. He had been sure they were the rogue Piijkij he had been tasked with hunting down. The fact that they dressed like soldiers had not swayed his conviction that these were the last of the Immortal Hunters, the last to challenge the power of the High Priest of the Order of Believers.

Staring northward, Niilán breathed in the cold. The air stung his lungs and cleared away false hopes. In hindsight, his decision to send his riders off to follow the fleeing Brethren had been ill-considered. He was sure those spurious soldiers were the men he sought. He also knew his men were no match for them. The best he could hope for was their safe return and a trail he might follow come daylight. Discouraged by an uncertain future, Niilán turned his attention to the snow-hushed valley. The last time he had been here, it had been a once-green field turned to mire by men and Jápmea, fighting and dying. While the battle seemed a lifetime ago, the moon had ridden across the sky for only six cycles. And yet his life had been changed more in that short time than in the preceding twenty-nine seasons of snow.

Once again, this valley proved to be the backdrop of death. Only this time it was not the Olmmoš fighting the Immortals. It was men cast against each other. Niilán believed he had seen the end of the fighting as an ordinary foot soldier and counted himself grateful to be alive. He had survived the last battle with the Immortals because of the skill of his Brethren commander. *They led us into battle, and then we turned on them,* he observed silently, regret foremost in his thoughts. Had these rogue Brethren simply been content to escape after their fortress had been sacked, they might have gone overlooked. But they had killed their own people, burned Believers' temples, and infiltrated the ranks of soldiers to further discord. *Their desire for revenge will be their end*, Niilán thought, wishing he had never been tasked with finding the last of the Piijkij. He had only ever had respect for them. But respect mattered little to a soldier following orders.

Niilán railed against the gods who had cursed him and then castigated himself for believing he could be more than a failed farmer and worthless handmate. His wife had not been sorry to see the back of him leave for war. His children had neither heart nor need for him either. How could they, when hunger shadowed them daily? With gratitude, Niilán understood that the battle had freed him from their recriminations. His wife had taken a new man. His children claimed a new father. And Niilán had finally found a trade in which he was skilled. So skilled, that he had come to the notice of the High Priest. He would have preferred to have stayed as another faceless soldier. The gods, it seemed, had other plans for him. They had singled him out for unwelcomed recognition.

A piteous howl called Niilán back from a past he could not change. The Immortal female cowered at the feet of one of his soldiers, shielding her babe from his rough tugging. She screamed something he did not understand, trying to pull away. He had enough burdens to bear without a Jápmea in their midst. An expedient end to this problem would be to kill the female and her infant. Niilán could even reason it would be a mercy. *Better to kill them than let my men use her cruelly*. An argument he knew he would never act upon. Despite his failings as a man, husband, and father, he could not kill a woman or her child. Nor did she deserve the violence of his men. *Too long away from home and too full of their undeserved arrogance*. Most of his soldiers were really just boys. Few had fought in the last battle against the Jápmea. Beneath the sheltering snow lay the bones of countless dead, human and Immortal alike. *What did they know of it?* Still these soldiers felt owed retribution for how the Jápmea had treated their mother's mother's mother.

"Give me the creature," demanded the bow-legged soldier, pulling on the yowling babe. "I will put an end to the spawn of your unnatural kind."

"Leave it!" Niilán ordered, stepping forward to yank the determined soldier away from their prisoners.

Under his commander's crushing grip, the young soldier relinquished his hold on the infant. Niilán pushed him toward the others, who stood watching. "Go make camp!" he growled, eyeing his men for further challenges to his authority.

"Osku," Nillán called to the one man he could trust to do what was asked of him.

He would have gladly traded half these boys for a couple more experienced ones like Osku—a man who knew what it was like to fight to see another day. The weathered soldier also understood that the true danger did not rest with the Immortals, rather with the High Priest. In the absence of the Jápmea and the Brethren, the Vijns's power had no limits.

He waved the man over. "Get my furs and cover her. Then dig her a snow-cave and stay with her."

Osku nodded, then headed to where the horses were tethered to forage.

Niilán regarded the Jápmea. She sat upon the snow, shivering. She held the infant to her chest, trying unsuccessfully to comfort it. Her golden hair lay plastered to her face. Even in the night's gloom, he felt her eyes watching him.

"You are safe," he said. He then wondered if the Jápmea understood him. He had never actually spoken to an Immortal. He'd only fought them on the battlefield. Fighting required no words, only a blade, and a fist.

"Can you understand me?" he asked, as much out of curiosity as a need to communicate with her.

She nodded, saying nothing.

At Osku's approach, Niilán turned away from her fixed stare. The seasoned soldier handed over the furs, keeping for himself the short, crude spade. Only when Osku set about digging a snow-cave did Niilán step toward the Jápmea. She shrank back. He raised his hand, then held open the furs. "I'm going to cover you."

She said nothing and watched him with shadowed eyes.

Niilán gently laid the furs on her broad, muscled shoulders, then stepped back. She grasped the ends around herself and the infant, her focus on him.

He put out his open hand to her. "I will help you stand."

She stayed hunkered on the snow, trembling. Niilán let his hand drop. His patience with her had reached its limit. "When Osku finishes, he will guard your shelter." He turned toward the snowy sweep of the valley floor and the dead who waited.

"I will ride out into the valley with some men," he said to Osku, adding to himself, "Perhaps fortune granted us a Hunter among those we lost."

~

Away from the shelter of trees and the heat of smoky fires, not even the reassuring sounds of men and horses could shake Niilán of a growing sense of foreboding. There was something in the air. He swore he could smell death, even though he knew the wind and the cold kept rot at bay. The dark shapes scattered upon the white snow seemed to shift before his eyes as if the dead were about to rise and accuse him for their end. He had not wanted to be a commander. Just as he had not wanted to cut off the heads of their own scouts, men he had once trailed behind as a foot soldier. He had assuaged this guilt by telling himself their scouts were already dead at the hands of the Brethren. It was his commander who had ordered their heads be passed off as those of the escaped Hunters. Niilán could have told the man the deception would end badly. It had. For all those involved. Now Niilán was the commander, promoted against his will. Charged with delivering the heads of the true Brethren, he could not escape the feeling he too had made a fatal error.

CHAPTER TWO

A PIERCING CRY TORE THROUGH the recesses of Marnej's mind. He awoke facedown in the snow. His head throbbed. His body was numb, as if he was made of ice and stone. He heard another scream. This time an image shattered the fog, imprisoning his thoughts. *Dárja.* Marnej coughed, choking on snow. His parched throat tried to sound out her name. Slowly he opened his frost-encrusted eyes. His vision swam, mixing with his memories. He struggled to move. The slow coursing of blood began to burn in his veins as he painstakingly bent his fingers to claw through the snow.

He recalled the soldiers riding down from the hills. There'd been too many of them for him to fight. There'd been others among them as well. Faces he'd recognized but couldn't recall. Marnej rolled onto his side. The effort took all his concentration. He felt something solid behind him, something that prevented him from shifting onto his back. The steam of his breath clouded his hazy view of his surroundings. He tried to concentrate on the pale shimmer of light in the dark sky. *The moon*, he thought, as if naming the parts of the world in which he found himself would help him to make sense of it. Faint voices reached him. *Okta?* Was the ancient healer in this world? Perhaps Úlla had not given birth. *No, no, no. That's not possible.* The sky had been light when he'd last seen them, when he'd ridden out into the valley to confront the riders—the Olmmoš soldiers. *How long have I been lying here?*

Marnej pushed himself up to sit. The pain in his head went from throbbing to pounding. He clutched his temples in his hands, taking in the shadowed shapes around him. Scattered bodies. Horse carcasses. The reindeer he'd been riding. The binna's forked antlers looked like a tiny, desolate tree upon the snowy plain.

Fear gripped Marnej's heart. What if Dárja were among these corpses? He'd been fighting next to her. He twisted to see what lay behind him. It was a dead Olmmoš soldier. Panicked, he scrambled toward the next closest body. Then he remembered that Dárja had been carried off. By a soldier. *No. Not a soldier.* It was Válde, dressed as a soldier. *Why was he dressed as a soldier?* Válde was a Piijkij, one of the Brethren of Hunters, like Marnej had been once.

Only Marnej was no longer a Piijkij. The Brethren had betrayed him. He'd escaped, with Dárja's help. She'd brought him to the Pohjola, where the other Immortals lived. Where his father had lived. But Irjan was gone. He'd died in the battle between the Olmmoš and the Immortals. Dárja was also gone. He'd tried to help her, tried to protect her. In the end, he'd failed her.

The sounds of horses and men shifted Marnej's interest to the dark contours on the eastern border of the valley. In the glow of smoky fires, men milled about where he'd last seen Okta and Úlla. *At their Origin.* This thought ripped the breath from him. *Gods! No!* he prayed, even as he knew what must have happened. He had left Okta and Úlla at their Origin. They were the life bringers. Okta's end time had come and Úlla was about to give birth. He'd promised to keep them safe as Okta ascended and his spirit stream passed into Úlla and the unborn baby. He'd honored the Jápmea ritual like the Immortal Elders demanded. At first, he hadn't understood why they needed to give birth away from the others. Later, he'd convinced himself he didn't need to know. It was enough to help Dárja protect Úlla, so she could return with her child to the Pohjola, to their kind. "Our kind," he whispered. Then a horrible realization washed over him. *The scream.* It had been Úlla. He was sure of it now, and he feared what it meant.

The pounding in Marnej's head grew louder. Before he could make further sense of what had come to pass, he became aware that the pounding came from somewhere other than his battered self. Mounted riders rode toward him. His anger surged. He longed to fight, to make right the injustices heaped upon him, the Immortals, and Dárja. He wrenched a sword from a dead soldier's frozen grip. He could barely hold the blade in his shaking hand. His strength had deserted him.

If I die here, I'll be of no help to anyone, he thought. Sick with defeat, Marnej used the last of his will to pull the two closest bodies on top of him. Their rigid weight crushed him into the snow's stinging chill. His breath caught, then released in short bursts. He made himself accept the feeling of death upon him. He heard the indistinct voices of men, then felt the snow shift as horses trod past him in a deliberate circle. Tensing, he prayed that men and beasts would lose interest in the dead. Then he heard the snow squeak as boots landed on its yielding surface.

"How are we supposed to know which are ours?" a low voice groused, close enough to where Marnej lay that he held his breath, convinced his beating heart would give him away.

"Sir, they are all wearing the yellow and brown of soldiers."

"Search them all to see if they carry any markers of a Piijkij," said a weary voice of authority. After a pause, the speaker added with the bite of annoyance, "A weapon. A talisman. Anything a Believers soldier would not carry."

Feet shuffled past Marnej's hidden body, then stopped.

"The dead don't need much," said someone so close to him he could smell the onion on the man's breath. A tremor ran through Marnej.

"When you are done searching the bodies, turn them on their stomachs," said the weary voice. "The ravens have already claimed these men's souls. They do not need their eyes."

The corpses on top of Marnej rolled away. He registered an onion-tinged grunt a moment before the stars suddenly came into view. He jumped up, startling the nearby soldier. The man fell back, hurling crude invectives into the night air.

Marnej didn't wait for him to stand for a fair fight. He raised his scavenged blade, intent on adding one more soldier to the dead in the valley. The sword slipped from his numb fingers, leaving him unarmed and facing a trio of soldiers. He briefly registered the shock on their faces, then turned to run, not wanting to know what they intended to do to a risen corpse.

"Run. Run. Run," Marnej hissed to his wobbly legs as they plunged deep into the snow. He ran like a man on the brink of falling forward, barely managing to stay upright. His lungs were near bursting with the effort it took to pump his arms and legs.

For the love of the gods! Why were the western hills so far away? They were like a horizon he would never reach. Only, in this case, he really might not live to see another day. If the soldiers caught him, there would be no mercy, no tomorrow. He would be dead upon the snow in this valley, like his father.

"You'll just have to wait," he shouted at the gods, then regretted his swagger when a wracking cough rose in his lungs. As he ran, he tried to dislodge the thick foulness blocking his throat. There was only a sustained wheeze. He hadn't the breath.

If I die, so be it, he thought, imagining his bones resting with those of his father. Perhaps then he would know the truth of the man.

While Marnej's steadfastness threatened to crumble, his body continued on, propelled by a will of its own. His eyes riveted on the trees ahead of him. *They were getting closer. Weren't they?* His vision blurred and for an instant he felt himself falling. The whole world around him seemed to be vibrating. *No. Humming,* some far-off part of his mind corrected. No sooner had he noticed this than every part of him resonated with the overlapping chorus of countless songs.

"Too many voices," he protested weakly before the interwoven refrains within him carried away further objections.

From a distant place, Marnej looked down upon himself. He knelt on the snow. A small part of him screamed to get up and keep running. Every other sound around him called for him to listen and add his voice to theirs.

My voice. It was a dreamlike thought that swelled to urgency. His voice cracked as he whispered, "I am the vessel of a father's soul."

Then he felt the very center of his being come alive and the words flowed from his heart.

I am the vessel of a father's soul.
I have journeyed into the realm of the dreams of the dark sky
And have traveled back in a blaze of light.
I enter into the world to meet my destiny,
Knowing that I have been touched by the gods.

When the last of his refrain entered the resplendent chorus around him, Marnej could no longer hold himself up. His forehead touched upon the snow. He waited for what would come next.

The mounted soldiers surged past him, their hooves churning the snow. Then they came to an abrupt halt. Voices cut the air with sharp rolling curses.

"Mother of demons! Where did he go?"

Marnej raised his head to meet the men encircling him.

"Eternal darkness, where he belongs." A soldier spat upon the ground.

Marnej saw the anger in their shadowed faces. There was also something fearful in their quick, shifting movements.

"He's here, hiding. A coward like all his kind!" said the rider, who passed by him.

Marnej lay back in the snow and laughed while the soldiers turned their horses in all directions. He had somehow left behind the world of men and entered the realm of the Immortals through the chorus of the Song of All. He was beyond the reach of these soldiers. They could be on the same terrain and never touch one another. He was like the wind now. Marnej let himself sink into the beauty of the songs, listening to the Immortals who lived far from here and wondering if it had been the will of the gods or some inexplicable aspect of the Song of All that had made it possible.

As a boy, these voices had been a comfort against a harsh life among the Brethren of Hunters. As a young man, Marnej had soon figured out the voices made him different. Wanting to fit in with the other Piijkij, he had shut his mind to their soothing presence. It had been a needless sacrifice because nothing Marnej did mattered. Not when he was the son of Irjan—the most skilled of the Piijkij and a traitor to the Brethren. He, however, was never gladder to have Irjan's Immortal blood flowing in his veins than at this precise moment.

Marnej slowly stood. He rested his hands on his knees. The mounted horses continued to snort and rear. He wondered if they saw him or could hear his song. He couldn't hear theirs. Dárja had said everything had a song. *Except for the Olmmoš*, he reminded himself. The Song of All was a gift from the gods to protect the Jápmemeahttun from the humans. Dárja had tried to explain things to him. She'd tried to help him live like an Immortal. And he had begun to make a life for himself among them.

The mounted rider closest to Marnej pulled hard on his reins. "We gain nothing by searching for the Jápmea. Our purpose is to find the Brethren." The soldier looked west once more, then turned to address his men. "Go back to the bodies. See if any are Piijkij."

With that command, they spurred their horses back the way they'd come. Marnej watched them retreat. On the valley's eastern edge, the fires burned. The sound of men, laughing and singing, caught the wind. Marnej stood frozen, chilled by wrongs he would never be able to right. Finally, he turned and reprised his journey west.

CHAPTER THREE

DÁRJA LONGED TO SINK to her knees in the snow. She wanted the cold to drain the life from her. Instead, her feet kept trudging on through the drifts. Her arms continued to push aside the branches in her way. In her way to what? To where? She didn't know. She looked up at the clear night sky, her eyes avoiding the North Star. It provided no guidance. It served only to remind her that she couldn't go home. Not after the promises she'd made to the Elders. To Kalek. Not when Marnej and Úlla lay dead upon the valley floor. The sound of Úlla's screams haunted her.

But it was the stillness, following the screams, that drove Dárja. Each step she took was out of an urgency to atone. She'd been so certain she could protect the nieddaš who traveled to their Origins. Now she wondered if her actions had been motivated by a desire to protect her friends. Or if this foray had been some grand gesture to prove that, though she would never give birth to become almai, she was Jápmemeahttun.

When she'd first learned that Irjan's attempt to save Marnej had robbed her of the life force she needed to mature, she'd been heartbroken. Irjan had been her biebmoeadni—her guide mother. He'd raised her among the Jápmemeahttun. And when she'd asked him, he'd trained her to fight like a Taistelijan. *No, not a warrior. A Piijkij—a Hunter.* When she'd finally confronted him, demanding the truth, his remorseful confession had confirmed her greatest fear. He'd always loved his son, Marnej, more than her.

The day she'd run away to fight in the battle against the Olmmoš, she'd resigned herself to her fate. She'd die upon the battlefield like a true warrior, and Irjan would suffer the loss. Dárja hadn't expected the gods would spare her. She'd been taken prisoner by the Olmmoš, then escaped, making it back to the Pohjola and to her kind. Her freedom, however, had not been the work of the gods. That had been Marnej. He was gone now. So was Irjan. And she was the one left to suffer their loss.

With plodding steps, Dárja began to cross the clearing ahead of her. Her feet were numb with cold. Her one boot was sodden from crossing a still-running stream. She heard the accusatory screech of an owl, coming from the trees ahead of her. In the treetops, branches rustled and shadows appeared to come alive for a moment. Then everything was quiet again. With each successive footfall, the silence grew more oppressive. A desperate need to seek out the Song of All arose within Dárja. She longed to hear the voices and feel the solace of being a part of something bigger than herself. But she didn't dare. She couldn't bear to hear the songs of Birtá, Tuá, Ravna, and Kalek. To stave off the tears that threatened to rise, she began to hum.

Step after step, the words came out of her in a halting mutter as if against her will.

Daughter of the gods.
Sister among the Jápmemeahttun.
You start your life at your Origin, with sadness and joy as your companions.
You braved dangers and met enemies and can see the truth of friendship.
Go into the world to meet your destiny, knowing that the stars watch over you.

Dárja was so engrossed in the measure of her song that she hardly noticed she once again wound her way through the trees. The branches buffeted her. She staggered first in one direction and then the other. She obsessed upon the falsehood inherent in her song. She was no longer a sister among her kind. The Elder had said she wasn't truly Jápmemeahttun. He'd said it in a way that told her he'd known this all along.

Dárja lurched to one side. Her arm pulled away from her body. Stumbling through sharp branches, she fell forward into the snow. A pressing weight landed upon her. Her first thought was she'd been attacked by a wolf, but she felt no teeth, no tearing of her skin. She struggled, kicking and screaming into the snow. She twisted around to see a body straddling her. A hand shot forward to cover her mouth.

"You are stomping around like a wounded bear," an Olmmoš voice hissed at her. "There are soldiers out there. Do you understand?"

Dárja shook her head, trying to clear her eyes from the snow.

"Be quiet, or you will get us killed." The man's whisper was more a snarl. His hand drew away from her mouth.

Dárja took a gasping breath. The shadowed face, hovering above her, came into focus. "I'm prepared to die," she scowled back at the Olmmoš soldier. He was the one who had pulled her out of the skirmish in the valley. She was about to comment that it seemed all he knew how to do was yank her about, then he brandished a knife. Its edge caught the moonlight, filtering down through the trees.

"I saved you once. Do not make me regret it."

"Why's an Olmmoš soldier hiding from his brothers-in-arms?"

"Why's a Jápmea saving the life of a Piijkij?"

"Marnej's not a Hunter."

The Olmmoš snorted. "No, he's one of you and no more fortunate for it." The man rolled off her. Awash in moonlight now, Dárja could see his large, wide-set Olmmoš eyes studying her.

His lips pressed into a grim line. His patchy beard did not conceal his disgust.

"Why did you pull me out of the fight?" she challenged, failing to find a reason for why an Olmmoš soldier would try to save her.

The man continued to stare at her. "You did not deserve to die out there," he said finally.

Dárja heard the judgment behind his words. Though she might never be a warrior in body, she was one in her soul, and no one could take that from her. "I am a Taistelijan. I fought in the battle. I killed as many of your kind as I could, just as I did today. I deserved to be there." She scrambled to her feet. Pushing against the Olmmoš, she lunged to free herself from the dense underbrush.

Unable to break her captor's grip, he pinned her to him. "Warrior among your kind or not, your bravery will be wasted if you die here because you were too proud to hear the truth."

Dárja's response was muffled by the man's hand clamped to her mouth. "Riders."

The Olmmoš dragged her down into a crouch. Dárja didn't resist. She had no weapon to defend herself if it came to a fight.

In the cold night air, the crack of snapping branches carried.

"He must've come this way," said a disgruntled voice.

"We're going to freeze, wandering around out here," complained another.

Through the gaps in the frozen thicket, the two riders came into view. Dárja's heart skipped a beat. If the soldiers continued on their current path, they would see her footfalls. Those tracks would lead the riders right to them.

"Gods be cursed," the man next to her muttered.

The foremost rider slowed. Leaning to one side of his saddle, he examined the area around him.

"Let's go back to where the tracks ended," suggested the soldier at the rear.

"I want to go just a little farther," said the lead, surveying the ground on the other side.

"I want to go back to the valley," said the soldier at the rear.

"And I want to be in my wife's bed. But I'm stuck here with you," grumbled the first.

The low grousing of his compatriot was cut short by the leader. "There! Footfalls."

He kicked his horse into a trot.

"It could be a trap," his friend warned.

The Olmmoš beside Dárja sprang up. "I am not waiting to see if they find their way here," he hissed, tugging her forward. Dárja dug in her heels.

He dropped her hand. "Stay here if you like. Be discovered by those two." He nodded his head in the direction of the approaching soldiers. "If you are as wise, you will not be so sow-headed that you turn down an opportunity to escape when it is offered."

He turned his back on her and began to wend his way through the opposite side of the snowy copse.

Dárja stood and took a few reluctant steps toward him. "Why are you willing to help me?"

"Because the enemy of my enemy is supposedly my friend," the man said, his whisper strained as he pushed his way forward.

"Who's your enemy?"

"You will have to follow me to find out."

Lacking a weapon to defend herself, Dárja followed, puzzled by this Olmmoš. Branches slapped her face and tore at her furs and breeches. Emerging from the thicket, she saw the Olmmoš had already untied a horse from its lead.

"Hurry," he encouraged. "Get on the horse!" He held his hand out to her.

From beyond the thicket, the voices of the soldiers accosted them.

"The tracks stop here."

"Wait for me."

Dárja took his hand. Using his bent knee, she vaulted onto the shaggy horse. The Olmmoš grabbed the saddle and pulled himself up. Dárja set the animal in motion. The Olmmoš pressed against her in the tight saddle. She couldn't move away without ending up on the horse's withers. She'd had enough of that when riding with Marnej. The thought of him, and what they'd gone through to escape north, made her breath catch. So often, she'd reminded him that without her he never would've escaped the treachery of his people. In truth, were it not for him, she never would've been reunited with those she loved.

"Give me the reins," the Olmmoš said into her ear, breaking through her sorrow.

Dárja felt the momentary pressure of his hands upon hers, then did as he asked. To steady herself, she gripped the front of the saddle. The man leaned in closer, pushing her up against the horse's neck. The beast's muscles rippled as the man urged it to go faster.

They broke through the thinning forest into a gallop. Dárja closed her eyes against the biting wind that brought tears. There were other reasons for those tears as well. She and Marnej had managed to overcome their mutual resentment. She'd finally let herself share her feelings for him, feelings that had made her unbearably weak and vulnerable. Dárja squeezed her eyes tight in a futile attempt to stop the images of Marnej from assailing her. His smile. The obstinate set of his chin. The way he reminded her of Irjan. The anguish in his eyes when she'd accused him of betraying her secret to Úlla.

Úlla had looked so sincere when she'd said she was sorry Dárja would never return to her Origin. Never give birth. Never go through transition. It had been maddening to hear sympathy from someone who had always despised her. In that moment, Dárja's rage had let her imagine Marnej, holding Úlla in his arms, sharing with her Dárja's darkest fear. The memory of her rage filled her with shame—a shame made more excruciating by the recollection of Marnej's last stand and Úlla's last scream.

The horse veered sharply under Dárja, bringing her back to the present. She managed to stay upright by virtue of the Olmmoš's encircling arms. Suddenly, his chest peeled away from her, and though she couldn't see him, she knew his gaze trailed behind them.

"You may have a chance to die today, after all," he said into her ear.

"I'm not afraid," she shouted, the wind tearing her words from her mouth.

An arrow sailed past them. Then another.

"How close are they?" Dárja called, her training winning out over the flutter of alarm.

"Close enough," the man grunted, snapping the reins again.

An arrow grazed Dárja's knee. Its sharpened point cut through fabric and into her skin. She grimaced. The horse veered again, and the man behind her was abruptly gone. Dárja fought against her instinct to look back. She gripped the horse harder with her legs. She leaned forward to grasp the dangling reins. As she sat up, the horse responded with a sharp, arcing turn back the way they'd come. Dárja bit back a curse, wishing she were on a binna, an animal she knew how to control.

Ahead, the Olmmoš who'd been riding with her staggered to his feet. He drew his blade. From the south, two mounted soldiers rode at him, one at full gallop, the other trailing with an arrow nocked to his bow. This was her moment to escape. She owed the man nothing. *I was ready to die fighting*, she told herself, watching the arrow fly wide of her into a snowdrift.

"Gods' curses," she swore, knowing she could not leave the Olmmoš to fight alone. She snapped the reins. Her only weapon was the speed of the beast beneath her. She kicked her mount's sides, urging the horse to run hard at the two mounted soldiers. "Ride with the wind," she said. "Ride with all your courage." The last part had been for her resolve. Dárja kept her eye on the soldier with the bow. He aimed for her Olmmoš. *Darkness take him!* Her fury exploded as a fearsome howl into the night.

Momentarily unsettled, the archer dropped his bow. Dárja rode directly at him. He sat stunned as if he didn't believe what he saw. Dárja launched herself at him. The two of them fell ass-over-head into the snow. The bow shattered as both bodies landed on it. Blind rage brought Dárja to her feet immediately. She kicked the soldier in the gut and then in the ribs. A frisson of icy pain shot through her frozen legs. Still she kept on kicking the downed soldier. The man, tangled in his quiver and bowstring, cried out, covering his head. Dárja saw the bone-handled niibi at his waist. She grabbed the knife and drove the blade through the Olmmoš's back with the surety of vengeance. Again and again.

Dárja jumped to her feet and spun in the direction of *her soldier*—because this was how she thought of him now. Her soldier fought the mounted rider with a practiced skill she recognized. She watched, bewildered why the humans were fighting amongst themselves. Less than a full turn of the heavens had passed since she'd been a prisoner of the Olmmoš. They had appeared united in their victory over the Jápmemeahttun. *The world can't have changed this much in such a short time*.

Dárja shook herself from her stupor in time to see the mounted soldier land a hit. Without thinking, she sprang into a run. The two Olmmoš blades clanged together like a tolling bell. The mounted soldier began to press his advantage. Dárja's anger gave way to strategy. She couldn't enter the fight with only a knife in her hand. Either of the men's swords could cut her in two before she could be effective.

Dárja stopped running. She planted herself and hurled the knife at the largest target—the horse. She despised the idea of hurting the beast who had no will in the matter, but it was the only practical option. Her throw went high, missing its mark and surprising the rider. Distracted, he overswung. Suddenly unbalanced, her Olmmoš easily pulled the soldier to the ground.

The two men grappled in the snow, grunting with the effort it took to move in their furs and leather armor. Dárja ran forward, then heard the crack of bone upon bone, followed by a sharp snap, and then the quiet of the forest returned. Her Olmmoš stared at her, his shoulders heaving. He slowly crumpled.

A hush as soft as falling snow enveloped Dárja. Her vision closed upon a single point. She swayed, feeling light enough to float away on the wind. Then a pounding in her chest pulled her back from the comforting darkness. Her mind reeled as she relived the last few moments. She looked back to where she'd left the corpse of the Olmmoš archer. She felt nothing. No anger. No regret. Then she turned to where her Olmmoš had fallen. The notion of him being hers seemed laughable, yet something compelled her forward, at first haltingly, then as fast as her spent body would let her go.

Reaching him, she knelt by his side. Blood oozed from more than one wound on his body and his nose was broken. If she left him here, he would die, if not from the wounds, then from the cold. She moved him onto his back, thinking she could pull him to the sheltering trees, then realized that in her exhausted state she might as well try to move a mountain as to move his limp body. She looked up, searching for the horse she'd abandoned, hoping it would be close at hand.

While their horse was nowhere in sight, the soldiers' horses stood together, head to head, as if they sought the reassurance of closeness. Dárja stood up on shaking legs. She slowly walked toward the animals, as much out of her need to preserve her strength as out of a desire to not startle the pair. Nearing, she held out her hand.

"Come. We are one," she murmured soothingly. "I'll give you my song if you give me yours."

One horse snorted and shook its mane. The other stepped back. Dárja cautiously leaned down to take hold of the closest reins.

"I've met your kind before," she said with a fondness for this animal that hadn't existed before her escape north with Marnej. Before that journey, she'd thought of these animals with a disdainful pity. To the Jápmemeahttun, horses had no will of their own. She knew better now. She'd learned these creatures had a generous and kind spirit.

Slowly she came close enough to the animal to brush its shaggy coat with her hand.

"The Olmmoš do not deserve you," she said, then added with heartfelt understanding, "I know of your longing to be with your herd and to run free."

A weak groan caught Dárja's attention. She glanced back. Her soldier had rolled to his side, his face half hidden in the snow. She hadn't asked for his help, and she hadn't asked for this fight.

Why do they always demand something of us? If not our death, then our aid.

CHAPTER FOUR

ÚLLA AWOKE TO A talon-like grip upon her ankle. She screamed, clutching her baby to her. She pushed against the frozen wall of her snowy cave and kicked at the hand that held her. The baby began to wail.

"Come away," said an Olmmoš voice from behind the grotesque face filling Úlla's vision. "Come, take your drink and place by the fire."

The grasping hand released her, and the leering smile widened. Úlla peered out through the opening to the shelter. The squat Olmmoš who guarded her nudged the ugly man toward the fire. He muttered something low and coarse. The men by the fire yowled like wolves, laughing. Úlla shushed her baby, her pulse slowing, even as her anger rose. She gathered her furs and scooted farther back into the cave. She could not stand to see the shadowed outlines of the thick-limbed Olmmoš who lusted after the blood of her kind. They had already taken her beloved Kálle in the last battle, and today they had killed Marnej, Dárja, and Okta.

Úlla tried to remake the horror of this day into an image of what it ought to have been. She had been happy to reach her Origin and relieved to be in the company of Dárja, Marnej, and Okta. Then Marnej had ridden out into the valley. She had seen the advancing riders but had not fully understood what it meant until Dárja had ridden out after him with her sword in hand.

Úlla had watched helplessly as the soldiers overran them. She had tried to follow Marnej and Dárja, wanting to pull the Olmmoš from their saddles and claw their faces so not even the gods would recognize them in death. Okta had stopped her. He made her go and hide in the thicket beyond their clearing. Like a frightened rabbit, she had remained hidden, helpless as she watched Okta raise his sword to fight the onslaught of Olmmoš soldiers. At the first clash of metal, she had closed her eyes against the violence. She could not, however, protect herself from the sounds of men shouting and cursing. Then, above it all, came Okta's clear and resonant voice.

I return to my Origin to share my life force.
My life ends so that a new life begins and another transforms.
I leave as I entered and the whole is unchanged.

Úlla's body had spasmed. The birthing came so swiftly she'd had barely enough time to shed her breeches before the child pushed through her in a bloody mass. The memory of her revulsion disgraced her now. She'd had to fight through her reluctance to release the babe from its still-pulsing sac. She had just cut the gods' cord with her teeth when rough hands had dragged her from her hiding spot. The recollection brought a fresh rush of blood to her ears, momentarily muffling the baby's cries.

"You are both safe," said a voice at the opening to her shelter.

Startled, Úlla reflexively pulled her legs in, cradling the crying baby to her. She squeezed her eyes shut and whispered promises and prayers. The infant's cries grew into a wail.

"Quiet her," said her Olmmoš guard, adding in a softer tone, "It's best they forget you are here."

Úlla opened her furs, awkwardly shifting the little one to her breast. The tiny searching mouth latched on. The pull of her suckling was at once powerful and heartbreaking. Úlla released a shuddering breath that shook the weak flame of a tallow candle.

She stared at her baby's face. In its shadowed contours, she saw the reflection of Kálle. *She has his willful chin and his dark hair.* Úlla brushed back the baby's dark downy strands, feeling grief's tendrils coil around her.

Tears blurred her vision. She began to rock back and forth. It was more an act of mourning than an effort to comfort the hungry babe. Part of her wished to die, to join Kálle in the gods' embrace. Another part knew she had to survive, if not for herself then for her baby—Márgu. She had to bring her child back to the Pohjola. Back to her kind.

When Úlla's milk dried up at the end of the next moon cycle, she would sing the child's birth song and give her to her bieb-moeadni. Márgu's guide mother would raise her, leaving Úlla to become an almai. The lifecycle of the Jápmemeahttun would continue in balance, the way it had been since the beginning of remembered time: one soul to leave the world, one soul to enter the world, and one body to transform from nieddaš to almai.

Úlla looked down at the tiny life clinging to her swollen breasts. She had believed Marnej when he had said he and Dárja would see her and the baby back to their kind in the Northlands. He had promised her. He had died trying; the dead could not be expected to keep their word.

The sound of horses halted Úlla's rocking. She peered through the opening of the snow-cave. The Olmmoš who had put the furs around her handed the reins of his horse to the one who had stood guard on her. He spoke words she could not hear, then nodded in the direction of her shelter. Finally, he turned to face those sitting by the fire.

Úlla released the breath she had been holding. She lay down, nestling the sleeping baby in the crease between her breasts. She took comfort from Márgu's warm body against hers. Wrapped in the furs, with the crown of Márgu's dark, downy head peeking out, Úlla closed her eyes, searching within herself for the Song of All. *Please*, she begged. To push back against the wretched silence of the Olmmoš world, Úlla began to softly sing the song gifted to Márgu by the gods.

> *Child of love, born in peril,*
> *You shall see the dawn of light.*
> *You shoulder the burden of journeys,*
> *but will walk as kin among many.*
> *The stars light the way beyond what any have known.*

Úlla fell asleep with the song echoing in her mind. She dreamed she was back at the forge. She felt the new strength of her body as it began to change. When called to the Chamber of Passings, she sat within the Song of All, listening to hear her new song. She saw the Council of Elders gather around her. The Noaidi held out his hand.

> *"Name yourself," he said.*
> *Without hesitation, she said, "Gunnár."*
> *"Share your song, Gunnár, and join the almai," the ancient Elder said.*
> *Son among the Jápmemeahttun.*
> *Master of the Forge.*
> *My hammer beats within the heart of us all.*
> *My fire burns away all but truth.*
> *I honor the fallen by taking their place.*

~

Niilán sat alone, warming himself by a smoldering fire, listening to his men snore. He did not know what to do with the Jápmea female and her infant. He had no desire to cart her around with his regiment. He also did not want to send them back to the High Priest in the escort of his men. Osku could be trusted. The others had proved they could not be. They would kill the infant and abuse her, if only for the novelty of it.

A sound behind him brought Niilán to his feet. He cast his fur cloak to the ground. His hand was already on the hilt of his sword when he realized it was the Jápmea female, crawling out of her shelter.

She saw him and tucked herself back into the snowy cocoon Osku had made her. Niilán eased his grip on his weapon, replacing it in its scabbard. He waved at her to come out. He sat down near the fire, watching to see if she would reappear. After a while, he saw the flash of her pale hair in the mouth of the shelter. He gestured to her. She gradually emerged, her gaze going in all directions. Niilán beckoned again. She stood but did not move forward.

She had clothed herself in the bloodstained uniform he had given her. In response to his frank appraisal, she glanced down to see what he was staring at, then she tightened the furs around her so only her boots showed.

"It's not me you should worry about," Niilán said, the tension of the night rippling across the surface of his emotions.

Her expression clouded. She shifted uneasily. Her head turned to see in all directions.

"I am sorry," Niilán said. "You are safe to come out. No one will harm you. Come." He encouraged. "Come sit by the fire. Are you hungry?"

She came forward slowly, then crouched within the firelight just out of his reach.

"Are you hungry?" he repeated.

She nodded.

He handed her a piece of dried reindeer meat. She took it and began to chew with watchful enthusiasm.

Niilán finished his piece of reindeer meat, then took a drink of warm water from his wooden bowl. Her green eyes caught the firelight as they flicked with interest to the bowl he held to his lips. He took another drink, then held the bowl out to her. She kept her eyes on him as she took it. She sniffed first before taking a swallow, then handed the bowl back to him to once again chew the tough, salted meat.

Niilán filled the iron pot on the fire with fresh snow, observing the Jápmea out of the corner of his eye. She had braided her honey-colored hair. The long braid had slipped forward to drape down the front of her furs. She had a full mouth and, given how she tore at the meat, strong teeth. Her wide shoulders and capable hands were at odds with her female form as if her beauty hid a dark force behind it.

"What do I call you?" he asked.

She stopped chewing. The pop and sizzle of the fire punctuated the void that grew between them.

"I am named Úlla," she said, the tenor of her voice proud.

When it was clear she would add no more, Niilán asked, "And your child?"

Úlla's head snapped back toward the shelter, then, seeming to be reassured, she said, "The gods have named her Márgu."

She edged closer to the fire beyond his reach. "Might you have more?"

It took Niilán a moment to understand her formal phrasing. He reached into his satchel and pulled out another piece of dried meat. Leaning forward, he handed it to her. She took it, this time with a slight nod of her head.

"What are you doing here?" he wondered aloud.

"I came to birth," she said matter-of-factly, before tearing off a piece of the meat with her teeth.

"Here?"

She nodded, chewing.

"Where is your handmate?"

Her brows furrowed.

"Your man," he said.

Her eyes widened. "He is gone," she said, her food forgotten.

"He left you alone?"

She shook her head. The firelight caught the shimmer of tears. "Okta was with me until the end. He fought to protect me, but he could do nothing when the gods called him. I was not left alone." The Jápmea's voice cracked. "Your kind did that." She began to cry.

Niilán looked around the encampment, relieved to see her outburst had not woken his men. "Be quiet. I know you grieve. If you anger my men by waking them, I will not stand in your favor. I have said you are safe."

She hiccupped, then glared at him as tears streamed down her face.

"Our purpose is not to kill Jápmea," Niilán said. "Enough of that has already happened."

She bared her teeth at him.

"Believe what you will," he said. "You pose a problem. My men see you as a prize. I see you as a burden. I don't want to bring you with us, and you don't want me to send you back to our High Priest with my men." His hard stare conveyed his meaning.

Her mouth quivered with anger. "Then let me go," she said. Her swollen eyes flashed in defiance.

Niilán regarded her. Her earlier beauty had vanished to reveal the darkness he had sensed. She pulsed with hatred. If she were armed, he had no doubt she would have skewered him.

"Why don't you disappear? Your kind is supposed to just. . . . vanish," he said, his irritation growing.

"Give me one of your beasts and I will," she said.

The possibility of a solution cooled his ire.

"Can you ride?" he asked.

"Of course," she said.

He overlooked her caustic tone. "I mean, are you well enough to ride?"

She nodded.

Niilán looked up to take the position of the stars, then dropped his gaze to meet her hooded eyes. "Prepare your child because I will be rid of you both tonight."

"You will let me go?" she asked. Mistrust lingered in her voice.

"I no more want you here than you wish to be here," he said. "What do you need to make it back to your kind? I will get you what I can."

She sat up straight. "I need food and more furs to keep us warm." She considered the matter further. "And tinder. An axe or sturdy blade."

Niilán watched hope and doubt take turns shaping her expressions. "I will gather what I can and meet you there." He pointed to an outlying stand of trees.

The Jápmea needed no more encouragement. She rose to her feet and retreated to her shelter.

Niilán stood, hoping this plan would work. He walked to where they had tethered the horses. He untied the closest, aware of the sounds around him. The animal proved to be quiet and yielding as he led it toward the stand of trees. Niilán tucked his supply of dried meat into the saddlebag. He added his water bladder, short axe, and tinder pouch.

The Jápmea emerged from her shelter, clutching the infant to her chest. She cast a wary sideways glance toward the rest of the camp, then scurried across the snow to reach Niilán and the waiting mount. In the moon's pale, slanting light, he thought he saw both fear and relief in her eyes when she took the reins from him.

Niilán laced his hands together, then boosted her onto the saddle. Once situated, she looked down at him. He was momentarily overcome by the realization that never in his life had he been this close to an Immortal and wished them to live.

"Ride hard. Do not look back," he said. "My men will not follow you, but I cannot guarantee others will not."

She nodded once, then tightened the slack in the reins. The horse huffed as she spoke. Niilán could not understand what she said. Perhaps it was thanks or perhaps a curse. As he watched her ride away, he was not sure what he deserved more.

CHAPTER FIVE

MARNEJ DUG AT THE snow until his hands were numb to the burning cold. He climbed down into the shallow depression he had carved beneath the spread of pine branches. The cleared area closest to the tree's trunk granted some shelter. Shivering, he thought longingly of the tinder pouch safe and dry within his furs. What he would give to make a fire.

The effort it took to pull his arms inside his furs left Marnej exhausted. He wedged his hands into his armpits, hoping the meager warmth of his body would stave off frostbite. He curled into a tight ball, tucking his chin so his breath warmed his flesh and not the infinite cold around him.

With each exhalation, Marnej heard the ragged sounds of regret. He squeezed his eyes shut. *There had to have been another way*. He should've argued with the Elders. He should've convinced Dárja not to go. They were all so blind, so unrelenting. All the Elders cared about was preserving their Immortal traditions. Even though there were so few Immortals left, the Elders insisted the life bringers had to travel to their Origin to give birth. And Dárja. She just had to prove herself. *So stubborn*. A vision of her as they had fought alongside one another rose clear and terrible before his eyes. The dark wisps of her hair whipped in the wind. Her face flushed with anger and the desire to meet death.

"I'm not a coward," she'd cried out.

Marnej's throat tightened. He'd begged her to run, begged her to leave. Then Válde had reached down to pull her up out of the skirmish. *What were the Brethren of Hunters doing there? Dressed as soldiers while fighting other soldiers?* Had the world of men gone mad in his short absence? Despite their soldiers' uniforms, Marnej had recognized Gáral and Válde immediately. When last he'd seen his fellow Brethren, he'd been leaving with the Avr's retinue to present their Jápmea prisoner to the High Priest. That prisoner had been Dárja, captured on the battlefield when the Olmmoš finally conquered the Immortals.

Even as a prisoner, Dárja had been unbowed by defeat. Marnej had both resented and admired her for it. But it had been her connection to his father that had seized his imagination. While Marnej had been abandoned by Irjan among the Brethren of Hunters, Dárja had been raised by him when Irjan chose to align himself with the Immortals against his own people. His whole life, Marnej had believed his father was a traitor: first to the Brethren, whose ranks he had deserted, and then to the Olmmoš for siding with their sworn enemy.

In reality, the true treachery rested with the Brethren. Their leader, the Avr, had known all along that both Irjan and Marnej shared Immortal blood. He had used them both. His father'd had the courage to walk away. Marnej, on the other hand, had done everything to win the Avr's favor—to prove he was loyal. Had Dárja not spurred him to action, he'd be standing in the great hall of the Order of Believers, stunned by the Avr's duplicity or, more likely, imprisoned in a Believers's cell.

"Run," she'd yelled at him, and he'd responded.

Together they'd fought their way out of the Believers' Stronghold. Together they'd managed to make it back to her kind. Or rather, their kind.

She's gone now. Taken by the Piijkij. She hadn't swatted away Válde's arm nor had she fought his grasp. He couldn't blame her. He knew what betrayal felt like and he'd betrayed Dárja. He'd shared her deepest secret, and she'd discovered his carelessness. There'd been no time to explain that he hadn't meant to tell Úlla. Frustration and a desire to defend Dárja had made him reckless. The rage in Dárja's eyes as she'd called him a liar had been like looking into a violent storm and fearing there would be no end. Then he'd seen riders in the valley, the yellow and brown of their uniforms against the white backdrop.

He'd ridden out into the open, remembering the last time he'd charged into the Great Valley. Then, he had wanted to kill every last Immortal who stood before him to prove himself worthy as a Piijkij. Today, he rode out fearing he'd lost whatever tenuous right he'd had to live as an Immortal. He'd be lying if he said he'd found welcome among them. He was at best a quarterling and a man trained to hunt and kill Immortals—a Piijkij, like his father before him. Irjan, despite his past, had proved deserving of his place among the Jápmemeahttun. He'd sacrificed his life upon the battlefield to defend the future of the Immortals.

What had Marnej done? *Nothing*, he thought bitterly. He'd tried to adapt to the strange ways and customs of the Immortals. He'd taken a place at the forge as an act of service to the group, suffering Úlla's badgering as she oversaw his work. He'd only just gained her grudging acceptance, wresting a promise to train him as an apprentice when she returned from her Origin.

How could he face the other nieddaš who'd called Dárja and Úlla their friend and their sister? Ello, who had laughed and teased. Tuá, who had trusted him with her knives. Or sweet Birtá, who saved food for him when Úlla made him work late into the night chopping wood for the furnace. Even her warm heart would turn cold to him were she to know of his failure.

And what would Kalek think of him?

"Irjan would be proud of you," he'd said at their parting. "You have his best qualities."

If we had succeeded . . . Marnej thought. It might have been different. But they'd failed.

A scream cut through his jumbled thoughts.

"Úlla." He breathed her name, his gut cold with remorse.

The raucous laughter of men rolled like thunder across the valley.

I have to go to her. She is alive, he told himself. For how long, he didn't dare guess. The Olmmoš soldiers would not let her live. One more dead Jápmea would be a testament to the Olmmoš victory over evil—a triumph for the once-oppressed. That's what he'd thought the day of the Great Battle, before he'd learned the truth, before he'd lived among the Immortals.

Marnej twitched. He had to get up. He had to help Úlla. He could retrieve the sword he'd dropped, or take another. If he stayed hidden in the Song, then he could sneak up on the soldiers, like in the old stories of the Immortal raiders. If he could get to Úlla, she could find the Song again. She could disappear as he'd done. If not, then at least he'd send a few more soldiers beyond the dark sky.

Marnej would never be as skilled a fighter as his father nor as faithful to those he loved. His one consolation was that he could die trying. This notion gave him a strange sense of peace. He'd spent his whole youth trying to be nothing like Irjan. Now, he could think of nothing more fitting than following his father's example. Marnej pushed against the furs protecting him. The effort emptied him of everything except purpose. *Get up*, he goaded, feeling the prick of cold on his exposed skin. A deeper voice within him said, *Just rest a moment. Then get up*. Marnej began to argue against it but it was getting harder to remember, harder to keep his eyes open. *Just a moment. Then I'll get up*, he promised.

～

Sitting opposite Ávrá in the healers' quarters, Kalek breathed in the reassuring scent of her vitality. She blazed with life, while he floundered in an abyss of dark days. Suddenly self-conscious, he looked up from the flames to meet Ávrá's intent gaze. With her hair the color of harvest rye and her frank manner, Ávrá was different from his first heart-pledge, Aillun, who, with her dark hair and eyes, had always reminded him of the night sky. In her last moments, before leaving for her Origin, Aillun had been a wild storm of emotion. At the time, Kalek had allowed his anger to cloud his judgment. *If only she had told me sooner, it could have been different*, he thought, repeating a time-worn excuse.

Kalek reached out and touched Ávrá's flushed cheek. The gesture signaled both a healer's concern her fever had returned, and the hesitant affection of someone who had not expected to find love again. *Not after Aillun and Irjan.*

"Dárja will return," Ávrá said, giving him a tentative smile. The mention of Dárja's name caused his breath to catch. He had been holding her absence at bay. He had not been able to stop Dárja from escorting Úlla to her Origin, just as he had not been able to stop Irjan from fighting in the last battle with the Olmmoš. Part of Kalek had died the day he found Irjan's broken and bloody body upon the battlefield. He could not imagine the same fate for Dárja and hope to survive.

When Dárja had returned to them after the battle, he had thanked the gods for sparing her. He should have known it would not be enough for her to be welcomed home or to become a healer under his guidance. She was Irjan's guide child. Irjan had raised her. He had taught her to fight. And she had made herself into a warrior. *She is also my daughter*, Kalek thought.

Even now, the Olmmoš word felt foreign to him. He had lived with Irjan and had loved him long enough to learn what it meant to be a father to an Olmmoš—the unconditional love, the willingness to sacrifice, the fear silently borne. When Kalek had embraced Dárja the last time, he had called himself her father and told her he loved her no less than Irjan. He had heard her promise to return and, in that moment, his heart broke. It was not a promise she could keep, and he could not stop her from going. Once again, Kalek had been powerless to protect those he loved. And once more, the depth of his love had not proved powerful enough to be honored.

Ávrá cleared her throat. Kalek came back to himself, painfully aware he despaired for love while Ávrá sat before him extending to him her heart.

"Perhaps if you gave more of your effort to healing, you will find some for yourself," she said.

The truth of her observation stung and Kalek could tell by the set of her jaw she meant to continue.

"I know that you fear for Dárja and Marnej and Úlla. But I believe Okta's absence is the greater heartache. It is something which cannot be changed." The tenderness in her eyes softened this harsh reality.

"They are all gone," Kalek said. "So many in battle." *Almai. Taistelijan. Irjan.* Piled one upon the other in the green field. All dead. "Now Okta." He shook his head, unable to express his sadness and unwilling to face his new responsibilities.

Ávrá took his hands in her slender ones. "You are needed. It is time for you to take Okta's place."

Kalek winced, hearing in Ávrá's gentle exhortation the echo of the Noaidi's counsel.

The Elder had been far less tractable when he said, "You must take Okta's place, regardless if Dárja returns or not."

"To what end?" Kalek asked of both Ávrá and the absent Elder.

Their numbers were so few and the Jápmemeahttun lifecycle so ordered that there would never be more. *The death of one. The birth of one. The life of one as All.* Dárja and Marnej had ridden out with the life bringers, believing they could protect them, believing they could make a difference.

"To what end?" Kalek asked.

Ávrá squeezed his hands, her strength surprising. "Our lives continue, such as they are."

Kalek took in Ávrá's expectant expression. In his heart, he knew she was owed reassurance. As a nieddaš, she faced the greatest danger. He had already traveled to his Origin to give birth. He had already been an almai long enough to see Guovassonásti, their Life Star, rise and set three times. *More than thirty seasons of snow.* He need never go Outside. He need never leave the safety of the Pohjola. But Ávrá would. Like Aillun before her. Like all the nieddaš who remained. As their kind had done since the gods had given them the first oktoeadni.

"You risk so much," Kalek said, profoundly aware of what their growing connection meant for Ávrá, and incapable of denying himself the comfort she gave.

CHAPTER SIX

NIILÁN STOOD BY THE glowing embers of his soldiers' celebratory fire. He glanced up at the Bear Star. The moon had set behind the eastern ridge. Dawn was still a long way off. The scouts, chasing the fleeing Piijkij, had not returned. A desolate certainty his men had become victims vied with a tenuous hope the gods would take his side and lead his men back to him. Short of this, Niilán wanted enough light to ride out and find tracks before they were lost.

He looked to the east, impatient for daylight. He thought of the Jápmea female. He hoped she had sense enough to get as far away as possible. In the next days, were they to come upon her in their travels, he would not be able to spare her again. His men would not stand for it, and he could not fault them for wanting some reward for their efforts. They had been repeatedly thwarted in capturing the last of the Piijkij. Yesterday's mêlée had been the closest they had come to success. Even so, the remaining Brethren had managed to elude them. The Jápmea female would have at least garnered some favor with the Vijns.

Near the sheltering trees, Niilán heard his men stirring, shaking the cold from their bones. He made out Osku's stout shape, striding toward him.

"She's gone," he said. His clipped voice betrayed no emotion.

"Yes," Niilán said, stepping back from the fire's drifting smoke. "I checked on her earlier and discovered she had disappeared."

Osku's frown suggested he understood what was not said.

Niilán erred on the side of caution. "I kept watch. She did not emerge."

"The men will be disappointed," Osku said matter-of-factly.

"Yes," Niilán agreed. Before he could continue, one of the men cried out.

"Riders from the north!"

Niilán and Osku drew their blades. The others scrambled to readiness. With weapons drawn, the soldiers closed ranks, awaiting attack. Niilán peered into the dark landscape, taut with tension, unsure of what he hoped for more: the homecoming of his scouts or the Brethren's return so they might bring an end to this damnable commission.

"It's our scouts," a voice called from the front of their small group.

"Can you be sure?" Niilán demanded, vividly recalling yesterday's subterfuge.

"They wear our colors, sir," the voice called back. "I think."

"Stand ready," Niilán ordered, tightening his grip on his sword.

"Hail the gods' chosen soldiers," a voice among the riders cried out, strong and cheerful.

The men lowered their weapons.

"Stand ready, I said," Niilán boomed.

The men tightened rank again.

"State your regiment," Niilán yelled.

"The Vijns's personal," the rider shouted back.

Another rider added, "We bring Piijkij heads."

A roar of excitement swept through the rank and file. Niilán stepped out of formation to greet the returning men. He counted six riders and seven horses. The last looked to have something slumped over the saddle.

Niilán strode forward. He felt the eagerness of his men behind him, and their desire for blood. The riders halted. The first to dismount addressed him formally. "Sir, we bring back two of the Piijkij." He presented a snaggle-toothed grin.

Niilán clapped the man on the back, making his way to the horse with two corpses draped across it. He lifted one head by its hair. Lifeless eyes stared out of the bloody, bearded face. He let the head fall back down, lifting the other. He recognized neither man. Then again, he hardly expected to.

"Osku," he called.

The man appeared at his side, eyeing the dead.

"Ours or theirs?" Niilán asked under his breath, unsure if, once again, Believers' soldiers had been passed off as Piijkij to gain reward.

Osku looked the two bodies over, then returned to Niilán's side. "Not ours," he said.

Niilán addressed the lead scout. "And the others?"

"We don't know," the soldier answered. The wariness in his eyes belied his calm expression. Perhaps the man believed he would be blamed for not capturing all the Piijkij. While Niilán disliked the heavy hand he had to use, he valued the results.

"Strip them of the cloaks and furs and anything else of use to our men. Then send them back to the Vijns," Niilán said, addressing the lead scout. To the soldiers from camp, he added resoundingly, "Tell him we will continue to send Piijkij corpses back until none remain." The men cheered. The rider smiled.

To Osku, he said, with genuine reluctance, "Saddle your mount and ride with them. Make sure the accounting is accurate."

"What of you?" Osku asked, his gruff manner easing.

Niilán considered the question, unsure of both its intent and his answer. "I will send their corpses back until none remain," he said, repeating his earlier declaration.

Osku held out his hand and the two clasped arms. "Don't freeze out there," he said, gesturing toward the northern stars.

"Keep your wits about you when you return to the Stronghold. Áigin, the spy, is sharp. Fair, with an eye to any advantage," Niilán advised.

Osku nodded, then walked away.

"Come. Let us build up the fire and get these men something to warm their bellies before we send them off to greet the Vijns," Niilán said to his men.

The riders dismounted, receiving raucous praise along with good-natured jests. Niilán left his men to their camaraderie. He studied the two dead Piijkij. Their arms hung limp and their feet dangled on the other side of the horse's girth. *Two*, he thought, his disappointment getting the better of him. Two were better than none, he reasoned, trying to avoid the persistent questions: *Two out of how many? And where were the rest?* He had boasted of success for the sake of his men, knowing the odds favored the Piijkij. They could be hiding anywhere.

Would they be content with that? he wondered.

After all they had done to plague the Vijns so far, Niilán doubted it. The Brethren of Hunters had lived by their oath for generation upon generation. They had been the first to pick up arms against the tyranny of the Jápmea. His father's father had sung the joik of his father's father, saved from the Immortals' blades by the Brethren. But joiks and stories would not help Niilán discern where the Piijkij were. Nor could he predict where they might next show up.

A deep, brooding resentment took hold of him as he came to terms with the fact he would be forced to wait for the Brethren to act before he could take up their trail. And the longer it took him to capture these men the more he risked the Vijns's ill temper. The High Priest was the voice of the gods. He was also a man who took pleasure in dispensing pain to make a soul wish for death.

Niilán surveyed the valley, recalling a field of green grasses and red blood. He had made a bargain with the gods that if he survived the battle, he would serve them by living an honorable life. He had honored his wife's decision to take a new handmate. He had honored his commander's orders, even when he feared their outcome. And he had honored the High Priest's directive to bring an end to the Brethren. Advancement had little to recommend it when it meant being the arbiter of harsh choices. He could not help wondering if the gods had spared him at all, or if they had merely delayed the sacrifice he would be called upon to make.

CHAPTER SEVEN

VÁLDE TRIED TO PUSH himself upright. The soft snow gave way with a squeak.

"Stop," the Jápmea girl said, kneeling at his side. "Save your strength." She looked him over. "You're bleeding. If the wounds aren't stanched, you'll die from blood loss or the cold."

He attempted to sit up again and failed.

Her dark eyes narrowed. "Why didn't you let me fight?"

Válde coughed, grimacing at the sharp pain. "The soldiers would have killed you."

She pushed back onto her heels. "I owe you nothing," she said. "I'm here for my own reasons."

He coughed again. This time he brought up the blood that drained into his throat from his broken nose. He spat, turning the white snow a lurid red. "Whatever those reasons, they are now gone. Believers' soldiers are there."

She sniffed. "Your comrades."

"Not mine," he wheezed. "Not anymore."

Looking to the heavens, the Jápmea exhaled. Válde could not tell whether frustration or resignation ruled her spirit. Finally, she said, "This isn't the place to dress your wounds. Come. I'll help you sit up and then stand."

With difficulty, she got Válde to his feet. She surprised him with the strength in her grip. As they staggered toward the tethered horses, it became clear that, despite her resilience, she would not be able to lift him into the saddle.

"You'll have to pull yourself up or stay here," she said, shifting his arm off her shoulder and onto the saddle. "I can give you a hand, but you must get yourself up."

With a graceless shove, the Jápmea helped Válde pull himself into the saddle. The effort robbed him of what little strength he had. He swayed. The girl grabbed his arm, jerking him straight and saving him from toppling over the other side.

She mounted her horse, ignoring his bellowed curses.

"If you can't keep yourself upright, I will tie you to the saddle," she said.

"I have been on a horse longer than you have been alive," he replied.

"Perhaps," she allowed. "But if you can't stay upon this horse, I'll outlive you today."

Válde's snort came out as a snuffle of blood, bubbling from his nose.

The Jápmea sat tall and straight on her horse as if to show both man and beast who was in control. He also noted her tight grip on the reins.

"A light hand is all that is needed," he said.

She nudged her horse forward with her heels.

"There is only death in the valley," he added.

The Jápmea stopped with her back to him, then with an easy flick of the reins she turned her horse to the north.

∽

Though weak and dizzy, Válde managed to stay conscious throughout their ride. When they paused to rest, he closed his eyes and slept. Each time he woke, he expected her to be gone. Against all odds, she had stayed with him, making shelter for them when needed, and filling him with hot broth to keep the cold at bay. Válde watched her across the rim of his steaming cup. He blew on the weak, scalding broth. She raised her gaze from the smoking fire. Her dark eyes blazed with hostility, obscuring the flash of concern he had noticed.

Earlier today, when he had seen her ride onto the snowy field to fight alongside Marnej, he had not recognized her. With her short mop of dark hair, she had, at first, appeared to be a boy. Then her voice and her uncanny fighting skill betrayed her. She could be none other than the Jápmea female from the bat-tle—their prisoner. Or at least that was what she had been when the Avr's retinue had left to parade her before villagers and the High Priest alike. Then, as now, Válde was at a loss to under-stand why the Immortals would let their females fight in battle. Nevertheless, he could not deny her abilities were formidable.

When he had pulled her out of the skirmish, he had rea-soned that an enemy of one's enemy was one's friend. Now, as he watched her, he had to admit some part of him had seen her greater potential in his plans to avenge the Brethren of Hunters. Her motives for staying were far less clear.

"This is the last of the broth," she said, pouring the dregs into his cup.

"You could have gone," he said, considering how far he might push her.

She transferred her weight and looked as if she might stand. "I still can," she said evenly, her words less a threat than a state-ment of fact.

"But you stayed."

She stood. "My reasons are my own." The rounded quality of her inflection took on a harsh edge. She stamped her feet and pulled up the hood on her furs. "How much farther to your camp?"

Although he suspected he would get nothing more from her, Válde felt emboldened to try. "Do you know who I am?"

Her laugh was sharp and derisive. "I saw the way you fought. I know those moves. I have seen them before. I have fought against them. You fight like Marnej."

At the mention of the youth's name she seemed to waver, then recovered herself, adding, "You're a Piijkij." Her chin rose in defiance as if daring Válde to contradict her.

"I am," he agreed. "So, why have you stayed?"

She kicked snow over the struggling fire. "I told you, my reasons are my own." The flames fizzled out with a hiss. "How much farther to your camp?"

Válde went to get up, then felt the earth tilt beneath him. His vision swam. The stars turned into a bright swirl just before his body hit the snow with a soft thud. A pair of hands hauled him up. He heard himself groan. Seated once again, Válde was aware of the exhortations and invectives flowing from the Jápmea's mouth. Then her sudden stillness sharpened his focus. He watched her scan the vicinity. His heart began to race.

"More soldiers?" he asked, surprised by the slurring of his voice.

"No. I need shelter to see to your wounds."

"We are less than four leagues from the cave," he said.

She shook her head. "Too far. You're bleeding. You won't make it."

"I will make it," he assured her.

"No. You won't."

He was about to protest when she cut him off. "Are all your kind this sow-headed, or is it something particular to the Brethren?"

He cracked a grin, then grimaced when a flash of pain shot through him.

"See," she said, her point made.

❧

Dárja cast an eye over the terrain. There were no hills or outcroppings to provide even a meager ledge for a shelter. She had no axe to trim branches for a lean-to. She stomped back to where she had built the fire and brushed away the snow she had thoughtlessly kicked over the embers. She cursed her temper which had driven her to douse it, but the Olmmoš had pushed her to it.

Of course she'd figured out who he was. She'd been raised by one of the Brethren. She'd been taught to fight as a Piijkij by a Piijkij. An image of Irjan flashed in her mind. Her guilt cut through her sure and deep as any blade. In their last moments together, she'd demanded to know his role in her mother's death, unprepared for how this knowledge would make her feel. *The hollowness.* It was as if an abyss had opened within her.

Irjan had been her biebmoeadni—her guide mother. He'd been chosen by her mother to care for her. She'd always known he wasn't like the others of her kind. He was a man, not a nieddaš, and his quarters were a prison cell. She'd taken the taunting of the other mánáid. She'd learned to pay no mind to the fact she was shunned because Irjan wasn't a true Jápmemeahttun. The company of others meant little to her when he had doted upon her.

When the troubles with the Olmmoš began again, Dárja was just past her seventh season of snow. She'd heard the older nieddaš whispering. They'd spread gruesome stories about the humans to scare the younger ones into good behavior. Dárja had been frightened when the older nieddaš had threatened to leave her for the humans when the battle started. Then they'd laughed. The next day she'd asked Irjan to teach her to fight.

Dárja had known by his expression he hadn't taken her demand seriously. She'd squared herself, placing her hands upon her hips. "I must know how to use a sword if I'm going to fight in a battle against the Olmmoš."

She remembered standing there before him, expecting him to praise her for her bravery. Instead, he'd kissed her forehead.

When he'd straightened, she'd seen sadness in his eyes. She wondered if, in that moment, he knew what would come to pass.

Dárja closed her eyes and swallowed hard, trying to keep the memories at bay, unable to stop his last words from repeating in her mind. *My love for my son drove my every step.*

"Marnej," Dárja breathed his name out loud. The spell broke.

The Olmmoš stared at her from where he sat. Dárja dug down into the snow covered embers to avoid his gaze.

"Gods' cursed stars," she swore, pulling her gloved hands back quickly and grabbing her knife to sift through the ashes.

"He's one of you now?"

"Who?"

"Marnej."

Dárja leaned forward to coax the embers back to life, ignoring the drawn-out way the man said his name.

"He fought alongside of you. He acted as your ally."

She sat back on her haunches, then rose to stand. The man's eyes followed her, searching her face for some sign to confirm his belief. She ignored him, stalking off to the nearest tree where she dug down below the snow for the pine needles and broken branches of past seasons. She scooped large handfuls of snow and tossed them to the side. The effort distracted her from her remorse. It also served to obscure the prying Olmmoš from her line of sight.

"He is like his father." The Olmmoš voice assailed her like the crack of a whip.

Dárja whirled around. Her breath steamed from her exertion. Her mind screamed, *He's nothing like his father!* But he was. Marnej was more like Irjan than she cared to admit. The childish part of her wanted to accuse them both of betraying her. It was a meaningless charge held up against the sacrifice they'd both made, not only for her, but for all the Jápmemeahttun.

She turned around, grabbing fistfuls of the exposed twigs and forest duff. She walked back to the smug Olmmoš. Without further comment, she knelt and carefully applied the new tinder for the fire, then set small branches upon it.

"Open your furs so I can see the wounds," she said, packing a battered iron cup from the soldier's saddlebag with snow. She placed the cup at the fire's edge.

When Dárja looked up, the man had taken off his furs and stripped off his woolens. His bloody linen undershirt clung to his torso. Dárja let out an involuntary gasp.

"Am I so gruesome?" the Olmmoš asked.

Dárja masked the heat in her cheeks by returning to the pine tree. Sap had oozed and frozen on its way down the bark. She dug her knife into the stiff amber track. "I prefer my Olmmoš dead and buried," she said.

The man let out a laugh.

He still smirked when she returned to the fire. She wanted to wipe the crooked grin from his ugly human face. She picked up the cup of melted snow. "Here." She handed it to him.

The Olmmoš accepted the heated metal cup, his hands protected by a corner of his fur cloak.

"Take a sip to warm yourself, but leave me some to wash out these cuts."

The Olmmoš did as he was told. Dárja knelt and took off her gloves. She probed his cut and bruised torso.

"Warrior and healer," he said with a sharp intake of air.

She gave him a withering glance.

"I do not mock," he said. "I merely acknowledge your skills."

She took the cup from him and poured the hot water onto one of his cuts.

"Gods' mercy!" he exclaimed when he finally regained his breath.

Dárja scooped a handful of snow and scrubbed the dried blood from his flesh, gladly leaving aside gentleness for expediency.

The man shrank back reflexively. "If you wish to kill me, then do so with a blade. Stop this torture you call healing. Please."

She hid her fleeting smile and busied herself, refilling the cup with snow. "I grew up among healers and fighters," she said.

"Is that common?" the Olmmoš asked with a semblance of interest.

Dárja watched the snow melt at the fire's edge. She shook her head.

"I was there when they took you from the battlefield," the Olmmoš said.

She picked up the cup and doused the man's cuts with scalding water as if she could wash away his arrogance.

Through gritted teeth he said, "You were bloody and unbowed."

Dárja grabbed another handful of snow and scrubbed the wound with renewed force.

The man gasped, managing to say, "I watched you leave with the Avr's retinue to take audience with the Vijns."

He'd left the question unstated. She knew what he asked. She packed the cup one more time, reliving the day she had been led out of her cell. Her heart had been pounding, not knowing whether her end had finally come. She'd tried to keep her fear hidden, not wanting to give the Olmmoš satisfaction.

Marnej had been there too, seated upon his horse. His eyes had bored into her. She knew questions about his father burned inside of him.

Dárja placed the cup on the fire. "I don't remember you," she said coolly.

The man chuckled. "No. I was one of many and you . . . you were . . ."

"A prisoner," she supplied sharply, testing the water for readiness. "As I seem to be again."

"I see no walls here," the Olmmoš said.

This fresh taunt was too much for Dárja. She grabbed the cup, ready to scald him anew. Searing pain flashed across her hand. She cried out, flattening her burning palm into the snow.

She felt his haughty gaze upon her. "Why were you fighting soldiers dressed as one?" she demanded through clenched teeth.

After a pause, the man said, "The High Priest sent his soldiers to slay us in our beds."

Dárja glanced up to see his far-off gaze. Except for the grim set of this mouth, she would have thought shock had set in.

"I watched old men and young boys put to the knife," he said, his voice faltering.

With added care to both her smarting hand and the man's cut, she resumed cleaning the wound.

"I fought beside the only friends I had known," he said, then broke off to exhale. "We don't know how many of us remain."

When Dárja said nothing, he added with revived conviction, "We will not hide like the bears and wait for spring!"

"Perhaps not, but you do make use of a cave," she said tartly, watchful of the knife blade warming in the coals. She didn't want to look into his eyes again. *Were they gray or green?* She couldn't tell. Whatever their color, they'd made her uneasy.

When the blade's tip glowed a warm red, Dárja placed a piece of the resin on it. She waited until the first drop threatened to fall from the knife's edge, then moved next to him. Her blade hovered over his skin. She hesitated. She could just cut his throat and be done with him. *One less Olmmoš in the world. One less Piijkij.* Her hand began to shake. The hot resin dripped onto the man's skin. He jumped.

"Sorry," she said, unnerved by the fact she had no desire to harm him. She had no desire to fight. It was as if the fire in her soul had gone out.

CHAPTER EIGHT

DÁRJA LEANED INTO HIM, *her dark eyes searching and hopeful. You have my heart, she said. Marnej tried to speak, to tell her the truth, to say, "I told Úlla your secret." Her lips were upon his, softly demanding, tasting of honey and anise. He was on fire now. Her heart pounded against the flesh of his palm. She told him she'd always be there for him. She'd always be a nieddaš. Marnej's mind tried to surface. His mouth sought solace for a lifetime of yearning. Just a little bit more, his body begged, feeling the heat of her skin upon his skin. Then tears and blood slipped past his lips, choking him. His skin burned. He tore at his clothes, calling out, "Forgive me."*

Now Úlla was in front of him. Her strong arms at her belly. Marnej touched the swelling life within her. She grabbed his hand, crushing it in hers, like the hammer upon the anvil. Marnej cried out in pain. The sound was lost in the rush of flames. The forge was hot. He was hot. He needed to be free of the clothes that clung to him.

He coughed, gagging on the snow in his mouth. *Forgive me. Please let me come home. I did what was asked of me.* He fought to open his eyes. He ached to see one face, a welcoming face. *Dárja. Kalek. Okta.* An internal voice screamed at him, "Wake up!"

Marnej's breath came back to him in short bursts. Distorted. Painful. Cravenly hailed. His conscience continued to plead for oblivion, his body demanded life. He clawed his way up to sit.

Daylight cut through the snow-wearied branches to which he clung. He heard the brutal sounds of human triumph. Fresh fear pushed him up onto his knees. Shaking with cold and effort, he crawled up the encircling snowpack and peered over the lip of his shelter, panting. The soldiers had broken down their encampment. Some men sat upon their horses.

At the side of the shifting unit, Marnej saw a tethered horse with two bodies draped across its back. Sickness gripped him. He tried to discern Úlla's golden plait or Dárja's long legs. At this range, he couldn't tell. *They could be fallen soldiers,* he reassured himself. Then again, they could also be Brethren. Válde. Gáral. Herko. Men he'd known. Men he'd fought against in the last skirmish. He searched for a feeling of outrage or a sense of loss. The Brethren of Hunters had been the only family he'd known. He'd grown into manhood believing pain and torment to be the beating heart of a family.

It had been Dárja and Kalek who had suggested a new understanding. They'd given him an idea of his father's devotion. At first, Marnej refused to believe them. He'd clung to the fact Irjan had discarded him to the Brethren, men whose only interest had been to turn him into a killer. The truth was Irjan had sacrificed everyone for Marnej. Dárja. Dárja's birth mother, Aillun. Kalek. They'd all paid a price for Marnej's life.

If he could have stopped his father before any of this had started, the lives of those he'd grown to care about would have been different. Dárja would be able to return to her Origin to give birth, become an almai, maybe even a Taistelijan warrior. Perhaps there would've been no need for warriors. No Great Battle. Úlla's love, Kálle, would be alive. All the Immortals would be alive, safely veiled by the Song of All. Perhaps even Irjan could've found happiness.

Gods. If I could take it all back, I would, Marnej thought, gazing with unseeing eyes at a faraway tableau. It was a futile wish. Worse than that, it was a lie. He'd give anything the gods asked to have more time among the Immortals and feel what it was like to belong.

Men shouting tore Marnej free from his longing, reminding him there was no place for wishful thinking. For an instant, the valley reverberated with the energy of milling soldiers. Four riders headed south, trailed by the horse with the two corpses. Marnej watched the limbs of the dead sway in a mocking wave as the horse cantered south.

To the north, the larger group of soldiers disappeared through the valley's craggy fissure. Marnej shifted his weight to climb up over the lip that shielded him. His legs seized. He crumpled down into the protected swale. Twisted by cramped muscles, he lay listening as peace descended upon the valley. In that moment, it dawned upon him he no longer heard the sweet cacophony of overlapping choruses. He'd lost his connection with the Song of All.

Briefly, he considered trying to find the Song, if only for the comfort of not being alone. But there were voices he feared hearing. *No.* He'd survive as he had before his time with the Immortals, before he'd discovered he was one of them. *I was trained for this.* The Brethren had seen to it. And his training told him he needed to get moving or he'd freeze.

Marnej grabbed on to the pine branches to steady himself. His arms protested the strain, threatening to lock in place. He kicked a foothold into the snowbank and then another. The soft snow crumbled under his feet. He scrambled up and over the lip, rolling onto his back. Mindful of plunging feet-first back into the tree-well, Marnej carefully inched away from the edge. Snow stung his scalp where his hood slid back. The cold crept down into his furs, seeking his sweaty warmth beneath all the layers. He had to clench his teeth to stop them from chattering. Slowly, Marnej stood, aware his legs had failed him once already. Swaying, he regarded the valley before him. The white expanse glistened where the weak winter rays touched upon the earth. He took an uncertain step forward, then another, retracing his way to the center of the field. The wind swirled around him like a warning.

Even at a stagger, Marnej soon reached the spot where the dead lay scattered. Yesterday, as he'd run, it had seemed an eternity before he finally reached the wooded edge. He wondered if the gods had been playing tricks upon his mind. If so, wasn't it possible he'd dreamed it all? *Dárja. The Immortals. Their Song. His part in it.* Perhaps it was nothing more than a madness that had overtaken him.

He knelt down and touched a snow-dusted body. The cold, rigid surface cured him of any doubts he might've had. This was no dream, no illusion conjured by the gods. Men died here. Some by his hand. With effort, Marnej removed the dead soldier's fur-lined helmet. He slid it over his own head. He wished there was no crossbar to block his vision. But warmth, not sightlines, was more important at the moment. He gave the helmet a solid thump with his gloved hands to make sure it was secure, then noticed a leather cord around the dead man's neck. Digging down into the soldier's uniform, the layers of frost-covered cloth crazed. He pulled free a bloodstained leather flask. The cord snapped like a brittle twig.

Marnej yanked open the stopper and sniffed the contents. *Juhka.* He'd never liked the heady drink, nor could he afford to cloud his mind further. He poured a yellow rivulet of liquor out onto the snow. It reminded him of piss. He'd wait until he'd passed beyond the boundary of the dead before he'd pack the flask with fresh snow.

His eyes strayed to the east—to Okta and Úlla's Origin. It was where they'd been born, where they'd come to give birth, and where they'd return to ascend. He'd promised the Elders he'd respect their ways. He'd promised Úlla he'd see her and her baby safely home. And he'd promised himself a life among the Immortals.

Marnej began to walk east, following the path made by soldiers and horses.

He had to know.

He had to know if his life held any promise.

~

Entering the area where the soldiers had made their camp, Marnej noted the charred remains of their celebratory fires. He recalled the victorious journey home after the last battle with the Immortals. The returning soldiers reveled in their exploits, the growing leagues adding luster to their heroism and righteousness to the gory triumph. Marnej suspected it had been the same for these men. One less Jápmea. One less Immortal.

They had no idea there were so few Jápmemeahttun left. And there would never be more. *The death of one. The birth of one. The life of one as All.* How many times had he heard the Elders say it was *their way.* He'd let himself believe Dárja when she'd said they could make a difference. He'd deceived himself. Disgusted, Marnej turned away from the abandoned snowcaves and uncovered piles of men's waste. Úlla had once called his people a blight. She'd been right.

He walked into the clearing where he'd last seen Okta and Úlla. He didn't know the exact spot they called their Origin. To him, this was all hallowed ground. He thought about the last moments of Okta's life. The essence of his spirit was supposed to aid Úlla in birth, then help her become almai. *Did it happen all at once?* he wondered. Would Úlla be so changed he wouldn't recognize her were he to come upon her? He tried to imagine what she'd look like as a man.

He'd promised the Elders he'd leave the life bringers to their sacred right. And he had. Not as he'd intended to, out of honor and respect. Rather out of need to defend them. Marnej closed his eyes, thinking about his father, Irjan, who had tracked the life bringers Aillun and Djorn. What had he seen? What had he felt as he thrust Marnej into the spirit stream of the ascending boaris?

Without warning, his song assailed him from within.

I am the vessel of a father's soul.
I have journeyed into the realm of the dreams of the dark sky
And have traveled back in a blaze of light.
I enter into the world to meet my destiny,
Knowing that I have been touched by the gods.

Each word cut Marnej to his core with its meaning, its portent. Even so, he let his song fill him, listening for an answer until he could no longer deny the silence.

"As it should be," he said, opening his eyes to what he hadn't wanted to see: the deep grooves in the snow as if a body had been dragged toward the encampment, and the glaring spray of blood against a snowy background. Marnej whirled around, searching for a sign of a body. He ran along the gouged snow until he came upon a bramble between two trees. Blood and viscera stained the trampled ground. *Was this what remained of Okta?*

A glint within the dull shadows of intertwining branches caught Marnej's eye. Without thinking, he plunged his hand through the crackling snap of winter twigs. His gloved fingers strained beyond his reach, pawing at an ornate dagger. The blade fell from its thorny nest, piercing the yielding snow to leave only the beautifully wrought hilt showing. Marnej dug down in a frenzy until he held Úlla's dagger, the one Kálle had made for her.

She'd shown him the blade before they'd begun this journey to her Origin. He'd praised Kálle's skill, and had asked Úlla to teach him this craftsmanship. She'd laughed at his honest desire, saying, "I liked you better when you were a Piijkij and not spouting wishful notions."

Marnej held the dagger in his gloved hands, an unspoken prayer to the gods upon his lips. To whom should he pray? Okta, who'd passed beyond their world? Or Úlla and her babe? The prayer died along with everything else. Love. Belonging. A future. They'd all perished here. On this spot. He committed to memory all the humble details. He would never forget this day. Still he wanted to ensure that when softness crept into his memories, the hard outlines of truth would carve away illusion to reveal the bone beneath.

Marnej gave the sky a quick glance. Its dull glow told him he had only a short time to climb to the ridge in daylight. He tucked Úlla's dagger into the empty sheath upon his belt. The blade's sharp point dug into his flesh. He canted the tip, then he stayed his hand. From this point on, each step would be a reminder of what he had lost in the span of one day.

CHAPTER NINE

THE STORM CAME UPON them suddenly. Dárja cursed herself for giving into the Olmmoš's demand to keep going when her instinct had been to find shelter.

"The cave is close by," he'd assured her.

For two days they'd traveled through increasingly rugged terrain. Had she known they'd be picking their way through craggy rocks and boulders, she would've pushed harder on open ground. At present, they risked injuring their horses, and without these shaggy beasts, they'd freeze here.

"We have to stop," she shouted over the shrieking wind.

"We are close," the man growled.

The only thing we're close to is breaking our necks, Dárja thought acidly. She brought her horse to a stop. Shielding her eyes from the blinding snow flurry, she squinted at the world around her, wishing for the promised cave. At this point, she didn't care if the hideout was filled with Piijkij. She'd choose walking into a bear's gaping maw over waiting for her limbs to freeze.

Growing hopelessness drove Dárja to seek the Song of All. Within its choruses she could find a copse of welcoming pines or an animal's burrow, whose occupant would grudgingly share. She closed her eyes, letting her mind quiet. A timorous voice rose within her.

Daughter of the gods.
Sister among . . .

Dárja stopped there. Her eyes flew open, heart hammering in her chest as if she'd run to save her life. The possibility of hearing Kalek's song was too much for her to face. She was no one's daughter, no one's sister. Not anymore.

"There," she said, pointing at the closest shape she could discern. She nudged her horse forward, trying to outpace the wretchedness which trailed her. "We can take shelter in those trees," she said, holding onto her conviction as the elements buffeted her. When she detected no movement at her side, Dárja edged back her hood. The thick-headed Olmmoš had continued farther to the west.

"You'll die out there!" she shouted at his hunched figure. Her sudden anger had transformed guilt into rancor. When he didn't answer, she thought, *So be it*. She'd survive without him. She turned back toward the trees, powerless to shake the sight of the Olmmoš, bent and canted to one side. Dárja might survive without him, he wouldn't survive without her. It was a fact that gave her no satisfaction. Despite her frustration with his single-mindedness, he'd become her last connection in the world.

Dárja made her way back to the Olmmoš. She blocked his path. He didn't look up.

"You're about to fall out of your saddle," she said, waiting for him to argue. When he didn't say anything, she took the reins from his slack hands. "Hold onto the saddle. I'll guide us to shelter."

The man mumbled something which she couldn't hear above the wind and let himself be led to the trees. Although grateful he no longer fought her lead, his quiescence troubled her. She worried the gods had already begun to claim him.

～

In a crevice made by two leaning boulders, Dárja crouched by the Piijkij. There was just enough room for the two of them to sit wrapped in the moth-eaten saddle blanket, hoping to preserve what little warmth was left to the Olmmoš. Even so, he shivered as if he were about to shake free from his skin.

Dárja scooted closer to the hunkered man, thankful he couldn't see her face. They'd been this close before, when hiding from the soldiers and when escaping on the horse. Dárja briefly wondered if this was how it had been with Kalek and Irjan—need becoming choice.

If we'd sought shelter sooner, she thought, then let go what could not be changed. He'd lost a great deal of blood before she'd stanched his numerous wounds. If the gods would listen, she would have prayed to them. But she'd stopped praying when she'd learned Irjan had died in the battle. She'd stopped because the gods had not spared Irjan and because her actions made her unworthy of their mercy.

Dárja realized that while she'd been wandering in the past, plagued by ghosts and cold alike, the man next to her had stopped shivering. She couldn't be sure how long he'd been still. She listened for his breath and heard only the wind moaning. She peered into the darkness, trying to see the rise and fall of his chest. Fear clouded her vision. She pulled off her glove, ignoring the cold's sting upon her exposed skin, and slid her hand across the man's cloak. She felt the scratch of rough wool, then the fur of his hood. Her hesitant fingers followed the contour of his scruffy face to brush against his cracked, parted lips. Her hand lingered there, relieved to feel his warm exhale.

"What is wrong?"

The soft Olmmoš words slipped through her fingertips.

Dárja withdrew her hand. Humbled by her weakness, she hid behind bluster. "What am I to call you?" she asked.

"Válde," he said, his voice a shadow of who he'd been in their first encounter.

"I am named . . ."

"Dárja," he said.

On guard, she asked, "How did you know my name?"

"Marnej."

The Olmmoš said the name as if it were his last breath. When he added nothing more, she feared the end.

"He called your name as we were fighting the soldiers," he said finally.

"You knew him?" she asked, mortified by her tentativeness.

The man's chuckle grew into a hacking cough. Dárja stayed quiet and watchful. When he settled, she surprised herself by saying, "Tell me about Marnej."

"Marnej," he repeated, then sighed.

Dárja held her breath, half-expectant and half-filled with dread with what might follow.

"I was a boy when the Avr brought Marnej to the Fortress," he said. "My parents had sold me to the Brethren to gain enough money to feed the family."

Another interminable pause followed this opening.

"Marnej was a baby. I was more interested in the boys my own age. I did not pay him much heed. As he grew older, he attracted more than just my interest." The man—Válde— dragged out the word as if he searched his memories. "He was odd. We all sensed it before we knew it."

Wind, whistling through the cracks in their rocky shelter, replaced Válde's hoarse whisper in her ear. Dárja recalled Marnej sharing with her his fears and confessing to an abject loneliness. She'd been stunned by his candor and, at the time, had been too taken aback to extend more than sympathy. Later they'd found a common understanding of belonging.

"We all had heard the stories of Irjan and his betrayal of the Brethren," Válde resumed his tale with a thick cough. "It clouded our judgment of Marnej, even if it was not deserved."

At the mention of Irjan, Dárja's body went rigid.

"He was always small and sickly when he was little."

It took her a moment to realize Válde had continued to reflect upon Marnej. She felt both relieved and bereft. She'd pledged her heart to Marnej. But she'd *loved* Irjan.

"We treated him harshly," he said, as she held on to images of both Marnej and Irjan, son and father.

"If he suffered in the beginning, there came a point when he gave back in equal measure."

Válde sucked in a ragged breath and stopped speaking. Dárja was immediately aware of his position relative to her, his breath, his pulse. Her hand trembled, ready to reach out.

Please don't let this be the end, she thought. Then his voice was in her ear again. "There was one time . . ." Her heart skipped a beat.

"A boy much older than me had beaten him badly for being Irjan's son. Marnej had curled into a ball. He took the kicks to his back and head. He never cried out. The next morning, they found the older boy with his throat cut. No one could prove Marnej did it and not one of us touched him again."

Válde's voice faded. Torn by wanting him to continue and wanting him to conserve his strength, Dárja touched his arm. "Rest," she said.

"It feels too much like death," he said. After a prolonged pause, he asked, "What is he to you?"

"I fought him once," she said. The vision of their first encounter loomed like a terrible premonition. "I didn't know it was him until I heard Irjan say his name." She stopped, hoping this man would save her from her sordid truth. But it seemed he'd finished with his tale.

Her eyes sought any detail of Válde's face. "I would've killed him if I could've," she confessed to a shadowed outline.

Time stretched out before and between Dárja and her Olmmoš.

Finally, she asked, "Why did you really save me?"

"Why did you take my hand?" he asked.

It was a question she couldn't answer.

~

Válde waited to see if the Jápmea would add something. When she did not, part of him wondered if he had pushed her too far. He needed her, not so much for his immediate survival, because he had survived worse. He needed her for the plan he had envisioned.

Although he could not see her face, he could tell by her voice something had stripped her of her fire. He tried to recall what he had said about the young Marnej. Hunger and the deep ache in his bones muddled his thoughts.

After a beat, she said, "He was everything to Irjan."

Unsure of what to say, Válde held his tongue.

"His son. His precious son."

He heard a bitter wistfulness in her voice that harkened back to his childhood memories.

As the lull in her tale dragged out, Válde leaned toward her. The effort taxed his limbs and wounds. He groaned.

He felt the pressure of her hand on his arm, her breath taut with fear.

"What is it?" she asked.

"Stiff," he croaked.

Her hand flew away like a bird startled from a branch. He felt the loss. He recalled how she had held onto his hand when he pulled her out of the mêlée. She and Marnej had fought side by side. But it was Irjan who somehow bound them together. *She is too young to be his handmate*, Válde reasoned through hazy recollections of the man. *Irjan would be gray and grizzled by now*. Then again, he had no idea how old she really was. The Jápmea were immortal. While she appeared on the verge of womanhood, she could easily be twice his age or countless seasons of snow beyond that.

"Tell me about Irjan," he said, his curiosity outweighing his judgment.

He felt her tense. Fearing he had lost her, he said, "I was there when he came to rescue Marnej." It seemed to him she held her breath, whether from alarm or anticipation, he could not tell. "The older boys were out training. The younger ones like myself were in the dormitory, honing weapons and polishing saddles."

He felt her shuddering exhale at his side. "Irjan burst into the dormitory, saying there was a fire. The old brothers who cared for us were powerless to stop the stampede he had started." Válde chuckled weakly at the memory of it. "Irjan had us all out in the corridor, and I was glad to be free from my chores, whatever the reason. I didn't know it was Irjan. I thought it was just another Piijkij."

The Jápmea's shoulder leaned against his. When she didn't move away, he let himself ease into her as well.

"He led us down to the Hall of Hunters," he continued, seeing it all as if it had happened yesterday. "Another Piijkij stopped us. Suddenly, the name *Irjan* echoed all around and the baby—Marnej—started to scream. Irjan and our Piijkij drew swords. We shrank back, transfixed by their fierce, quick blows. I don't know what happened after. He must have made it back to your kind."

Válde let his unstated question disappear into the sounds of the storm beyond them. It had been a gambit, to test her trust. As the silence stretched out, he began to regret the ploy.

He thought of her hand upon his face. The way her fingertips had trembled as they traced the hollow of his cheek to his blistered lips. Her hand had lingered for a moment intertwined with his breath.

"I saved you because your fate does not lie upon that field," Válde said.

"Then where does it lie?" she asked without interest.

"Where you choose," he said. "But not there."

She scooted away from him. "I chose to fight," she said, her enmity restored.

"If you wish to die, then walk out into the cold. Be done with it," he said.

"If I die here, so do you," she said.

Válde let this certainty sink into his weary bones, then made a final wager with chance.

"If you let me die now, why did you bother to save me before?"

CHAPTER TEN

I DIDN'T THINK I WOULD miss Úlla's sharp tongue," Ello said. Ravna looked up from her mending to scold Ello for her unkind comment. When she saw the nieddaš's downcast expression, she knew there was nothing teasing or heartless in her observation. She truly missed Úlla. As they all did. Ravna flicked her gaze in Tuá's direction. Tuá's hands wove colorful strands of wool into the intricate pattern of a welcoming for a mánná. Her heart-shaped face reflected none of the worry that plagued her sleepless nights. Only the sharpest eye would have caught the hesitation as Tuá entwined the red strand with the white.

Ravna knew of Tuá's nightmares because she slept beside the nieddaš, as she had done since they were mánáid. Their guide mothers could not separate them as children. Even in rest. So they had given in and joined together to live in one space. Tuá was older, into her sixth measure, while Ravna was in her fifth. Not so many seasons of snow separated them. Perhaps enough for Tuá to believe she needed to hide her concerns.

"I know you're all thinking the same thing," Ello said abruptly. Her red hair stood out like a flame against her drawn pallor.

"Enough, Ello," Ravna cautioned, her throat tight with fear.

"Maybe a different topic," Birtá suggested, nervously looking from Ravna to Ello.

Tuá's gaze fixed upon the knot in her threads. Her fingers shook as she used her needle to tease apart the tangle.

"I know you're all scared," Ello said, undeterred. "But Dárja's with her. And so is Marnej. I know they'll bring Úlla and the baby back. Did Úlla choose a guide mother before she left?"

Tuá's needle slipped from her quaking hand. The *ting* of metal upon wood rang out in the brittle calm.

"Ávrá's looking well," Birtá said, breaking the tension, her smile forced.

"She is," Ravna agreed, determined to spare Tuá further heartache. "Kalek did a fine job of caring for her."

Ello muttered something under her breath. Ravna chose to pay her no heed in favor of praising Kalek. "We are blessed to have a healer who has such skill and concern."

The other nieddaš nodded, though none added to the conversation. Ravna fought against her rising dismay by counting her stitches. Her eyes strayed to Tuá. From where she sat, she could no longer see her beloved's expression. The subtle curve of Tuá's normally straight back made Ravna ache to be at her side, to put an arm around her and hold her close. She held back for fear that if she attempted to comfort, she might shatter the illusion of Ello's optimism. Úlla was with Dárja and Marnej. It was more than any nieddaš had ever had for protection. Then again, it had never been more dangerous to be Outside the Song of All.

"I grieve for Kalek's loss," said Tuá.

The fragile tenderness of her voice pierced Ravna's heart like a knife. She swallowed back a sob that longed to rise. *It is so like her*.

"She will come back," Tuá said, straightening herself and looking at each one of those gathered. "She will return with her baby. And we will all love her with open hearts." The pronouncement hung in the air like a prayer.

"Kalek . . ." Tuá began, her voice shaking. "Okta will not return to us." She swallowed, raising her chin. "Lejá will. Úlla will. Their babies will."

Tuá's hard-edged smile looked more like a grimace. Fresh fear blossomed within Ravna's already-stricken soul. More than anything, she wanted to believe her beloved's words. At the same time, she could not stop herself from thinking, *What if they do not return? What if Tuá does not become a guide mother to Lejá's baby?*

~

Ávrá sat before her loom. The wooden shuttles lay in her lap. She rubbed their edges, worn smooth over countless seasons of snow. She stared at the taut wool strung for the warp. Its evenness stood out in contrast to the haphazard array of her feelings. She had been a nieddaš longer than most. She had grown accustomed to the routine of her life. Ávrá felt lucky to have been a biebmoeadni. Her guide child, Gáre, was grown and spent less and less time visiting. She apprenticed as a smith in Úlla's forge. *No longer Úlla's forge*, Ávrá reminded herself.

Úlla had gone to her Origin to give birth. As many times as Ávrá had imagined what it might feel like to give birth and become an almai, she gave thanks to the gods she was a nieddaš, unvisited by the quickening. Now, with Kalek, there was that possibility.

Ávrá counted the strands upon the warp and planned the sequence the next shuttle must follow. The process of pattern repeating pattern provided reassurance. Her life had mirrored this repetition thus far. And truth be told, she was fulfilled as a nieddaš. While the idea of giving birth intrigued her, she did not hunger for something different to take shape in her life. And the notion of becoming almai was an abstraction. She'd enjoyed the fullness of this body since her blood-moon. She could not see herself with the hard features and the beard of an almai.

Hidden in a corner, Ávrá slid her hand along the curve of her breast to her waist and from her waist to her hip. She thought about lying beside the long, angular lines of Kalek's frame. The attraction between them was not some fanciful imagining. Ávrá knew Kalek's need for her was as sure as weft for warp. She too felt the pull of desire, one qualified by an unspoken warning that the longer she let their hearts weave together, the greater her risk of change. Once already, she had believed herself heavy with the god-seed. Fear had made her sick with fever. She did not know if she could withstand the panic should it prove real.

Is it not enough to be a nieddaš? Ávrá wondered. She honored her oktoeadni. She had loved her biebmoeadni. And she had cherished her time as a guide mother. To become a *birth mother . . . ?* It scared her. She could not deny the pressure to honor their traditions, even with the new reality of what it meant to bring home a child from one's Origin. It was so much more tenuous than what past generations of oktoeadni had faced. Yes, there had always been the understanding that only the strong would continue on. But now birthing depended not on one's strength. It was in the hands of the Olmmoš.

Ávrá had never been Outside. She had been born after the gods had gifted the Jápmemeahttun the Song of All. Like the others, she knew the stories of the Olmmoš. They had feigned innocence, affecting helplessness. All the while, their dark hearts carried hatred and treachery.

Ávrá cast one of the shuttles through the vaulted warp with more force than she needed. She caught it just before it would have clattered on the floor. Her heart raced. She wished she'd had the power and conviction, like Dárja, to pick up a blade. She looked at the shuttle in her hand and tried to see it as the hilt of a sword. But the shuttle was more like a bird, flying through branches, trying to escape to sheltering shadows.

"Ávrá."

Startled by the sound of her name, she dropped the shuttles waiting in her lap. She hurriedly bent down to pick them up.

Sitting again, she saw Ravna, staring down at her. The flickering candlelight cast shadows across the nieddaš's drawn expression.

"I am sorry, Ávrá," she said.

Before Ávrá could offer reassurance, Ravna sat down next to her. Her hands, made hard and cracked from tanning hides, twitched in her lap.

"I need your counsel, Ávrá," she said. Then, without further explanation, she asked, "What am I to tell Tuá?"

Ávrá wished she could close her eyes and open them to no expectant faces, no questions. She wanted the surety of her loom, not the uncertainty of the Jápmemeahttun life of late. She took the nieddaš's hands in hers. She felt their tension and their hard life of work. Ávrá could not turn away from Ravna's dark, imploring eyes.

"What does Tuá ask of you?"

"Nothing," Ravna answered. Her anguish transformed her whisper to a plea. "That is what worries me," she confessed in a rush. "If she asked anything of me, I would do it. The problem is she hides what troubles her heart, so I cannot suggest a word of support without questioning her strength."

Ravna sagged. Ávrá gathered the nieddaš into an embrace, unsure if she was called to give comfort or honesty.

"So much has changed," she began, weaving her way through competing thoughts and feelings. "It is hard to know what to do or what to say." An image of Kalek came to her mind. She understood the weight of guilt and powerlessness which came with counseling the nieddaš.

"Tuá believes Lejá will return with her baby," Ravna said.

Ávrá heard the misery hidden in her friend's hopeful inflection. Somewhere in her dark internal landscape lay the real question in Ravna's heart. Ávrá rested her head against the nieddaš's and waited.

"What happens when Lejá does not return?" Ravna finally asked.

And there it is, Ávrá thought, overcome by profound sadness.

"Tuá will not be a biebmoeadni," Ravna said, answering her own question. In her mind, Ávrá began to construct a consoling response, then succumbed to an even more disturbing thought. *What if there were to be no more guide mothers at all?*

～

The Noaidi breathed in the cold night air. He felt its sharp sting as a call to task for being sheltered for too long. He raised his eyes to the waning half-moon. It cast a hopeful glow across the vast black sky. The contrast reminded Einár of the duality of their world, filled with light and dark, and the partition of their lives, experienced first as nieddaš and then as almai. As he searched the heavens for the familiar starlit shapes of Bear, Eagle, and Rabbit, he began to recite the hallowed story of the first oktoeadni.

Einár had never questioned the story of the first of their kind to transform. It had been a gift of the gods that saved the Jápmemeahttun. Harmony had been restored to the world and their kind had gained a deeper understanding of each other, both as children of stone and as guardians of seed. As a nieddaš, Einár had never dreamed of becoming the Noaidi. Life had been too rich with experiences to sit idle and imagine the future. Now, as the gods' oracle among the Council of Elders, he struggled to remember the substance of his days as a nieddaš, named by the gods, Siru.

I was happy, he thought, his feelings closer to the surface than individual memories. Thinking of the nieddaš he must guide, he wondered if they would or could say the same thing. While there had to be moments of happiness in their lives, he doubted the nieddaš would say they were content. His ancient eyes might be failing him, but he was not blind to their struggles and fears. Of late, he had felt pulled to act without knowing what was best. Time and again, he had sought the counsel of the gods. They, in turn, revealed less and less. Tonight, he had come outside, forsaking warmth and comfort, to find a connection he could not find through the sacred smoke and chanting of the Elders' circle. He had come outside to hear the purest version of the Song of All, free of presumption and compromise.

With surprising difficulty, Einár let the song of the Elders quiet within him. *Have I been Noaidi too long that I have forgotten how to be one soul and not a guide for all souls?* he wondered.

When the first notes of the song of Einár rose, his weary heart fluttered with recognition. It was like being reunited with a dear friend. Even though if felt as if a lifetime had passed since he had last sung these words, it was only a moment before his song soared, all hesitancy lost. In return, Einár listened to the song of snow, subtle and layered, pierced through by the song of wind, beckoning him to fly away. One after another the songs took hold of him, sharing their essence and their spirit. They filled him up until Einár believed he could hold no more. He held on steadfast, taking in the faint choruses of far-flung forests and shorelines, aware, even in this exalted state, of the sadness at the boundary of his consciousness. *So many lost*, he mourned, acknowledging the absence of one song in particular—one he would never hear again.

Einár thought of his old friend and healer, Okta. He had kept the healer's chorus close to his heart in the days after Okta's departure to his Origin. When, three days ago, he last heard his friend's noble song, he had wept. Okta had been many things to him in this life, not all of them pleasant. Yet, even in their thorniest moments, Einár knew he'd had the healer's respect, if not reverence, gained over a lifetime of shared experiences, first as nieddaš and then as new almai pledged to fight against the Olmmoš. It pained him to think his friend had never understood what it meant to be chosen the Noaidi. *How could he*, Einár reasoned, wishing, of all his friends, it had been Okta to stand by him without contest.

This regret made the Noaidi eager to turn away from the past to the present and the song of the lynx in the fore. Einár's heart found solace in the soft padding upon the snow and the scent of hunted and hunter. There was also a flash of boldness touched with conceit. The lynx's surety stirred Einár's envy. Then the lynx's song ebbed as another took its place. Einár felt the undercurrent of desolation in the faint refrain. *Daughter of the gods. Sister among the Jápmemeahttun.* The chorus ended abruptly, leaving a void in the Song of All. As the singer of all Jápmemeahttun songs, he knew this one by its yearning and heartbreak.

Though her voice had gone silent, Einár continued to sing the song of Dárja. *You start your life at your Origin, with sadness and joy as your companions.* He wavered on the next verse, seeing an ill-omen rather than a blessing in its meaning. With more force than intended, the Noaidi, the Singer of All Songs, sang to the night sky, *"Go into the world to meet your destiny, knowing that the stars watch over you."*

CHAPTER ELEVEN

MARNEJ LOST COUNT OF the number of steps he'd taken, trudging down through the sloping forest. He started over. *One. Two. Three. Four.* He tallied silently to trick his mind into ignoring the deep ache in his muscles and the gnawing emptiness in his belly. Step after step, through deep pockets of snow and menacing branches, he counted. *Thirteen. Fourteen. Fifteen.* After a while, his eyes strayed to the east. *Twenty-eight. Twenty-nine. Thirty.*

A charred scent in the air shook Marnej from his torpor. He scanned the sky, hoping to see smoke, curling upward. All he saw were the sagging tops of snow-burdened trees. Searching for a welcoming beacon, he became reckless as he descended faster and faster. *There*, he said to himself as proof he hadn't imagined it. Through the thinning forest he saw a white plume against the somber gray of the darkening sky. The billowing smoke appeared too thick to be a homestead. Fear seized Marnej. Had he led himself to a garrison? He had been sure he walked east. Then again, the forest had been dense and he'd had to wander to make it through.

Homestead or garrison, he needed to get warm. Marnej pressed on, alert to what was around him. Emerging from the cover of trees, he discovered what he'd thought to be a clearing was in fact the main trade route dividing Davvieana into its eastern and western halves. He walked out through the broad swath of felled trees that lined the cart path. Caution tempered his relief. The open area on either side of the path protected traders and travelers from being set upon by thieves and wolves alike. The wide-open space also made it hard for a man to take cover if the need arose.

Marnej slowed. He examined both north and south bound tracks. He found himself caught in the sticky web of memories. He and Dárja had passed along this route in the eternal days of summer when they'd fled north. He'd wanted to keep to the forests. Dárja had chafed at their slow progress. They'd argued. More than once. Marnej remembered their escape to the Pohjola as one protracted contest of wills. But there'd been companionable moments as well. He recalled the unexpected pleasure of her laugh the first time he'd heard it. The startling mirth had caught them both off guard. His surprise had made her peal with a belly-shaking roar that had ended in their breathless wheezing.

He wished he could hear her laugh again, wondering about her fate. Instead, he heard a crack that could've been the snap of a branch or the flick of a whip. He hoped it was a trader, traveling by sled. One who might allow him to ride on the runners. Just as likely, it could also be a soldier, pressing his horse onward with brutal urgency.

Marnej's fatigue made him both curious and resigned to what might emerge around the bend in the cart path. He waited until the cold convinced him he was alone. A perverse regret centered upon him as he reprised his shuffling steps through fresh falling snow. To have it all done with—the struggle, the remorse, the futility of wishing for a different outcome—appealed to him. In the end, the ingrained nature of his training proved more forceful than his impulse. He walked south, one foot in front of the other, with the same obdurate tenacity that had formed his loyalty to the Brethren. *Blind loyalty*, he thought disparagingly.

On their journey north, Dárja had asked him if he'd wanted to be a Piijkij. It was the first time he'd actually considered the question. The only thing he could think to say in response was it was all he'd ever known. It wasn't until Kalek had pressed him to find a purpose which suited him that he'd asked himself what it was he truly wanted. Admittedly, it had been Úlla's goading that made him choose smithing, just to spite her. But it had been a choice and he'd made it.

~

The hospitable outlines of a travelers' hut were a welcome sight after the tedium of the tree-lined trade route. Marnej's shaky legs momentarily forgot their exhaustion in anticipation of a warm fire. Coming closer, he regarded the upward drift of smoke as two men ducked out from under the overhang of the hut's sloped roof. Marnej hesitated, his caution winning out over his eagerness to rest. He stepped off the path. From the safety of cover, he watched the two men. They stood, facing his direction, in what he feared was frank scrutiny.

Reasoning a direct approach would better serve his cause, Marnej pushed back his hood and removed the soldier's helmet. He slipped back into view and hailed the men with what he hoped was a cordial note. As he came closer to them, he saw they'd squared themselves and widened their stance. Marnej slowed. He eyed his surroundings with a quick appraising glance. He stopped a safe distance away from the two men.

"Is there shelter for a traveler to be found here?" he called out.

The shorter of the two burly men came forward. Marnej noted his compatriot's hand had found the knife on his belt.

Marnej kept his hands away from his body, showing he meant them no harm.

"My wife is the hutkeeper," the short man said. "What business do you have?"

"I'm traveling to the Stronghold," Marnej lied. "I'm pledged to become an acolyte of the Believers."

"Then why are you covered in mud?" the bigger man challenged.

Marnej glanced down. *More dried blood than mud*, he thought, hesitant to correct the man. "I was set upon by wolves as I camped last night," he said, spinning a tale. "I killed one and fought off the rest with fire until they tired of me."

The squat man frowned. "How does an acolyte have the fortitude to fend off wolves?"

"Four older brothers makes you quick, strong, and wary," he said with a loose smile, marveling at how easily lying came to him.

The man snorted. "True enough." He eased his stance. "My wife is inside. Ask her for what you need."

Marnej inclined his head in a gesture of thanks. The two men turned, heading around the side of the hut, one saying to the other, "Let's get your sledge tended to before the snow sets in for the night."

Marnej tucked his helmet deeper into the folds of his furs. He was an acolyte. Beyond the low door to the hut, the two men harnessed the tilted load upon the sledge. Marnej stooped to open the door. Catching sight of his bloodstained furs, he hoped the hut was dark and smoky and the other travelers were not attentive. He opened the door, then ducked under its low frame to be hit with warmth and the smell of food cooking. Marnej closed the door behind him and leaned against its solid surface until his legs felt strong enough not to buckle with gratitude. As his eyes adjusted to the gloom, he saw the hut was four timbers across, with a beckoning fire in the middle. The room, as he'd hoped, was full of smoke. The smell of man and beast and cooking meat intertwined. He squinted to see who else was about. Relieved to see no soldiers, he shrugged off his outer layers, stashing them and his helmet under a crooked bench near the door.

Fireside, the hutkeeper stirred a pot. She glanced up at him, the firelight catching the glint of suspicion in her eyes. Marnej nodded to her. She was almost as square as her husband. Near her, two men sat on low stools. One was old, the other a boy. They spoke to each other in hushed tones. In the corner, two men played stones. An occasional comment or jest punctuated the sounds of clicking pieces.

The hutkeeper left her stirring to take down a clay pitcher that hung above a stack of three barrels. Marnej heard a careless splash. The sound made him painfully aware of his parched throat.

The thickset hutkeeper came back to her fire and poured the liquid into the pot. "Food for you? Or drink?" she asked, her head cocked to one side as if presenting a good ear to hear his answer.

Marnej was about to say both when it occurred to him he carried no coin on him, nor much to barter with. "I have little with which to repay you," he admitted, "save my strength to do what work might be needed."

The woman resumed her stirring. She eyed him as if looking to cull the weak in her herd. "You can muck the stalls for your meal," she said finally. "And you'll get no juhka. Only tea."

Marnej bent to pick up his furs to head to the stables.

"The food is hot now," she said, not unkindly, but with no suggestion of nurturing. "You can eat first and then muck the stalls."

"Thank you," he said, truly grateful.

Marnej sat on one of the low stools facing the door. It had taken the last of his strength to not collapse. He doubted he'd be able to stand again. A worry he'd confront later. First he'd eat the hutkeeper's soup and then face the consequences.

To his left, the old man and the boy slurped from their bowls. Marnej noted the old man and the boy had the same sweeping forehead and blunt, upturned nose. *A boy and his áddjá*, he thought. The man looked too old to be the father.

Caught staring by the old one, Marnej bobbed his head in respect. "I greet you, Grandfather."

"I greet you, my son," the old man responded, then sucked his teeth, savoring the last of his food.

The boy said nothing. The hutkeeper handed Marnej a bowl. He took it in both hands, his palms soaking in the heat. He breathed in the aroma and with it the rising steam. When he looked up, he met the boy's hard stare over the lip of his bowl. The flames of the fire gave light to the whites of the boy's mistrustful eyes. He looked to be less than ten seasons of snow. Although, with a grim life and little food, he might be older. Marnej sipped from his bowl under the boy's watchful gaze. He remembered the robust tables of the Brethren of Hunters and going hungry while others ate.

Marnej let the meaty broth sit upon his tongue just long enough for his stomach to demand more. There might've been a time when his honor would've obliged him to hand over his bowl of food to the boy. But no longer.

"Tea," the woman said. The word was both a question and a command. Marnej took the clay mug from her, then placed it between his knees to allow him two free hands to eat his stew.

"Either this pottage is the best you've tasted or the gods are chasing you."

Marnej looked up to see a toothless grin twist the old man's gaunt profile.

Startled, it took him a moment before he answered truthfully, "Grandfather, this meal is as gratifying as a visit from the gods."

"High praise coming from an acolyte of the Believers," said a new voice in the murky room.

Marnej's head shot up. He squinted into the smoke and shadow to see who had spoken. The hutkeeper's easy laugh suggested it had been her husband. Marnej held out his empty bowl as proof of his penitent standing.

The woman snickered, her florid face creased into a smirk. "All right, hand your bowl back and I will fill it." To her husband she added with more asperity, "This one here may claim to be an acolyte but he has the appetite of an ox."

The old man by the fire chuckled. Marnej realized he no longer heard clicking stones. Slowly, he peered into the corner. The two men regarded him for a fraught moment, then called to the hutkeeper, "The gods call upon you to fill our cups too!"

The woman motioned to her husband. The man dipped a pitcher into a barrel, then approached the men in the corner with a broad grin. Marnej watched furtively, trying to determine their trade or interests.

"You are an acolyte then," the old man said.

Marnej nodded absentmindedly, then corrected himself. "No, Grandfather, not yet. I'm traveling to the Stronghold to become one."

With a sage bob of his hoary head, he said, "There is honor in serving the gods."

Marnej was instantly reminded of Okta. The ancient healer had said something similar as they'd travel to his Origin to meet Úlla and Dárja. *Gods, why couldn't we've traveled together?* he agonized, not for the first time. *It might've been different then.* He'd let the Elders' needless traditions and rituals take precedence over strategy. They'd not been there when he'd ridden into the valley to fight off his own kind. And they hadn't been there when he'd found Úlla's dagger in the bloody snow.

"You do not agree?" the old man croaked.

Marnej shook his head. "No, Grandfather. You mistake me. There's honor in serving the gods," he said. "I just don't think I'm worthy."

"Bah." The old one waved a dismissive hand. "We all doubt."

Marnej lifted the mug of tea he'd nestled between his knees. He downed the lukewarm contents, then stood and handed both bowl and mug to the woman. "I'll go rake the stalls now."

"He'll likely run off," the hutkeeper muttered under her breath to her husband.

"He is a Believer. He does the work of the gods," the husband said loud enough for the room to hear.

Marnej bent down to retrieve his furs and helmet by the door.

"We are all Believers, dear husband," the hutkeeper said. "It doesn't mean the work will get done."

CHAPTER TWELVE

VÁLDE POINTED TO A rocky incline ahead. "There. To the right."

"Can we bring the horses?" Dárja asked.

"We cannot ride up. We will need to lead them."

She leaned forward in her saddle. "Can *you* make it up there?" she asked, her doubt evident.

"I can make it," he said, answering his qualms as well as hers.

Dárja brought her horse to a stop. She swung one leg over the saddle's rise, then landed in the snow, sinking past her ankles.

"Well. Here's your first test," she said.

Válde stared down at her. The frank challenge in her expression made him question his nascent plans. He had enough of a rivalry with Gáral that to court Dárja's aid seemed like sheer folly. He leaned back, then lifted his leg up over the horse's head in an awkward arc. The stalwart animal dropped its nose with a nervous shake of its mane.

"Easy now," Dárja said, giving the animal a few reassuring pats.

With his teeth gritted against the pain, Válde managed to get both his legs on the same side of the saddle.

Dárja extended her hand up to him. He hesitated, wanting to show her he was able. Finally, he grasped her hand, trying not to crush it as he eased himself down. Dárja held fast, supporting his full weight until he got his feet under him. Winded, Válde rested briefly, feeling their hard journey in each of his muscles.

Dárja glanced up at the rocky incline. "I don't see the cave entrance."

"It would not be a safe place to hide if it was in plain view," Válde said.

She leveled her dark eyes on him. "If I don't know where I am going, I can't help lead you there."

"You will not need to lead me," Válde said, taking hold of his horse's bridle. He used the animal to steady himself as he walked toward the uneven slope. He did not know what his men would say or do. He did not even know if there were men waiting for him. He could only hope they had survived and he would be able to convince them a Jápmea in their ranks was the key to their success.

"You have nothing to fear," Válde said, turning to face her. "You will be safe. You have my word to the gods."

"It's not your word I doubt," she said.

Válde straightened. "My word is sufficient."

She stood her ground. "I can take you up there, then leave."

He shook his head. "You risk yourself and the animal. You have had little rest and no food."

"I can make it," she said.

"Just like I could make it," Válde said. She looked ready to protest again. He raised his hand to stop her. "Shelter with us. I ask this as much for my own needs as I do for yours."

He stepped toward her and turned his ankle in the soft snow. She steadied him until he regained his footing. This close to her, Válde saw the indecision in her watchful eyes.

"Tomorrow, if you feel your path lies somewhere else, I will not stop you," he said.

Dárja and Válde were both breathing heavily by the time they reached the top of the craggy trail. Twice he had lost his footing on the icy slope. Were it not for Dárja, he would have slid down feet first and helpless. She had been right to suggest they leave the horses behind to forage until they could be retrieved. In truth, he knew not what awaited them at the top. It was wiser to not risk the horses.

Dárja came alongside him. Her hood fell back, exposing her mop of dark hair. She pushed the errant strands out of her face as she surveyed the area around her.

"I don't see your men's horses," she said warily.

"The corral area is around the overhang on the left. Look." He pointed to the tracks in the snow, a surge of relief washing over him. "They are here."

Válde knew her doubts were valid. He had pledged her safety, believing he could control his men. Given everything that had happened since the battle . . . to bring a Jápmea into their midst might prove too much for them to accept. *I need to make them see her value.* Otherwise, Herko's predatory nature and Gáral's contentiousness could prove too much for him to control.

Dárja pulled up her hood, obscuring her face from Válde's view. Splattered with mud and dried blood, she stood like a natural fighter, her hand resting on her sheathed sword.

"I will go in first," he said, "and prepare the men for your arrival."

She cleared her throat. "I'll go and retrieve the horses. Now that I know what to expect." She paused, then added, "From the trail."

Válde watched her disappear over the precipice, unsure if she would return. She had fought at his side, treated his wounds, and sheltered with him. Her reasons were her own. She had said as much. He could not begin to imagine what they were. He only knew that, from the moment she took his hand, he had glimpsed what was possible. *This gamble, if it pays off, will be worth the risk*, he told himself. *If she returns. And if I can convince the others.*

Válde bent his head under the low overhang. In the deep, shadowed recesses, he saw the orange glow of a fire. From the entrance, he called, "Válde greets the Brethren."

He heard muttering and movement within but could not discern the nature of it. His men should have responded. He retreated, his hand on his blade, sensing a trap. Válde looked to the precipice where Dárja had disappeared. He doubted he could descend on his own. When he looked back to the cave, Edo and Feles came out from under the overhang with their weapons drawn.

"We had given you up for dead," Edo said matter-of-factly.

A weary, uncharacteristic smile peeked through Feles's red beard. "I told them you would return."

They grasped arms in greeting.

Válde felt heartened to be once again among his men. Entering the cave, his eyes tried to make out their shapes. Mures huddled by the fire. Two men were lying down near him. From their backs, he could tell one was Herko. Mures stood. The two clasped arms.

"What is our count?" he asked, fearing the answer.

"Redde fell to the soldiers," Mures said. Válde felt the man's sorrow like a blow. The two had been inseparable since they were boys.

Herko rolled to face him. He grimaced, then lay back down. "The others?" Válde asked.

"Beartu and Daigu are missing," Gáral's voice came from the other side of the fire. "We assume they are dead," he said. "We had assumed you were dead as well."

Gáral made no attempt to sit up. Válde believed the man was secretly disappointed to see him. In his absence, Gáral would have been the natural leader of their group, a role he had coveted since their escape from the Believers' soldiers.

"Why did you go back?" Edo asked, sinking down opposite the fire.

The gash on his cheek looked red and angry in the firelight. The youngest and most guided by conscience, he would likely be the hardest to convince.

The recklessness of his plan hit Válde full force. "How many sustained wounds?" he stalled, his mind racing to find a way to broach the subject of Dárja before she materialized at the mouth of the cave.

"We all did," answered Gáral pointedly. "Herko and I received the worst."

"Broken leg to show for it," Herko grumbled.

"And you, Gáral?" Válde asked, cutting Herko off.

"A deep slice along my side," he said.

Válde's gaze dropped to the dark stain on the man's furs.

"I believe I might have something to ease our present condition," he said as a preamble to his larger intent.

"If you carry a barrel of juhka with you, Válde, I don't see it in your furs," Herko said, rolling onto his elbow with difficulty.

A couple of snorts greeted his remark.

Válde pressed on. "Edo, you asked why I went back. I will tell you truthfully it was for the Jápmea."

"You went back for that spawn of treason?" Gáral exploded.

"To kill him, I hope," Herko said.

"I left Marnej to his fate," Válde said, the implication momentarily lost on his men.

Gáral was the first to react. "Did you receive a blow to your head, Válde? Because you sound like you have lost reason."

"I took the Jápmea female," Válde boomed over the outrage of the others. Quiet descended like a felled tree. "The one who had been our prisoner."

Questions and demands erupted from all sides.

"Why would you?"

"You brought her here?"

"What good is she to us?"

"Why did we fight them if we continue to seek their company?"

"We fought them because the Avr believed it was our sacred right," Válde said.

The voices around him fell to a low grumble.

"The Avr is dead," he said, his exhaustion creeping up on him "And so are the Brethren." Válde's heart pounded with the effort it took to stand among his men and exhort them to go against all their training. "Yes, we breathe and act, but we are all like the living dead. We agreed we would exact our revenge upon the High Priest for what he has taken from us. And he takes more and more each day. Our numbers are paltry. The only way to find justice is to see the Vijns dead before us, and the Jápmea girl is a weapon we can use."

"Weapon," Gáral scoffed.

"She fought in the battle," Válde reminded him. "She fought the same soldiers you and I fought a handful of days ago."

The man balked. Válde continued, knowing his next words had to win his men over. "What is her greatest skill?" he asked, looking from one to the next. "What can the Jápmea do that none of us can do?"

Válde let the question linger until it was clear none of the men were willing to answer.

"They disappear," he said.

"What good does . . ." Mures started to say.

"Why would she help us?" Gáral interrupted. "We killed her kind."

"We share a common enemy," Válde said, then waited for the comments to die down. To conclude, he added, "I can convince her to act for us."

"Well, I can achieve this with the tip of my sword," Herko said.

"No!" Válde said, his frustration mixing with fatigue. "The point is for her to willingly do what we want. It is the only way we will ever be able to control her actions."

"And you believe this is possible?" Feles asked, breaking his silence.

"Yes," Válde said with more confidence than he actually felt.

"And if you cannot?" Edo asked.

Válde hesitated.

"Then my sword will get the chance to kill one more Jápmea," Herko said.

~

Dárja descended the treacherous path, feeling the Olmmoš's eyes upon her, seeking out her weakness. Using her hands to hold onto the rocks on either side of her, she dug the heels of her boots into the icy ground. *There is nothing special about him.* Just another Olmmoš. It was she who'd wanted him to be special. Not like Irjan or Marnej, with their Jápmemeahttun blood and ability to enter the Song of All. But like an oracle. One who had all the answers and could show her a way to keep going that was not running away. *Someone who knew what it meant to lose everything.*

Dárja lost her footing. She slid down the jagged incline, her hands scrabbling through snow and gravel to arrest her fall. Her cheek scraped against the granite boulder that formed one wall of the chute she found herself in. The raw heat of pain tore through her, then she landed with a jarring thud at the bottom of the path. Dárja sat frozen, fearing she'd broken a bone. Carefully she tested her limbs. When they proved sound, she raised her gloved hand to her smarting face. She flinched at the touch. She stared at the fresh blood on her soiled glove, thinking about what had led her here—crumpled in a pathetic pile, trusting some Olmmoš to keep his word.

Dárja scooped up a handful of clean snow and rubbed it against her cheek. She bit down on her lower lip. She'd felt worse than this. She'd felt cold metal cut her flesh and bone. Why were there tears welling in her eyes? *I survived worse. I can survive this.* Disturbed that her silent assertion felt more like an entreaty to the gods, she stanched her rising panic. The words "I can. I can. I can" coming to life as a desperate whisper.

"I can take a horse and leave him to his men," she said, testing her resolve. *He showed me the tracks.* His men were there. *I wouldn't be abandoning him to die alone in the cave.* Dárja stood up, her knees trembling with the aftershock of the fall. She walked to where she had tethered their horses to forage. The squeak of every snow-packed step acted a counterpoint to her reasoning.

"He'll be fine."

He's weak and wounded.

"His men will care for him."

There are none left to him.

"I owe him nothing."

He saved me. And I saved him.

Dárja untied the reins from the lead she'd secured to a high-branching birch. She'd made her decision. The horse whinnied and snuffled against her hands. She breathed in its warm, musky breath, wishing she had something to gift the animal before the ride ahead of them. The beast had been pushed hard. It was likely tired and in want of more forage. As was she, if she were honest with herself. She leaned in and rested her forehead against the horse's damp, shaggy neck. A gust of wind swept its dark mane into her raw cheek. The coarse strands stuck to the blood that continued to ooze.

If she were home, Kalek would lecture her on the proper care of wounds, however slight. *It is easier to engage what is minor, than to heal what has become serious due to neglect.* She thought of the many times Kalek had healed her cuts and comforted her bruises. While Irjan had been her bieba, Kalek had been just as important.

He'd called himself her father. If pressed, Dárja couldn't explain the full meaning of the Olmmoš word: *father.* She understood it held power. She'd unknowingly lived under its shadow her whole life. Irjan had been her guide mother but he'd been Marnej's father. Irjan had raised her but he'd sacrificed everything for Marnej. It was an old wound and it stung. She'd told Marnej it had been forgiven and forgotten. The truth was she couldn't forget. Her body wouldn't let it happen. She'd always be a nieddaš because of a father's love for his son.

When Úlla had ridden ahead to her Origin, heedless of what danger might await her, she'd said Dárja didn't understand the call of the Origin—the connection. She was right. Dárja would never feel the call of her Origin because she'd never give birth. Úlla had said this too. Not without pity. She'd been sincere in her sympathy. But her compassion contained a trace of her deeper loathing. Dárja wasn't like Úlla. She wasn't like the other nieddaš. She was as foreign and despicable as an Olmmoš.

Dárja searched within herself for any sign that Úlla's meanness had received a just end. She felt only the misery of her part. She was the one who chose to ride with the nieddaš to protect them. Just as she was the one who chose to go with the Taistelijan to fight the Olmmoš. No one had told her to do these things. Her fate was of her making, not the result of Marnej's existence or Irjan's action. *My own making.* If she could, she would go back to be with Kalek and listen to him speak to her of plants and their medicinal properties. *How simple and rewarding it would've been.* She could've become an apprentice healer and lived a peaceful life.

Only there was no going back. Not after what had happened. And, this too, was of her own making.

Dárja looked up at the darkening sky. There were no gods or stars to guide her in this world of her making. She had no dream to follow, no personal wrong to right. All that remained to her was a promise of rest and shelter from an Olmmoš Piijkij.

CHAPTER THIRTEEN

NIILÁN SAT IN FRONT of the garrison commander's fire drinking juhka. Over the past days, he had come to appreciate the overly spiced version drunk here in the north. There was little else to do other than stay warm and drink. That and obsess upon where the last of the Brethren had hidden themselves. The commander of the Mehjala garrison had been accommodating of Niilán and his men upon their return. The fact the Brethren had earlier infiltrated this garrison, stolen horses, and set fire to the stables was a failing Niilán had let the commander assume, while assuring the man the High Priest would hear no report from him regarding the events that had transpired. Although Niilán doubted much escaped the Vijns's spy, Áigin.

Niilán swirled the dregs of his cup. The sediment of herbs coated the sides of the carved wooden vessel. The dark stains took shape in his woolly thoughts: a snarling wolf, a crow on the wing, and Niilán as the plump autumn hare caught between predator and scavenger—both winter-starved. Niilán shook himself free of the dark premonition swirling around him. He thumped down his cup, turning a resentful eye to its bottom, chiding himself for finding augury in the leavings.

This was what he had come to. Idleness and baseless portent. At the root was the frustration of needing to wait for the Brethren to act before he could act. Niilán could chase his tail around the snow-blanketed forests like a kit fox in the first season of snow. But hungry and exhausted men were even more worthless than the rested drunkards he currently had. A sot could sober in a day to ride. A spent man would fall from his saddle to never rise again.

Nonetheless, Niilán felt the building pressure of indolence. Osku, along with the two Piijkij they had killed, should be nearing the Believers' Stronghold. Whatever gratification the Vijns would derive from this tribute, Niilán was sure it would not be enough for the man. He regretted sending Osku as the escort. At the time, he could think of none other more trustworthy to return their bounty. Now he saw the error of making Osku a prize as well.

I am no commander of men. I am a wind-pissing dirt farmer, Niilán thought, holding up his cup to be refilled.

❧

"I'm armed," the Jápmea girl called from the entrance of the cave. "Upon my honor, I am no threat."

A hush fell across the heated conversation that had taxed Válde to the limit of his strength and command.

"Honor," one of the Brethren sniffed.

Válde overlooked the comment even as he registered the snick of knives being unsheathed.

"You are safe to enter," Válde spoke up, his ears pricked to the sound of shuffling feet. A shadowed figure crept slowly forward, then stopped.

"Keep your sword ready if it gives you comfort," he said, coaxing the Jápmea girl onward.

A chorus of protests assailed Válde from behind. He shouted, "I say you are safe to enter." The word *enter* resonated in the hollow cave, sounding like more of a command than an entreaty, and had the effect of silencing the others.

The Jápmea cautiously came forward until she faced Válde, a short, sharp blade between them. A blade he recognized as his own. Instinctively, his hand went to his belt. His niibi was gone. *When had she taken it?* He marveled at how, even after all their trials and travels, she had her wits about her. She had relieved him of his knife, anticipating the sword she carried would be a hindrance to her in close quarters. This kind of forethought deserved admiration. It also merited caution.

"You could have used a blade on me at any time," he said, making no mention of the fact it was his niibi, adding with unexpected bravado, "I have no cause to fear it now. The others will learn." He turned his back to her as proof of his trust.

When he did not hear movement behind him, Válde said, "We have two men badly wounded." He limped further back into the cave. "Your skill as a healer would be appreciated. In return, we can offer you a fire, some food, and rest."

"I'm not letting some Jápmea touch me," a graveled voice rasped.

"Then suffer from your wounds, Herko," Válde answered without hesitation.

The man continued to gripe under his breath.

"Gáral, do you object to the healer looking at your wound? Or are you scared as well?" The question hung upon the stale, smoky air as Válde turned to face the Jápmea girl.

"I do not object," he said coolly. "Although I do not welcome it."

The girl came within the fire's glow. Her sinewy shadow curved up the cave wall, reminding Válde of a cornered pine marten. The fire caught the whites of her eyes as she furtively took in the men behind him, her energy that of a watchful mountain hare.

Without advancing farther, she asked, "What are your wounds?"

To Válde's ears, her voice sounded strong and steady. Nothing like his racing heart.

"I am cut upon my left flank from stomach to mid-chest," Gáral answered.

Válde added, "He has lost some blood though the cut is not deep."

She peered around Válde once more. It seemed to him she had reached the moment of decision. He waited, curious as to what scales she balanced. He offered a quick entreaty to the gods for his men to see reason. They were six to her one. But both Gáral and Herko lay prone with their injuries. That left four Brethren. *Three, if I am honest about my own state.* She was skilled and his memory of her savagery made him anxious. *None of us might leave here*, he thought.

The Jápmea girl stepped forward, shifting around Válde, meeting his gaze. What was it he saw in her dark eyes? Determination? Resignation?

Before he could decide, she asked, "What supplies have you?"

"Few," Válde said, matching her curt cadence.

She moved toward Herko and Gáral, holding the knife. Válde caught movement out of the corner of his eye. His three able-bodied men shifted. To his great relief, they did not rise. Feles stared at her, his face unreadable. Edo looked away. Mures nodded once, warily.

"I need both hands if you want me to treat your two wounded men," she said to the three seated by the fire. "I'm sheathing my knife." She held both hands away from her body. Slowly and visibly she loosed her grip, letting the knife tip drop downward. She eased the blade back into its casing at her side. She did this with her eyes trained on all except Válde, who stood at her back. He read trust in her disregard of him and fervently hoped nothing would test this hard-won faith.

With the weapon tucked away, she pulled off her fur mitts. "I'm going to examine the wound," she said to Gáral. "I need you to lift your arm."

"I cannot," he answered as a grunt.

Válde saw Gáral's jaw clench as he spoke. It was unclear how much of his discomfort was the wound and how much was wounded pride.

"I'll move your arm to the side so I can see," the girl said with surprising mildness.

She waited patiently for Gáral to nod, a forbearance she had not shown Válde on their travels. When she gently held aside his arm, Válde was dismayed to see the dark wetness upon the earthen floor. Gáral had lost more blood than he had let on. "Ass-end of a—" he began. The girl's request for light cut short his reproach.

Chastened, Válde took a flaming branch from the fire. He held it far enough away so it burned neither healer nor patient, but close enough it shed light upon the uneven gash.

The girl sat back on her heels.

Válde replaced the branch in the fire. "Well?"

She looked up, her expression unreadable. She said nothing as she held his gaze. "It's an ugly cut," she said finally. "With proper tools and herbs it's survivable. Provided the foulness does not set in."

"You can do something." Válde made the question into a statement.

"Do you have any herbs? Honey? Anything?" she asked, a note of exasperation coming to the fore.

Válde shook his head. "We fled with little more than our weapons. We have only stolen for our immediate needs."

The girl cursed under her breath, eliciting an appreciative chuff from Herko.

"Her mouth is not as honorable as she claims," he said.

She ignored him. "Do you have salt in your food stores?"

"Do we?" Válde asked the others.

"Beartu kept track of supplies," Mures said.

She looked around expectantly.

"Beartu's dead," Gáral said.

"What stops the rest of you from checking?" Válde growled, lashing out at the censure he heard, unable to deny his responsibility. He led these men. He had exhorted them to avenge their fallen brothers, their Avr.

Edo and Feles stood. They retreated toward the back of the cave.

"Are there any bogs near here?" Dárja asked.

"Are you planning on tossing Gáral in?" Herko chuckled.

"If any would find a bog home, it would be you, Herko," Mures said. His normal humor had turned churlish.

"Are there?" she asked again.

"In the valley. A league, maybe two, to the west," Válde said. It was impossible to fathom her thinking.

"The other one." She nodded to Herko. "What's his injury?"

"A broken leg," Válde answered.

"Have the bones broken the skin?"

"No." Herko spoke for himself with disdain.

"He'll live," she said. "He'll probably walk like a goose for the rest of his days, if I don't set it. But he'll live."

Gáral managed to bark out a laugh. Herko added some choice words which were cut short when Edo called out, "Salt."

The girl bent down and retrieved her gloves. "Excellent. Raise him off the floor as best you can, and strip him to the waist. Use furs to cover him so he does not chill." She scrambled to her feet, giving orders. "Clean the wound first with plain water. As hot as he can stand it. When it runs red and bright add salt to the water and pour it over the wound." She scanned the men. "Have any of you clean cloth?"

When none answered, she said, "Cover him with the furs. Watch to see if the blood flow stops. If it doesn't. . ." She left off, donning her mitts.

"Where are you going?" Válde heard the shock and alarm in his question.

"To get what I need," she said as if the answer were evident.

"You must care for Gáral. I will go," he said.

"You don't know what I need or what to look for," she said.

Her reasoning sounded like a rebuke to Válde's ears. Pulling tight his loose hanging furs, he said, "Then we both go."

"You're weak from your wounds," she said. "You'll only slow me down." There was no rancor in her comment, only cold appraisal.

"I am well enough to guide you," he said.

"Two leagues?" she asked.

"Two leagues."

She raised her brows at him. "And the terrain, once we descend this ice-spire?"

"Sloping forest into the flat of the valley," Válde said.

～

Riding out into the exposed valley, the wind picked up, adding a flurry of snow to Válde's already unsettled thoughts. The girl had not run off when she'd had the chance. She could have ridden back to her kind, and it would have been the end of his plan. But here she was, riding behind him, willing to help heal his men— men who had not welcomed her of their own volition.

He had told his men choice and not force was the key to gaining her skill to their aims. He needed her to stay. He needed to find a way to convince her. He thought back to what she had shared during the time they had sheltered together in the storm. She had admitted she would have killed Marnej at one time. Yet, they had been fighting side by side. Marnej had told her to run, caring nothing for his safety. Then there had been the tender way she had said, "Tell me about Marnej." There had been jealousy as well. Not like a lover. More like a child who sees the inequity of a parent's love among their children.

They are siblings, he realized, annoyed he had not seen this sooner. *Marnej is her brother.*

"There. That stand of trees!" she called.

Válde turned in his saddle to look at her. She pointed to birch trees just to the south of them. While he could not see her face beneath the hood of her furs, he had a picture of her in his mind's eye. Dark, angled eyes and hair the color of coal. She looked nothing like Marnej. And still, there was something about both of them reminiscent of a wolf, hunting outside of its pack.

Without thinking, he blurted, "He is your brother."

~

"My brother?" Dárja repeated, lost to the Olmmoš's meaning.

"Irjan is Jápmea, like you. As is Marnej. And Marnej is Irjan's son."

Dárja sat astride her horse, stunned.

"You obviously care greatly for Irjan. Not like a handmate," the Olmmoš continued.

"Not like a handmate," she echoed, shock giving way to meaning. "Irjan is *not* my father. He is my biebmoeadni."

Dárja slid off her mount and stomped toward the stand of towering birch trees. Her indignation at the Olmmoš's suggestion grew with each step. Abruptly, she halted and turned to face him. "And Marnej is *not* my brother." She wheeled back around and trudged ahead through the deep snow.

My father? My brother? she fumed silently. *Gods, this Olmmoš is . . . is . . .*

She turned on her heel again and shouted, "Enfeebled!" Then resumed the heavy going to the birch trees.

"What is a biebmoeadni?" he shouted at her.

Dárja dismissed him with a rude gesture. He had said "guide mother" as if it were caught in the back of his throat.

Were they all this thick-minded and croaking?

"My brother," she scoffed aloud. If the Olmmoš heard her, he had no response.

An image of Marnej came to the forefront of her mind. Dárja almost lost her footing. The thought of him stung like nettles. His betrayal fresh and smarting. His sacrifice undeniable and condemning.

Irjan's love for Marnej brought him back to life and my love for him . . .

"Killed him," she admitted, the confession disappearing like mist into the cold. Gone.

Dárja reached the trees with the sweat of her effort coating her back. "Focus on the task at hand. Think like a healer," she whispered to herself.

To be a healer meant putting those you cared for first. It was one of Kalek's many admonitions. She'd watched both Kalek and Okta work this way. Her stomach twisted, thinking about Kalek without Okta.

"Focus," she hissed at herself.

She needed a nice supple section of bark. It was best to harvest the bark once the snow had thawed. Doing it now, she risked removing the inner layer along with the outer, damaging the life-force of the tree.

Focus to the exclusion of all else. The rote lesson of a lifetime ago sprang fresh in her mind as she examined the tree within her reach. Her efforts went unrewarded. She stood back, looking around her. *Where. Where. Where*, her internal voice demanded. Then she realized her blindness.

All she needed to do was listen to the song of these trees and they would tell her what she needed to know.

I am as slow-witted as the Olmmoš, she thought, sure her short-sightedness was the result of remaining in the human realm.

She rested her hands on the trunks of two trees. She took comfort in their solid presence beneath her fur mitts. She released a long, slow breath, then closed her eyes, turning within to find her song. She sang the verses softly, out loud, waiting to hear the overlapping voices of the Song of All. Then a sudden fear of hearing Kalek's song stopped her. She opened her eyes, her body pulsing with alarm. *What if he hears me?*

Dárja had worried about Okta's absence in Kalek's life, never letting herself consider what *her* absence would mean. He'd thought her dead once. He'd tried to talk her out of leaving again. She'd left anyway, promising to return, knowing she might not, and unwilling to think of what it would do to Kalek. *Her father.*

If he heard her voice, would he find comfort in it, knowing she was alive? And when she did not return. What then? She had no answers to her questions, only misgivings.

She thought of the two wounded Piijkij, waiting in the cave. Their lives were in her hands. They had killed her kind. She owed them nothing. No pity. No mercy. But Marnej had been a Piijkij. As had Irjan. How different were these men from either of them? They were as defeated as she. There was no valor in letting them die. And perhaps there was absolution in honoring her training as a healer.

Dárja placed her hands upon the tree trunks once again. She closed her eyes and released a shaky breath. She searched for the voices around her, her own song taking shape within her. She waited. She listened. Hearing the wind. Hearing the treetops creak. Time passed, dragging on, heavy and unbearable, like her first moments in the Olmmoš world. Fresh panic prickled her skin. She'd thought the choice to rejoin the chorus of all voices belonged to her. She'd been wrong. This realization pressed down on her, driving her to her knees.

Then, like a fire roaring to life, awareness blazed in her hands. Dárja found herself pulled in through the bark and down into the searching roots. The trees' chorus shot her skyward to where the stars reached down to her fingertips. Dárja spread out her arms. Pure joy flowed through her and out of her, along with her song.

> *I am daughter of the gods.*
> *I am sister among the Jápmemeahttun.*
> *I started my life at my Origin with sadness and joy as my companions.*
> *I have braved dangers and met enemies and can see the truth of friendship.*
> *I go into the world to meet my destiny, knowing that the stars watch over me.*

As much as she wanted to stay like this forever, listening to the wind and the pulse of every living thing, she had a purpose.

She had a task. Dárja concentrated on the trees before her, asking for their permission and guidance to take what she needed without harming them. In their slow, penetrating hum, she felt the dark journey of roots and the warm caress of sunlight upon the highest branches. The trees shared the patience of rings upon rings of time, speaking directly to her soul.

Act with a gentle heart and remove only the barest necessity. What is taken may never be fully replaced.

~

The Olmmoš sat astride his horse. Fresh snow dusted them both.

"You picked a strange moment to be done with me," he said, handing her the reins to her horse.

Dárja hesitated, unsure of his meaning.

"I thought perhaps you had truly gone or something had befallen you on the other side."

"On the other side of the grove?" Dárja asked.

"No. Where your kind hide," he said bluntly.

Gods protect me from my feeblemindedness, she thought, realizing she'd not considered how it would appear to the man when she entered the Song.

"Either way," he said, "I decided to wait and see what would happen."

"How long was I gone?" she asked tentatively, then added, "I mean, from your sight." She looked up at the sky. It was as dark as it had been when they'd stopped.

"Long enough for my limbs to grow stiff as I waited," he said, his eyes upon her, studying her. For what, she couldn't say.

Snow swirled into her face. Dárja shivered, ducking her head until the gust settled.

"We did not betray Marnej," the Olmmoš said. "The High Priest did."

The man sat motionless upon his horse. Dárja could not see his expression in the rising moonlight.

She looked within for the flame of indignation that had guided her to become a Taistelijan. The one which had been so quick to come to the surface with Marnej in the early days of their escape to the Northland. Dárja could come up with any number of reasons for righteous anger. The Olmmoš had hunted and killed her kind. This man, Válde, had been trained for that purpose. Their two kinds had just fought a battle, intending to bring an end to one or the other of them.

Now the Jápmemeahttun were at an end.

And so was she.

She was done with fighting. She'd thought that her sword would give her purpose, give her power. Instead, her sword had only taken from her. It had taken what she'd sought to protect—those who loved and cared for her. Her sword had left her with nothing.

"I have what I need," she said.

She looked back to the birch trees, standing like silent sentinels, then said, "I will heal your men and then I will go."

Part Two

ONE LIFE TO CHANGE

CHAPTER FOURTEEN

THE HORSE'S GAIT FALTERED, then settled back into a lumbering rhythm. Úlla blinked her heavy lids. *How long have I been on this animal*, she wondered. *Days? Weeks?* She tried to recount how much time had passed as she guided the unwieldy beast with nothing more than her instinct. *It cannot have been weeks*, a distant part of her reasoned. It had to have been days. Just how many she could not be sure.

Úlla's head lolled back down. Her mind caught on the thread of a lingering dream, sweet and beguiling. They were all together. Ello was smiling, laughing. She was making fun of Birtá. Úlla looked around in her internal world, seeking out Birtá's round contours and flushed cheeks. The vision vanished into darkness.

In her dream, Úlla called out, "No! I want to see Birtá." Terror gripped her.

She jerked awake to hear the scream outside of her, raw and feral. She pulled back on the reins. The horse stopped and looked back at her as if questioning her judgment. Márgu continued to wail.

Úlla wanted to shout at the unfamiliar beast, "No! I don't want to stop! I don't want to be here!"

She wanted to be home, with Birtá, Ravna, and Tuá. She wanted to be at her forge where she felt in control and capable.

Not here, on this lumpish brute, with Márgu's hunger draining what little life was left of her. But in a tiny, huddled part of her thoughts, she was grateful to be alive and free of those Olmmoš. The idea of them made her stomach churn with fear and disgust. She could feel their grasping hands on her body and hear their cruel laughter.

Úlla fought back the urge to be sick. *Gods! There is nothing in me to bring up*, she thought. The food the Olmmoš had given her was gone. A fact that made her stomach fold in on itself with want. Úlla eased herself off the horse. The snow beneath her feet sent cold radiating up her legs. She wished for her own boots, with their fur and felt and dried grasses, to keep her warm. The Olmmoš clothing and boots she wore were ill-fitted and threadbare. She led the horse under sheltering trees. Tying the animal to a sturdy sapling, the reins slipped through her half-frozen hands.

Úlla bent to pick up the reins before the beast could wander off. With effort, she righted herself. Her head pounded. It felt like a herd of binna ranged across the expanse of her skull. Blood coursed through her veins. In her mind's eye she saw Olmmoš soldiers. Their grotesque faces had been a blur as she had kicked and bitten any who grabbed at her baby. The desire to cut them down where they stood took control of Úlla. Her rage blazed. Her body felt as if it were on fire. She reached for her dagger at her side, ready to fight. Images flashed before her eyes. *Battlefields. Blood.* She felt within her the chant of Taistelijan warriors. A growl escaped her lips. Then as quick as it had begun, the feelings were gone, replaced by Márgu's agonizing howl at her chest.

"Shh. Shh. Shh." Úlla tried to soothe the baby, longing for comfort herself. She had listened to the guidance from the Council of Passings before her departure, believing she knew what to expect, what it would be like to have Okta's spirit within her, taking control. Now she was not so sure. Did this mean her body was already becoming almai? It was supposed to happen after her milk had dried. Screened from the wind by the horse and the neighboring pines, anxiety gripped her. *Has it been weeks and not days after all?*

Úlla opened the outer layer of her furs, revealing the dark crown of Márgu's head. She fumbled with the knotted length of cloth that held the babe's writhing body to her own, then ripped off her mitts with her teeth to free Márgu. Her child's red, angry face turned upward, eyes squeezed tight and mouth wide open, wanting so much. Úlla struggled to open her shirt, unused to its Olmmoš cut and fittings. Cradling the inconsolable Márgu with one hand, she loosened the leather ties, exposing her swollen breast for the babe to latch onto. Márgu's screams ceased, replaced by a soft snuffling. Úlla sagged against the horse's flank and closed her eyes. The forest around her throbbed with silence. Úlla felt the pang of absent voices. She opened her eyes, blinking back tears, and looked down at Márgu, nuzzled to her breast. Her heart swelled with tenderness.

From the moment she had realized what was happening to her body, Úlla had tried to pretend her quickening had not come. She had feared not only giving birth, but also traveling to her Origin. She had never been Outside the Song of All. She had never even seen an Olmmoš until the soldiers had discovered her and Márgu, hidden in the bramble. She touched her babe's cheek. *Thank the gods we got away from the humans*, she thought, knowing her freedom came at the behest of the Olmmoš commander. He had let them go. He had supplied her with food, water, and furs; most importantly, he had given her his animal, when he could have just killed her and been done with it.

She could not reconcile this mercy with the fact Olmmoš soldiers had killed Kálle. Úlla briefly considered the possibility her beloved could have died by his very hand. She felt herself flush. Despite the cold, she was on fire, her mind filled with violent images not her own. *I should have killed him and not taken his scraps*, she thought bitterly. *He is as guilty as any Olmmoš for what had happened to the Jápmemeahttun. To Kálle. To me.* As quickly as her anger flared, it ebbed, leaving Úlla shivering and spent, fearing what it meant to live with Okta's spirit within her and wishing for Kálle's reassuring embrace.

While he lived, they had often spoken of their lives together, entwined by love, made stronger by friendship and their shared skills in the forge. They had imagined the joy they would experience when she became a biebmoeadni. Úlla recalled with affection her guide mother, who had made her feel she was the sun, shining above. She had wanted a mánná to love in this way—to raise her with Kálle. When he had been killed, she was sure she could not become a biebmoeadni.

Úlla pictured Kálle's dark eyes, merry with laughter, and his dark hair, flecked by soot from the forge. In her mind's eye, she saw him run his hand impatiently through his cropped locks before he turned to her, his face clouded with concern. Sweet gods, how she wanted to reach out and touch him one more time. Úlla raised her hand as if to caress the image. It disappeared before her fingers could feel the rough stubble of Kálle's beard.

Just a while longer, she begged. Then to the dark sky above her, she whispered, "Please."

The stillness of the Olmmoš world rebuked her. Úlla had never felt so slight or so unsure in all her life. She imagined staying out in the cold to embrace her end and go beyond the stars, to Kálle. Márgu squirmed, bringing Úlla back to her reality. She had a baby to care for and make sure she survived. There was a nieddaš waiting to become a guide mother. And Úlla would become almai. Although, if what she felt happening in her body continued, she was not sure that she would survive with her reason intact.

She cradled the sated baby on her shoulder, then awkwardly tied the shirt closed. She repositioned the child on her chest, wrapping Márgu snuggly against her breast with the length of fabric. Without warning, a sob burst from Úlla's lips. Hot tears began to stream down her cheeks. Through the haze of self-pity she heard a voice, faint and fragile. She held her breath, fearing the power of her exhalation would shatter the far-off murmur. Then the voice grew in strength. *Kálle.* Úlla's heart ached at the thought. Another voice added its tenor. Followed by another. Before she could grasp what was happening, the full resonant power of the Song of All washed over Úlla. She opened her tear-frosted eyes. The world around her glowed with life. She felt the unfamiliar thrum of the horse at her back. She heard the susurrant chorus of falling snow and the enduring, low hum of the trees around her.

The Song. I am within the Song again. Úlla trembled, her heart beating with excitement and apprehension. She searched within for her own voice. For one brief moment, she feared she had forgotten her song. Then, with the power of a hammer, the opening refrain broke through, threatening to rend her where she stood.

> *I am the daughter of the gods, made of flesh and fire.*
> *I carry the heart of all my kind within.*
> *My will is strong.*
> *My guide is ready.*
> *My journey stretches beyond the heavens.*

And then she heard:

> *I am the child of love, born in peril.*
> *I am destined to see the dawn of light.*
> *I will shoulder the burden of journeys,*
> *but will walk as kin among many.*
> *The stars light the way beyond what any have known.*

Úlla began to weep anew. This time her tears were of joy. She bent forward and pressed her lips to the warm crown of Márgu's head. For the first time since she had stepped Outside, Úlla let herself believe there might be a future for her.

❧

Ravna stood in the archway between the butcher's shed and the tanning barn. She watched Tuá, who hummed to herself as she worked trimming the cuts of the boar for Birtá. Ravna knew the lullaby she hummed. The soft, lilting melody turned her stomach to stone. How many times had her biebmoeadni sung this to put her to sleep as a mánná? She sang the words in her mind, feeling sadness where once she had felt comfort.

Tuá laid down her knife. She wiped her hands on her stained apron. The bright red of fresh blood stood out against the darker patches. Recalling her purpose, Ravna stepped forward. Tuá looked up. A smile graced her heart-shaped face.

"I have the pelts for you," Tuá said, reaching behind her for a stack of boar skins.

Ravna accepted them, acting as if everything was as it was supposed to be. Staring at the bristled gray of the boar hides, she knew she had to say something. Tuá could not go on like this. It had been more than three moon cycles since Lejá had left to give birth. She was not coming back to them with her babe. Tuá would not become a guide mother.

Ravna glanced up, ready to speak her piece, then stopped the instant her gaze met Tuá's. Her expectant expression reminded Ravna of a doe. She appeared curious without being suspicious. A rare moment of reserve rose between them as the sounds of the kitchen came to the fore. Ravna heard Birtá's hearty laugh. Its mirth stood out in stark contrast to her dismal state of mind.

A line of worry creased Tuá's wide brow. "Is there something wrong, Ravna?"

Though she wished with all her heart she could say there was nothing wrong, Ravna could not let this opening pass by.

She cleared her parched throat, watchful of her beloved. "I want nothing more than your happiness," she began, then hesitated, wanting to steady the waver she heard in her voice. Tuá stared at Ravna, unblinking.

"My fear is that the longer you hold onto this dream, the harder it will be to accept the truth." Ravna hedged around the heart of the matter, as unwilling as Tuá to engage the inevitable.

Even in the shadows, Ravna witnessed Tuá's normally full lips harden into a thin line. Without answering she turned on her heel, busying herself with cleaning her work area.

There is my answer, Ravna thought, saddened, knowing she could not leave things as they were.

"It has been more than three moon cycles. Lejá is not coming back," she said.

Tuá spun on Ravna. She held a knife in her hand. "You do not know that!"

Shaken by the ferocity she heard in Tuá's normally gentle voice, Ravna stepped back. "None have returned to us from the Outside this late," she said softly. The finality of her statement held the two of them locked in a battle of wills.

Tuá placed the knife on the carving block in a slow, measured motion. Her eyes trailed the movement. "Úlla has been gone a full moon cycle."

Ravna was about to point out one moon cycle was not three, then held her tongue, sensing Tuá had more to say, and hoped her beloved had seen her way to reason.

"Úlla has been gone a full moon cycle," Tuá repeated with more force. "You all believe she will return. I will not give up hope for Lejá and the baby until you all give up on Úlla." Tuá raised her chin, which seemed as sharp as her declaration.

"Please, Tuá," Ravna pleaded, putting down the boar skins to approach.

"No!" Tuá shouted, stopping Ravna in her tracks. "You cannot deny me this. No one can. Lejá chose me to be a biebmoeadni to her mánná and I will be. I think you are just jealous Lejá chose me and not you."

Ravna gasped. The cruel sting of Tuá's accusation was like a slap across her face. Never had she been this monstrous, not even when they were little and fighting over a favorite doll.

"I chose to speak to you today because it pained me to think of you hurting. You speak only to hurt me," Ravna said, then gathered up the boar skins. She walked with unsteady legs back to her tanning barn, fearing not just the loss of Lejá and Úlla, but also that Tuá would never forgive her for what she had said.

Ravna dropped the boar skins down in a heap by her feet. She picked up the worn birch paddle and began to stir the vat before her. *Once stirred*, she worried, then left the thought unfinished as a shiver ran down her spine. She stopped stirring and watched the softened pelts sink below the surface. *It could all go back to the way it was before*, she thought, resuming her stirring. Straining against the tug of the submerged pelts, a thought crept to the surface of her mind. *Perhaps it is I who will not be able to forgive Tuá*.

CHAPTER FIFTEEN

MARNEJ HAD AVOIDED TRAVELING with the old man and his grandson, who, as it turned out, were headed to the village outside the Believers' Stronghold. The old man had endeavored to persuade him to join them. Marnej remained resolute, saying he needed to keep to a quick pace not suited for a laden sledge with three riders. Now, he cursed himself for the lie, because he'd need to keep a quick pace or risk running into the pair again. Something he wasn't keen to do. Although the old man was fair company, he asked too many questions. And the boy's sullen expression reminded Marnej too much of himself as a child.

As Marnej shuffled along the icy cart path, he tucked his head deeper into his furs, letting only his eyes peek up above the collar. Nonetheless, the wind sliced at him. He pulled his hood farther down in front of him, leaning forward into the rising gale. *The trouble with lies is that they have a will of their own*, he thought, at once resentful of the old man and the boy, and abashed at his stupidity. He wouldn't have minded traveling with speed if he had an actual destination, but he didn't. He had told a lie and was stuck going to no particular place in a hurry.

In truth, he resented not just this one lie. His whole life had been built on falsehoods, ones he'd believed and fought to defend.

Then Dárja had brandished the truth like a blazing sword, to cut through the shadows of his life. *She was the truth*, he admitted to himself. A vision of her receding into the distance played before his eyes. He trudged forward; the pointlessness of continuing slowed his steps. Irjan was dead. Dárja was lost to him. There was no place for him among the Jápmemeahttun. He saw that the life he had struggled to build among the Immortals was as much a deception as anything he'd known with the Brethren. He wasn't a blacksmith. He wasn't a protector. He was a Piijkij—a trained killer. But this too was a lie, because he'd betrayed the Brethren of Hunters. He'd fled north to the Pohjola with Dárja rather than fighting alongside his leader.

All of it lies, Marnej thought. The worst of them were the ones he'd told himself. *Over and over again*, he brooded as the merciless wind tore at him. *So desperate to belong*.

"Come on! I'm here," he shouted into the storm, thumping his chest with his fists, his exposed face turned skyward. "Blow through me if you can," he crowed, wishing the wind would sweep away the past.

～

Marnej stumbled into the next travelers' hut half-frozen and lucky to be alive. The storm had done its best to punish him. When he'd seen the sloping roof of the hut through the relentless snowfall, his bravado had given way with a whimper.

"Looks like the storm nearly claimed you for the gods," the hutkeeper said as she eyed him, blocking his way to the fire. She was young with hard-set features that suggested she had experience beyond her years.

"A drink or two should thaw you out," she said, smirking. Marnej felt the cunning behind her welcome.

"I'd be grateful for a place by your fire," he said.

Her crooked smile disappeared. She put a hand to her hip, her suspicious eyes upon him. He felt the stares of the others gathered by the fire. The hutkeeper stepped aside. Her smirk had returned. "Let me know if you change your mind," she said, turning on her heel, trailing the scent of pine and onions.

Marnej noted the four soldiers in the corner of the hut. His instinct told him to leave. His exhaustion and the warm fire convinced him to stay. He removed his cloak and the outermost layer of his furs, hoping the bloodstains hadn't been noticed. He rolled them up and held onto them. By the looks of the soldiers, they were well into their cups, but if he needed to, he could escape into the storm. For now, he didn't want to arouse suspicion by acting as anything other than a weary traveler.

He sat down on the stool closest to the door, near enough to the fire to warm himself. He watched the hutkeeper walk back to the soldiers. The sway of her broad hips reminded him of a lumbering bear. He was not fooled by her placid appearance. If angered, he was sure she would prove dangerous. He leaned forward and rubbed his hands over the fire, alert to any movement among the soldiers. Reaching the corner, the hutkeeper had put her hands on her hips. She said something low and guttural Marnej couldn't make out. The men roared with laughter and called for more juhka. These men would make up for the lost coin Marnej represented. She'd make sure of it.

Assured the soldiers took no interest in him, Marnej set his rolled furs on the floor next to the stool, then met the inquisitive looks of the three men who shared the fire. He gave them a nod. Each in turn responded likewise. To discourage the possibility of conversation, he lowered his eyelids and slouched to give the impression he rested. Through lowered lashes, he could see enough to know the hutkeeper had put the ewer down on the trestle table with a sloshing thump. The soldiers cheered as one. Then grousing voices layered one over the other, until Marnej heard, "All this fuss for a handful of Piijkij. What can they do?"

He fought against the impulse to sit up. *Don't move. Just wait*, he counseled himself.

"They've killed our men and burned temples," a higher-pitched voice said. "We can't let this go unpunished."

"What do we have to show for it?" came a glum response.

"Two of them are dead," someone else chimed in. "I'd say it's a start. I wish I could've been there when they brought the bodies back to the Stronghold."

"You think the Vijns will be satisfied?" the first scoffed.

The disagreement among the soldiers turned heated, until a gruff voice cut off the others. "He'll accept the tribute. And then he'll want to know where the rest of them Hunters are. When them soldiers say they don't know, they'll be lucky to come back with flesh on their bones."

"Well, if we'd been able to bring back the carcass of the Jápmea and her runt . . ." one of the soldiers started to say.

Marnej's eyes flew open. It was all he could do not to bound off his stool, blade in hand. Then the knowledge that Úlla's babe had been born sank in and it crushed him where he sat. *They're both gone*, he thought, his unseeing gaze upon the flames before him.

"Well, we don't," the gruff one interrupted. A chastened quiet settled among the soldiers.

Marnej thought of his last glimpse of Úlla, supporting Okta with Dárja's help. He'd never seen her look frightened until that moment. He shook his head to clear the image, heedless of who watched him. *Let them think I'm witless from the cold*, he thought. He wanted to remember Úlla as the fierce nieddaš who had spat in his face the first time she'd come upon him, her green eyes flashing with hatred. Gaining her acceptance had been hard fought and all the more meaningful for it. With Úlla, he was certain pity played no part in his welcome. He'd had a place in her forge because he'd earned it.

"They'll think twice about coming down here to spawn their foulness," the high-pitched soldier said, bringing Marnej back to his flesh and his failings.

He cast a hateful eye in the man's direction. Of slender build, with hair the color of mud, the squeaking soldier sat up straighter in his chair. "I was there, you know," he said, his nose high and arrogant. "I was at the Battle of the Great Valley."

The others started to jeer. "You weren't there."

"The Jápmea had us trapped," he said. "Great big beasts they were and savage." The taunting subsided and even the hutkeeper had stopped to give an ear to the wiry man.

"Worse than wolves," he went on. "With teeth as big as a bear's. But the gods steadied our hands, and we cut through them Immortals. Their blood sprayed on us, as black as night and as foul as a reeking bog. We showed no mercy. They deserved none for the violence they visited upon generations of men. Each of us on the field answered the call of the gods to avenge our lost loved ones. We held the Immortals' fate in our hands and we crushed them like ants under our boots. Once and for all, we showed the Jápmea they were not our masters. Never again shall men be chattel. The land we till is ours. Our sweat and tears, our own."

His tale finished, the soldier emptied his cup, then brought it down on the table with a loud bang. The two soldiers closest to the scrawny storyteller clapped him on the back. The fourth soldier regarded the others with a sneer. "And they say only the strong survive." The gruff tone cut through the merriment.

A hush descended upon all in the travelers' hut. Marnej heard the crackle of the fire and the creak of a stool. Then the space erupted with shouts and jostling bodies. The hutkeeper screamed. The three travelers who sat adjacent to Marnej jumped back to give the fighting men room. None of them went to the aid of the hutkeeper, who waded into the scuffle with her stout bread paddle.

Marnej snatched up his bundled furs. Moving to the door, he unrolled his cloak and wrapped it around himself. He slipped out into the darkening day, feeling like he'd barely avoided a trap. He looked ahead at the cart path heading south. The white snow before him turned gray and menacing. *I'm done with walking*, he thought, the cold seeping up his spent body. *And done with pretending to be something I'm not.*

Marnej knew he couldn't go around saying he was a Piijkij. The Hunters had somehow become the hunted. This explained why Válde and the others had been fighting soldiers in the Great Valley. But not why Válde had pulled Dárja from the skirmish. Crossing to the stables, it occurred to Marnej that Válde might use Dárja to bargain with the High Priest. He pictured Dárja back in the Believers' Stronghold, standing tall, her arms bound, her long, dark braid down to the small of her back. *No, that's how she was*, he reminded himself. He'd cut off her braid as they'd made their way north. She had a short mop of hair now, not much longer than his own. Shouting erupted from the travelers' hut. The brawl was about to tumble outside at any moment.

Marnej slipped into the stable and untied the nearest horse. The animal puffed and stomped, then reluctantly followed him out into the elements. He pulled himself up onto the saddle, preparing himself for an uncomfortable ride in the storm. Far better than walking, he knew. He nudged the animal forward with a squeeze of his knees. He was unsure of where he should go. There was no way back to the Pohjola and the Immortals for him. Not now, with Úlla and her babe gone to the gods. And there was also no place for him among the Olmmoš. The illusion of taking up an ordinary life disappeared with the recounting of the battle. Too Olmmoš to live among the Immortals, Marnej was now too Jápmemeahttun to live like a man.

CHAPTER SIXTEEN

O SKU KNEW HIS LIMITS. He wasn't a clever man. Not like Niilán. So he'd taken his commander's caution to heart. So much so that dread had been his constant companion on the journey south to the Believers' Stronghold. Bringing back the bodies of two Piijkij should have been a coveted task. Niilán had warned him of the potential danger the Vijns posed. And Osku had heard enough rumors of the High Priest's cruelty to wish Niilán was the one to address the Vijns and not himself.

Niilán, however, had stayed in the north to track down the Piijkij. He'd placed his faith in Osku to present a favorable account of their regiment's actions. Osku didn't want any reward or notice. Accolades were for other men. He wanted a warm billet, some decent food, and a few friends he could trust. At the Stronghold, he would find food and shelter. Those he could trust remained to be seen. Passing through the fortified outer picket, he wished he could just vanish like the Jápmea female they'd found in the Great Valley. Or, perhaps, slowly drift to the back of this procession and trail off into the woods. There was no wife to miss him. No woman had chosen him for her handmate. What family he'd had were east of the Blue Lakes, tending their struggling crops in the hard, rocky soil. He wouldn't return to them. He could resume his life as a trapper. It wasn't much, but it could sustain him until the ache in his old bones was too great. When that happened, he'd let the cold claim him for the gods.

In place of the gods, a sentry challenged Osku at the Stronghold's gates. With an exhale, he resigned himself to what was asked of him. He owed Niilán this much for shielding him and the others from the Vijns's wrath thus far. He'd deliver the Piikij bodies, along with the news of his regiment.

He cleared his throat. "I am Osku of the Vijns's personal regiment."

"State your purpose," the sentry boomed.

"To deliver these slain Piijkij and give my commander's report to the High Priest."

The gates opened slowly. The hinges creaked under the weight of the sturdy wooden planks and iron bracers.

"Enter and await your escort," the sentry called down from the parapet.

Osku did as he was instructed, aware of the growing unease among his tight group of men. They'd cocked their heads and begun to mutter under their breath. Niilán had assured him responsibility rested with a regiment's commander. An empty reassurance when he wasn't here. Reconciled to lead by example as Niilán had done, Osku sat up straighter in his saddle and hoped he'd be able to protect these men under him.

A mounted guard, bearing the Vijns's sigil on his breastplate, stopped in front of them.

"My men need rest and provisioning," Osku said with an authority that surprised even himself.

"They will be cared for," the guard said. He didn't go on to elaborate and Osku didn't press him. He merely followed the guard, first through the battlements, and then through the bustling activity of villagers and soldiers alike.

Riding to the left of their escort, Osku asked, "Is there an occasion to be marked?"

"The Vijns's orders," the guard said, his focus ahead.

Osku noted the grim expressions of those who hurried past.

Their guard came to a halt before the doors to the keep. He pointed to one of the trio of soldiers present. "Take these men to the barracks for quartering and provisioning." The foot soldier came forward to stand alert. Osku turned to his men and gave them a nod of dismissal, wishing he could join them.

He was about to inquire who would assist him with the bodies when two soldiers pulled the Piijkij off the horse. The blood-blackened and rotting corpses landed with a sickening thud on the frozen ground. The soldiers lugged the bodies inside the keep. A grateful Osku took the rearguard of this grisly parade. As they wound their way into the cavernous gathering hall, all eyes trailed them.

Atop the dais at the far end of the hall, two pillars in the shape of snarling bears rose on either side of a seated figure. Even at this range, Osku was certain this was the Vijns. He swallowed, his throat suddenly dry. Drawing closer, he was sure the Vijns could see into his soul. With an unceremonious *thunk*, the soldiers dropped the corpses before the dais. Osku flinched, feeling wholly unprepared. The bold came forward to stare at the bounty. He'd expected to see horror and disgust. To his dismay, he sensed expectancy behind inquisitive glances, as if the new arrivals were a spectacle of entertainment.

Movement on the dais attracted Osku's attention. A gaunt figure, more scarecrow than man, strode across to the seated Vijns. He leaned down and spoke into the Vijns's ear, then stood straight as a reed. Osku recognized the man but couldn't say from where. The High Priest rose from his seat. Despite his embroidered robes and ornate chains, he wore no beard to honor his wisdom and connection to the gods. Everyone around Osku bowed their head. He promptly followed suit. The clean-shaven lines of the Vijns's face reminded Osku of a ferret, only with more menace than playful spirit.

"Rise," a voice commanded.

Osku stood up. He clasped his hands behind his back and waited, unsure of how to proceed. A darting glance around him gave no clue. He finally decided it was better to be slow and humble than quick and proud. So he waited to be told what to do. The sound of shuffling feet and stifled coughs circulated through the large hall.

"Do we stand here patiently and guess what news you bring? Or will you speak and save us this tedium?" the High Priest asked. The gaunt man to his side leaned in. The Vijns cut him off. "Not now, Áigin."

Osku knew the name. Niilán had told him to seek out this man.

"Well," the High Priest said.

Intimidated, Osku stuttered, "My Vijns, I . . . I . . . bring word from Niilán, the commander of your personal regiment."

"I know who the commander of my personal regiment is," the High Priest snapped.

Osku bowed. "My apologies. Niilán presents these two Piijkij in tribute."

"Piijkij?" The Vijns dragged out the Brethren title, peering over the end of the dais. "If they are Piijkij, why are they dressed as my soldiers?"

Osku felt himself sweating. "My Vijns, these men stole the uniforms of your soldiers to disguise themselves," he began to explain. Then, flustered by the suspicion he read in the Vijns's arched brows, he blurted, "We fought against them in the Great Valley. When we gained the upper hand, they tried to escape. In the end, we tracked them down."

"Two!" the High Priest disparaged. "Two of how many?"

"I can't say," Osku said, feeling the flush of alarm clear to the soles of his feet.

The Vijns narrowed his eyes. Osku froze, unsure of what to do. Should he look down or meet his gaze? Or should he stare into the offing and risk offense?

"How many moon cycles have passed since your regiment departed?" the High Priest asked, his question like a whip. Before Osku could answer, the Vijns went on, "And how many attacks have these Piijkij perpetrated? Unopposed." Osku opened his mouth to answer, then closed it when he realized the Vijns was not done. "You supply me two and I ask what of the others? Why are they not all here before me? Why is Niilán not here before me?"

Osku hesitated, uncertain of which questions required a response. He didn't have all the answers. But he *could* answer the last one.

"My Vijns, Niilán stayed in the north to hunt the Piijkij," he said, adding, "Their ruse caused confusion." The rest of the explanation Niilán had supplied him was lost now. He finished, saying, "My commander is confident their end is imminent, either by capture or sustained injuries."

"And by ruse, I assume you mean their appropriation of our soldiers uniforms?" the High Priest asked tartly.

Osku dropped his eyes and bowed his head. "Yes, my Vijns."

"And the capture of the remaining Piijkij is imminent?"

Osku kept his head bowed. "Yes, my Vijns."

"Does anyone, other than Niilán, know what he means by imminent?"

Osku raised his eyes furtively, trying to figure out the man's intent. To his surprise, the High Priest appeared to address the man named Áigin. The one Niilán had called a spy.

"My Vijns, I do not know," the spy said, his face impassive.

"I suppose we must all wait for Niilán's imminent return," the Vijns said with a tight smile and an emphasis on *imminent*. With a withering look he added, "Remove the bodies before they begin to thaw and reek."

"Yes, my Vijns," Osku replied, bowing as he listened to the receding swish of the High Priest's heavy robes. When he saw movement on either side of him, he rocked forward and grabbed a leg on each corpse. The circle of spectators opened to allow him to exit. None offered assistance. Osku struggled back the way he'd entered, the weight of the two bodies straining his exhausted muscles.

Almost as an afterthought, the Vijns commanded, "Strip them of those uniforms. Let their naked bodies be a reminder of what befalls the enemies of the Believers."

~

Bávvál sat upon the dais fuming, his face a mask of confidence. He heard the supplications of those who rushed to seek his audience. In his thoughts, he obsessed upon the most recent development. *Two. He sends me two. And expects me to wait. I have waited too long already to be done with the Brethren of Hunters.* It was not enough that he had seen to their leader's broken and bloody end. The fact any faithful Piijkij existed rankled like an open wound. He had sent a regiment after them. Yet they had managed to elude capture to roam freely. *Their ruse caused confusion.* Bávvál silently mocked the weak excuse. *More like feebleminded gullibility.*

"My Vijns?" a solicitous voice prompted. "Do you have comment on the proposal before you?"

Trifling, was what Bávvál wished to say. The wide-eyed posturing of the counselor only served to further annoy him.

"Restate the positions requiring consideration," he said pointedly.

"Stores in the northern villages have been reduced to dangerously low levels," a priest of middling rank spoke up. "Between the fires set by the Piijkij and the sequestration enacted by the soldiers engaged in the north, villages fear for their livestock and, indeed, their survival."

This poorly disguised complaint stoked Bávvál's smoldering ire. He glanced among the men gathered. They were like so many stripling trees in an already overgrown forest. None of them understood what it took to be High Priest. Countless generations of fear and struggle had ended through his efforts. All of them wanted the homage. None of them knew what it truly took to hold this much sway. In part, no one understood because none before him had held as much power. Not even their Olmmoš ancestors—the ones who had answered the gods' call to leave their mountain-ringed plateaus. His bishops professed piety. His counselors preferred their wealth. Both lacked the finesse to rule. To govern, a man needed coin and devotion. To rule, a man needed to know when to ladle the honey, when to apply the whip, and when to wield the sword.

The joik of the Olmmoš was no longer merely the ancient tale of migration, from the womb of the gods to this harsh world of ice and darkness. Nor was it the lamentation of their subjugation by the Jápmea. It was finally the tale of glorious victory and Olmmoš dominion. The reign of True Believers would be marked by his name and his deeds, and rightly so. He had transformed the title of Vijns from servant to master.

"I am sure those of us in the south, who have not experienced these troubles, can open our hearts and coffers to the care of northern brothers and sisters," said someone in the gathered group.

From the corner of his eye, Bávvál observed the generous benefactor with equal amounts of curiosity and suspicion. He smiled at Siggur, the priest from Hemmela, then applauded lightly. "There, you see. The gods have given us a sound resolution to this question." He stood and smoothed his robes. "Members of the Court of Counselors, let us withdraw to more intimate quarters to discuss recent developments."

Descending the dais, Bávvál adopted a pace befitting his station and the weight of his vestments. In deference, his counselors trailed, respectful of the gap he had created. As he neared his private chambers, Bávvál felt a rushed presence come up alongside him. Expecting to see Áigin, he was momentarily taken aback to find his bishop, Rikkar, flanking him.

"My Vijns," the bishop began, then hesitated, his bony hands clasped in front of him. Their footfalls echoed one another while Bávvál waited for the man to continue.

"You have something on your mind, Rikkar?" he prompted, tiring of his draggling company.

"I request a private audience prior to convening the court," the bishop said in a rush.

For all his power, Bávvál could not resist needling the pretentious man—a habit of a lifetime. "I believe this is what we are currently engaged in."

"My Vijns, this is hardly private," Rikkar said, looking around.

Bávvál regarded this man he had known since their youth. He tried to see what remained of the pale-haired, fiery zealot who had prayed and denied himself in the name of faith in the gods.

Rikkar's hair had become white as the seasons of snow. Ambition. Betrayal. Repentance. They had been hard masters. Rikkar had learned. He had served Bávvál well, in the end. And he had been rewarded for it.

"Privacy in the Stronghold is a matter of degrees," Bávvál said, reflecting further on their many years of acquaintance. "Speak your mind."

"My Vijns, is it wise to bring Siggur to the Court of Counselors?" Rikkar asked in a low, hurried manner as if the speed of his sibilant inflection could somehow conceal its venomous intent.

Bávvál let out an amused laugh. "My dear Rikkar, is it wise to question my decision?" He let the levity with which he posed the question fall away. "I will remind you and all who might be similarly disposed to impertinence that Siggur is a member of the Court of Counselors because he has provided tribute well beyond his counterparts." He stopped short of his chamber door to hold Rikkar's gaze. The man's pale eyes wavered with undisguised fear. "I suggest you forget your petty squabbles with him. As I have forgotten your duplicity."

~

Alone at last, Bávvál paced the length of his private chambers. *Two. I have sent hundreds and they have sent me two*, he silently raged. Aloud he muttered, "They are a handful and we are thousands."

His meeting with the Court of Counselors had proved as much an irritation as the simpleton Niilán had sent in his stead. *Worthless. Every last one of them*, he thought, giving his vexation free rein. He alone had taken a governance divided between Believers and Hunters and brought it under a single rightful leadership. The Vijns defended both body and soul of the Olmmoš. It maddened him that he needed these petty counselors to tighten his control. But he could not be everywhere at once to voice the gods' will. And temples and garrisons often favored their needs over their duty to him as True Believers.

A knock upon the door prompted a hasty, disgruntled "Yes!"

The door swung wide on silent hinges. Áigin entered without Bávvál's leave.

"You take liberties," he warned his agent.

The man stopped. He inclined his head. It was not a true bow. Rather, it was just enough of an acknowledgment to count. "My Vijns, my haste to serve overwhelmed my nobler intention."

In spite of the provocation, Bávvál appreciated the man's ability to twist words and meaning to suit his purpose. A begrudging grin broke through his peevish mood. He chuckled to himself. "I trust your unsolicited presence will provide substance to counterbalance the intrusion."

Áigin frowned. "Substance I can supply. Your pleasure I cannot guarantee."

"Gods curse you, Áigin! Speak plainly," Bávvál exploded, stomping his foot.

The spy raised his large, slender hands in an expression of forbearance. Bávvál sat down in the chair by the fire, hardly noting the comfort of warm furs beneath him.

"I have received word confirming the report from Niilán's man," the spy began, his voice mild and controlled as if he spoke of the weather and not the challenge to Bávvál's rule.

"There was a skirmish upon the battlefield of the Great Valley. All save two appeared to be our soldiers."

"All save two?" Bávvál repeated.

"By all accounts, a young woman and a young man engaged the soldiers in the mêlée," the spy said slowly, giving the words time to sink in.

"The Jápmea and the bastard Piijkij," Bávvál surmised.

"The descriptions fit," Áigin allowed. "Our soldiers also captured another Jápmea and her infant."

Bávvál waved off the last piece of news. "What of the other two? What became of them?"

"One recounting said a soldier seized the young woman in the skirmish."

"So, she is our prisoner."

"No, my Vijns. She has disappeared."

Bávvál slammed his hands down upon the chair's wooden armrests. "The Jápmea are defeated. Yet this one female comes in and out of our grasp, not once, but twice."

"If she is Jápmea," Áigin said, his tone even and reasonable.

Bávvál was in no mood to accept reason.

"Dávgon's plans . . ." the spy began.

"Dávgon's plans were those of a child who believed he understood the game he played. He didn't and he lost," Bávvál said.

Áigin took the lash of anger without flinching. He stood tall and impassive, like a tree waiting for a storm to pass. "I would not confuse the merit of the man with the merit of his calculations," his spy said without malice or censure.

"What are you saying?" Bávvál asked, edging forward in his seat.

Áigin shrugged. "I am merely suggesting Dávgon saw a purpose in her. Otherwise, why spare her life?"

"She was a prize to build his pride upon, something he thought he could use to bolster the Brethren's claim to power."

"Perhaps." Áigin shrugged again.

"What is so special about her, beyond her immortality?" Bávvál demanded.

"I do not know," the spy said with an air of regret. "I suspect Dávgon did."

"Enough," Bávvál said, leaning back, tired of chasing ghosts. Then he recalled the mention of another Jápmea. "What became of the other one, the one with the infant?"

"She was found hiding in a bramble on the Great Valley's eastern border," the spy said.

"Then we can question her," Bávvál said with renewed expectation.

Áigin pursed his lips.

"You disagree?"

"I would not disagree, except for the fact she too has disappeared," Áigin said, betraying no emotion.

"Is there nothing you can say that does not reek of ill-tidings and the Jápmea?" Bávvál said, slumping back into his chair with disgust.

"There have been no new reports of Brethren action since the skirmish in the Great Valley," Áigin said.

Bávvál sniffed. "Which is like saying the chuoika are not biting today."

Undeterred, Áigin agreed. "Yes. And like midges they are destined to be crushed under our hand."

Looking to find fault with his agent, Bávvál inquired, "What of the man charged with bringing us the bodies? What duties have you given him?"

Áigin hesitated, his eyes shifting ever so slightly. "He has been assigned to daily patrols," he said, then added, "pending your word."

Bávvál smiled inwardly, having managed to ruffle the man's cool demeanor. "I believe we can make much more use of him than just another body for the patrols."

His spy bowed his head. The inclination had the air of doubt disguised as deference.

"We should promote him to a regiment commander and have word of his deeds and reward broadcast through the outposts," Bávvál said, keen to see his man's reaction.

Áigin started, for once speechless. The High Priest continued, "The Brethren have waged a campaign to challenge my power. But you are right, Áigin, they are gnats, an annoyance. We have the strength of the soldiers and the gods behind us. Let us show these holdout Piijkij the only thing they have accomplished is to raise a humble Olmmoš soldier from rank and file to commander. It will inspire others to rise to the occasion."

CHAPTER SEVENTEEN

"I F YOU DON'T LET me look at your leg, I can't set it properly," Dárja said, moving away from the irascible Piijkij called Herko.

"I didn't want you to touch me in the first place," the man grumbled.

Dárja knelt by the fire, placing the moss she'd gathered in the boiling salt water.

"Gods pity us, Herko! Just let her do what she must," the other prone man croaked.

"I cannot fault you for wanting to live, Gáral. The rest of you are too blind to see what is happening," Herko warned.

"Válde, make him stop," said the young Olmmoš with a sparse beard framing his pointed chin. "We are all familiar with Herko's opinions."

"And what of yours, Edo?" Herko asked, propping himself up on one elbow to glare past Dárja to the back of the cave. "You, who always clamor for honor and our oath, what of our oath to kill her kind? Or have you been bewitched by her and seek her warmth in your furs?"

The young man lunged forward, his anger catching the fire's glow. Dárja's hand went to the knife at her waist. Válde interceded, pushing the young one back to where he had been sitting, motioning for calm.

"Perhaps, we are no longer Brethren," he said, looking around the cave to each of his men. "Perhaps we are simply Olmmoš, willing to forget our fallen brothers, our slain Avr, and the injustice enacted upon us by the Vijns and his soldiers." His eyes came to rest on the one called Herko. "You can leave, join the ranks of the faceless, and live the life of a coward. It is your choice. If you stay, then you will do what is best for us all. And this means, if your leg is useless, then you are useless to us, so either let Dárja look at it or crawl out of here and live your life as a coward."

The fierceness of the Piijkij's words surprised Dárja, who'd begun to look upon the man as fair, if not noble, for an Olmmoš. A furtive glance around at the others suggested they were also taken aback. For what felt like a lifetime, the only sounds in the cave were the wind outside and the crackle of the fire.

"I'll see to the wound and then to the leg," she said, meeting Herko's eye briefly.

Válde withdrew to the other side of the fire, indicating Dárja should continue with her work.

Without asking permission, she carefully lifted up the furs from the man named Gáral. When he made no complaint, she moved his arm away from his body so she could again examine the long cut. It was deep and inflamed. *At least the dried blood and dirt has been cleaned off.* She applied firm, gentle pressure along the edges of the gash. The skin felt hot. The man recoiled and cried out.

"I want to see what flows from your wound," she explained, aware the others watched her.

"My guts if you are not careful," he grunted.

Dárja rubbed her thumb and forefinger together, testing the thickness of the seepage. Then she leaned in close to the man and sniffed the wound. Behind the strong odor of an unwashed body, mixed with smoke, she smelled the sweet scent of bell-heather.

She sat up, brushing back her hood.

"Your cut has turned," she said aloud to the man, who grunted again.

Válde spoke up, drowning the half-voiced mutterings of the three hale Olmmoš. "What does that mean?"

Dárja heard in his question both the concern of a leader for his man, and the desperation of a man for his future. She briefly considered telling him only time and the gods could answer with certainty.

"I'll need something to bind him," she said, busying herself with the birch bark she'd stripped from the tree. "Something long enough to tie around his chest," she added. Válde sat unmoving, his expression stoic.

Finally, he signaled to the three able-bodied Piijkij. "Find her what she needs."

Dárja waited for these Olmmoš to question her. To her surprise, they proved to be helpful, if not solicitous. She cut a strip of the bark, placed it into her mouth, and began to chew. Válde's brows arched, but he said nothing. She scooped a cup of the hot salt water and waited for it to cool, all the while chewing on the tough, bitter bark.

The prone man didn't hide his suspicion. Dárja ignored him in favor of testing the water on her bare palm. She flinched, shaking her hand free of the scalding water. The man sucked in his breath, his nervous attention on the iron pot above the fire. He'd already experienced the water's stinging bite. Dárja spat out the contents of her mouth into her freshly cleaned palm. The bark resembled a thick, gray pulp which she spread across her palm with her thumb.

The man tried to shift away. "What are you doing with that?"

"Healing your wound," she said, lifting the sodden moss from the hot water with the tip of her knife.

Dárja worked swiftly to apply the remedies as the the man twitched and writhed. Then she took the remaining length of birch bark and pressed it firmly against his side. "Do we have the bindings?" she asked, glancing up.

Beyond the fire, the young Piijkij, the one named Edo, held out his hand wordlessly.

To Válde she said, "Lift him to sitting. I will hold the covering over the wound."

Válde leaned in, ready to act.

"Carefully," Dárja cautioned him.

He nodded, gingerly sliding his hands under the prone man's back before shifting him into as much a seated position as he could manage.

Dárja directed her next instructions to the young Piijkij. "While I hold the poultice in place, you'll need to wrap the binding around him."

The young man hesitated before rocking forward to kneel behind Válde. He encircled his comrade with two lengths of leather. When his wrist brushed against Dárja's he recoiled as if burned.

"Her touch is not tainted," Válde said.

"Tie the ends securely," she said to the young Piijkij, shifting the straps to hold the poultice in place. He fumbled with the cordage, then retreated when he'd finished. Dárja signaled to Válde to lower the man.

With Gáral resting once again, she replaced the furs across his exposed chest, then pulled on her fur gloves to place the fire-heated stones along the length of his torso. "They'll replace the heat you lost," she said to both the injured man and those watching her.

Válde pulled a leather flask from his furs. He held Gáral's head and tilted some of the liquid into the man's mouth. "For the pain," he said.

Dárja rose, stretched her stiff body, and then slumped down against the cave wall, saying, "I'll examine the leg in a moment." She reviewed her efforts, looking to find anything she might have missed. Her training as a healer had been intense if not complete. Kalek had spent her whole life under Okta's tutelage; she'd studied only a quarter turn. Having grown up in the apothecary, she had a natural affinity for healing which gave her the confidence to try to care for the wound. And she had to admit it had felt good to have purpose once more, even if her satisfaction was restrained by the fact the man's life was in her hands. *If he dies, they'll blame me.*

She regarded the men in the cave. Those well enough to move about busied themselves with tasks that kept them with their backs to her. Even Válde had turned away. She took his unguarded stance as a sign of his faith in her, as well as her skill. This level of trust wouldn't last should his man succumb to the wound. She needed to be gone before that happened. *I'll slip away when these Olmmoš rest*, she thought, her eyes closing. *No. I'd better set the broken leg, then leave.*

The last thing she heard before sleep embraced her was, "And what about my pain?" followed by a dry laugh and "Herko, you are the pain."

~

"Are we just supposed to trust her?" Edo whispered, glancing over at Dárja, slouched against the cave wall. "What's to say she won't cut our throats when we sleep?"

"If she meant to kill us, why would she work to save Gáral?" Válde reasoned.

"To gain our trust, before sticking us with that knife of hers," Feles said without emotion.

"She might be Jápmea," Herko said, "but she's no match for the four of you."

"There are easier ways to be rid of us," Válde argued. "She could have run off yesterday. She could have taken word to the soldiers of our location. She did not."

"Then what are her reasons for staying with us?" Feles asked.

Her reasons are her own, Válde thought to himself, repeating her answer. It was no answer he could give to his men and hope to convince them she would be their weapon against the High

Priest and his Believers. For centuries the Brethren of Hunters had dedicated themselves to tracking and killing the Immortals, who had once enslaved the Olmmoš. He had killed her kind in war and in peace and had never questioned whether their actions were just. He had merely trained and believed and killed. He had no reason other than duty. *I swore an oath*, Válde thought. *We all did.*

And yet, here she was. No abomination, just some strange puzzlement he could not quite grasp. She could have killed him at will or betrayed him to the Olmmoš soldiers who sought them. Instead, she'd put effort into saving more than one Piijkij life. He watched the firelight shadows dance across Dárja's hollowed cheeks, touching upon her soft mouth. A knife peeked out from the folds at her waist. His knife. The one she had taken from him. The one he had let her keep in hopes his gesture would gain her trust and sway her intent.

Gods above, how will we ever succeed? They were a ragged lot of six men, two of whom were wounded, and one Jápmea girl. In her words, it could take several moon cycles for Herko's leg to fully heal, and Gáral needed a proper place to rest and decent food, neither of which they had at the present. Though Válde was loath to consider it, they would have to find a true source of shelter, which meant risking discovery. *With only four Piijkij and a Jápmea*, he thought, amending his previous accounting.

"What was she doing out there?"

The whispered question brought Válde back to his men. He had no answer, so he skirted the unknown with what he did know. "Fighting Olmmoš soldiers, like us."

Despite the confidence of his of response, Feles's question stayed in the forefront of Válde's thoughts. *She fought in the battle and escaped from the Avr's retinue, taking Marnej with her. And she was there again in the Great Valley, fighting alongside Marnej against Olmmoš soldiers.* Was it happenstance? Or did her *reasons* mask a greater, unforeseen threat to the Olmmoš from the Jápmea?

Válde harbored no hatred toward his people. In truth, he took pride in the fact the Olmmoš spirit had freed men from their Immortal overlords. What he sought was justice for the Brethren betrayed by men who chose power over the protection of their own people. He cast an appraising glance in Dárja's direction. Her head had lolled to one side, slack-jawed, like a careless child. Válde looked back to his men, reminding himself that she was no child. She was a Jápmea, one who might be spying to find a way to reprise an Immortal offensive against the Olmmoš. He had seen her disappear into their other world and come back.

A low voice asked, "Do you really believe we can use this Jápmea for our purpose?" Válde looked up to see Mures had leaned in close to the fire as he spoke.

"For the moment, her skill as a healer is useful," Válde answered. To himself, he added, *Her other uses remain to be seen.*

CHAPTER EIGHTEEN

MARNEJ SHOULD'VE GUESSED THAT after the last travelers' hut, the trade route, this far south of the Stronghold, would turn out to be rough and rarely traveled. The last travelers' hut had been a forlorn place, more of a hovel than a seat of respite. The hutkeeper had been a kind old woman with failing sight. She'd been generous with her fire and tea. Marnej had paid in kind by chopping trees felled by the last storm. The old woman had been grateful enough to supply him with food and dried muorji for his journey, along with a bit of unsolicited advice.

"There isn't much south of here for a stripling like you. Best make amends with your father and mother and return to your kinfolk."

Marnej had nodded his thanks, saying nothing further about his plans. As he'd guided his resigned horse south, he'd felt the woman's milky eyes upon him. He'd peeked back at her. She'd stood by the door to the hut for a moment, shaking her head at what she'd deemed the folly of his youthful pride. He could not tell her that it was dishonor and not pride pressing hard upon his heels.

Leagues beyond the travelers' hut, the gray midday stretched ahead, unwelcoming and unrelenting. On either side of Marnej, the thick forest closed in as if it meant to crush him in its heavy silence. He tucked his chin, his eyes squinched above his collar. Despite his best effort to let the tedium of the passing landscape dull his mind, the question of what would happen when he ran out of road nagged at him. With no easy answer, he tried to avoid thinking about the inevitable future until he found himself before a horizon of bluish ice.

Marnej sat upon his horse, staring into an endless vista his mind could barely fathom. Ahead of him lay nothing. No trees. No hills. Nothing but ice and air. He slid off his horse, stunned and unsure. His cold-stiffened limbs protested. Their ache was a welcome reminder he was alive and this was no dream.

A gust of wind from the south brought with it an eddy of snow as if it cast back to the land what was not wanted upon the frozen water. Marnej inhaled. The biting air held no trace of scent. No pine. No smoke. No animal musk. No hint of green slumbering beneath the deathly blue. *Have I truly come upon the southern shore of Davvieana?* It had been his unspoken goal to reach it, with the understanding that, once he arrived, his next step would be revealed. Marnej scanned the distance again. There was no sign from the gods, no sense of purpose awaiting him, only a whistling wind which, to his ears, sounded like solitude. Perhaps this too was a trick of the sea. He recalled the fireside stories of seals that swam upriver from the sea to steal Olmmoš dreams. Men and women would chase after them, swimming out into the deep water where the gods could not stand and hold them safe. Marnej shivered, seeing himself sinking, his dreams just outside of his grasp.

There's only one way to know if I've come far enough, he thought. He tied the reins to his belt. He didn't want the horse wandering off, leaving him alone to wait for the spring thaw. He closed his eyes upon the vast nothingness ahead of him. Even as he tried to slow his breath, his pulse raced at the impossibility of water meeting the heavens at some unfathomable point. Marnej listened to the wind, mumbling to himself assurances he'd come far enough to be free of the Song of All—free of its connection and its promise of belonging. The far-off cry of some distant bird seemed to mock him.

"I don't belong," he said out loud, answering the bird and his own lingering hope. *Not to the Brethren. Not to the Immortals. Not to Dárja, or even my father.* He thought of Irjan, and what his father had looked like the one time he'd seen him. Dark, tired eyes and gray-streaked beard and hair. He'd shouted at Dárja to leave and escape back to the Immortals' realm. Just as Marnej had done in the last skirmish. *I'm not my father's vessel. I'm not touched by the gods.* He chided himself for once believing in a destiny. To prove he was free of fate, love, and belonging, he began to chant his song, silently promising, *This is the last time the world will hear my joik.*

As his final refrain trailed off, stillness reigned, rich and comforting. He'd passed beyond the Immortals' reach. He'd found freedom, one where his heart would never again experience the surge of hope and the pang of loss. Marnej drew in a deep breath, feeling the sting of cold air for what it was—cold air. No whispered entreaties. No promises of clear skies to roam. Tightness gripped his throat. He swallowed hard. He called this freedom. His soul said otherwise. Hot tears brimmed and cooled in his eyes. He began to shake, not from the cold but from the sobs that wracked his exhausted body. As a boy, Marnej had never cried. Tears only garnered pain and derision among the Brethren. A Piijkij was never weak, even when defeated. Now, Marnej cried for the mother he had never known, the father he had hated, and his own inescapable failure.

I only wanted to belong. To be accepted, he pleaded, lost to the first voices upon the wind. Then he found himself overwhelmed by the cacophony of competing choruses, too many to take in all at once. Marnej's heart leapt. His skin prickled as if touched by the rays of an unfettered sun. The Song of All embraced him. It coalesced into a melody that revealed he'd never been alone or separate. He'd always been a part of every living thing.

How can you be adrift when you never left? they all seemed to ask.

No! some part of Marnej objected.

They beckoned him. They wanted him. They were him. All of it was true.

No! It's not true. They wouldn't want him when they learned of his failings. He pulled back from the voices, trying to find his own.

"No!" he shouted, his denial echoing in his head. Marnej came to himself on his hands and knees, panting.

From behind him, he heard, "You have nothing to fear from me."

Marnej scrambled away, alarmed to see a man, leaning over him.

"You've nothing to fear from me," he said again.

Marnej's head spun.

"Strange to find a soul out here," the man said. "Stranger still to find them sitting in the snow, shaking. I thought you'd been taken by a fit. So, I stopped to look upon you. Gods be thanked you came back to yourself. You would've frozen out here before I could've ever moved you on my own."

"I've been traveling," Marnej managed to say.

"Can't go much farther," the man said.

As his features coalesced into something solid, Marnej studied him. He couldn't see his eyes beneath brows as thick as a bramble. A bulbous nose hung between a pair of drooping cheeks which might have once been plump and cheerful.

"I can give you shelter and not much more," he said, then arched his brows revealing frank blue eyes, the color of the ice at the end of this world. "Just so we're clear, I'm meager bounty for a thief, unless your currency is salted pike."

Woolly headed as he was, it took Marnej a breath or two to gather the man's meaning.

"I am no thief," he said.

The bulbous nose sniffed. "No need to find offense in a man's caution. Few souls come this way. Those who do are either lost or running."

On guard, Marnej asked, "And which are you?"

The man barked out a laugh, only just muffled by the woolens wrapped about his lower face. "Fair question. Best answered with something to warm the belly."

~

Marnej bent down to look into the snug, log-stacked hut. The man shuffled to the hearth.

"Be welcome," he said, rebuilding the fire.

Marnej stooped his head further and took a hesitant step forward. The man lit a candle. It cast a weak glow in the cramped, dark space. *Barely enough room for the two of us,* he thought, pulling shut the door behind him. He stood up, his head poking through the ranks of dried fish, hanging from the roof. Their dry, lifeless eyes stared back reprovingly.

Marnej ducked away from their rasping touch. The man let out another laugh.

"They're not much for company," he said, amused by his comment.

Marnej looked around, unsure of what to do. Fishing nets draped from nails on the walls. A bearskin lay across a low pallet in the corner. Two iron pots hung above the fire. When he'd run out of walls and corners to stare into, he regarded the man. Shadows made it hard to tell his true age. His beard was mostly white, but his brows were black like the feathers of a ruffled crow.

"Sit!" the man encouraged.

Marnej squeezed onto a squeaky stool between a rough-hewn ladder, with no apparent purpose, and an empty brining barrel.

The man stoked the fire, saying, "Good thing you weren't out there too long."

"Mmm," Marnej agreed, pulling his hands from his mitts to warm them with his breath.

The man took down two fish carcasses and placed them in a large pot suspended over the fire. From a basket on the floor behind him, he produced an onion that he peeled with surprising dexterity, carving half-moon pieces into the pot.

"I don't doubt you are chilled to your core," he said, grabbing another onion. "Fish soup will bring you back to yourself. Now, what do I call you?"

The man's expression was inquisitive without being intrusive as if he expected his guest to lie. Which, of course, is what Marnej did.

"Kálle," he said without thinking, then struggled to free himself of the vision of Úlla, round and full of expectant life.

The man inclined his head, "I am Jusse," he said, cutting wrinkled turnips and pale roots Marnej didn't recognize.

Banishing Úlla's ghost, Marnej said, "You're a fisherman."

"When the light shines," Jusse said, seemingly unaware of his guest's disquiet.

"And now?" Marnej asked.

Jusse grinned over his pot. "I am half a fisherman."

Marnej frowned. "And the other half?"

The man's grin widened, revealing long, yellowed teeth. "A man who fishes for things that don't always come from the water."

Marnej stiffened, wary of his meaning.

Jusse laughed again. He gave the stew a slow stir, then rested the wooden spoon on the lip of the pot.

"You're looking at me as if I've stepped out upon cracking ice?"

Marnej shook his head, not wanting to give offense.

"Well, I don't fault you for it. I spend most of my days in my own company." He held up his hand to stop Marnej from speaking. "And, before you sow a garden of pity for me, I do so by my choice. I like others just fine. I just like my company more." He picked up the idle spoon. "Although, another voice is occasionally welcomed."

"How long have you been here?" Marnej asked.

Jusse eyed him. "Most of your life, I'd imagine. Before that, I felled timber and milled wood." He sat down on a low stool, his legs bent like a frog waiting to spring. Pulling out a short knife with a thick bone handle from his belt, he said, "Old man that I am now, I prefer projects to keep me by the fire." He picked up a creamy piece of wood off the floor and began to whittle the wood, casting curled shavings toward the flames between them.

Marnej reexamined the overfilled crevices of the cramped hut, seeing it with new eyes. "Why did you come here?"

Jusse shrugged, concentrating on the wood he carved. "I grew up not far from here. My father fished the reef waters like his father before and his father. My father expected the same of me. I, to the contrary, was certain I wasn't a fisherman. When I was old enough to believe I knew better, I left. I traveled north, relying more on strength than skill. I enjoyed the traveling. Then I met a woman who stole my heart. She kept me in one place until the gods took her. I didn't see much reason to stay after, not with soldiers pushing their snouts into my grain sacks like rooting spiidni." Jusse coughed. It was a deep rumbling hack that shook his frame. When he recovered he added, "I could see there'd be no end. I wanted no part of it. And you, Kálle?"

Marnej started at the unfamiliar name. Jusse looked up from his whittling. He rested the knife and carving wood in his lap, then leaned over to ladle from a smaller pot of steaming liquid. He held a cup out to Marnej. "Here, I find something warm always helps a story along."

Marnej hesitated, then took the cup. Their eyes met. Jusse smiled. Had he guessed Marnej planned to weave a tale in place of the truth? He took a sip, delighted by the tart berry flavor tinged with a bite of something stronger. He took a deeper drink. A relaxing warmth began to trickle through his veins, starting in his chest and ending in his tingling fingers.

Jusse blew across his cup. "I'm not partial to either muorji tea or juhka. But together, they make fine friends." He leaned back. "It's been many a season of snow since I've heard a joik."

"I'm sorry, I've no voice for singing," Marnej said, thinking of his part in the Song and fearful of what Jusse might've heard.

The man took another sip, then smacked his lips. "It's not the quality of the voice that matters. It's the story you tell."

Marnej's ears reddened. "My story isn't so different than yours." He went to drink from his cup to hide his flush, then realized it was empty. Reluctant to ask for more, he held the cup in his lap.

He cleared his throat. "My father loved me. I didn't know it until it was too late. We had no time to speak, to clear the ill will I'd harbored. Then I betrayed someone." He broke off, reliving the transgression. "She hates me now. I couldn't go back to her kin."

He'd almost said "kind." It was only by gulping back the last letter that "kin" had come out in its stead. Marnej eyed his cup, disturbed by the truth he'd just shared.

Jusse sighed. "We learn, don't we. But at what cost? And for whose benefit?" He shook his head, holding out his hand for Marnej's cup. Marnej gave it to him, warning himself to treat this next helping with much more care and respect.

"So you came to the end of the world to cast yourself into the waters?" Jusse said, handing the sloshing cup back.

"Yes. Perhaps I did," Marnej admitted, embarrassed he'd been so easily divined. He chuckled. "It wasn't a very well-thought-out plan."

"The frozen sea does make it difficult," Jusse said, smiling as he leaned in to test the bubbling stew. Satisfied, he waved for Marnej to drink up. Jusse traded the empty cup for a bowl of stew with a carved spoon sticking out.

Marnej pulled out the spoon, taken aback by the intricate design. He caught Jusse's eye.

The man shrugged. "I've had many nights to practice."

The two sat and slurped the stew, which Marnej found as tasty as anything he could remember. Jusse coughed, then wiped his chin with the back of his hand.

He lowered his bowl. "I'll grant you the wisdom my father gave me. And because you've shared my meal, you'll listen. That said, because you're young, you'll like as not heed it." A knowing smile graced his creased face. "You gain nothing by running away. You only lose."

Marnej opened his mouth to speak.

Jusse held up his hand. "Yes, I know you've well-reasoned excuses and wish to argue them. But I'm full and content and have no desire to debate. I'm a man who sees more shadows behind him than in front of him. This allows me to say I understand the world better than you. I also know the power of youth and know I can't conquer it."

CHAPTER NINETEEN

THE GRAY LIGHT OF day broke through low on the horizon. Marnej gave it a fleeting look. Jusse's boat creaked with each broad stroke of the oars. But even this monotony was an improvement over his journey across the ice. Fresh snow had clung like mud to the wooden rails of the laden rowboat. The leather harness he'd used to drag the boat forward toward the open sea had dug into his shoulders. Marnej had soon developed a new sympathy for cart-nags. On his second day, walking out upon the ice, a fierce headwind slowed him. He'd leaned into the gale, his eyes trained to the south, expecting to see the Southern Teeth jut out of the protected waters of Davvieana. His second day had passed much like his first out on the desolate expanse, his senses alert to the trembling that would precede the loud crack of solid ice giving way. Jusse had said a wise man would do well to have his boat ready when he heard the ice murmuring.

What the old fisherman had not warned Marnej about were the tricks his mind would play on him. Several times, he'd found himself teetering on the verge of panic. He'd unhitched the boat and climbed in more than once, believing the ice ready to break, only to have the wind taunt him for his fear. The last time he'd gone through the motions of preparing for the water, the ice had cracked like the thundering sky. The boat had pitched to one side. Marnej had held fast to the oars, staring into the open mouth of dark waters. He'd had no experience rowing a boat. But he'd convinced himself it couldn't be any harder than riding an unwilling horse.

He'd been wrong. Jusse had cautioned him that the oars would be unwieldy and the boat unsteady. The most miserly movement sent the vessel tilting one way and then the next. His stomach had sloshed along with the sea beneath him, leaving Marnej sure he'd never eat again.

"Plenty have gone," Jusse had cautioned. "I've not met one who's returned from the Breath of Gods."

Marnej had listened to Jusse's detailed instructions about the wind and currents, aware of the man's doubt.

"How can you believe you will survive when you've never been on the water?" Jusse had asked.

Marnej had clung to the belief that his strength and resolve would carry him through. He had to believe because he couldn't go back and he couldn't stay with Jusse in his little hut. Even if he failed, it wouldn't be a loss, as Jusse assumed. Because death, in its way, was a form of freedom he could accept. Mercifully, time and repetition had transformed Marnej's initial flailing into smooth, confident motion. Dip the oars. Pull back, arms aching, legs straining. Raise the oars. Sweep. Over and over again.

Marnej leaned back, the oars gliding through becalmed waters. The sun broke through the parting clouds, turning the water dripping off his oars golden, like summer honey. He dipped the oars again into the smooth waters, pulling farther and farther away from the past he'd left behind. To the future which awaited him he promised, "I *will* make it."

~

When night descended, Marnej used the bright North Star as his guide. He kept the Goose's Back to the far west of the dark sky and the Fox's Tail to his east. And, although Jusse had cautioned him against falling asleep, lest the Breath of Gods push him west to the limit of their domain, Marnej dozed.

He dreamed he was back with the old fisherman, warm in the hut, a bowl of fish stew in his hands.

"So where will you go"? Jusse asked.

He shrugged. "South, I guess."

Jusse snorted. "Onto the sea?"

"Yes," he said, beginning to doubt his answer.

"What do you know of the sea?" the fisherman challenged.

"Nothing," he said.

Marnej awoke from this dream with a start, his heart pounding, vowing he'd stay awake. Then the days stretched on, one into another. He stopped expecting to see a remote shoreline. He stopped worrying about the Breath of Gods. There was only ever water. Sometimes gray. Sometimes black. And none of it could quench his growing thirst.

Initially, Marnej had been careful with his supplies of food and water, taking only enough to keep him going. When those supplies dwindled, he became even more sparing. He let his stomach rumble long and loud, appreciating that at least his hunger helped to break up the tedium of ceaseless rowing. His thirst was another matter. It was more than a distraction. It became his constant companion, even in his dreams.

"Wait for the rain, my boy," Jusse said.

He looked at the clear, cloudless sky. "When?"

The fisherman dipped his bowl into the white snow. "Soon enough."

"What if it never rains?"

Marnej woke, blinking into a fog as dense as a wool blanket. It hid all save the patch of sea upon which he and the boat rocked. It was useless to wonder how long he'd been asleep. It could've been a moment or half the morning. On the western horizon, buried behind both winter sky and mist, there was a faint glow, hinting at the sun. He pulled harder with his left hand to keep the boat on an easterly track. Behind him, the sky darkened to the color of ore from Úlla's forge. He pulled harder, trying to outrun the memories closing in. Mist clung to him, becoming drops that slid down his nose onto his cracked lips. Marnej's thirst came alive with new urgency. He lapped up the precious water, tasting the salt crust upon his beard. He grimaced. *Always salt*, he thought, wishing for the fresh streams and lakes he'd left behind.

From the murky east, a fierce gust rose, bringing with it the first promise of rain. Whatever joy Marnej felt at the possibility of fresh water, it disappeared into the white crests, battering his boat. Convinced he'd swung west, he steered harder to his right. The sea sluiced over the dipping sides, drenching the sleeves of his furs. Cold dampness soaked down through his many layers to act like a lash upon his skin.

The wind tore at Marnej as he labored at the oars which were like twigs in the watery valleys and mountains that rose and fell all around him. He looked down into the dark trough of water where once there had been a peak. His stomach lurched. He held on to the useless oars, fighting against a rolling sickness. As he plummeted down the face of a rising wave, he let go of any hope he might regain control. He was at the mercy of the sea. His mind flashed to Jusse's warning that none had returned from beyond the Breath of Gods.

Rising again toward the sky, Marnej prepared for the moment when up became down. But he kept on rising. The supplies in the boat's prow tumbled into him. He glanced over his shoulder. A black wall of water towered above, its lip curling toward him like a twisted grin. Marnej's blood ran cold with the certainty of his death. He shouted at the gods. They roared back with wind and water, sending the rowboat hurtling over.

Plunged into the cold, dark abyss, Marnej clawed at the water, reaching for the surface. His fingers scratched something solid that eluded his grasp. Salt stung his unseeing eyes. Blinded

in this black world, the furs which once protected him now
dragged him down. He thrashed, trying to free himself of them.
He kicked and lashed out with his feet. His lungs ached to burst.
His every thought screamed for air. Then his head popped above
the churning sea. Air and water mixed together in his instinctive
gasp. Marnej choked, his arms flailing through the wave's foamy
crest. Again his hands brushed something solid. He squinted
against the spray. The unfamiliar shape of his overturned boat
came into view. It was earthen brown rising up the leaden surging
sea. Marnej kicked with the last of his energy. His hands caught
the boat's ridge. There he hung like the last wind-bedraggled leaf
in a winter storm.

CHAPTER TWENTY

T HE DOOR TO THE apothecary swung open with a bang, startling Kalek, who stood grinding herbs at the work table. Ello came rushing in, her face almost as red as her hair. The gust of wind she brought with her rustled the dried leaves upon the table.

"She's returned," the nieddaš gasped between breaths.

Kalek dropped the stone pestle into the mortar bowl, his herbs forgotten. He rushed around the wood table and grasped Ello by the hand. "Dárja has returned?" He whirled the nieddaš toward the door she had just burst through. "Show me!"

"No, Úlla has!" Ello cried out, racing ahead to leap over obstacles and slip around pillars with the speed and grace of a deer. Kalek followed, making up for a lack of finesse with force and determination. When they reached the fortified doors of the gatehouse, they broke through the murmuring crowd. On the smooth earthen floor lay a fur-shrouded body in Ávrá's arms.

The coiled figure shook like a wounded animal. For an instant, Kalek hesitated, waiting for Dárja to appear beyond those gathered. Ashen faces stared back at him. Like a tree, carved from within by time and elements, Kalek slowly fell to his knees, his gaze resting on the blurred outlines of Ávrá's face, its familiar angles hovering over the shaking body. *Above all else, I am a healer,* he reminded himself. He reached out his hand. A tremor passed through his palm as it touched Úlla's arm. Gently, he turned her toward him, worried by the concern in Ávrá's expression. Half-hidden by a tangled mat of hair, Úlla's eyes stared out of her dirty, tear-streaked face as if haunted by horrors. Kalek fought back his revulsion at the smell of blood and neglect to take her into his arms. Úlla cringed, clinging to Ávrá.

"You are home," Ávrá said, smoothing the hair away from Úlla's face. "You are safe."

Kalek watched a spasm ripple through the shell of the once-powerful nieddaš. Only Úlla was no longer a nieddaš. She had given birth. She was an oktoeadni. *This is no homecoming for a birth*, he thought. No music. No joy. No celebration of new life. Or honoring of the soul that has passed beyond this realm. Gods, how he wished Okta was by his side.

"The baby?" Kalek asked, desperate to avoid his loss.

Úlla whimpered. Her grip on Ávrá tightened. Ávrá shook her head, her eyes imploring Kalek. *To do what?* He did not know.

"You are safe, Úlla," Kalek said, loud enough for all to hear. "And you need care. Ávrá will stay with you." Kalek looked to solemn-faced Ello, who stood next to him. She nodded, her mouth a resolute line. "Ello is here to help, as well. We need to take you to the healers' quarters, Úlla. Where I can care for you," he said, adding hesitantly, "and the baby."

Ello knelt opposite him. She laid her hand on Úlla's still-trembling body. "I'm going to pick you up," she said, glancing to Kalek for her next cue.

"I will stay with you as well," Ávrá said.

Kalek looked to Ávrá and Ello as he waited for a sign from Úlla. Their eyes met, their dismay undisguised. When Úlla finally spoke, she was muffled by the folds of her fur. Kalek could not understand her. Ávrá waved him off.

"I'm going to pick you up now, Úlla," Ello said, "like you used to pick me up when I was a mánná." Her voice cracked at the end. Ello bent, slipping her arms under Úlla's body, lifting her as if she weighed no more than a bird. Kalek shuddered, thinking about what Úlla must have gone through to be so transformed. She had left as Master of the Forge. Now she appeared as thin and brittle as a barren seed.

Leading the way back to the apothecary, Kalek's thoughts both jumped ahead to what would be needed, and trailed behind to wonder what had happened. He checked to see if Ello struggled. Her quiet determination revealed no strain nor bore no resemblance to the boisterous nieddaš who took pleasure in teasing him. In the time between when she had burst into the apothecary and now, Ello had aged.

Kalek picked up his pace, pressed upon by duty to care for Úlla and his aching need to learn from her what had become of Dárja. Reaching the apothecary, he pushed wide the door, thankful the room was empty. This season of snow, there had been few illnesses and those who had been afflicted had rapidly recovered. He motioned to Ello to rest Úlla upon the pallet before him. When she tried to slip away, Úlla held on tight.

"Sit," Kalek said, gesturing to Ávrá to join them.

"Úlla, we must clean you," he said, his calm tone at odds with his racing pulse. "Will you let Ávrá remove your furs?"

Ávrá met Kalek's gaze briefly, then she gently peeled back the outer layers of the bloodstained furs. Beneath, Úlla's chest writhed. Ello gasped. While the stench assaulted Kalek, it was his heart that took the brunt. How had it come to this? Ávrá continued to soothe as she unwound the cloth to reveal the dark crown of the babe at Úlla's breast. *Where is Marnej? Where is Dárja?* He needed to know. The infant's wail shattered the swell of unanswered questions.

"May I wash her?" Ávrá asked.

Kalek nodded, staring at the tiny body, freed of fabric and filth. In the babe's dark hair and pale visage, he could not help seeing Dárja. Child of Aillun. Also child of his god seed. He knew Dárja as battle-hardened and determined to protect Úlla. She had promised to return and he had allowed himself to believe her, letting her go, as he had Irjan.

"Úlla?" a voice stricken with alarm called from the threshold.

Kalek reeled around to see Tuá, her heart-shaped face distorted by fear and hope. Behind her, Ravna trailed, trying to hold the nieddaš back. Tuá shook herself free. Before Kalek could stop her, she pushed past him to confront Ávrá, who held the red-faced infant.

Tuá reached out her hands to the baby. Touching the infant's body, she turned to Ravna, her eyes beaming. "She is alive!"

Ravna hesitated at the threshold, her arms crossed in front of her, her expression drawn.

Tuá turned back to Ávrá. "May I hold her?"

Árvá looked to Kalek. His words of caution caught in his throat, recalling Dárja in Irjan's arms.

"Úlla and the baby both need our care," Ávrá said, her timbre that of a stern bieba instructing her child. "You and Ravna can light fires in the baths. We will need hot water for both oktoeadni and mánná."

Wide-eyed, Tuá nodded. Ravna came forward, taking hold of Tuá's outstretched hands. "We will do what is best for them," she said.

"We will wash you and care for you and the baby," Tuá added.

"Go," Ávrá encouraged, but Tuá lingered for a moment longer.

"The baths will be ready," Ravna said, her sad eyes on Tuá.

Kalek recovered himself enough to say, "Go now. We will follow shortly."

The two nieddaš left, with a longing backward glance on Tuá's part.

"I thought I would die." Úlla's shaky voice cut through the infant's cries.

Kalek looked away from the stricken figure in Ello's lap, seeking the apothecary's familiar details. The herbs. The jars. The scarred work table. They gave no grounding. This was Okta's apothecary and he was gone.

Alive with grief and fear, Kalek knelt before Úlla. "You and your mánná are safe and with us," he said, choking back the questions no one had asked. *What of Dárja? Why was she not here before him? What had happened?* Kalek heard himself say, "We should clean you and the baby." Even to his ears, he sounded lost, but he forced himself to continue, "We must make sure you are both well."

Kalek held out his hand. Úlla stared at it before meeting his eyes.

"Can you walk?" he asked, his outstretched hand unmet.

Úlla nodded. With Ello's help, she stood. Kalek curled back his fingers, their tenuous need rejected. He stepped aside as Úlla shuffled past with Ello's guidance. Ávrá trailed, holding the baby. Her eyes stayed on him long enough for Kalek to feel her pity.

～

Ávrá layered fresh linens and then warm furs upon Úlla and Márgu, thinking of the tears that had streamed down Úlla's cheeks as they had washed her and the baby. Úlla had let them tend her without will or comment until the clear water turned brackish. Now, a peaceful calm had fallen on the room. Ávrá had persuaded Kalek mother and baby would find more comfort in their own bed than on a pallet in the apothecary.

Ello had returned from the kitchen with food for the mother. A steaming bone broth to start, until Úlla's body could handle more. Tuá had also been persuaded to leave Úlla's side to fetch a bladder of fresh goat's milk for the baby. Although Úlla's breasts appeared full with milk, she needed rest and a chance to regain some strength. Ávrá sat down beside Úlla, feeling her tension turning into fear. Not for Úlla, who she felt would regain her former self. Nor Márgu, who, in spite of the ordeal, looked hale. Ávrá's concern centered on Kalek.

When he had come upon her, cradling Úlla, Ávrá had watched his eyes dart about the gathered crowd. She knew he searched for Dárja. When he had faltered, she had tried to help him find his way. At the time, Úlla had been her focus. She was the one in Ávrá's arms, a ruin of the nieddaš she had known. Now, Ávrá began to imagine the worst. She wanted to believe Dárja was safe. She could turn up any day, as she had after the battle. She wanted this to be true for Kalek. She wanted it for herself. Without Dárja, Ávrá feared Kalek's darkness would overwhelm her light.

As if reading her thoughts, Úlla said, "She rode out to protect us." Her voice was even and detached. Ello gaped in horror. Before Árvá could think of what to say, Úlla went on in the same dream-like manner, "I was never kind to her. Or Marnej." This truth, so softly spoken, pierced hopes and hearts alike.

Ravna regained her composure first. She moved to kneel next to the bed, resting her hand on Úlla's cheek. "Let us speak of this another time. When you are stronger."

Úlla shook her head slowly. Tears glistened in the candlelight. "No. It must be said. I must say it. They died protecting me so I could return with Márgu, so we could all continue on. We are here and they are not."

"You and the baby are here. You are home." Tuá's impassioned voice came from the threshold. "You will become almai and Márgu will have a biebmoeadni."

Ravna whirled on Tuá, her shock giving way to disgust. "Tuá," she breathed the name as if it caused her pain.

"Tuá is right," Ávrá said, wanting ease returned to them all. She wanted to eat a meal where they feasted on bounty and not grief. She wanted to look at these dear faces and not see worry etched upon them before their time. She wanted to work upon her loom with joy and not see it as the worrisome symbol for what she was becoming. But there was no going back. She was the warp upon which others wound themselves.

"Tuá is right," she repeated, resolved to her purpose. "Úlla and Márgu are with us. Our precious lives continue. When we give thanks for this gift, we honor all who have come before and all those still to come."

~

Kalek felt the Elder's knowing gaze upon him. When the healer could take it no longer, he said, "I don't know why you asked me here if you have nothing to say. If you have no need of me, I have other matters I can attend to."

The Elder pursed his lips. "I asked you here to drink tea with me, Kalek." The ancient leader sipped from his cup to make his point.

Kalek shook his head. "It is never that simple." Memories fresh and faded flooded the healer's mind. Irjan. Okta. Aillun. Dárja. They all seemed to be threads in some tapestry, woven by the Noaidi.

The Elder lowered his cup. "True. Where you and I are concerned, matters have rarely been simple." He faltered. Kalek waited for him to continue.

As the moments stretched, the healer crept to the edge of his seat, shifting his cup of cooling tea from one hand to the other and back again.

"You have done much in the time since Okta left us," the Elder said.

Kalek's hand wavered, spilling some of his tea. He shot forward to wipe it up. The Noaidi brushed off his efforts. "I have waited for you to speak. Since you have not . . ."

Something within Kalek snapped. "Did you know she and the baby were covered in their own foulness? Úlla could do nothing for either of them other than stay alive and try and feed the baby. When the nieddaš washed her, Ávrá said she cried in shame. She blames herself for Dárja's death." Here Kalek stopped, too overcome with emotion to continue.

"Yes," the Elder said. The one word contained the weariness of countless ages.

Kalek shot to his feet. "She is gone. As is Marnej. And Okta." He gestured angrily off into the distance. "Dead upon that wretched field. Like Irjan. And the others." His arm dropped under the weight of his guilt and grief. "I should have forbade her. I should have stopped her." He glared at the Noaidi. "You should have never agreed to let them go."

"Imagine if I had said no to her plan and you had forbade her," the ancient one began. "Imagine if we had placed her in prison for her own good. Do you believe we could have truly stopped her?"

Kalek blinked, unable to hide his hate.

The Elder sighed with more sadness than resignation. "Did prison stop her biebmoeadni? Did you make Irjan see reason? They were sewn from the same cloth though Dárja was of your seed."

A vision of Dárja flickered before Kalek's burning eyes. She had assured him she would be back before he realized she had gone. Her voice had trembled as she spoke. "I know you don't approve," she had said.

Kalek had interrupted, trying to give his blessing even though his heart argued he might lose her.

"I *will* come back," she had said.

Kalek sank onto the stool across from the Noaidi, defeated by the truth. "She is not coming back," he said, then halted. "None of them are."

He searched the Elder's face for an answer beyond words. His ancient eyes held Kalek's. What was behind the look? Acceptance? Kalek was sure he would not find the same acceptance within himself. Acceptance required forgiveness and he could not forgive them for his heartbreak.

"I have lost them all," Kalek said aloud, knowing that, if they had loved him as he had loved them, they would not have gone.

CHAPTER TWENTY-ONE

ODS STOP ME!" MURES shouted, stirring the thick layer of smoke in the air. "If he does not stop his grousing, I'll shove a fur in his mouth."

"We have faced greater trials than this," Válde said, his tone as sharp as the knife he honed. "We are warm. Well-provisioned." The snick of iron upon the whetstone punctuated the man's words. "Gáral's wound has knit. And Herko . . ."

"Herko is no more nor less a thorn-in-the-saddle than ever." Feles supplied his usual sober appraisal of the situation.

"It's fine for you, isn't it?" Herko grumbled. "You can move about. You can go outside. Meanwhile, I shit in a bucket like some teat-suckler too young to leave his mother's side." He looked at Dárja in foul regard as he said this.

She scowled back at him, unsure of which was worse: trying to ease him down the treacherous ravine from the cave or being sequestered with him in this trapper's hut. The seven of them, existing stacked upon one another like rats, was an ordeal of both patience and filth. Dárja never thought she'd think fondly on the cave. At least there they'd had some room to move about, some meager sense of privacy. Here the only reprieve any of them had from each other was when they went to hunt for food, tend to the horses, or relieve themselves. Except for Herko. *Belly-aching Olmmoš.*

"Enough!" Válde said.

"What we need is action," Gáral said from his dark corner. "We have been cloistered like doleful priests for too long. The Believers will have grown arrogant in our absence. It is time we remind them they are worms to be squashed under our heels."

"We still have our soldiers' uniforms," Feles said.

"It's time to put her to work," Gáral said, with a touch of malice.

A fraught lull descended in the tight space. Dárja felt all eyes on her. "I can care for the wounded," she said, her disapproval coming to the fore. "I'd hoped there'd be no more."

Válde met her gaze. In his eyes, she saw a resolve she had believed to be honorable.

"We are grateful for your healing skill," he said.

Dárja heard the unspoken caveat beneath this recognition. A chill ran through her despite the stifling heat of the hut.

"It is your skill with the blade we seek," Válde said, his features hardening. "And your training as a Jápmemeahttun."

Dárja's breath caught, taken by surprise not only by the implications, but also by the dignity he'd afforded the word. He'd not said *Jápmea*, the foul perversion of their gods' given name. She blinked. The outline of his face suddenly transformed before her. The wide eyes and the burden-curved back she'd begun to trust slipped away. In their place were the sharp focus and loose joints of a prowling wolf.

"You can do what none of us can," Válde said, his voice rough and insistent like a growl.

Dárja edged back from his intense stare.

"You can disappear into nothingness and then reappear when you want," he pressed.

She glanced at the door, planning what it would take to make it out.

"Can you see the havoc this will cause with the Vijns's soldiers?" he asked.

She met the Piijkij eyes boring into her. Some were merely curious; most were filled with suspicion and resentment.

"You can help us bring the Believers to their knees," Válde said.

Dárja's internal fires roared to life, full of anger toward these scavenging Olmmoš and toward her gutless credulity. She had told herself these Piijkij—these Hunters—had needed her in their ranks for her abilities as a healer. She'd even let herself believe they'd accepted her because of a shared history of battle and bloodshed. In truth, they'd sought to keep her because she was Jápmemeahttun, because she had a part in the Song of All. She was nothing more to them than a pawn. As Marnej had been. As Irjan had been.

Dárja grabbed her furs and blade and stood. "I'm not some specter you can dangle before your enemies to taunt and scare as you wish," she said. She pushed through the bodies in the way of the door, using the jab of her elbows to mask the wobble in her knees. Outside, in the welcoming peace of snow and ice, she dug her nails into the braided leather of the hilt at her side. These men had promised no refuge. It was only a trick of her desperation.

She breathed in the bitterly cold air. She felt as if a part of her had been cleaved away. But when she wrapped her furs about her, she found herself to be in one piece. Dárja donned her gloves and pulled up her hood, then strode through the knee-deep snowdrifts to the stable abutting the trapper's hut. The shambling structure couldn't house all the horses. She felt a kinship with the shaggy beasts tethered outside, huddled together, waiting their turn to go inside.

Dárja stroked their necks. "It's better out here where the air and forage are fresh than inside were foulness breeds." She slipped inside the lean-to stable. The horses within stirred. The creak of leather and wooden saddles reassured her they were ready to ride. This was one Piijkij precaution that would serve her purpose. The horses outside would be brought in at some point, and the saddles transferred to their backs as they warmed themselves. She'd be gone by then.

She untied the reins of one of the horses and led it out, whispering her appreciation. Outside again, she took pity on the snow-covered animals. She hobbled her mount, then led one of the snow-dusted horses into the stable.

"I know what I said," she muttered, tethering the beast to the wooden trough. "It's also good to be warm, with your feed before you." She gave the horse a stroke along its back, wiping the snow from the rough pelt. The animal's muscles shivered under her hand.

They can saddle it if they want, she thought, leaving the lean-to with its scent of wood and hay and dung.

Outside, Válde stood abreast her horse.

She narrowed her eyes at him. "Have you come to stop me with your words or your blade?"

"Planning to steal a horse?"

The accusation in his question reminded her of their earliest exchanges. Before she'd forgotten an Olmmoš could never be trusted.

"Consider it payment for services given," she said, stepping around him.

He moved to bar her way again.

Dárja instinctively widened the gap between them. "So, you are here to stop me."

"Only if you run away."

She placed a hand on the pommel of her sword. "And if I fight?"

"Then the blood of one or both of us will fall here." Válde pointed in a circle, his eyes never parting from hers.

A watchful stillness surrounded them. Dárja had once mistaken his calm for sadness but not again. *No. Never again.*

"Neither of us will gain from it," he said, taking a step forward to close the gap.

"I will. I'll take the satisfaction owed to me."

"For what? For insults you suffered at Herko's hand, or the—"

"For the deceit you knowingly constructed," she cut him off. "Mutual assistance," she hooted. "This was it all along. This was the plan. Keep me occupied. Keep me tied by my word and their need." She pointed accusingly to the hut, to where Gáral and Herko sat healing thanks to her. "Did you think I'd trust you? A Piijkij."

"Yes," he said, coming to stand directly before her. "Yes, that was the plan. The others would have preferred a knife at your throat. I told them it must be your choice."

"So I should be thankful to you I'm alive and free to move about," she scoffed, shaking her head in disgust. "I don't need your mercy or protection. I act for myself."

"Then answer me one question and I will gladly send you on your way," Válde said, the dark centers of his eyes pinpoints in the deep green.

Dárja felt his hot breath on her cheeks like the bellows of Úlla's forge.

"What then?" she shouted, her resolve grounded in righteousness.

"Why did you stay?"

The disdain in his voice was nothing compared to the bite of the words themselves. It was all Dárja could do not to stumble back, while he stood tall and imperious, just waiting for her to speak.

She wanted to yell at him. She longed to shout her reasons were none of his concern. Her reasons were her own. She'd always said so. What right had he to a truth she'd kept hidden even from herself? Still here he was, staring down his Olmmoš nose at her, so smug. *Well, let him choke on the truth*, she thought.

Instead, it was she who choked upon all the reasons she'd conjured. Her bravery had been an act of fear, her determination a reflection of her desperation.

"I stayed because I have nowhere left to go!" she hissed, fending off the more painful truth with a hardened piece of honesty.

In the pulsing quiet that followed, Dárja felt her racing heart-beat disappear into the pit in her stomach. She willed the gods to claim her where she stood. Spent, she swayed, listening to the wind howl for more of her, sure she would blow away. She closed her eyes and waited to drift into nothingness, confessing to herself, *I stayed because you're all I have left of Marnej. All I have left of Irjan.*

When she opened her eyes, Válde was there. He reached out a hand. Dárja watched it, convinced it would pass right through. There was nothing left of her. Then there was a solid weight on her shoulder.

"Dárja."

The way he said her name, with the unmistakable Olmmoš accent, stirred her spirit. It was like hearing Marnej, as she'd first known him. Arrogant. Brazen. As if he owned her name when he spoke it. Later, she'd heard Marnej's lilt as well, the one that reminded her of Irjan—her bieba.

"Dárja." He spoke her name again, his hand resting now on her arm, keeping her tethered to him. "What did you mean, you have nowhere else to go?"

She felt mocking pity creep under her skin where he touched her. She pushed his hand away. But the feeling tarried like a poison making its way through her.

"What did you mean?" he asked.

She heard the insistence, the underlying demand. *They always want something of us.*

"What do you want of me?" she heard herself ask, a lifetime of doubt behind the question. "Do you want to hear I can't return home because Irjan's gone and I'm heartbroken? Or that I'm an outcast because I'll never give birth or become an almai? Or perhaps you wish to know I'm breaking the heart of the dearest soul remaining to me because I failed to protect those entrusted to my care."

~

Válde felt the sting of Dárja's recrimination as if she had shouted and not whispered. When he had taken her hand on the battlefield to draw her up onto his horse, he believed she was a means to an end. He had assured his men she was something he valued and protected for this reason alone.

But her combination of fearlessness and compassion had made her something more than a weapon against the Believers. As much as she had tried to present a hardened front, she had been gentle in her care of Gáral's wound. Even Herko, for all his foul bluster, had prospered under her ministrations.

"Where do you plan to go?" he asked.

She shook her head, looking up at the sky. "I don't know."

"Where?" he pushed, wanting her to fight back so he could keep his concern for her hidden.

"To die," she said, pushing past him.

He shoved her back. "And waste what you are given?"

She sneered at him. "You mean waste what you can use?"

Válde grabbed both her arms and shook her. "I mean waste an opportunity for one last stand against your enemies."

Dárja pulled free of his grasp. "*You* are my enemy."

"We are dead already," Válde whispered fiercely. "We only pretend to walk a few more steps. Can you not see? With you we can bring about the end of the Vijns. We will avenge both our peoples."

"You're all Olmmoš."

Válde shook his head. "We are Piijkij. And before you cast our sins before us, hold our honor, our valor, and our willingness to sacrifice our lives in equal measure. Each of those men in there have killed Jápmemeahttun. It was what we were trained to do. We must do what is right. Just as you must."

Dárja's dark eyes flashed. "What is right? You can't bring back all those you killed on the battlefield."

"And what of you?" he shot back, wanting her to understand, needing her to see what he proposed was bigger than either of them. "You were there to fight, were you not? Do you regret what you did?"

Her chin jutted forward. "You hunted us. We had no choice."

"We owed allegiance. We had no choice."

Her denial was writ across her face.

"Do you regret what you did?" he pressed.

"No," she said without hesitation.

"And yet, you expect me to." Válde threw up his hands. "You want me to undo a past, stretching back to a time neither of us witnessed nor had a part in." He grasped her shoulders again, staring into her unforgiving eyes. "I cannot. We are the product of that past, not its creators. We have the chance to make it right."

"By killing one man?"

"By acting together to kill the Vijns," he exhorted her. "By showing that Olmmoš and Jápmemeahttun can work as one. By proving even the defeated can rise again."

"I'm one Jápmemeahttun. You're six Piijkij," she said, a dull languor to her voice. "We're like midges for the Olmmoš soldiers to swat."

"Legends have been built on less. Look at Irjan." Válde watched Dárja's reaction, fearing he had pushed her too far.

"He was a traitor to you," she said, a fresh sadness taking hold of her.

Válde shook his head. "Before that he was a legend. He was one man. Look at how he shaped the future."

Válde stepped in, closing the gap between them, wanting more than ever for Dárja to see his point, to understand what he was asking. The cloud of her breath rose to meet his. He lowered his head to inhale the warmth she cast off.

Dárja shuddered. Válde stepped back, aware of the tender thread between them. Mentally, he brushed it aside. But like a cobweb, it clung to him, promising something more than a means to an end. For a moment, he let himself wonder what it would be like to feel her strong arms embrace him. Not to hold him steady in a saddle because he was wounded. He was whole and so was she and they were together. The hopeful vision faded like a snowflake into a flurry. Too much hung in the balance for him to disregard the calling they both shared.

"Irjan was an Olmmoš and a Piijkij. He did what he thought was right and fought for your kind. I am asking you to do the same," Válde said, fresh snow beginning to fall between them.

CHAPTER TWENTY-TWO

MARNEJ COUGHED. THE SALT of seawater mixed with the curdled emptiness of his gut. He retched, then took a gulping breath, expecting the wall of dark water to pull him under once again. The smell of his own sickness wound its way back through his nose. It was the scent of rot and death. He coughed again. The pain in his chest threatened to break him wide open. He blinked his crusted eyes. He lay upon his belly, his cheek pressed into grit. An askew shoreline stretched into a misty expanse. Marnej clawed at the solidness beneath him. His hand filled with wet sand but he didn't move. He lifted his head to right the world around him. The effort caused his vision to spin. He sank back into the roughness below him, more rock than sand. A monstrous roar drove a fresh jolt of fear through him. *It's coming for me*, he panicked, the water dragging on his legs.

The terror of what awaited in the dark, cold depths behind him pushed Marnej up onto his elbows. The fearsome sound of waves chased him. He dug his way forward on his belly, thinking only of getting away until the raw skin on his feet stopped him. He rolled onto his back, expecting to see the white spray of cresting water above him. A stark blue sky blinded him. He squeezed his eyes shut, seeing light where there should have been darkness.

Somewhere beyond him, he heard voices.

No, he thought. The Song couldn't possibly reach him here. He'd come too far. *If it's not the Song, then is it the gods speaking?* Through slitted eyes, Marnej let the light in, unsure if he were dead or dreaming. Dark shapes passed over him. He flinched. The ravens had come to claim his soul. *Or do they have it already?*

If the gods awaited him, Marnej must greet them with truth upon his lips. "I have only done what was asked of me," he pleaded with the sky above him, his throat aching with the effort.

Judging silence spoke louder than the waves in his ears. He'd come before the gods and he'd lied like a man with a life before him.

"I hated my father," he whispered, half hiding his truth in the incessant crashing upon the shore. But the gods could hear him. *Couldn't they?* "I abandoned the oath I made to my people," he said, seeing a wavering image of men he'd called comrades. Marnej let long-awaited tears slip from the corners of his eyes. "I betrayed the love given me." *Salt upon salt, upon salt*, he thought, unable to say her name, hoping the slow progress of his tears might atone for his deeds.

~

An insistent shushing stripped away the feeling of the oars in his hands. Dripping with water as he leaned forward. Dipping into water as he pulled back. Again. And again. And again. Marnej blinked open his eyes. Pale sunlight greeted him. He slung his arm across his face to block it. He swallowed painfully, his tongue as thick and parched as summer earth. He rolled onto his side. His cramped muscles groaned like the boat that had brought him to this shore. On his side, staring back at the waves, edging ever nearer, a powerful thirst overtook him. *Why do the dead have need for thirst?* he wondered. He rolled onto his hands and knees, noticing his gloves were gone. Coarse sand squeezed up through his fingers. The ready water just below the surface oozed up, bitter and undrinkable. Marnej crawled, his thirst compelling him forward until the sand gave way to smooth, rounded stones.

Getting to his feet, his body throbbed with weakness. Ahead of him, beyond the rocks, colors and contours appeared as remote and unreal as any dream. Marnej swayed. His clumsy step bashed and twisted his tender feet. He canted forward, his hands breaking his fall on the rocks. One hand slid across slick green curves. The other scraped against rough edges. Slowly, rising to his knee, he saw the shimmer of water in a time-gouged stone. He dipped his cracked lips to drink from the puddle. He tasted the tang of fish without the bite of salt. He drank greedily. Choked. Coughed. Then drank some more, his pain momentarily forgotten. He sat back down on the stones, unwilling to leave what was left of the fresh water despite his inability to drink more.

Freed from maddening thirst, Marnej surveyed the shore in both directions, looking for signs of gods or men. North of where he had dragged himself across the sand, he saw his boat. Its broken staves pointed skyward, calling to mind spiked ribs. Nothing else remained of Jusse's provisions. Marnej understood the depth of his generosity. The man had given what he'd had with the understanding it would all be lost. A greedy soul would never have done that.

Marnej turned away from the sea. It offered him nothing. The sand and rock of the shoreline upon which he sat gave way to tawny reeds and tall brown grasses, flecked here and there with patches of green. Beyond, a slope angled up to a high bluff, layered in red and yellow soil. Nothing like the pale blue and gray of ice and snow he'd expected. Then again, perhaps the gods lived beyond the season of snow.

The wind picked up, bringing an unfamiliar scent to mix with the smell of his wet furs. Though the sun shone, Marnej shivered. He briefly wondered if this was where the sun rested when men slept. Then he began to worry if he should await the gods or if he should seek them out. Although reluctant to leave these rocks and the promise of fresh water in their carved surfaces, he also wished to be out of the wind. As a compromise, Marnej moved closer to the sloping bluff, where the tall grasses swayed and suggested a softer place to bed down.

~

Marnej awoke with the sun to the east and shadows stretched across the sand. The ocean continued to rage. Wave upon wave crashed to be pulled out to sea once again. He didn't know how long he'd slept. The clothes he'd stripped off to dry had an unwanted dampness to them. His thirst had returned, and with it came hunger as a companion. Marnej dressed with difficulty. His muscles protested as he pulled on his tunic and breeches. His fingers fumbled with ties. Finally, he shrugged on his furs, leaving them open to the air, which felt surprisingly mild under the rising sun.

He stood slowly, balancing with outstretched arms. Solid land felt strange to him after all his time in the rocking boat. He looked about for water to drink, returning to the rocks where he'd first slaked his thirst. He gave thanks when he found another hollowed rock with water for him. He drank his fill, hoping to quiet his hunger, at least for the present. Glancing up to the bluff, he saw what looked like patchy snow between brown grasses.

Marnej became curious about what opportunities he would discover from a higher vantage. Perhaps he'd see who claimed this shore, if not the gods. And if this was the home of the gods, then surely they'd be able to find him with ease. Marnej made his way through the reeds and grasses, then scrambled up the unstable slope. His toes dug into sliding dirt, pushing him forward onto his bare hands. The interspersed rocks had sharp edges that scraped and cut his exposed flesh.

At the top, he pulled himself up to standing. Marnej found himself looking at a barren plateau of grasses, stretching ahead for leagues. He turned back to the shore. Little was left of the boat to attest to his journey or to remind him of what he'd left behind. After some time, Marnej gave up on the hope there was anything for him on the shore. Facing into the sun, he began to weave his way through thin stalks that rustled like whispers. The brittle frost crunched under his bare feet.

The farther Marnej retreated from the shore, the less it felt like he was running away. Whether this was the lands of gods or men, he was no longer Marnej, son of Irjan. He was no longer a man with a duty chosen for him. If he walked among the living, then he was a man of his own making, one with no history other than what he chose to give himself. His life was his own. If he walked among the gods, then he wanted to do so as he hadn't done among men and Immortals. He wanted to make each step his own.

A new lightness took hold of Marnej. As he continued across the plateau, he let go of all the limitations he'd lived with—the doubt and the blame. And he began to suss out who he was without his past. He'd been a Piijkij. But no longer. He could be a tradesman. If the gods had no need for a tradesman, he could choose something else. With those decisions ahead of him, Marnej walked east until the grassy plain ended abruptly in a wide, dry path, running from north to south. *Perhaps a riverbed in the melt*, he thought. Then revised his assessment. With its shallow sides, it had more the feel of a cart path than a natural formation. Stream or cart path, it didn't matter. What was important was he chose the direction he traveled.

~

Marnej peered up through the ominous trees with thick branches like dark spires. The overcast sky gave little indication of how long he'd been walking. His sea-softened legs made him think it had been leagues already. While his initial enthusiasm had flagged, he found himself amazed at how different this world looked. He inhaled. Even the air smelled different. There was something curious and pleasurable in it, like crushed herbs that almost lulled his concern about the deepening gloom of the forest ahead.

Who knew what dangers awaited. Behind him lay a desolate shore. A past he no longer wished to claim. *No.* The path continued on and so would he. He listened to the sounds around him as his footfalls tamped the earth. He'd seen neither man nor beast nor gods. He had heard birds call to one another and once the graveled caw of a raven.

Well into the shadows, Marnej glanced up at the overhanging branches. They arched and wove together to obscure the sky. Even with quick steps to keep him warm, he felt the cold making inroads. Mist rose from the ground as if the earth itself had exhaled. The path disappeared only to appear once again. Marnej wrapped his dank furs tighter about him, aware they wouldn't protect him if he were set upon. Nor did he have a weapon to fend off the unseeable.

He picked up his pace, craning his head this way and that. The chatter of birds had been replaced by an unsettling calm. Not even his footfalls made a sound. It was like walking on sand once again. A twig snapped. Marnej stopped, waiting for movement on all sides of him. When nothing followed, he resumed his steps, scanning the path, unable to see through the rising veil.

A far-off scurrying caught his attention. The sound skittered away from him. It was something small and quick. *A fox or a rabbit*, he thought, then reminded himself he knew nothing of the beasts lurking in these woods. Before his imagination could fashion a vicious predator, a slow repetitive creak from behind came to the fore. He glanced back to see an indistinct, looming shape, coming ever closer.

Marnej stepped to the side of the path, intending to hide in the trees. But the uncertainty of what else sheltered in the woods caused him to hesitate. He squinted back in the direction of the sound. Large and unrecognizable, whatever it was, it was not swift moving. Marnej's growing curiosity bolstered his daring. He decided he had time to dash into the undergrowth if he felt a threat approached. The creaking sound took on an alternating pitch. At first deep and low, then high and piercing. Caught between his desire to see what approached and the very real possibility it represented danger, Marnej looked at the uninviting mist to his left.

A sharp call broke through the quiet. It took Marnej a moment to realize it was a voice because the sound had no meaning to him. Surely, if it were the gods, they'd make themselves understood. And if what approached wasn't the gods, then it was a man and perhaps many more beyond him. In the absence of a weapon and the strength to wield it, Marnej's skill as a fighter meant nothing. His best recourse was to slip into the woods and let the fog shield him. The voice called out again. This time it sounded like a song.

Marnej froze. The hairs on the back of his neck bristled. He'd let himself believe he'd traveled far beyond the reach of the Song of All without actually testing this truth. He hadn't taken the time to try and find the voices. He stood there with a growing pit in his stomach, waiting for the chorus to take hold of him, dreading to hear Dárja's song or Kalek's.

Marnej reached out his hand to a neighboring tree, cringing in expectation. His hand met the rough grooves. He felt the bark and nothing else. No thrum. No sense of oneness. He bowed his head. His hand dropped away, shaking. Then the lone song repeated, shattering the hush. Marnej's eyes flew open. A figure emerged from the mist. A horse. And behind it a laden wagon. Set in the middle, shrouded beneath a hooded cloak, loomed a stout shape. The voice rang out again. No others joined in. Pushed to decide whether to stay or run, Marnej heard himself call out. He'd kept the nature of his greeting light to avoid being mistaken for a threat, which in his current condition seemed laughable. Nevertheless, he was relieved to hear the sound of welcome from the oncoming figure, even if he couldn't understand the words.

When the horse drew close enough, Marnej saw a great, big beast with a snorting breath that rose like steam from a cookpot.

As tall as him at the back, the beast was bigger than any of its kin to the north. And the animal's large hooves looked as if they could till a field. The cart-driver called out a deep, soothing sound. The great beast slowed. The towering stack of bundles swayed. Marnej jumped back, alarmed at the horse's presence.

Gaping, he slowly held up his hand in a greeting, hoping the wave would be understood. The figure on the cart pushed back his hood and stared down. Marnej stiffened. Even in the dim light, the man's skin glowed golden, as if he were part of the sun himself. Marnej dropped to his knees, sure he was before the gods, because no man he'd ever seen looked like this. The sound of deep resonant laugher made him lift his eyes up from the ground. A smile as white a snow broke through the man's beard of dark ringlets.

Marnej looked down, aware he again stared. The horse snorted, its giant hooves pawed the ground. Marnej scrambled back, fearing he was about to be crushed.

A low, rumbling voice said, "North man."

Beneath the "r" sound that stretched the first word lean and the "a" in the second that sighed like an exhalation of air, Marnej grasped the meaning.

"Yes!" he said, his pulse racing.

The man frowned. Marnej's eagerness gave way to apprehension. Maybe his kind were unwelcome in the south. His sudden hesitancy must have shown, because the man smiled again, this time not as broadly. Suddenly self-conscious, Marnej looked down at himself. With damp furs, bloodstained and tattered, he must have looked like a bedraggled, wild animal.

He glanced up, both hands raised. "I'm no threat to you." As he spoke, Marnej's eyes sought out the man's armament. Though there was no visible blade about his waist, there could easily be one tucked into the load.

Marnej kept his arms raised.

The man put a hand to his chest. "Aage," he said. With his other hand he motioned to join him upon the cart.

Marnej hesitated. Not because he feared the man would do him harm, but because with one gesture the possibility of living a new life had become a reality.

With his hand to his heart, he said, "Marnej. Friend."

CHAPTER TWENTY-THREE

E INÁR STOOD WITH THE sacred drum inside the circle of
the Council of Elders. The last tremor of the taut deer-
skin tingled in his fingers. Even with his eyes closed, he
could see the world spiraling out from him: the Elders, drawn
together to honor the dark sky of this season of snow, the other
Jápmemeahttun, the livestock in the stables, the fallow snow-
covered fields beyond, and the natural world at the periphery.
He heard all of their songs and in their chorus he glimpsed the
greatness of the gods.

Einár asked the gods for their guidance. In return, he felt the
swelling power of the Jápmemeahttun song take hold of his body.

We are the Jápmemeahttun.
We are the guardians of the world.
Our memory stretches back to the start of days.
Our vision reaches beyond all tomorrows.
We sing together as one, so that our one may always survive.

The refrain stayed within the forefront of his mind, while
others came through, fleeting and suggestive. The striking bone
in his hand had become heavy, as if he held not a bone but the
whole of a body.

We are the Elders.
We are chosen to guide.
We listen to the voices of the gods.
We seek to avoid the mistakes of the past.

Einár stopped drumming. Although the voices within him continued on, his own had fallen silent. He opened his eyes to look upon the other Elders, held within the sway of the Song's power. His muscles twitched and ached like one who had run for leagues. Parched, he wanted nothing more than a sip of cool water and a moment to savor it. That pleasure would need to wait. The awakening Elders on all sides needed him. Their heavy-lidded eyes looked apprehensive. Had they seen what he had? Or had they merely sensed it?

Einár lay down the drum and striking bone. His fingers alighted upon the ancient drawings. *Do we continue to be at the heart of this world?* he wondered, letting his hopeful eyes rise to greet the other Elders. He expected to see something in their expressions. Doubt. Challenge. Judgment. He saw only familiar faces. One by one, he took the hands of these guardians. He felt the cold in their fingers. It chilled his heart. He pulled them into an embrace, not caring if it was unseemly or unexpected. He wanted to feel their heartbeats joining with his. He needed to feel their life as his own.

"May the gods continue to bless us," he said, the rote words imbued with fresh will.

"As we are always grateful," the gathered Elders intoned together.

Einár watched the Elders retreat, feeling spent. In recent days, it seemed like he had joined the boaris, too old to stay among company, too connected to the Song to renounce life. He had seen the birth of war with the Olmmoš and lost friends and loved ones too numerous to count. He had also lived long enough to see the end of war and the destruction of their kind. There were times when he woke, hoping to feel, among his numerous aches, the first crushing tremors of ascendance. On those occasions, he believed the crippling pain of the end would be more merciful than witnessing the subdued passing of their numbered days.

Though he wished it were not so, Einár knew the Jápmemeahttun had no future. While the nieddaš seemed healthy and vibrant, the almai were few in number and low in spirit, and the boaris were more like ghosts than the life bringers for future generations. With their numbers so diminished, each birth represented the last vestige of hope or the harbinger of final ruin.

Not since the days of hunger and death, before the first oktoeadni, had the Jápmemeahttun braved a future as dire as the one Einár saw before him. "The death of one. The birth of one. The life of one as All," he muttered to himself. Their way had brought them into balance, into harmony with the world around them. Now their numbers were so few. And there would never be more. And yet, who was he to mourn, when those he guided had lives ahead of them? And who was he to say the time was short or doomed, when so many worked to serve others and continue their way of life?

Einár stopped walking, seeing his feet had brought him to Okta's door. He raised his hand to knock, then let his hand drop to his side. Okta was gone. His spirit lived on in Úlla and her child, Márgu. It was a consolation and it was also not enough. Einár needed the familiar comfort of the tea Okta had always made. And it was wrong to ask Kalek for respite when he himself had such need of solace.

Einár had said to Kalek that Dárja would have gone with or without his approval. Which he believed. What he had not shared with the healer was that, in allowing her and Marnej to travel Outside, he had wished they would both find a path better suited to them than remaining in the Pohjola. Dárja had always struggled to fit within the weave of their community. In part, this was because of Irjan and the Olmmoš ways he had shared with her as her guide mother. The bigger problem was she could not live by their ways. And Einár had not wanted to see Kalek's face when they confronted the fact she would never give birth. He did not want to be the one to declare her rivgu to her kind. He knew this was cowardly of him.

It is better this way, Einár thought, feeling, more than ever, the burden of his role as Noaidi.

"Do you seek my services?"

The voice startled Einár. He turned to see Kalek at his side.

"I find myself at a loss," he said with candor.

The healer's solemn expression relaxed into a smile, revealing the youthfulness of his eight measures, as compared to Einár's twenty-some-odd measures. Nevertheless, lines had begun to crease Kalek's angular features. *A testament to his grief*, Einár thought, hoping Ávrá could ease some of his sadness. He inwardly acknowledged the bittersweetness of love in these times.

"Would you care to come in and share some tea?" Kalek asked, opening the door to the apothecary.

Einár sighed. "Tea would be welcomed."

Kalek hurried ahead to the stone hearth. He lit a candle and from it another, placing them upon the work bench. He indicated to Einár to sit.

Hunched by the fire, Kalek asked, "Is there an ailment which bothers you, Noaidi?"

"No, Kalek. I am sound in this body, regardless of its protests to the contrary."

Einár breathed in the familiar scents in the room, all of which he associated with Okta.

"He was willful," he said aloud, without meaning to.

Kalek stiffened noticeably as he ladled water into a pot.

Einár winced at his misstep. "I am sorry, Kalek."

The young healer shrugged, sitting down opposite Einár to stare at the fire. "It is true. Okta was willful." He looked up, his eyes searching. "I miss him."

Einár nodded. "As do I." He paused, struggling with the truth. "We were often at odds, but had reconciled ourselves by the end. I know you felt the brunt of this strain. I am not proud of my actions in that respect. As the Elder, I had a duty to all of us." He trailed off, his thoughts wandering back to an earlier time.

"He valued life above all else," Kalek said finally. "I did not understand this at first." He stood abruptly and stepped to the work bench, where he reached for one among many jars. His fingertips brushed the label. He whirled around, the jar forgotten. "I would have killed Irjan, you know?" The almai's lips pressed into a grim line.

Einár said nothing, sensing more was to come.

"Okta insisted all life was important," Kalek said. "Even an Olmmoš's. And he was right. With Irjan, I experienced true friendship and love." A rueful smile broke through the sadness. "Even if it was not always easy or accepted."

Einár nodded in encouragement. "He was a challenge."

"Did you know?" Kalek asked.

Einár frowned, unsure of what the almai wanted to hear.

"Did you always know he was Jápmemeahttun? That he was out there?"

Einár released his breath in a slow exhale. This day was leading him into the darkest corners of his conscience. "It must seem to you the Elders have knowledge beyond this world, that we spend our time in conversation with the gods. In truth, we listen, we watch, and we try to understand what we hear in the Song. We rely on experience and the stories of our past to help us. We are just guides, not gods ourselves." He stopped, thinking back to the moment when he had first heard Irjan's song. "We did not know of Irjan until he met with Aillun."

Kalek's frown deepened, his gaze straying to the fire.

"When we heard his song it was confused and mixed with those of Aillun's and Dárja's."

The healer twitched to life, striding to the hearth, where he ladled steaming water into two wooden cups.

"If this is too painful, I do not need to recount it," Einár said.

Kalek shook his head. "No. I wish to know." He brought the cups to the work table, keeping his back to Einár.

"When Aillun's song waned and only Dárja's went on, we were able to hear Irjan's song."

Kalek turned to face him. "How?" he demanded, echoing Okta's disbelief of so long ago.

Einár sighed. The past, it seemed, needed a voice today. He took the cup Kalek presented him. Behind the concern he saw in the healer's pale eyes, there was a greater need to understand. He inhaled the warm scent of the tea.

"I was a mánná when the Olmmoš appeared," Einár began. "They had walked from where dawn began and made it through the eastern passage that no longer exists. I was excited to see something new and strange. And surprised to discover they were like us in many ways. My biebmoeadni did not share my keen interest. She kept us apart from the Olmmoš. Others did not share her reticence. The Elders of that time said the Jápmemeahttun could care for the newcomers the way a guide mother cares for her child. But the lives of our two kinds became entwined. The Elders' warning against the mixing of our life seed came too late."

Einár sipped his tea. The recollection of the past was like the steam before his eyes. "I was too young to understand or care. I remember the older nieddaš whispering about the Olmmoš and ourselves. The offspring, they said, were hideous and malformed. It was just the imagination of young ones and the pleasure they take in shocking each other."

"What about Irjan?" Kalek pressed.

"When the Elders heard his song clearly for the first time, we were stunned. He was no monster. He was, though, a male offspring. We could only believe his oktoeadni, Mare, had borne Irjan from a relation with an Olmmoš."

"And Mare?"

"Mare died at her Origin. We had assumed the baby had died as well because we never heard its song."

Kalek's long fingers knit together like roots. "Did Irjan know this?"

"We explained the truth of his birth to him."

The almai raised his eyes to meet Einár's. "What if you had heard his song at birth?"

"I wish I could say we would have brought him to live among us. As a male mánná, he would have been the seed of the enemy. And he would never give birth. He would have been rivgu. As Noaidi, I would have been compelled to cast him out to die."

Einár rose to his feet. He placed a hand upon the young healer's cheek. "It is in the past now. At present, we both feel the keenness of loss. You and I also share a responsibility to the future of all those in our care. It is a heavy burden. One which should be shared. I am often thankful for the other Elders who stand with me and lend me their strength." He stopped, looking into Kalek's unseeing eyes. "I think it is time for you to do the same and choose a new apprentice."

~

"Let me hold her," Birtá said, opening her arms.

Ello batted them away. "I'm next."

Tuá shushed them. "She is asleep."

"All the more reason I want to hold her," Ello whispered.

Úlla smiled at them. "All right," she whispered back. "Do not wake her. She only just fell asleep." Úlla stifled a yawn. "She is like an owl at night, never resting."

Úlla placed Márgu in Ello's hands. The bold nieddaš's eyes widened, transforming her normally impudent expression into one of quiet awe. A wisp of her red hair came loose from behind her ear and fell across one eye as she continued to stare open-mouthed at the babe. Finally, Ello looked up at Úlla. "She's so . . ." and here words seemed to fail her. Ello turned to Birtá and then to Tuá before managing to say, "She's so tiny."

Birtá gave her a gentle thwack to the arm. But Úlla understood Ello's meaning. The perfection of something so small was almost beyond imagination.

"Enough, Ello," Birtá whispered. "You have fallow fields that don't require you and I'm needed at the kitchen. Let me hold her."

Ello grimaced, gently placing the baby in Birtá's plump arms. Birtá smiled with satisfaction, humming under her breath as she rocked Márgu from side to side.

Then Birtá began to sing aloud.

"Three pots of water, three measures of barley, salt for those who cry. A fire, a ladle, and time to stir, 'til hardness passes by. When my porridge is ready, within my bowl, it waits for honey's kiss, but only when the butter's laid is it ready for my miss."

Márgu smacked her tiny mouth. "See, she understands!" Birtá beamed. "She's got a good appetite, this one. Mark my words. She'll be stronger than any of us." Birtá tickled Márgu's belly. "You'll be a strong one, won't you?" As if in agreement, the babe burbled, then settled. Her dark lashes fanned across her rosy cheeks.

"The kitchen calls me," Birtá said, looking to the others. Tuá stood apart. Úlla saw the longing in the way she watched Márgu.

"Let Tuá hold her," Úlla said, adding, "I could use some more rest."

Tuá came forward. Her whole body blazed with need. Úlla understood this. She had shared it once. Before Kálle had died. It hurt to witness it. Birtá placed the baby in Tuá's arms and stroked her head in parting.

Márgu began to fuss. Tuá rocked her gently, singing to her. The babe quieted again.

"Motherhood suits you," Úlla said.

Tuá's gaze snapped up to meet hers. She blushed. She opened her mouth to speak, then closed it, having said nothing. A tentative smile peeked out from under her awkward nod. Úlla loved Márgu, maybe more so than a birth mother should. She also knew Tuá would love her even more.

"At the end of the next moon cycle, I will sit for the dákti," Úlla said, surprised at her sudden sadness. "My milk will have dried by then," she added, looking at the dark, downy head of her daughter. *So much like Kálle. So little of me*, she thought. Úlla cleared the lump in her throat. "Márgu will need a biebmoeadni. When the time comes to share her song, I want you to sing it, Tuá. I want you to be her guide mother."

Tuá began to shake. Ello rushed forward to steady her. "See, Tuá. The gods haven't forgotten you. They are with you, just like Ravna." Ello stopped rambling long enough to look around her. *Where is Ravna?* she mouthed. Before Úlla could respond, Márgu let out a piercing wail. Tuá adjusted the babe. Her dark eyes glistened with unshed tears and an uncertain smile graced her mouth. She caressed Márgu's cheek. The infant's cries became insistent. Tuá looked to Úlla.

Úlla held out her hands. "Let me feed her," she said.

Tuá hesitated.

"I will return her to your care when she is sated," Úlla reassured her, unfastening the ties of her tunic.

Tuá placed Márgu in Úlla's arms. Her trembling hands moved to cover her mouth. Márgu latched on eagerly to Úlla's breast. On their journey home, Márgu's need had almost been too much for Úlla. Now she found the infant's powerful hunger heartening. Tuá crossed her arms in front of her chest.

"Your milk will come," Úlla said.

"Should I go?" Ello asked, uncharacteristically shy.

Úlla shook her head, her heart full. "No. Stay, Ello," she said, a part of her wishing she could remain among these friends, sharing dreams and whispered confidences. The other part of her took comfort from the fact that when she became almai, Márgu would be cared for by Tuá until she came of age and no longer needed a guide mother. Then Márgu would join the other nieddaš and choose a skill to suit her and serve all the Jápmemeahttun. Then, one day, she too would become a guide mother.

Úlla imagined a future for her daughter, aware it was more a vision of the past, one where the ways of the Jápmemeahttun were a blessing from the gods. She would not be there to ease Márgu through the challenges she foresaw. *Those challenges will be Tuá's concern and not mine*, she thought, watching Márgu's eyes grow heavy with contentment.

CHAPTER TWENTY-FOUR

ARNEJ HELD THE CART reins lightly in his hands. The immense horse seemed to need no prompting to keep to the straight path ahead of them. Next to him, Aage slept, leaning against the secured load. His snoring snuffled along with the creaking cart and the even clop of the beast's massive hooves. After a week of traveling together, Marnej was getting used to Aage's sounds, which were varied and exuberant.

Through a combination of signals and the few words they spoke in common, Marnej had learned he traveled through Morallom. Aage was, as far as Marnej understood him, from somewhere farther south—a village or a land he called Halakzan. Aage traveled between villages, where he mended what was broken and fashioned what was needed. In return, he took coin or kind.

Marnej's skills as a smith had been welcomed with a broad smile and deep rumbling laugh as if Aage had understood something he hadn't. Marnej also suspected that the man quite enjoyed his company. Aage certainly took pleasure in parading him before the villagers they visited. At first, Marnej had been too exhausted to care. Then he'd become irritated, though he'd tried not to show it. At present, he just accepted he was like a prize of war to be ogled, poked, and commented on. He had survived his time with the Immortals; this place could be no worse. So far, no one had spit in his face, as Úlla had done. Rather, these people gave him food and a place to rest. Sometimes the elders laughed at him, calling him *fremdu*. The word was spoken without contempt or mistrust. When he'd asked Aage, in a mix of words and signs, what *fremdu* meant, the tinker had grinned, pointing at Marnej's hair and eyes and clothes. Marnej understood he was different. He could not hide his height or the color of his hair or shape of his face. He in turn pointed at Aage, saying, "Fremdu." For his traveling companion was as different from these villagers as he was, and always welcomed.

Aage had raised his hammer. "Martelu."

Marnej had taken up the bellows. Trying to match the rolling *r* sound, he'd answered, "Martelu."

Aage had let out a full belly laugh, shaking his head. "*Fuelluz*, fremdu Marnej."

Marnej was different. Only this time, he wasn't trying to belong. And here, like in the north he'd left behind, horses needed shoes and carts needed nails and he could craft both, thanks to Úlla.

Coming upon a fork in the road, Marnej slowed the horse. There were no villages or huts on the horizon. He prodded Aage, amazed how the man could sleep so soundly.

"Aage," he called, shaking the tinker more vigorously.

The man snuffled to wakefulness, grumbling.

Marnej did not understand the words, but he could guess their meaning by the irritation in Aage's voice. With no desire to argue, he pointed ahead and waited for the man to figure out his meaning.

Aage rubbed his hands across his face. Marnej peered ahead. Although the sun barely shone, compared to the north, this world was as bright as a spring day. The tinker muttered something, pointing to the left.

Marnej snapped the reins and clicked his tongue. The giant horse reprised its lumbering step. The cart groaned in protest. Aage stared off into the distance. Marnej looked to see what had caught the man's eye. He saw only rolling hills and tall, withered grasses.

"What do you see?" Marnej asked, knowing the man couldn't understand him.

Aage frowned. Marnej became instantly alert. He scanned the terrain. He saw nothing beyond the unremarkable landscape. He poked the tinker, pointing to the knife he wore at his waist. Aage shook his head. Marnej let himself relax, trusting Aage understood the dangers upon these roads and would tell him should they arise.

The man gestured to a hillock with a tall stand of trees to their left. "Stop," he said, with a rounded *ohh* and short punctuated *puh* sound. Marnej nodded, urging the horse in that direction, curious as to why they would be stopping in the middle of the day with no settlement in sight. The difficulty in trying to communicate these questions caused a familiar frustration to flare, reminding him of how he'd had to rely upon Dárja on their flight to the Pohjola.

To distract himself from the past, Marnej gestured in the direction they were headed. "Trees," he said, mimicking the branches with his arms.

Aage looked to where he'd pointed and then watched Marnej repeat the awkward motions.

First the man's brows knit, then his eyes widened. He nodded, saying, "Arbu."

Marnej repeated the word.

Aage shook his head.

"Arbu," the tinker said again.

Marnej heard the elongated *arr* followed by the short *boo*. He tried to copy the sounds with a tongue that felt like a stone in his mouth. Aage laughed and signed for Marnej to try again, which he did until Aage held up his hand. Had his life depended on it, Marnej was certain he couldn't tell the difference between his first attempt and this last. And he wasn't quite ready to accept his shortcomings graciously. He tapped Aage on the shoulder, looked him in the eye, and said, "Trees."

The tinker waved him off. Marnej repeated himself, raising his brows. Aage huffed, then spoke the word, trying to imitate the lengthy *eee* of the word followed by the hissing *esss* at the end. Marnej clapped his hands, shaking the reins, which slowed the horse. Marnej pointed at the animal, saying, "Horse."

Aage mouthed the word, rolling the *r* like his native tongue. Marnej began to laugh, finding pleasure in the release of his tension. Aage stared at him, his eyes narrowing. Concerned he might have given offense, Marnej held up his hand in supplication. Then he pointed at himself. "Northern man."

The hard edges of Aage's expression crumbled into a loud guffaw that startled the horse. The animal lurched forward in a trot, sending both Marnej and the tinker rolling back into the cart load behind them. Once righted, they both burst out into a fresh round of raucous laughter.

Aage tapped his chest and then Marnej's. "Amikuz."

Marnej smiled. "Amikuz."

The horse evened out its gait, resuming the plodding pace it seemed to prefer.

Without thinking, Marnej said, "Thank you, Aage."

The tinker met his gaze with a questioning expression. Marnej faltered as he searched for a gesture to match his words. Then he put both hands to his heart and bowed his head.

❧

From the stand of trees on the eastern hillock, Marnej looked out over an impossibly wide plain ringed by low rocky mountains. The wind kicked up dust from the cart path and rustled the leaves above them. Marnej looked up, shielding his eyes from the sun streaming through.

Aage poked him, then pointed. "Karkut."

"Karkut," Marnej repeated, trying to match Aage's pronunciation.

The tinker nodded his approval. Marnej could only guess at what it meant.

He rested the reins on the bench, grabbing the cart-side to climb down. The load canted. Marnej glanced up as Aage's head dropped out of sight. Marnej took hold of the giant beast's harness collar. The animal snuffled and eyed him, then allowed itself to be led ahead toward the overhanging trees. Marnej ground-tied the horse and patted its neck. Aage came up behind him with the animal's food satchel.

"Grada evalu," Marnej said, hoping he had said the words for "big horse" correctly in Aage's tongue.

The man grinned as he slipped the feed bag around the horse's head. "North horse egrada," he said, mixing both their languages, as he lowered his hand from his head to his waist.

Marnej pretended to be outraged at Aage's declaration that northern horses were small. He reached over and raised Aage's hand to his chin.

"Egrada," the tinker declared.

"And shaggy like you," Marnej joked, even though the man wouldn't understand. He waved off Aage's inquiring look and pointed out to an irregular shape in the south, west of the valley.

The tinker followed his line of sight and nodded, saying, "Karvaluz." He picked up a stick off the ground. In the dirt, Aage drew a tight circle and touched Marnej, then traced a winding line between larger circles. He pointed toward Karvaluz with his stick, then drew a large open circle on what Marnej realized was a map.

"Big," Marnej said in Aage's tongue.

The man nodded.

⌁

While Aage busied himself with setting up their camp, Marnej looked toward Karvaluz, imagining what it would be like. Eventually, he began to gather twigs and fallen branches, placing them in a pile. Then he gathered the stones that scattered about the ground where they would sleep. He set them by the mound of kindling. It was early, but Marnej wasn't opposed to a meal and some rest. He heard the clang of metal against metal. Aage mumbled to himself. When the tinker came around the cart, he smiled. The two had established a routine of unspoken, shared tasks. Marnej cleared the ground and built the fire. Aage prepared their food. Marnej opened the tinder pouch Aage had given him. He took out the flint and fire steel—the fire steel he'd made himself, under Úlla's exacting guidance.

"Horseshoes are big and oafish like you," she'd said. "The curve of a fire steel must not only fit your hand, it must bring out a spark."

Marnej fingered the straight edge of the steel, letting his memories settle back into the recesses of his regret. Little was left to him of his life among the Immortals: his furs, at which Aage had turned up his nose, his tunic and breeches, and his fire steel secured to his belt. Marnej struck it with the flint. Sparks shimmered and skittered across the dry leaves and duff. He blew softly upon the glowing points until tiny flames crackled to life.

He added fuel to the growing fire, watchful not to overload it before it was ready.

"Aage," Marnej called to the tinker, his thoughts on a question that had quietly plagued him since his arrival upon these shores.

The man looked up from the bits of food he had cut and arranged.

"Northern man?" Marnej asked, holding up one finger, then five, and finally all ten of his fingers.

Aage seemed to consider Marnej's question. He held up five fingers and said, "Karvaluz."

Marnej felt his heart leap at the news there were others like him here. He wondered if this was why they were headed to Karvaluz. He didn't know how to ask this, so he placed his hands over his heart and said, "Thank you."

Aage looked up, nodded, and then went back to chopping the onion-like plant into the pot.

Marnej looked back out toward Karvaluz. In the fading sunlight, it was a spot on the horizon, distinguishable only in opposition to its surroundings. It was neither the brown of the grassy plain nor the rocky gray of the hills, but perhaps it would be a place for him to finally stop.

CHAPTER TWENTY-FIVE

THE DAYS OF IDLENESS wore upon Niilán until his irascibility drove his men to avoid him. He knew this, but he was not inclined to change his temperament. His frustration consumed him, and worry gnawed upon him like a starving rat. When he had divided his regiment outside of Hassa, he had told his men he would travel south to the Stronghold once he had the Piijkij in his hands. That was before the Brethren managed to escape him once again in the Great Valley. All save two. *Two*, he thought bitterly. A pathetic showing for the time and effort they had spent hunting these men.

And how many more remained? The question tormented him. Some must have survived and those who did must be close. They had to count some wounded in their ranks. It stood to reason, even with their skill, the rogue Piijkij had been outnumbered and that meant at least an arm or flank had been grazed or worse.

It was also possible their wounded had died in the escape or else these Brethren were desperate enough to abandon those who might slow them down. *No*, he thought. He had served under their leadership in the Great Battle. When the fighting had become a swell of brutal savagery, he had seen his commander in the thick of it. And when it was over, Válde had walked the ranks of the dead and dying looking for his own. Niilán had been fortunate.

His injuries had been superficial. He recalled with gratitude how Válde had held out his hand and assured him he would receive care.

No. They are together. The Piijkij act as one.

Even though there had been no word of banditry or even sightings, he would be the blighted son of a five-teat sow if he returned south empty-handed. Niilán grimaced. He was already cursed: feckless farmer, worthless handmate, and long-forgotten father.

But he had been a good soldier, if reluctant at first. *Good for something*, he thought, then grumbled aloud, "Better to sow your seeds than cast good deeds." It was an old Olmmoš saying Niilán's mother had favored. One she had lived by. He was beginning to see her wisdom. The only problem was, Niilán had no skill with seeds and no farm to claim. For better or worse, he was a soldier. Nonetheless, on days like this, he was sorely tempted to turn his back on the High Priest and his spy, Áigin, and leave them pissing in the wind. Then he thought of Osku, whom he had sent south. He did not want to add the man's head to his conscience. He'd had enough of that already. His stomach churned, full of juhka and little else.

Unable to sit still any longer, Niilán burst from his lavvu, shouting, "Hárri!" The leather tent flap beat against him in a gust of frigid wind. "Which scouting parties have returned?"

The soldier jumped up from where he hunkered before a struggling fire. "None, sir."

"Any word from the outpost?" Niilán demanded.

"No, sir," the soldier answered, sharp as a whip.

"None sir and no sir," Niilán mimicked the man, then saw in the soldier's expression the ugly truth about himself. He had become as arbitrary as the commanders he had once condemned.

"As a good soldier should answer, Hárri," Niilán said. "I will take the watch. You warm yourself. No need for us both to be cold when only I suffer for news." He gave the soldier a rueful smile.

The change in Niilán's demeanor had the effect of unnerving the man even more. "Sir, I'm as anxious for word as you."

"I know, Hárri," Niilán cut him off. "It is an order. Go and warm yourself."

The soldier afforded him a long look before heading off to his tent. Even then, he cast one more questioning glance back.

Niilán waved him on, aware he was quickly becoming a man he neither recognized nor much liked. *Men have revolted for far less*, he thought, clapping himself about the arms to ward off the rising cold. His men had been sorely pushed when the Jápmea female had escaped. Were it not for the two dead Piijkij as a prize, her disappearance might have turned out very differently for him. Osku had said as much. *But I made a bargain with the gods to live an honorable life*, Niilán mocked himself. Still, it had been the right decision, maybe even the honorable decision to make. Women and children should not bear the brunt of the hatred between men and Immortals. The war was over. The Jápmea defeated. There was no praise to be earned in brutalizing those weaker.

~

"So I'm to be left behind while you lot go traipsing off to kill the Vijns's soldiers," Herko complained. "Even Gáral?"

"Herko, you can hardly go hopping along with your sword drawn and ask soldiers to fall upon it," Feles said, packing his satchel with care.

"I can do more with one leg than most of you can with two," Herko said, earning himself hoots of derision from the others.

"Imagine what he could do with three."

"And what if you don't come back?" Herko demanded.

"You just said you could do more with one leg than most of us with two," Mures said. "I'm sure you will find your way."

"Oso," Herko sniffed. "Not much of a village."

"If you mean not overrun by reinforcements after a recent fire we caused, then yes," Válde answered, tired of the banter.

"Not much of a test for her, is it then?" Herko eyed Válde. "How will she know what to expect if you are playing in the pastures of Oso?"

"She escaped once from the Believers' Stronghold," Válde said.

Herko waved off the reply. "This time she's got to break *into* the Stronghold, crawling with soldiers, find that weasel-faced High Priest, slit his throat, and slip past those same soldiers."

Válde leaned forward. "I don't want to risk losing her in a test."

"If you don't risk her now, you surely risk losing us at the Stronghold," Herko said.

"I can speak for myself," Dárja spoke up. "He's right." She looked over at Herko, who sat with his splinted leg, resting on a barrel. "You're right. What would be a true test?"

"Mehjala," he said, without missing a beat. "The garrison is large and fortified. Not like the Stronghold . . ."

"I broke free from the Stronghold," she interrupted.

Válde frowned. "It won't be easy. They've learned their lesson."

Dárja shrugged.

Gáral cleared his throat. "The outpost commander is at the top of the defense tower. The stairs are guarded. Likely the entrance to his quarters."

Dárja looked from Gáral to Herko. "You wish me to kill him and make my way out without being seen?"

"No," Válde said, uncomfortable with the direction of the conversation and Dárja's casual tone. "The death of some soldiers in Oso is one thing. It would signal we have returned. If Dárja kills the commander in Mehjala it will only serve to raise the concern for safety in the Stronghold. We want to test our plan, not give it away."

"What do you wish me to do for you?" she asked. "Steal more uniforms or set fire to stables?" She arched her brows at Herko, who scowled back.

"We need no more uniforms," Gáral spoke up, "because we will not be able to help you."

Válde nodded, "If you go into Mehjala, you will have to act alone. If we were to try our earlier trick, we would put ourselves and you in danger." He hesitated before continuing, "Oso would be a different matter. We would be able to assist you because we have not been seen there and they are not likely to expect that kind of subterfuge."

Válde watched Dárja weigh the options before her. It made sense she should try Mehjala. On the other hand, to do it alone gave him cause for concern. What if she failed to disappear? She would be alone and exposed within the heart of the garrison.

Oso gave her their backing, but Herko was right. It was hardly a proving ground for the Stronghold. He thought back to their earlier argument. He felt himself flush with guilt, aware his worries had strayed from strategy.

"I'm going to Mehjala," she said. "The rest of you can go to Oso."

Válde opened his mouth to protest. She cut him short.

"If we act on two fronts, we can serve two purposes. Let me try to prove myself in Mehjala, while the rest of you draw the interest of the Believers toward the west." She looked to the others. "If I'm caught, you don't risk yourselves. You can continue to harass the heels of your enemies."

Válde shook his head.

"Don't say *no*," she said, her stance squared like a badger before its burrow. "Just tell me what I need to do to further *our* chances at the Stronghold."

Gáral nodded. "Her plan has merit."

Válde said nothing, unprepared for her to say *our*.

"How are we supposed to trust her to act for us?" Herko demanded.

"Do you want me to go to Mehjala or not?" she snapped.

"We would not be able to help you within the garrison," Válde repeated his earlier warning, considering the advantages of her proposal.

"You weren't there to help me at the Stronghold either," she said.

"True," Válde answered, turning his back on her scorn. "Gáral, what do you recall of Oso?"

"The village and garrison are nothing worthy of note," he said. "The garrison is on the eastern side, where the river widens. The village is on the western side. The river will be frozen by now."

"How many men in the garrison?"

"Fifty. Maybe a little less. Mostly young and inexperienced by the look of them."

Válde frowned. "Can the village support that many in the season of snow?"

"Unlikely."

A plan had begun to form in Válde's mind. "So there could be fewer?"

Gáral agreed.

"Take Mures, Edo, and Feles to Oso," Válde said. "The damage you do is your own choice. Remember that the less hardship to the village, the more we save ourselves their acrimony." He turned and faced Dárja. "I will give you what support I can."

"I won't need it," she said with an ugly smirk.

Válde turned to his men. "We will give you five days, lead to reach Oso before taking action in Mehjala. This should allow for enough time to show them the finer points of your swords and retreat to safety before returning here. It should also give the Oso garrison time to send for assistance to the closest outpost."

"Skaina and Mehjala," Gáral said.

"Will lend aid," Válde added.

"Making it all the easier for our little Jápmea to slip in," Herko concluded.

Dárja watched Feles trail Válde. She'd offered to go check the traps. Válde had chosen Feles. She waited outside the hut until she could no longer make out their shapes. Inside, the rest of the Piijkij were huddled together—more a pack than any wolves she'd ever seen.

Although she'd never admit it, Dárja was nervous in Válde's absence. Herko resented her most. Her efforts to heal his leg fell short of balancing out her birthright. She was Jápmea to him. The coarseness of the word rankled. This was how they thought of her—vile and base. Gáral wasn't much better. He hadn't spoken out against her, but she'd noted his aversion when she'd examined his dressings. Mures still mourned the loss of his friend, Redde. Edo, though shy, would lend a hand when she asked. And Feles was unreadable.

At best, alliances were divided. And Dárja knew she couldn't count on any of these Olmmoš. Her efforts to heal Gáral and Herko had earned her a begrudging gratitude. She didn't want to test their allegiance. It was one of the reasons she'd chosen to go to Mehjala. At least there, she wouldn't have to rely on any of them. And maybe, if she succeeded on her own, they'd finally trust her.

Dárja looked back to the sagging, snow-laden outlines of the trapping hut. The moon had waxed and waned since Válde had stopped her from leaving. Each night, she'd gone to sleep, listing what she'd need to take with her when she left the following day. Only to stay on another day. This was due to more than the power of Válde's inexplicable pull upon her. The truth was, she'd no other place to go. At least here, she wouldn't be pitied. There'd be no furtive stares and no censure disguised as sympathy. She'd fought against these men. She understood them. They didn't know or care that she'd remain a nieddaš for the rest of her life.

A cough behind Dárja startled her. She whirled around, her hand instinctively reaching for her knife. Mures stood against the backdrop of the hut. Above him, a thin line of lazy smoke curled up into the sky. She let her hand fall to her side, her body buzzing with alarm.

"Why don't you want to be with your kind?" he asked, breaking the hush that had fallen upon them.

The question, so reasonable and calmly stated, left Dárja speechless. How could she answer? Her reasons were too revealing. They struck at the very heart of what it meant to be Jápmemeahttun. Despite the kindness Mures had shown her, he had no actual interest in the details of her life, nor had she the desire to explain.

"I no longer have a place with them," she said, choosing the simple truth within the larger, more complex one.

"They cast you out?" he asked.

Dárja shook her head. "I can't remain with them without causing discord."

The Piijkij nodded. "We've struggled with discord."

Dárja searched his face for a sign he referred to her presence among the Hunters. Time stretched out as snow began to fall.

Mures looked to the sky. "We were trained as Brethren. We had a purpose. Now . . ." He trailed off. After a short-lived pause, he added, "Válde has a vision. It's what keeps us together." He looked directly at her.

Dárja felt the intensity of his scrutiny. Before she could respond, the Piijkij went on. "He believes you're the key to our plans."

"And what do you believe, Mures?" she asked.

The man shrugged. "I believe in Válde. And he believes in friends of shared enemies."

He tilted his head, silently challenging her.

"There's wisdom in aphorisms," she said, carefully. "But friendship can be as fraught as enmity. Perhaps more so. As enemies, the lines are clear."

"Does this mean you stand with us or against us?" Mures asked, brushing aside her attempt to twist words.

Dárja watched the snow catch upon the man's thick beard, turning it almost white. "I am Jápmemeahttun," she said, feeling the loss of all her kind. "Jápmemeahttun and Olmmoš have fought each other longer than either of us can remember. It is also true that, in many ways, I understand your struggle and I share it." She stopped. An image of Marnej came to mind. He was seated upon a horse, among the other mounted Piijkij. She too was there. Their prisoner. Then they'd escaped. Together. What came after was too hard to bear. "I add my skills to your cause," she said, thinking, *There, I've said it.*

"Does it pain you to side with us?" Mures asked.

"No," Dárja said, watching the smoke rise up through the falling snow. "It's all in the past."

"The past often revisits us," he said.

Dárja took his meaning as a warning.

Then, looking through her, Mures sighed. "I find I'm never able to stay there very long."

CHAPTER TWENTY-SIX

FOR THE LENGTH OF the grassy plain they'd traveled, Marnej had eyes only for Karvaluz. He'd made silent observations as they followed the winding road from slightly east to west again on the southern track. He'd noted the differences in morning, midday, and evening light, though he could discern little of the unknowable place awaiting them. When he found himself within its breathtaking walls, he gaped. No picket. No palisade. No defense tower he'd ever seen matched the imposing bulwark of stones, reaching toward the clouds. The people of this place seemed to have had the ability to turn rock into thread and weave fine designs into the bastion that stood against the vast open plain behind them.

Everywhere Marnej looked there was something strange and captivating. His head swiveled like an oarri with plump seeds all around. One thing was clear to him: Karvaluz was no village. It was as if a village had spread like mushrooms across the forest floor. Except the buildings around him were hardly small and couldn't be knocked over by a careless step. The structures were as tall as they were wide, as big as the Brethren's Fortress and the Believers' Stronghold and made of stone, like the fortified walls he'd just passed through.

The cart path they followed was made of stone the color of river sand. The wheels of Aage's cart clacked as they rolled along. His horse's hooves clopped rhythmically as if someone beat upon a drum. All manner of people and carts trundled around them. None seemed to notice Marnej rode beside Aage.

Although the air was cold and a dusting of snow rested on the northern-sloped roofs, these people didn't wear furs. Both men and women swaddled their heads in cloth. Some wore woolen cloaks with brightly colored patterns sewn on them. There were shades of color Marnej had never seen before. He wanted to ask Aage what they were, but with his limited vocabulary in the tinker's language it was too hard. His eye caught markings on the faces of those who wore plain robes and wrapped themselves in colors like the stones and earth. He had so many questions with no way to satisfy his curiosity.

At a fork in the road, Aage turned down a slender path to the left. The horse willingly traveled the shadowed lane without the reins to guide it. A chill prickled Marnej's skin as the sun fell behind tall structures on either side. The wide openings in their fronts puzzled him. Most were dark patches within facades. Occasionally he'd glimpsed an unnatural shine that made him wonder if this place had another sun in the sky.

In the Brethren's Fortress, window slits had been cut high into the walls to observe those who approached. Admittedly, none had been so wide. So unprotected. Not even the High Priest in the Believers' Stronghold possessed light like this and he spoke for the gods. Marnej felt as if every structure stared at him like the wide eyes of owls at twilight. He could not escape the glint of them. Marnej pointed at the windows, unable to understand how ice covered them. Aage nodded, more concerned with the ground upon which they traveled. Marnej looked again to see if his eyes had tricked him. They hadn't. Weak sunlight bounced off the surfaces as if the windows were covered in a cascade of water. Marnej tapped Aage again and pointed upward. The man's attention was winnowed to the path ahead of them. Above, the structures reached across their heads like the branches of trees. Only a spare strip of pale sky kept stone from meeting stone. There were still a few people on either side of the cart, moving about with purpose.

Aage brought them to a shuddering stop with a sharp exhale of "Hazz."

An unexpected corral encircled them. The familiar smell of dung, animal, and fodder greeted Marnej. Aage handed him the reins, then descended the cart. Aage's groaning protests matched those of the sagging struts. Men stopped their work to approach. The conversation, rich with energy and gesticulation, was largely lost on Marnej, and soon held little interest. To occupy himself, he observed the men around Aage. They were shorter than his traveling companion, lean and wiry in frame. They wore similar clothing: knee-length leather vests atop a thick woven tunic and dark breeches made of a material he couldn't identify.

Their faces were also as distinct as the phases of the moon. The man who currently spoke to Aage had markings on his cheeks and chin. Standing nearby, with his weight resting on a tapered pole, was another man similar in features, with dots upon his skin in place of a swirling design. But it was the figure standing far to the right that held Marnej's fascination. As tall as the other men, with full hips and the shadow of breasts beneath the tunic and vest, Marnej couldn't tell if the person was a man or a woman. Wide-set eyes above high reddened cheekbones peeked out from under a cap with a colorful border.

The conversation stopped and all eyes were on him. Aage pointed to the ground. "Here northern man," he said, then signaled for Marnej to descend. Marnej did as he was told with wary curiosity. Aage grabbed a bag from below the cart bench and flung it over his shoulder. He ambled back down the path they'd come. Marnej stood by the cart, aware the others watched him. Aage stopped by a green door, above which curled a painted symbol.

Aage opened the door just as Marnej reached him. The smell of food cooking wafted out onto the stone threshold. Marnej's stomach growled with unabashed hunger. Aage flashed him a toothy smile, then disappeared within the interior shadows. He heard the creak of stairs before his eyes adjusted enough to make out Aage's shape ascending ahead of him. Marnej followed and his foot caught on the plank, sending him onto his hands. Cursing the stairs that were too short for his feet, he scrambled up the rest of the steps, feeling like a bear cub fresh from its mother's den.

When he emerged onto the next floor, Marnej froze. In the smoky, candlelit room, men and women laughed and talked as they ate and drank at a long table. In the center of the room, a man as tall as Marnej stood with a ewer in his hands. He had pale yellow hair and skin the color of goat's milk in winter.

Aage had said there were others like him. But Marnej had shrouded his hope with so much doubt that his elation was muddied by incredulity. Voices assailed him, hearty, happy, and foreign. He understood little and let it pass by him, his eyes on the man with the ewer. It had been at least a full moon cycle since he'd last spoken his own tongue and he was surprised to realize a man's heart could hunger for words the way his body did for food.

The man smiled and hailed Aage with a flourish of another foreign tongue, as if glad to greet someone dear and long-missed. He put the ewer down on the table with a loud *thunk*. He raised his open palm to Aage, then placed it on his chest. He came around the crowded table and he reached out his arm to be clasped. Marnej stared, noting the calluses and scars on the man's hands. He looked up, grasping the man's arm, feeling himself grin from ear to ear.

"I greet you, traveler. Be welcome in the home of Lávrrahaš," the man said.

To Marnej's starved ears, it was if the gods had spoken. Instantly tongue-tied, he struggled to recall the simplest greeting. In a rush, he said, "I am called Marnej."

Lávrrahaš laughed, then spoke to Aage in his own tongue. To Marnej, he said, "Come. Sit and rest. Eat your fill. We have no juhka here in the south, but I make a mulled wine I hope you will find pleasing."

Aage dropped his bag in a corner, while Marnej slid onto the bench at the end of the long table. Aage joined him, pushing Marnej close to the neighboring man.

"Excuse me," Marnej said, anxious he was trapped. The man gave him a broad, gap-toothed smile and said something Marnej didn't understand.

Lávrrahaš brought over two battered metal cups filled with rich, red liquid. Marnej sniffed the heady fragrance before taking a tentative sip. The taste was unlike anything he'd experienced. He took a deeper draw, his body beginning to relax. He caught Aage observing him. He smiled, truly grateful to the man for bringing him to this place.

Aage downed his cup. He grinned at Marnej, then tapped his chest, before pointing at Lávrrahaš. "Northern man," he said with apparent satisfaction. He took the freshly filled cup and turned to the woman across from him, entering into what appeared to Marnej as an immediate and animated debate.

Marnej looked up at Lávrrahaš, curious if he was at all surprised to see one of his own people. The man continued to pour drinks and pepper his conversation with a robust, good-natured laugh. When he approached to refill Marnej's cup, he held it out.

"What does the sign above your door mean?" he asked, recalling the curling figure.

Lávrrahaš chuckled softly. "It is the symbol for us here in Karvaluz. We are the sea monster to them." He laughed again.

Marnej frowned, unsure of what this meant. Lávrrahaš leaned in and whispered, "It is a conversation for when the others have gone." He stood up and nodded his head at the other patrons, pouring from the ewer the heady liquid that made all agreeable.

~

By the light of two dwindling candles, Marnej sat with Aage. Lávrrahaš poured them all more forrá. While Marnej had never cared for juhka, he quite enjoyed the sweet spiciness of this drink.

Aage said something to Lávrrahaš which made the man smile. The lines of his face were deeply etched. "Aage says you are a good traveling companion, except for the fact you snore like a bear."

Marnej sputtered, "I snore! This one here"—he pointed to Aage—"he's the one who snores."

The tinker let out a loud guffaw at Marnej's outrage, adding something further in his own language.

Lávrrahaš translated. "He says you are an able ironsmith and is surprised a northern man, stuck in ice, learned to work with fire."

Marnej, who'd been ready to protest another insult, inclined his head to Aage. "Boné."

"Ha!" Lávrrahaš exclaimed. "You speak some Bissmená."

"Only *egrada* words," Marnej answered in a mix of the two languages.

"Well, if you plan to stay here, it will be useful to learn some more Bissmená," Lávrrahaš commented. "But your skills as a smith will be welcomed. Especially in this quarter of the urbej."

Marnej frowned. "*Urbej.* What does it mean?"

"There is no word for it in our tongue," Lávrrahaš said. "The best I can do is to say it means a mother village, with her daughter villages surrounding her."

"I've never seen anything like it. Even the Stronghold of the Believers is tiny in comparison," Marnej said.

Lávrrahaš snorted. "That is because it *is* tiny. There is nothing in the north to compare. Karvaluz is at the heart of Karkut's prosperous trade routes, from Morallom, where Aage found you, to Halakzan, where Aage is from, and east to the Falkuj. Many of the Bissmeni from Morallom and Aeopo of Halakzan have come to trade here and stayed. And many Irkati from the outlying areas of Karkut have been drawn to the urbej with tales of wealth and an easy life. The reality is that most work hard for what we call our own."

"Is that why Aage's here?" Marnej asked.

Lávrrahaš translated the question for the tinker, who shrugged and spoke rapidly.

"Aage says he is content to stay in Morallom. He has been to Karvaluz enough to know it is not for him."

"In a place as big as this, there must be great opportunity to trade," Marnej said.

Lávrrahaš agreed with a tilt of his head, then sipped some of the forrá. He smacked his lips. "Sometimes it is not about the coin."

"Why did you come here?" Marnej asked.

Lávrrahaš's pale eyes glowed colorless in the candlelight. "Why did *you* come here?" he asked in return. His question had a bite to it.

Marnej quickly added, "I mean no offense. It's just, I thought I'd be alone in the south. Well actually, I didn't know what to expect, other than I'd be far away from the north. When Aage said there were other northern men here, I didn't really believe him." Marnej stopped short, embarrassed the drink had dulled his better judgment and loosened his tongue.

Both Lávrrahaš and Aage laughed and shared a private conversation in Bissmená.

Regarding Marnej once again, Lávrrahaš said, "Aage told me how you met, but he could not tell me how you came to be in the forest."

"I walked there from the coast," Marnej said.

Lávrrahaš's brows furrowed. "You were on the sea?"

"A fisherman gave me his boat," Marnej said, watching doubt play across his host's face. "Didn't you come by boat to the southern shores?"

"I have never seen the southern shores," Lávrrahaš said. "I traveled the land route."

"Land route?" Marnej repeated, his suspicion aroused. "How's that possible? What land route is there?"

"Perhaps if we share our stories, we will both be the wiser," Lávrrahaš said, pouring more forrá.

When Marnej held his cup back, Aage urged him to share another round with a friendly clap on his back.

"I will translate for Aage," Lávrrahaš said, putting down the earthen ewer, "so he does not believe himself excluded from the plotting of two northern men." He spoke to Aage, who nodded in agreement.

"In the south, they mark the passage of time differently," Lávrrahaš began. "So, perhaps I err when I say I have been here near thirteen seasons of snow. In the north, I was a badjeolmmoš in the Pohjola. Like my father before me. After calving season, I returned to Ullmea to visit my mother and sisters. The talk in the travelers' hut was of armies and another war with the Jápmea." He spoke to Aage. When he finished, he drank from his cup. "I had no ill feelings toward the Immortals. I knew they were there with us in the Northlands, though they never once harmed me, nor did I ever gain sight of them. And I had no desire to be a soldier or be a part of any war." Lávrrahaš hooted. "If the Immortals even deigned to appear."

"They came," Marnej said quietly, swallowing his words behind a gulp of forrá.

Lávrrahaš looked off into the darkened corner of the room, the comment unnoticed.

"I kissed my mother and sisters," he continued, "and headed back to the Pohjola, fearing it would not be far enough." He tilted back his cup with a slurp. "So, when we followed the reindeer to their farthest eastern track I continued on. I thought there had to be lands beyond our borders, regardless of what the priests had said. I traveled for days, with only the wind and the occasional bird to keep my mind occupied. Then I reached low hills that gave me plenty of forage. I thought to stay there. Build myself a hut. Then the mountains beyond called to me. I climbed. I nearly lost my life more than once on the treacherous rocks, but I made it to the other side."

Lávrrahaš translated for Aage. His explanation was more succinct, which made Marnej think Bissmená was a tongue that required fewer words to convey meaning.

"The first people I came upon were shocked to see me stumble into their camp. I do not recall exactly how it happened because I was beyond myself with hunger and thirst. They brought me back to life. I traveled with them south and west until we reached Karvaluz."

In the flickering light, Lávrrahaš's expression softened. "Much like you, I am beholden to the ones who found me."

He translated again and, at the end, Aage waved him off with his hand, saying, "Nesdané."

"So if you traveled over land, why do they call you the sea monster?" Marnej asked.

This time Lávrrahaš's laugh shook the table. The candles wavered. One guttered out.

"Darkness take me," their host swore under his breath. He stood and retreated to the sturdy counter along the wall, muttering curses, until he found what he was looking for. He returned to the table to light a new candle, saying, "Old legends and stories have lived well in these lands. There are tales from the ancient days of ice creatures beyond the sea who dwell in darkness and eat souls."

"We've no tales of southern monsters," Marnej sputtered. "Or men with dark ringlets of hair who come out of the forest mist to eat a man's soul. We've never seen anyone from the south."

The tavernkeeper held up his hand. He translated for Aage. The tinker chuckled and made a quick reply.

Grinning, Lávrrahaš said, "Aage does not believe the souls of northern men would be very flavorful."

Marnej let the jest pass in favor of what troubled him about Lávrrahaš's tale. "If the south is full of trade routes plying faraway borders, why haven't they come north by now?"

Lávrrahaš shrugged. "Perhaps the old legends hold some weight."

"But you've been accepted," Marnej persisted. "And the others."

"There is room for acceptance here."

"Even for sea monsters?"

Lávrrahaš held up his cup to toast Marnej. "Even for true sea monsters."

CHAPTER TWENTY-SEVEN

AT THE FULL MOON of Cuoŋománnu, the last of the season of snow, Úlla awoke early from a fitful dream. Nestled at her side, Márgu slept soundly. Úlla lightly rested her hand upon the baby's round belly. Márgu had grown and flourished since their return to the Pohjola. The awareness of this transformation made Úlla mindful of her body. She rolled onto her back, asking herself, *Do I feel different?*

In the weeks preceding, she had not felt a change building within her. Just recently Úlla had noticed she had begun to regain her energy and her unexplained shifts in temperament had eased, as had her disturbing dreams. In fact, this morning's dream filled her with hope. Careful not to wake Márgu, she pushed off the weighty coverings and sat up. She stretched out her arms, feeling her skin prickle in the chilled air. Her muscles lengthened, becoming pleasantly taut at their farthest reach. Then she hugged herself about the shoulders, finding the hard sinew beneath her hands gratifying. Today she would share Márgu's song with Tuá, then she would sit the dákti. Three days hence, she would begin her life as an almai.

As an almai, she would work at the forge as she did now, resuming her calling with more strength and command. When she'd first returned, she could barely lift the hammers or work the bellows. In the past days, she had observed her strength growing measurably. What had winded her previously now presented no challenge. She was sure it was a sign. Even so, as she released her hold, she could not ignore the feel of her breasts beneath her tunic. Surely, their softness would give way to hard muscle soon.

Her calloused hands explored the smooth contours of her face. No beard bristled at her chin or cheeks. Her voice was firm, deep even. As of yet, it had not wavered nor cracked. Úlla counted the days since her return. It had been a full moon cycle already. Unease spread like a fever under her skin. What if the Elders did not let her sit the dákti because she did not look ready to be almai? She was ready. There was no doubt in her mind.

With fresh clarity and resolve, Úlla wrapped her shawl around her, then gathered her clothing and noiselessly padded through the room. She slowly opened the door, which sighed with age. She looked back to Márgu, who continued to sleep as did the other nieddaš and mánáid. If the babe woke before she returned, the others would care for her needs. Gingerly, she closed the door behind her. She walked directly to the sávdni, listening for the sounds of any other early riser. The kitchen, forge, and baths all required fires to be stoked. Soon those tasked with laying the fires would be about. Glancing furtively behind her, Úlla entered the sávdni, conscious of the sounds she made. She had never had cause to be in the baths by herself before, especially when they were cold. Bathing was a time to relax together; to talk and slough off the day's grime and toil. The steam, fragrant with oils, had always eased her cares. On this dark morning, there was no steam creeping along the wooden ceiling, no smell of mint or spruce embracing her.

Úlla stood alone in the cold antechamber of the nieddaš bath, grateful for the privacy. She had always cherished the companionship of her friends. But if she was to be accepted as almai, she would need to take action. In a corner, hidden from the entrance, Úlla dropped her clothing and woolen shawl upon a washing stool. She slipped her linen tunic over her head. Keeping hold of the garment's hem, she ripped a wide strip of fabric from the bottom. She would mend the frayed edges later. For now, she slid the length of fabric across her bare back and around the front, just under her arms, cinching the strip hard against her breasts. Úlla tied the ends tight, tucking the remaining length under the taut bandeau. When she finished, she could barely get enough air into her lungs.

Satisfied her new armature would stay in place, Úlla dressed, stuffing what was left of her tunic into the leather breeches before securing her belt ties. She already felt more almai. Úlla pulled on her worn leather vest, hooking the loops around the bone buttons. She took the knife from her belt, checked its edge for sharpness with her thumb, then hacked off her lush braid with sure strokes.

～

Úlla entered the Chamber of Passings with Márgu in her arms. The last time she had been within these walls, she had been preparing to leave to give birth. Back then, fear had clouded her eyes to the beauty of the chamber. This time, though, her heart fluttered with anticipation. She took in, with reverence, the painted images sacred to all Jápmemeahttun. Her fingers touched the rays of the sun. Outside these walls, the sun rose higher and higher, breaking the grip of darkness. Úlla rejoiced in its return and the new life awaiting her.

She moved forward to walk alongside the scene that depicted the arrival of the Olmmoš. Her anger flared, hot and blinding. All at once, she wanted to avenge herself upon these humans who had brought with them only death and hatred. The pulse in her neck throbbed. Úlla had made many knives and swords in the forge. She had shaped the raw metal into fearsome blades, measured the tang for balance, and had honed the edges until they drew blood. But she had never drawn blood herself. She felt vengeance swelling within her. She wanted to stand with a blade in her hand and feel the power to take an Olmmoš life.

She thought of Dárja, unsheathing her sword, telling Úlla to ride ahead to her Origin. Dárja had fought that day, as she had in the battle, to protect her kind. She had given her life, just as Kálle and countless others had. Dárja had been a nieddaš, yet unlike any other. Úlla recalled their days as mánáid. It was true she had never been kind to Dárja, who spent her time either with her Olmmoš bieba, Irjan, or the healers, Kalek and Okta. When Dárja began training with a sword, Úlla had scoffed and teased her in the presence of the others. She had called her an Olmmoš and a traitor, echoing the whispers of those older than her. Only now, facing her own change, could she admit she had been envious of the world Dárja had lived in—one which had taught her how to think and fight like an almai.

Dárja was gone now. Had she lived, she would still be a in world of her own. Unlike Úlla, who would soon sit for her dákti, had Dárja returned, she would have eventually been cast out as rivgu, unable to bring new life to their kind. *Perhaps it was better this way.* The disgrace and loneliness of not being Jápmemeahttun was too much to imagine. Úlla vowed that when she emerged from the ceremony, she would honor the sacrifice Dárja had made. Márgu yawned in her arms. Behind, the sound of footsteps approached. Úlla turned to see the Council nearing, first the nieddaš, those who were already guide mothers but had not given birth. Behind them would be Tuá and her chosen witnesses. The Elders would enter only after she had shared Márgu's song.

Úlla stepped out into the middle of the room to acknowledge the beginning of the ceremony. Among the nieddaš was Ávrá, who smiled warmly and nodded her greeting. Once the Council encircled her and Márgu, Tuá came forward with Ravna and Ello on either side of her.

"Your hair," Ravna gasped, then clamped a hand over her mouth.

Úlla saw a flicker of irritation in the set of Tuá's jaw.

"It was time," Úlla said. "An almai should not wear the braid of a nieddaš."

"What about Kalek?" Ello commented with her usual disregard for sensitivity. "Ow!" she exclaimed, looking around to see who had pinched her.

The Voice of the Council came forward, bringing a hush to all gathered. "Are you ready to share Márgu's song with her biebmoeadni?" she asked, her tone gentle and commanding.

"I am," Úlla said, without hesitation. She looked down at Márgu. The babe's eyes were open, watching her with the sweet intensity she shared with Kálle. Úlla swallowed down the lump in her throat.

The Voice of the Council held out her hand to Tuá. "Will you accept this song as part of you? To share with Márgu the essence of her life?"

"Yes," Tuá said, her voice a hallowed whisper.

Úlla began to chant softly to Márgu, then for all to hear. When she finished, the last word trembled like the birch leaves in a summer wind.

Tuá stepped forward, her hands clasped to her heart. She closed her eyes and began to chant.

Child of love, born in peril.
You are destined to see the dawn of light.
You will shoulder the burden of journeys,
but will walk as kin among many.
The stars light the way beyond what any have known.

Tuá chanted it once more, then blinked open her eyes. They glowed with love.

Úlla came forward, placing Márgu in Tuá's outstretched hands. "She could have no better guide mother."

Tuá gazed in reverence at the baby. Márgu burbled and cooed in the blessed circle. Finally, Tuá looked up, tears glistening. "She will be loved," she said.

No longer Márgu's oktoeadni, Úlla stepped back. The Council of Passings fanned out into a larger circle, their hands intertwined. Through the opening, the Elders entered one by one, radiating the wisdom of their age and experience. The Noaidi was last to approach. He held the sacred drum in his gnarled hands. The Elder smiled at her, the lines of his face crinkling together.

"Be welcome, Úlla, and sit before us," he said.

The sound of shuffling feet filled the chamber as the nieddaš withdrew, taking Márgu with them, safely in her bieba's arms. Behind Úlla, the Elders laid pillows and furs upon the ground.

"You enter the dákti a nieddaš but will leave an almai," the Noaidi said. "Your body has changed by the gods' will. So too does your spirit transform by their will." The ancient Elder beat upon the drum in a rhythm that matched Úlla's heart.

"Listen to the Song of All. Listen for the voice of the gods," he intoned.

"We wait. We watch. We rejoice," chanted the Elders in unison.

Úlla sat down on the furs, her legs comfortably crossed. She took a deep breath which she let out in a slow stream, then closed her eyes and listened. The Song swirled around her as it always had. A comfort. A wellspring of all Jápmemeahttun life. For one brief moment, she relived the terror she had felt being Outside and lost to the Song. Her belly tightened thinking about the unbearable silence and the feeling her body had been turned to stone.

To banish her rising fear, Úlla brought her song to the forefront of her mind, turning each word into a weapon against the Outside and the Olmmoš who had claimed it as theirs.

I am the daughter of the gods, made of flesh and fire.
I carry the heart of all my kind within.
My will is strong.
My guide is ready.
My journey stretches beyond the heavens.

Úlla chanted her song until she felt herself floating away on the current of its sounds—deep into the heart of the Song of All, where the gods waited. Where her life as an almai would begin.

~

"Gods' curses," Kalek swore under his breath, heating the hardened honey to heal a cut upon his hand. "I don't care if he is the Noaidi. The Elder has no right to ask it of me."

The light was returning to their world, even though he felt shrouded in darkness. Dárja had only been gone two full moon cycles. *How could I replace her?* Kalek trembled, his cut forgotten, as images of Dárja came to him. She was his light, his student, his last connection to Irjan, his last connection to Aillun. And he was her father. That Olmmoš word, originally so hard for him to grasp, stuck in his mind.

As a biebmoeadni, he had loved and nurtured his mánná, Kearte. But he had never considered her as a part of him. He was her guide mother. Even when he gave birth to Ravna, she did not feel a part of him, though she had come from his flesh. Once he sung her song to her biebmoeadni, his duty to Ravna had ended. He had seen her grow and run through the hallways, and had never once thought to himself, "There goes my child."

With Dárja it had been different. Maybe it was his guilt over Aillun's death or the effect of Irjan's strange ideas, but Dárja held his heart like no other, not even Aillun, or Ávrá, if he were wholly truthful. Dárja had taught him love was not defined by roles. Rather, the role one played grew out of the love shared.

Irjan had once asked him, "Is she yours?"

Kalek had said, "She is all of ours. We all have parts in her life."

Irjan had not grasped the importance of Kalek's point. He had persisted with his own understanding, as he always did, insisting, "You are her father."

At the time, Kalek could only answer he'd had a minor part in Dárja's life. He had not been her birth mother. That had been Aillun's role. He had not been her guide mother. That had been Irjan's role. Nevertheless, for eighteen seasons of snow, he and Dárja had shared their lives. As a mánná, he had worried for her safety, reveled in her victories, and held her when she cried from whatever hurt had brought her to the apothecary.

If Irjan were here this day to ask him the same question, Kalek would, without hesitation, say, "Yes. I am her father. She is my daughter."

Only he is not here. And Dárja was not there. Realizations made too late were worthless. He'd had mere moments to appreciate what he and Dárja meant to each other. And he would have a lifetime to regret that it had not been longer.

Kalek watched the honey bubble with heat. In this moment, the sweet balm was liquid and golden, like dreams and wishes. When it cooled, it would solidify and harden, like sorrow. Kalek turned from the fire. Hunched over, his head in his hands, he pressed his palms against his eyes.

"She cannot be replaced," he whispered to the fire behind him, the walls around him, and the gods above. It was a truth with the power to transform the very essence of his part in the Song.

～

Ravna did not follow Tuá back to their quarters. Tuá had Márgu now. The others wished to celebrate the first biebmoeadni since the battle. Ravna understood the need to give voice to this moment. She longed to share in their joy, but she had heard something in the Chamber of Passings that made her seek the familiarity of the tanning barn. She needed the reassurance of something solid, simple, and within her control. She joined the others who worked with hides and dyes, nodding to them as she slipped her leather smock over her head. She looked to the stretching bars. The reindeer skins were almost ready to come down. In their place, more would soon be strung. Solid and simple. One action followed the other.

Ravna's hands and body moved out of long established habit, while her mind kept circling back to the song she had heard in the Chamber of Passings. She could not disregard it. She had heard the song within her. Not as though she listened to Úlla or Tuá sing Márgu's song. It had been as if Márgu sang within her. The babe's words were those of Ravna's own thoughts and she did not know what to make of it.

Leaving the ceremony, Ravna had almost convinced herself she had imagined it. Then, when she had parted company with the others, it had happened again. She had plainly heard:

I am the child of love, born in peril.
I am destined to see the dawn of light.
I will shoulder the burden of journeys,
but will walk as kin among many.
The stars light the way beyond what any have known.

She had looked to the others to see if they too had heard Márgu's song. So caught up talking to each other, they had noticed nothing, not even Ravna taking her leave.

Ravna worried she should say something. *But to whom?* She could not approach Tuá—the one soul to whom she had confided everything, since they were old enough to have secrets to share. Tuá would see it as more of Ravna's doubt and would say Ravna was spinning spider webs in clean corners. *No. I cannot tell Tuá. She has her mánná. She is happy.* This realization made it all the worse for Ravna, who knew in her soul she should not be able to hear the babe's song within her. The song was a gift for the biebmoeadni, one the guide mother would share with her child until she grew old enough to sing for herself. Ravna was not the guide mother. *So why can I hear Márgu as if she is part of me?*

CHAPTER TWENTY-EIGHT

DÁRJA STOOD AT VÁLDE'S side, watching the comings and goings of soldiers at the Mehjala garrison. Her tension was obvious in the way her weight bounced between her feet in the too-big Olmmoš boots. If Válde suffered as she did, he didn't show it. He stood as self-possessed as a hawk upon the wing. With their plan well considered and in place, they'd had to wait out a series of storms in the hut. Piled one upon the other, with no chance to escape outside, the Piijkij had grown as mean as cornered badgers. It was a relief when the weather broke and the others had headed to Oso. Herko, of course, had complained about being left behind, despite the fact he was well provisioned. And, in truth, he was able to hobble quite effectively when given enough room to try.

"It's time," Dárja said, sounding more confident than she felt. They'd delayed as long as they could. There'd been no large movement of soldiers out from the Mehjala garrison to suggest that the others had succeeded in Oso. Dárja would have to enter with the full complement of men on duty at the outpost. It was either that or freeze tarrying.

"I will give you to the next change of guard to get in, find out what you can, and get out again," Válde said. "If you have not returned by then, I will send as many flaming arrows into the garrison center as I can. After that, you will have to make your own way."

Dárja nodded. "I know. I'll make my way back to the cave and from there to the hut only if it is safe."

She smoothed the soldier's tunic and tightened the cloak about her. "Do you think this is necessary?" she complained. She sniffed at the cloak. "It smells like a rutting moose."

Válde smirked. "Be glad it is Edo's and not Herko's."

Dárja screwed up her face.

Válde shook his head. "Of all the things you could choose to complain about, it is this?"

"The fact the uniform smells and fits poorly isn't a trifling matter," Dárja said. "The smell alone is enough to distract me from the Song and this garb will hinder me in a fight." She batted at the cloak with both her arms for effect.

Válde pulled up her hood so it covered her newly shorn head. "This garb will also help you hide among the soldiers should you need. You'd be young for a soldier, perhaps." He frowned as if considering the matter further. "Youth and inexperience may work to your advantage."

"If they see me, they'll know I'm not one of them," Dárja said.

"Soldiers cannot see what they cannot believe. And no soldier would ever believe one of your kind would enter an Olmmoš garrison of their own will," Válde said. "So play the role of a young soldier if you must. Remember this is about subtlety."

"There'll be no subtlety when it comes time for me to hold a knife to your High Priest's throat," she said.

Válde frowned. "He is not my High Priest. And that is still ahead of us. If you make it out."

"I've been in worse positions," Dárja said.

Válde hung his head briefly before looking up at her. "True. But without you we are all at an end."

His eyes held an intensity reminiscent of Kalek. Her immediate instinct was to assure him she'd return, just as she'd done with Kalek. Then, as now, there was no guarantee she would. While she'd do everything in her power to make it back out, there was a chance she wouldn't succeed. She'd already lost the opportunity to make things right with Irjan, and she'd never be able to explain herself to Kalek. In this moment, she realized she'd been given another chance to speak her truth. Her heart began to race.

Before she could find a way to begin, Válde said, "You should go. They are about to change the guard."

With a doleful nod, Dárja let the moment slip away from her. She stepped away from Válde, aware his presence was strong enough to hold her in this Olmmoš world.

~

In the shelter of a ring of pine, Dárja released a deep, shaky breath. She closed her eyes, willing away the image of Válde's penetrating stare. She searched deep within herself for a calm center where she could call upon her voice and those of everything around her. *I am daughter of the gods. I am sister among the Jápmemeahttun.* She silently reminded herself of her chorus. Waiting for the rest of her song to emerge from her soul, her knees began to tremble in the cold. How long had she been standing there? It felt like mere moments to her mind. To her body it seemed a lifetime. A wave of panic rose within her. *Why did I think this would work?*

It had to work or nothing bound her to Válde and his men. She swallowed down the sickness she tasted upon her tongue. She searched deeper inside herself than she'd ever gone, pushing her awareness down into the snow beneath her boots, into the frozen ground below. Like flames catching fire, Dárja felt the rush of her song take over her body. Her heart rejoiced in its comforting chorus. Her mind sought out all the profound and subtle meanings.

One by one, the songs joined together until she was one with the All. She was the roots, the ground, the tendrils of ice, the snow, the trees above. Blood rushed through her veins, like swollen spring rivers. She was full and alive and bursting with clarity. She was meant for this.

Dárja opened her eyes on the world with new vision. She stepped out from under the pine trees, listening to their voices. She acted for them. She acted for her kind. She acted for the All. Dárja strode across the open ground, sure of her purpose. The thrum urged her on. Sweeping through the garrison gate, she looked into the Olmmoš faces around her, those with the clean lines of youth, others older with beards and scars, signs they'd been in the battle. Despite her time with the Piijkij, she felt no more kinship with these humans than she had upon the battlefield. They were her enemy. She would walk through them, while they were none the wiser. But if it came to it, they'd die by her hand, without a moment's consideration of their hopes and fears or family waiting for them at home.

The power to resurrect the specter of the Taistelijan burned in Dárja's veins. Like them, she could use the Song as a weapon. Ambush. Attack. Disappear. It'd be so simple, if it weren't for Válde's admonitions; his words nagged her like those of an overly cautious guide mother. *Ambush. Attack. Disappear. It would be simple.* Before she could act on her desire for swift vengeance, Dárja reached the rise of the defense tower. Ahead, as Gáral had described, one guard stood at the base and one at the top stockade. They looked young and overly confident. She could easily take them. Struggling against her desire to engage, Dárja passed by undetected onto the wooden stairs, leading up and over the defensive ditch. She counted some fifty steps to reach the top of the hill, then tried not to race up them and wind herself in the process. She'd be able to make up time in a quick descent.

Within a matter of a dozen steps, Dárja had risen high enough that a glance downward caused a peculiar uneasiness in her belly. *I've climbed higher than this on a tree with no ill effects.* She shot a queasy look back over her shoulder. The activity on the lower level of the outpost went on as before. Reassured, Dárja took another step up and then another, her song growing in strength.

At another time, this might have comforted her. But here, rising above a garrison of Olmmoš soldiers, the power of her voice, relative to all the others in the chorus, disturbed her. Climbing higher, she struggled to listen to the overall melody.

In an instant, the hollow pit of her stomach gave way to a gnawing abyss. Dárja fought against the fear that urged her to run back down the way she'd come. When her next footfall landed, the voices within her disappeared. She'd lost the Song. Unable to control the leaden weight of her body, she stumbled onto her hands and knees. Desperation screamed for her to move, to no avail. It was as if she were outside of herself. When she finally managed to look up at the sentry above, she'd expected to see him charging down on her. To her great relief, he continued to gaze off into the north. Dárja righted herself, praying he wouldn't look down. She climbed upward, aware of the spare sounds in the human world: the lifeless planks beneath her feet, the dull clang of metal on metal, and the guttural utterances of Olmmoš men. Counting the last steps to the top stockade and waiting sentinel, she kept her movements even and purposeful, like any other soldier.

From among all the shouted orders and responses, Dárja heard, "Identify yourself and purpose."

I am Dárja of the Jápmemeahttun and I have come to steal your secrets, she laughed to herself, giddy with the new challenge. She ran up the last five steps with her hand on the knife beneath her cloak, unsure if the soldier's uniform she wore would give her the advantage of doubt. She'd only need a moment. *And it's likely all I'll get.*

Dárja came upon the upper sentry, her hand on her blade, ready to run him through. As she cast aside her cloak, movement from behind distracted both her and the confused sentry. A clambering mass of soldiers jostled past her, grumbling orders Dárja couldn't understand. She seized her chance to slip through them. When they veered left, she hurried forward, keeping her stride to that of a harried messenger. Crossing the upper stockade to what she hoped was the commander's quarters, Dárja fixated on the possible obstacles ahead. What if the commander was not there? What if she was turned away? Even if the commander was inside, and she were permitted in, she needed to find something of value for Válde and the others. And then she'd need to make it out.

Dárja stopped in front of a door, cursing herself for believing Válde's plan would work. Then, for good measure, she cursed the gods for their spitefulness. She banged on the door, then waited an eternity before a clear voice rang out, "Enter."

Dárja opened the door slowly, anticipating the man seated at the table would look up and call her out as an imposter. The man scowled. "What is it, boy?"

Dung-brained fool. She hadn't considered the possibility that when she spoke she'd likely give herself away because she'd been sure she wouldn't need this Olmmoš guise. Her mind raced to find a reason for being there.

"It's the cooks, sir," Dárja sputtered, trying to imitate Herko's coarse accent. To her own ears she sounded like she talked around a mouthful of rotten berries. Her gaze wandered down from the commander's ruddy face to scrolls and parchments scattered in front of him. She couldn't tell if they were of any value. *If I'd been within the Song, as I'd planned, this would've been a simple matter of standing behind the man and looking over his shoulder.*

She couldn't do any of this now. All she could do was to try and get the commander to leave while staying behind.

"It's the cooks, sir," Dárja repeated.

"You already said that, boy," the commander snapped, his eyes narrowing on her. "What are you called?"

"Herko," she said.

"Get on with your message then, Herko." He waved his hand.

"The cooks haven't enough supplies to feed the men," Dárja said, grasping for ideas from her time with the Piijkij.

"Then tell the supply captain. Don't bother me with these concerns," the man shouted, pushing back his chair.

"Yes, sir. It's just that . . ." Dárja hedged, trying to act the part of an Olmmoš as Válde had instructed her. She hoped she could continue with this crumbling subterfuge. "The supply captain already knows and he's done nothing to procure more stocks. The cooks say he's drunk, sir."

"Drunk!" the man roared, banging his hand down on the table.

"That's what the cooks say," Dárja said, bowing her head and keeping her eyes on the man in front of her.

"Thieving rogues steal horses from an outpost not my own and I must fix it. And now I have a drunken supply captain in my command!" The man's voice rose with each grievance. "Fighting the Jápmea was the least of our problems." The man spoke that word as if it fouled his mouth.

"I'd take skinning their hides in battle over being the teat-maid to good-for-nothing soldiers." The man broke off. "What are you looking at, boy? Tell the cooks to throw the supply captain in the water trough and sober him up. I've got other more pressing matters to attend to."

Without thinking, Dárja crossed the gap between them. She vaulted over the table and tackled the man to the floor. Sitting on his chest, she leaned forward and looked him in the eye.

"I am not the least of your problems," she hissed. A dawning realization replaced the man's shock just before Dárja slid her knife between his ribs. She watched blood burble up through his lips, then spat in the man's face.

When anger's haze released Dárja, she pushed herself up off the corpse. On her feet and conscious of how far she'd strayed from Válde's instructions, she scanned the desk for what he might need. The Olmmoš words blurred in front of her. *No time.* She grabbed what she could and stuffed the scrolls and parchment into her uniform, praying the belt at her waist would hold it all in place. If she managed to survive and make it back to the Piijkij, they could sort it all out.

Dárja ran to the door. She pressed her ear to listen before cracking it open. Relieved no one waited outside, she slipped out, shutting the door behind her. The stockade sentry would be her next test and he'd set the precedent for what would follow. His back appeared before her sooner than she'd anticipated. In the tight space, she'd rely upon her knife. Afterward, if she made it down to the ground below, her sword could cut a wide swath through any opposing Olmmoš soldiers.

Advancing on the man, Dárja gave Válde's warnings rushed consideration. In a single-minded fury, she'd killed the commander. Her actions had jeopardized the future plans Válde envisioned. But the instant the Song had abandoned her, Válde's plan had failed. Killing the commander made no more difference than if she'd let the coward live. She'd have to feign or fight her way out with nothing to lose now. Dárja took a step forward. The sentry suddenly jerked, then tumbled down the stairs in front of him. A hue and cry of warning came from below, followed by the whistling of an arrow. Its flaming arc lit up the dusky sky.

～

"A rider from the garrison approaches, sir," said the soldier, poking his head through the leather tent flaps of Niilán's lavvu.

Niilán jumped to his feet, grabbing his cloak. He threw back the tent's opening, his cloak barely about him before the rider came to a stop.

The garrison soldier dismounted, his horse snorting from a hard ride. "The commander has received word from the Oso garrison that the Piijkij have raided their horses. Oso is without enough mounts to pursue them. Our commander requests your assistance."

"Tell him we are ready to ride," Niilán replied, his blood coursing through his veins.

The messenger pulled himself back up in the saddle, turned the horse without further fanfare, and galloped back the way he'd come.

"You there," Niilán called to the closest man. "Get me Hárri and get yourself ready to ride."

Niilán returned to his tent to gather what he would need. He would only take a contingent of his men and leave the rest behind. He could not afford the delay that breaking camp would entail. Oso was several leagues' ride from their current location. And while he was excited to be moving, he also acknowledged the possibility any signs of the Piijkij would be gone by the time he and his men arrived. *Still, I have to go. This is the first action they have taken since the skirmish.*

"Sir," a voice called out from behind.

Niilán turned to see Hárri at the tent's entrance. "Gather ten of the men and have them pack quickly—we ride for Oso," he said. "The Piijkij have attacked, stealing the outpost's horses."

"Oso is many leagues away, sir. Do we ride for speed or do we bring the supply train as well?" Hárri asked.

"We ride for speed. Bring one supply horse for our needs," Niilán replied. "The others can hold camp for our return."

Hárri's departure left Niilán alone again with his thoughts. He doubted he would find much in the way of useful tracks in Oso, even though the incident at the garrison told him the Piijkij continued to roam the north. It bore out what he'd suspected. *They are not finished with their campaign.* This meant there was a chance he might catch them and bring this whole farce to an end.

Niilán rolled up the parchment maps of the region between Mehjala, Oso, and Skaina. Unfortunately, the maps did not include features like caves, overhung ditches, and abandoned farms, places where men might hide which were not on the map. And the region was large enough that, with his small party of soldiers, it would be impossible for him to check out each nook and crevasse between here and Oso. Fortune, as never before, would rule the day. And Niilán suspected the little he had been afforded was about to run out. He cinched down the ties to his bedroll, then slung his satchel onto his back. Uneasiness hung upon him like an unwanted stench. From outside, a voice beckoned. "Sir! Another rider approaches."

Niilán pushed through the tent flaps with force enough to sway the entire structure. Standing there, he could not shake the feeling this second rider presaged an ill omen.

Horse and rider skidded to an abrupt stop, with a spattering of cold mud. Without dismounting or offering the respect due to Niilán, he cried, "The garrison is under attack!"

Niilán stood his ground. "We know of Oso," he said, irritated another rider had been sent to waste his time.

"No, Mehjala! Flaming arrows have been launched into the lower stockade. There are fires. And the commander has been killed." One calamity rolled on top of the next in a disastrous stream.

Niilán's outlook instantly transformed. "How many attack?"

"We don't know, sir," the soldier said.

"How do you not know?" Niilán berated. "If there are many, say many. If there are a few, say that."

"We can't see them," the rider confessed. "They're in the trees."

"Hárri, have the men mount immediately," Niilán shouted. "Weapons only. We ride to Mehjala."

CHAPTER TWENTY-NINE

VÁLDE LOOSED ONE LAST arrow, then mounted his horse. He waited to see if Dárja would appear among the pines. *Come on. Come on*, he urged. His horse pawed the ground, sensing the danger, wanting to be off. He could no longer delay. To stay was to risk capture. *I should have never made her do this.* He nudged the horse with his knees. The animal needed no more encouragement. It bolted across the open ground. Válde fought the instinct to look behind to see if Dárja had indeed made it out. Entering the thick woods, he slowed his breakneck pace. He had no desire to get a bash to the head and end up on the ground with a soldier's sword to his throat.

Moving deeper into the forest, Válde led the animal on a winding path he hoped would confuse any who tried to follow. What he could not elude were the fears, trailing in his wake. Had she escaped? Had she died within? Was she injured in the woods, waiting for him? He had told her she was on her own. *But the look in her eyes before she had disappeared into the woods.* Was it fear or hesitancy he had not wanted to see? He should have found another way. Válde snapped the reins, the pang of loss alarming. *Gods! I am like some lovesick wolf, whimpering after something I cannot have.*

She was Jápmemeahttun. He was a Piijkij. He could not wipe away the entirety of their history, even if it was not of their making. To allow sentiment to guide him was worse than pointless. It was dangerous. Even if Dárja survived this day to fulfill her part in his plan, there was nothing to bind them. If they prevailed against the Vijns, she could return to her kind, her honor restored through her valor. While he would languish, without purpose or place. Perhaps the others would be able to find a way to exist beyond this one final act. He would not.

The sound of men's voices brought him back from an untenable future. Pushing the horse to go faster, Válde looked in the direction of the garrison. He saw no sign of movement. Then, with a sickening dread, he realized the sounds came not from behind, but from ahead of him. He tugged on the reins, pulling the horse hard to the left. He gave the animal a swift jolt with his heels. Man and beast wound their way through the trees. Obscuring branches snapped him in the face. Saplings scraped his legs. He tucked within himself to avoid the worst. To the west he heard a shout, "Someone rides south."

"Surround him!" a voice commanded from the trees ahead.

Válde threaded his way east, breaking onto the open ground of a fallow field. He pushed his horse into a gallop over the even rows of tilled soil beneath a brittle layer of snow. Behind him, he heard the thundering sound of horses, pounding through the field he had just crossed. He cursed the men who chased him. *Scavengers with the scent of blood in their noses.* He would not fall to these men. If he could make the cover of trees beyond this open terrain, he could rise to the top of the ridge. From there he hoped he could double back to find the cave. He could hide there until the soldiers passed. If they managed to track him, then at least it was a defendable spot with a spare opening. If he had to, he would cut them down one by one until they were gone or he was dead.

Knowing the horse could not gallop at this speed forever, Válde leaned close. "You can do it," he encouraged. "Just a little farther."

"Do not lose him!" a voice shouted from behind.

～

Niilán had watched the rider crouch close to his horse as the animal tore across the open ground. Convinced he trailed one of the Piijkij, he vowed he would not let this man escape. *Not again*, he had sworn, the wind whipping about him, taunting him with its whistling.

That had been four days ago.

The man had just vanished. One instant he was in front of them and then he'd disappeared through the trees, never to reappear again. They had, of course, followed the tracks until they too dwindled away into nothing. Even after, Niilán had ordered his men to fan out from the last point of visible tracks. Methodically, he'd had them venture out in pairs, waiting for reports of signs or sighting. Each time, there had been nothing to report that was of interest to Niilán.

They had searched and camped and risen to search again these past four days and all for naught. They were like a sightless man, tapping his foot ahead to see if anything blocked his way forward. It infuriated Niilán, who muttered to himself the many injustices that had troubled him since beginning this ill-fated quest to rid the world of the Piijkij. He had just wanted to be a soldier—one among the multitude who served. He'd had no need for rank or glory to set his life to rights; he had just needed the occasional warm bed, a meal, and a fair commander.

Fair commander. He snorted. *Hardly*. His men were cold and beleaguered. He knew they had already given up hope of finding the man. They had even started to refer to him as the Jápmea. The man was no Jápmea, and Niilán had kept his men in pursuit long after it had proven wise. In the end, he had admitted his folly and given his men the break they deserved.

Niilán, as the commander, could not afford the same respite. At first light, he rode up toward the ridge with Hárri, who had elected to come. The way had been difficult. Thawing snow had made the rocky path slick with mud. More than once his horse lost its footing on the downhill. Climbing again toward the gray sky, an occasional patch of blue hinted at a returning sun. But not even the promise of lasting days and a sun to warm his bones could lighten Niilán's gloomy outlook. *Gods! These Piijkij have become a thrice-cursed tick burrowed under my skin.* If he could just get his hands on this one, he could perhaps use him to find the others.

A branch snapped in the distance. Niilán looked to see if Hárri followed. He called out to the man. In response, he heard the scream of a terrified horse that sent chills down his back. His own mount pawed the ground, matching Niilán's tension. He rode forward, scanning the trees to his right and left, dreading what awaited. If Hárri's horse had fallen, the man might well be injured.

Niilán made his way through a sparse larch forest into a dense stand of pines. His horse shook its head, sidestepping as the sound of struggle and pain continued. Coming around the blind of trees, he heard a man's grunt. Hunched before a prone and thrashing horse was the back of a bedraggled soldier. The horse, however, did not have a soldier's saddle.

Niilán drew his blade. "Rise," he ordered.

The crouched man paid him no heed. His hands braced the trap, clamped upon the horse's foreleg just above the hoof.

"Rise," Niilán shouted, "or die where you squat."

The man rose slowly, his back to Niilán all the while. He pivoted away from the wild thrashing of the injured animal, his emblazoned cloak cast back. Niilán's eyes flicked from the brandished sword to the man's soot-stained face. The triumph he felt at finally catching his quarry died the moment he recognized the man before him.

"If you mean to fight then let it be done, so I can tend to my mount," the cornered Piijkij said.

Niilán sat upon his horse, his arm raised, sickness churning in his gut. Here before him stood the very man who had led him into battle. The one who had held out his hand when Niilán had been injured and assured him he would receive care. He was also one of the men who had killed scouts and messengers and had burned temples. Niilán could not reconcile the two actions within the man—a man he had sworn to kill in the name of the Vijns.

Niilán lowered his sword. *Of all the sorrow-ridden souls.* In this moment, he could not have been more certain of the gods' disdain for his vow to serve them by living an honorable life.

"I served under you, sir," he said, answering the Piijkij's unspoken confusion. "I fought under your command in the Great Battle. I honor the name Válde and the courage you gave your men."

The sodden Hunter lowered the tip of his blade, his suspicious eyes on Niilán. "I know your face, but not your name."

"I am named Niilán."

"You serve the Vijns," the man said, neither wholly a statement nor a question.

Niilán nodded. "I am sworn to bring to justice the Piijkij who have acted against the gods and their voice in this world."

Válde disparaged. "Justice. What does he know about justice? We are like this beast. Brought to our knees, savaged. We honored our oath. We fought to protect the body and spirit of our people."

Niilán looked away to the man's horse. Its eyes were wide and wild.

"Are you supposed to be the merciful blade to put us out of our benighted existence?" the man asked.

Niilán heard mockery behind the demand. "I took an oath as well. And I fought. I did not ask for this blighted honor. I only wished to remain a soldier, with my head upon my shoulders and my eyes within my head."

"You may not have asked, but you have accepted what was tendered," the man said, as cold and judging as the gods themselves.

Niilán swung himself off his horse. He landed with a thud on the ground, with no clear idea of what course he had set for himself. He only knew he needed this one man to understand. "I did what I had to do to protect the men under my care," he said, widening his stance. "It is what I learned from you."

"I do not serve a traitor," Válde shouted back.

"You do not have to serve. Just stop," Niilán pleaded. "End these actions. Live out your lives as men among many."

Válde shook his head.

Swept up in the passion of his entreaty, Niilán stepped forward. "You served the Avr. You served us all. That service is over. The Vijns will not rest until you are all brought down." Racing ahead of his pounding heart, he said, "There is a place for you as men, who lead ordinary lives and do not burn temples and steal horses. You disgrace your rank with these acts. There is no place for the Piijkij anymore."

Válde lashed out with a warning strike. It just missed Niilán's thigh. "What do you know of our disgrace? You sit at the heart of the rats' nest, scurrying about, looking to glean a bit of rubbish for yourself."

Niilán cut through the insult with his sword. The Piijkij blocked. Blade ground upon blade. Standing close enough to clasp arms in friendship, Niilán saw determination, flashing in the man's eyes. While his own conviction could not match it, his animal desire to live was as fierce as any half-hearted belief. He pushed his former commander back with all his strength.

"If by rubbish you mean my life, then yes!" Niilán shouted.

Válde stumbled, then regained his footing. He sliced.

Niilán jumped back. "You have a choice to live. I do not!"

"There is no other life for us," Válde said, readying his weapon.

Niilán swallowed down his anger, his frustration. *Why will he not see reason?* The two circled. Niilán tightened his grip on his sword, promising himself the only way to redeem his life was to take the life of the man in front of him. The Piijkij had no place among the Believers.

Válde attacked with brutal speed. Niilán parried, keeping his eyes on the man's torso. He ducked as the Piijkij sliced high. Niilán shot his blade forward, nicking the man's shin. He darted back out of striking range. Válde lunged forward with the speed of an arrow. Niilán barely countered a thrust to his chest. The blades slid upon their edges. Niilán had no more breathed in Válde's warm, stale breath than pain exploded in his groin. He doubled over, unable to stand, his vision blurring as Válde lowered his knee. It was the last thing Niilán saw before darkness descended upon him with a crack to his head.

Part Three

ONE LIFE TO END

CHAPTER THIRTY

ÚLLA SAT WITHIN THE Song of All, adding her chorus, anxious for the change. The Song had brought her deep within its resonant melodies. At times, she felt as if she understood the sublime essence of life. There was also a part of her that she kept separate from the All. This had not been her intention when she began the dákti. But the longer she sat, the more aware she became of this divide within her.

At first, it was just a sensation at the base of her neck. Then, as time swam by in a lazy current, the subtle thrum crawled down her spine. It burrowed into her belly like the seed of new life. She felt worry growing just as she had felt Márgu inside her over the many months before her birth. Relying upon the strength of her song, Úlla denied the feeling. All the while, the agitation grew, threatening to pull her down into its depths. Then she seized upon the possibility that this was the moment of her full metamorphosis. *This is what I have been waiting for.* A true test of her readiness to leave behind the fears of a nieddaš and take on the demands of an almai. *I am changing in body and spirit.* With an expectant joy, she cast out her song with renewed vitality. Her soul's declaration echoed back in a myriad of layers and inflections. Her heart swelled. She felt the beat of every word, cast in bright colors, evoking the warm wistfulness of what was to come.

Úlla listened until the last whisper of her song subsided into the whole, thinking, *It is my time*. She remembered a far-off dream of this moment. She could almost taste the new refrain that would guide her into her future. It was there. Waiting. She just had to find it in the current of voices moving through her. She tried to quiet the watchful part of her mind. It raced ahead of her, pulling up tendrils of alarm, wrapping them around her like cobwebs. *It is my time*. She saw herself standing in the forge as Kálle had done. As she had done. She was no longer Úlla. That name was ash upon the fire. How could it be then that her song continued, unchanged? Her heart fluttered in her chest, like a bird caught in a cage.

There must be a new part for me. Fear clawed its way into her throat, choking her. *The words must come*.

Úlla's pulse throbbed in her neck. She raised her hand to stop her fear from going any farther.

They must come.

Her fear pushed down on her tongue, sticking to her silent plea. Úlla came to herself repeating, "They must come."

She rocked back and forth, faces swimming in and out of focus, frightened by the fitful and dark dream, holding sway over her. A gentle voice echoed her name. Úlla cocked her ear, observing the vision from afar. She watched a robed figure walk toward her. A hand reached out. She felt a cool touch upon her cheek. The Noaidi looked down on her. Tears flowed along the care-worn lines of his face.

"They will come," she said.

～

Úlla awoke on her cot. Her throat ached. Her eyes were sore and swollen. The cold certainty of her dream told her that her new song had not come. She was not almai. Her breath caught. A hiccup escaped. Úlla dug her fist into her mouth to keep herself from screaming. She shut her eyes against welling tears. I am rivgu. I am an outcast. She felt the weight of someone sitting down. The touch of a hand upon her hand stopped her rocking. Before a word was spoken, Úlla knew it was Tuá who sat beside her. She could smell the blood from her labor in the abattoir.

Úlla had always found Tuá's company a salve for her harsh frame of mind. On this occasion, her friend's light touch was more painful than any blow she had ever received. She shrank back. Tuá withdrew her hand but did not stand. She sat next to Úlla, not touching her, radiating an undeniable presence.

"Úlla."

Her name, said in a soft, understanding voice, flayed the skin from Úlla's bones.

She curled in upon herself, her knees tucked to her forehead, her arms wrapped around them.

"Úlla, please."

So soft. So excruciating.

"Leave me be," Úlla sobbed, pleading with Tuá, with the gods, and every hope she had harbored in her heart. "Please, leave me be." *And let me die.*

~

Kalek broke off his conversation with Ávrá when the door cracked open. His smile faded. Ávrá turned to see who had entered the apothecary. A part of her expected to see Dárja standing in the doorway; she tried not to let her disappointment show when she saw it was Tuá, not Dárja.

Wavering in the doorway, the nieddaš's stricken expression brought both Ávrá and Kalek to their feet.

"She will not talk to me. She will not even look at me," the nieddaš said.

Kalek looked to Ávrá for guidance, asking, "Who will not talk to you?"

"Úlla," Tuá said, anguish drawing out the name.

Kalek came forward and embraced her, saying, "Give her more time." When she said nothing in return, he released Tuá to see if his advice had any impact.

She shook her head, her dark eyes tremulous. "I do not know what to do."

"Just give her more time," Kalek repeated. "Friendships can be mended."

The surety with which he spoke told Ávrá that Kalek had missed the underlying tenor of this visit. She could not distract him now without hurting Tuá.

"Should I give Márgu back to her?" Tuá asked, wringing her hands.

Kalek looked to Ávrá once again, his confusion yielding to alarm.

Ávrá stepped forward to take the shaking nieddaš into her arms.

"It is too awful," Tuá's faint voice pierced Ávrá to the core. "I must do something."

Ávrá held Tuá apart from her, demanding the nieddaš's full regard. "No, Tuá. Do not do anything yourself. Let the Elders guide and counsel us."

Tuá shook her head in forlorn defiance.

"Trust me, Tuá," Ávrá said, her command coming to the fore. "Go and care for Márgu. She needs you. You are her bieba."

In place of words, relief shadowed Tuá's fragile smile.

"I will approach the Council of Passings," Ávrá added, knowing something more needed to be said for both their hearts.

Tuá left the apothecary, allowing Ávrá to confront a transfixed Kalek.

"What has happened?" he asked, his tone wary.

Ávrá tried to form the answer in her mind. It was too awful to think, let alone say.

"Tell me what has happened." The authority in Kalek's voice twisted Ávrá's heart, torn between honesty and what it might mean to Kalek.

"Úlla has failed the dákti," she said.

Kalek blinked, then sat down as if he lacked the strength to stand.

"I did not know Úlla had begun the ritual," he said, in a daze.

Wavering between her compassion for Kalek and her own distress, Ávrá said, "There are many things you choose not to know." This truth, spoken without recrimination, still hurt.

For a moment, he looked within himself, then nodded. "You are right."

Árvá sat down opposite him. She took his hand in hers, interlacing their fingers. Were any to come upon them now, they would think it a moment of private love and not deep mourning. A slow, inescapable need for change had taken hold of Ávrá. She loved Kalek. She knew this without a doubt. She also perceived a greater calling within her, undefined and undeniable. She started to give voice to its nature when Kalek spoke first.

"More than ever, I feel Okta's absence," he said. "I know I lack a mentor's wisdom. I do see that a strength of conviction is needed more than ever."

Kalek gripped her hand tighter. He shared her urgency. Heartened by this, Ávrá had to share her tenuous vision. "I assured Tuá the Elders would provide the needed answers. But I am concerned those answers will not serve us." Ávrá hesitated, taking in Kalek's furrowed brows and sad eyes. "The Elders uphold tradition while our future is no longer built on an honored past. Our future is a fragile as spring ice."

As Ávrá made her way through muddled thoughts and feelings, they became clear. They became a plan that was as simple as it was unthinkable. She could only hope Kalek had the strength to stand with her. A quiet moment passed with only the pop and sizzle of the dying fire. Ávrá inhaled the scent of unknown herbs and curatives. She did not need to know their names nor their concoctions. She simply held faith in their power, just as she had faith in what was right and true for her.

"Úlla remains a nieddaš," she said finally. "I stand by her. I will not let her be cast out from us . . . alone."

Kalek hung his head, holding on to her hand. Ávrá stroked the hard angles of his face. It was a face that, when smiling, appeared hopeful. In this dark moment, she saw only shadows and bones.

"Once," he said, his voice pensive, "during the time Irjan lived and Dárja was a babe in arms, I asked Okta what would have happened if Aillun had lived to return with Dárja." Kalek stopped. The slow bloom of sorrow spread across his prominent features. "Okta had said there were many things to be proud of as a Jápmemeahttun . . ." He trailed off. After a long pause, he added, "This was not one of them." He looked up. His pale eyes caught the last of the fire's glow. Pain shone bright, a brutal candle to illuminate them. "Given what had happened, with Irjan and Marnej, had she returned, she would have been cast out." Kalek's spirit seemed to collapse. "She would never be almai. She would never bring life back to us at her end. It is better that she did not return," he finished.

Ávrá was unsure if Kalek referred to Aillun or Dárja, and she could not ask without shattering their connection in this moment.

"They would not cast her out. Not now. They could not." Kalek reasoned with the unseen.

Ávrá, meanwhile, could not imagine a future without Úlla. She had a place within the Jápmemeahttun. As much as Ávrá. As much as any Elder. They might be life bringers in the end, but Úlla's strength and skills could help them survive now. *Úlla must remain among us*. Ávrá did not know if she had the power or authority to challenge the Elders. She did know she had to try. She hoped Kalek would support her. Even if he did not, she would go ahead and speak with the Noaidi. If she could not persuade him, then their kind would lose more than Úlla.

As if Kalek read her thoughts, he said, "If Dárja had returned to sit the dákti, she would have faced the same outcome as Úlla." He stood abruptly. "I cannot stand aside and do nothing while she is cast out into the world alone."

Ávrá stood as well. Her fears of facing the Noaidi alone eased with Kalek's presence. "We will not let it happen," she said.

"Every life is important," he said as if answering a greater debate. He turned to her, holding her face in his hands. Ávrá held his wild gaze, afraid to blink, afraid to witness his will crumble.

"Whatever it takes," he said, passion resonating. "Úlla must remain with us."

~

Einár sat with the other Elders. Their mood was as somber as his own. Furtive sidelong glances told him most were reluctant to begin the difficult discussion ahead. In the length of his life, Einár had witnessed the casting out of a handful of his kin. Of them, three had been for crimes against their own. The others had been for failing the dákti. Those nieddaš, who had given birth, then failed to transform into almai, were rivgu, neither nieddaš nor almai, and the ancient rites were explicit. Unable to become a life bringer at their end, the rivgu broke the cycle. They could not be allowed to remain within the group.

The fact that this was well defined did not make it any easier for Einár. All the rivgu were known to him. In his life, he had watched them grow, had listened to their songs, and waited for them to return from their Origin. And he had born witness as they were cast out from hearth and community to wander Outside until the gods claimed them. Einár acknowledged the cruelty and the injustice of surviving childbirth, only to be faced with a prolonged and certain death. On the other hand, these customs had helped them survive through all their struggles, even their war with the Olmmoš.

One of the Elders coughed. Einár looked up. All eyes were upon him. He cleared his throat. "Úlla has failed the dákti. Our traditions call for her to be cast out from us." A murmur of agreement rose among the Council. "We have kept our customs because they have sustained us," Einár continued. "We honor the gods who gave us the first oktoeadni."

The Elders began to chant the story of the first oktoeadni. Einár did not join in. He listened to his heart argue for mercy, for leniency. *What will we gain by making her leave us?* It was a question he had asked himself each time it was his duty to uphold the ritual of rivgu. In the past, he'd had the conviction of the gods' will. Today he lacked the self-assurance.

A hush fell upon the gathered Elders. They had finished the chant and awaited his decree. Einár could not free himself of the question.

Aloud he asked, "What will we gain by making her leave us?"

"She will not bring life to us at her end," said one of the Elders haltingly.

"It is what the gods wish," another Elder interrupted.

"Is it?" Einár asked of both the gods and the Elders.

"It is our way," another Elder answered.

"We are witnessing our end," Einár said. "We are already so few. To cast Úlla out would destroy what little hope we keep to ourselves."

"As Noaidi, you must honor the gods." The first Elder raised his voice. "You must follow their guidance."

"What do we risk in allowing her to remain?" Einár argued.

"We listened to you when Dárja and the Olmmoš wished to accompany the life bringers." The first Elder spoke again. "They failed. And Úlla has failed the dákti. The gods have judged us. It is our duty to think upon our mistakes, so they shall not be repeated."

A murmur of agreement spread among the gathered Elders. Einár sat quietly, feeling the sting of censure and trying to see a way forward. An insistent knocking caught their attention. Before Einár could react, the door to the chamber slid open and two figures emerged from the shadows. Einár was not surprised to see Kalek. But Ávrá's presence was unexpected.

"I can tell by your expression, Kalek, you mean to berate me," Einár addressed the healer, then held up his hand. "I will stop you before you do and remind you that you have interrupted the Council."

"There is no reason for Úlla to be forced to leave," Kalek said, his eyes boring into Einár. "She has already brought us new life in Márgu. She is skilled. A burden to no one."

"She has failed the dákti," one of the Elders pronounced, getting to his feet. "She will not bring life back to us at her end. She is rivgu. She is barren."

Ávrá stepped around Kalek to face the Elder who had spoken. "What Kalek says is true. Úlla is a skilled smith. The best among us. She is no burden. She has brought life to us. Tuá is a guide mother to Márgu. If we are to survive, Úlla must stay."

The standing Elder sputtered, "It is the gods' will."

"Is it the gods' will we do nothing until we are all gone?" Kalek demanded.

"This is a matter for the Elders to reflect upon," Einár said, endeavoring to restore peace.

"I believe it is a matter for all of us to consider," Ávrá said. Her resolve had the weight of a physical blow. Stunned, the Elders regarded the nieddaš before them. Undaunted, she went on, "You decide the value of lives based upon what we once were. We are no longer those Jápmemeahttun. We will never be again. We must find a different path to follow."

"It is not for a nieddaš to decide," an Elder said, his face pinched into a scowl.

"It is, in fact, for *every* nieddaš to decide," she calmly corrected him. "It is within *our power* to bring an absolute end to our kind."

"You threaten the Council?" Einár asked.

"Ávrá," Kalek warned.

The nieddaš ignored them both. The fine angles of her face caught the candlelight. Her determination was at once impressive and disturbing.

"I choose to remind the Elders of their lives as nieddaš," she said. "How they chose to give birth. You may say it is the gods' will. I say it is more so a nieddaš's decision."

Blustering among the Elders threatened to overtake the Council.

"Quiet!" Einár shouted.

In the void, Ávrá's clear voice resonated. "I choose to remain a nieddaš."

"Ávrá, no!" Kalek breathed out in shock.

"Others may follow," she said, undeterred.

"You would act against us?" Einár asked, unsure of what answer he preferred.

"I act *for* Úlla," Ávrá said without hesitation.

CHAPTER THIRTY-ONE

DÁRJA HAD BEEN CAREFUL to cover her tracks by criss-crossing north and south, all the while listening for the sounds of pursuit. She'd had a brief moment of panic, fearing she'd been discovered. In the end, it proved to be a hunter more interested in gathering the gains of his traps. She hadn't hidden in the cave as Válde had suggested. The ground showed recent signs of horses traveling in that direction. Two perhaps. Maybe more. She didn't want to chance coming upon soldiers as she made her way up the steep path to the cave. Instead, she'd built herself a shelter in a circle of trees with good forage for the horse.

This had been three days ago. Now she waited on the border of where the Piijkij hut sat, hemmed in by thinned birch and larch. Smoke curled up from the sagging roof. The smell reminded her of home. The word caught in her mind, wringing from her regret she'd thought discarded. There should be no place for grief to hide within her. Just as there would be no home for her to return to. *This place is fleeting shelter*. There would likely be others until she fulfilled Válde's plan and killed the Vijns. After that, who knew.

Dárja surveyed the area ahead, looking for signs of an ambush. But she couldn't see into the hut, just as she couldn't see into the future, and she couldn't be sure she'd succeed. Válde's plan was flawed. He'd made dangerous assumptions about her skill. The Song had been strong within her, then it just died out. It had failed her. Or she had failed the Song. These Hunters were relying on her to remain hidden from Olmmoš eyes, then strike out and disappear again. Her recent foray had proved their faith had been misplaced. As had her own. *Still, what does it matter?* She'd be alone in the Believers' Stronghold, as she'd been in Mehjala. If she didn't succeed against the Vijns, only she'd be lost. The Piijkij could continue on, nipping at the heels of the Olmmoš soldiers.

Looking at the placid smoke, rising from the hut, Dárja decided that if this was a trap, then so be it. She'd fought her way out of the garrison. She could take on whomever awaited her, friend or foe. Dárja nudged her mount with her knees. The cache of parchments and scrolls she'd stolen chafed against her chest—an irritating reminder of her promise to Válde. She hadn't planned to kill the commander. There'd just been no other option. *Let him be angry with me. It's my neck at risk.*

Dárja slid off her saddle. She landed with a bone-shaking grunt. She ground-tied the animal to forage, noting none of the other horses were outside the stable. Inside, four mounts sheltered. She ticked off those who'd acted in Oso, plus Válde. Herko had not ridden and she had left her mount behind. *There should be more. Unless something went wrong in Oso.*

Dárja trudged across the gap between the stable and the hut. Exhaustion dragged her down as if she carried boulders and not parchment. Outside the low door, she hesitated, expecting to hear Herko's grumbling. There were no sounds from within. At another time, she might've erred on the side of caution. Today she had little to lose. Knife in hand, she pushed against the door. Her tired muscles protested. She shut her mind off to her aches, stooping to enter the dim, smoky interior.

Expectant faces caught the firelight, then fell back into slumped bodies. A sinking feeling threatened to bring her to her knees. "Where's Válde?" she asked.

Herko glared at her from his corner. "He hasn't returned."

"He should be here," she said.

"Well, he's not here, is he?" Herko said with contempt. "And you are."

"He said he'd leave me to my own efforts," she protested.

Gáral sat forward, blocking her view of Feles and Edo. "Did you succeed?"

Dárja sheathed her knife, wary of those she'd called allies. She unbuckled her belt and sloughed off her outer layers. The cache of parchment and scrolls fell to her feet. She scooped them up and handed them to Gáral. "I didn't have the time to be selective."

Gáral said nothing as he gathered the material. Dárja refitted her belt and cloak, aware of the fact her standing with these Olmmoš was tenuous in Válde's absence.

"Is there anything in there worth the effort?" Herko asked, his manner dismissive.

"There are maps. Rosters of men. A supply request. And correspondence from the Vijns." Gáral listed off the content of the bounty, then paused as he read at length. When he'd finished, he turned to the others. "The Vijns commands the garrisons to the increase the máksu from the villagers."

"The High Priest was greedy before," Mures said, sharpening his knife.

Herko puffed. "His appetite has only grown."

"There is a limit to what the people will accept," Feles said.

Dárja let the men continue uninterrupted. Her thoughts strayed to Válde. *Where is he?* He'd stayed to give her assistance with the diversion she'd needed to make it out alive. What if he'd stayed too long? Had he been captured by soldiers? Dárja's mind spiraled down through all the bleak possibilities. *Surely he'd left himself time to escape.*

"Tell us what happened in the garrison," Gáral said, cutting off Dárja's dire speculation.

Wanting nothing more than to drop where she stood, she began to slowly recount the events. "I entered the garrison within the Song," she said as if embarking on a tale. "I made it to the defense tower stairs."

Herko was ready to interrupt. A cautioning hand from Feles stopped him.

"Near the top, I lost the Song," she said. "I was in your realm again, visible. The lower sentry saw me. I managed to slip by the stockade guard at the top when he was distracted." For an instant, she thought about censoring her tale, then saw it was pointless. These men would think and act of their own accord. "I entered the commander's quarters under the guise of a messenger from the kitchen. He proved quarrelsome. I killed him. When I made it back to the defense tower stairs, Válde had already sent flame arrows aloft. I stole a horse and broke out in the confusion."

Dárja left off the part of taking as many Olmmoš lives as she could. Without Válde there, she couldn't be sure these Piijkij would see her actions favorably. They'd been soldiers. It was too much to explain and she was too tired for a fight. She stared at Herko. He met her gaze. His broad face was pinched and oddly pensive.

From a dark corner, the pale head of Edo leaned forward. "What action do we take now?" he asked, his inquisitive eyes darting from Dárja to Gáral.

～

Marnej unloaded the ore from the back of the crude but sturdy cart. Lávrrahaš had negotiated the job for him, explaining that in Karkut nothing was straightforward. The Irkati enjoyed a lengthy bargaining period for everything from fruit to husbands. In Aage's absence, Marnej was grateful for his kinsman's help. The tinker, having come this far south, had decided it was time to go back to Halakzan to visit with his family.

"I might be away for some time," Aage had warned Marnej with the help of Lávrrahaš's translation. "I come from a big family." Then he'd laughed heartily.

Aage had assured him he would stop back on his way north to Morallom. In parting, he'd instructed Marnej to learn Bissmená, pointing to Lávrrahaš, saying, "When I return, we will not need this one between us."

Marnej missed the burly tinker. In a few more days, it would be the new moon and a full moon cycle since he'd left. In that time, Marnej had learned quite a few words in Bissmená with Lávrrahaš's assistance and could make simple sentences.

Although the Irkati laughed at the way he spoke, by and large, they were friendly and curious. At first, Marnej had expected to be treated with wariness and suspicion. But these people seemed willing to accept him as just one of many who traveled through their lands. On more than one occasion, he'd been greeted by grandmothers, wanting to touch his face. They'd cackled with laughter, saying "Be welcome, sea monster" in their language.

Marnej filled the waiting barrow with ore, then transferred it from the vojetu to the furnace. *Vojetu*, he repeated the Bissmená word for *alley* to himself. He didn't have a word for it in his tongue. To the people here in the south, he spoke Glaciuvortoz. And while there were as many tongues as there were states and realms in the south, only he and Lávrrahaš spoke with the "frozen words"—Glaciuvortoz—of the Northern Ones.

"Urgu!" a voice bellowed from within the forge.

Marnej picked up his pace, laboring under the weight of the ore. He performed the simple, burdensome tasks, as he had in his early days of working with Úlla. His mind turned away from the remorse of this recollection. There was nothing he could do to change what had happened. He wished the Immortals well, knowing they were better off without him.

"Urgu!" the gruff voice boomed again.

Marnej brought the ore close to the man who worked the smelting fire. He unloaded the rock onto the rising mound.

The man pointed back to the cart. "Again."

Marnej retraced his steps, moving with the ease of no load to carry. He loaded the cart again, estimating it would take him the better part of the day to shift the contents of the wagon. He was content to do the work and earn some coin. Lávrrahaš had given him a bed in exchange for his help in the tavern. For the first time in his life, Marnej wasn't defined by who his father was. He didn't need to prove himself worthy of the Piijkij title or struggle for his place among the Immortals. All he had to do was move rocks from one place to another until the task was complete. The simplicity of this existence was a revelation to him and he took to heart the fact tomorrow would bring the same freedom.

~

"So you like Georyus?" Lávrrahaš asked, handing Marnej another earthen ewer to wash. Marnej accepted the vessel, noting his calloused hands had become as wrinkled as dried berries in the sun.

"Georyus or virta virulu," Marnej agreed in Bissmená.

"Well done, my friend," Lávrrahaš cheered, placing a trio of cups before Marnej. "Georyus is a good man."

He plunged them into the water, then wiped them with the sodden chamois before handing them back to Lávrrahaš, who dried and placed them on the wooden shelf. Lávrrahaš sang something low under his breath. Although Marnej couldn't understand the words, he thought it might be part of the tavernkeeper's joik. Marnej felt a longing he'd come to associate with the Song of All. In the Olmmoš realm, he'd had no song of his own. Raised by the Piijkij, he had no individual destiny, no life song to be sung and shared by the hearth.

"Is that your joik?" he asked.

Lávrrahaš turned abruptly to face Marnej, his eyes wide with surprise. "Old habits, my friend," he said with a slow and wistful smile.

The tavernkeeper draped his chamois over his shoulder. He sank down onto a stool close to the fire. "It has been many seasons of snow since I have heard that word."

Marnej joined him, wiping his hands on his tunic. "Would you sing it for me?"

"Bah." Lávrrahaš waved him off.

From the man's expression, Marnej suspected it was his modesty which tempered his inclination to share.

"I have no voice for it," Lávrrahaš added.

"It's not the voice that matters," Marnej said, echoing the fisherman Jusse. "It's the story it tells."

"If it will please you . . ." the tavernkeeper hedged.

Marnej nodded, suddenly not trusting his voice.

Lávrrahaš cleared his throat and closed his eyes.

In the firelight, shadows accentuated the lines that creased the man's brow. It occurred to Marnej that Lávrrahaš was older than he had realized, perhaps closer to Irjan's age, had his father lived. The possibility both were men of the same age unexpectedly changed the way he perceived the tavernkeeper. Until this moment, he'd been a kinsman and a friend in a land of strangers and unfamiliar sites. Now, in his mind's eye, Lávrrahaš's weathered appearance spoke to the wealth of the man's experience in this life: his hardships and his triumphs, and the quiet and perhaps dull moments he'd experienced in between.

In the pause before Lávrrahaš began his joik, Marnej once again felt the loss of a father he'd never known.

When the tavernkeeper began to sing, his deep voice washed over Marnej like the sweeping winds they described. Marnej closed his eyes, feeling the thunder of reindeer hooves as his own pulse. In Lávrrahaš's crescendo he heard the cry of birds, nested in mountain tops. From there, the man's voice fell, sweetening and rounding into contentment with a life at the center of the trading crossroads.

Marnej opened his eyes, watching Lávrrahaš repeat his joik's last refrain. The map of the man's soul appeared to be etched upon his face. His lips curved up, framed by the lines of a strong laugh. His eyes wrinkled more from merriment than anger or disappointment. The man blinked once and then again, coming back into the present moment.

"Well. That is my frog's croak," he said, slapping his knees as he stood and stretched.

Marnej looked up at the tavernkeeper, whose pale hair hung like the halo of the moon around his shadowed face.

"Do you ever regret your decision?" he asked.

Lávrrahaš coughed out a laugh. "No."

He grew serious as he sat back down and regarded Marnej. "Coming here was the right choice. I made my peace with my family. They know I carry them in my heart and wish them blessings in this life. I ran from the war, it is true. I did not run from myself."

Marnej felt those last words lash his bones. His mind raced to find reasons to protest. He wasn't running from himself. There was simply no place for him any more in the north. A gentle nudge to the arm stopped his scrambling for excuses.

"I say this as a friend," Lávrrahaš said, tossing the chamois over onto the drying ewers. "Listen like a friend, ehh."

When Lávrrahaš walked away, Marnej was alone with his thoughts. He tried to dredge up outrage for being wrongly accused. He hadn't run away from himself. He'd run from the memory of Dárja leaving him alone to fight upon the battlefield. He'd told her to run when he'd wanted her to stay by his side, the way he had stood at her side when she approached the Elders. He'd argued with Kalek for her cause. Marnej once again saw her grab onto Válde's hands as if she'd never held his hand and called upon him to believe in her and believe in the voices she'd said were their kind, awaiting him.

CHAPTER THIRTY-TWO

DÁRJA SAT HUDDLED IN the corner, her head propped against the wall. She'd spent most of the night on sentry, ostensibly looking for signs of soldiers approaching. In reality, she watched for Válde. They were on the cusp of a new moon cycle, which meant Válde had been absent a full week, and Dárja's guilt had been building with the passing of each day. The grim expressions of the other Piijkij had added to her self-recrimination. *If I'd been able to stay within the Song of All, then there would've been no need for Válde to stay behind and provide the distraction.*

At the sound of scraping wood, she lifted her head. It was only Herko, shifting the stool upon which he sat. Disappointed, she once again rested her head and closed her eyes, replaying the infiltration of the garrison. The song had been powerful and her voice had woven in so easily. She couldn't imagine how she'd lost it. *Unless*, she thought, then stopped, afraid to voice her concern even silently.

Dárja revisited every step she'd taken until she saw Válde in her mind's eye. She'd wanted to tell him the truth and not risk another unspoken ending. He'd been determined and aloof, saying, "You should go. They are about to change the guard." Still, there'd been something in his eyes. Hadn't there? A flicker of concern she held onto, even though it caused her more pain. What was he to her? And more importantly, what was one more soul tallied against what she'd already lost? Irjan, Okta, Kalek, her friends. Marnej.

The kiss she and Marnej had shared had set alight a fire within her that had carried her across the vast expanse from the Pohjola to Úlla's Origin. She'd crafted a future for them in her mind. She'd imagined moments together, the tender opening of their hearts to one another, the exploration of the desire she'd felt. She'd fallen asleep sheltered from the tyranny of the cold by reliving that kiss. And she'd woken to start a new day's journey with Marnej's name upon her lips.

The memory of his sweet taste turned to ash in her mouth. They'd shared a destiny because of Irjan's actions. They'd been linked by her jealousy and his hatred. Then enmity had finally given way to love. *Yes, love*, she affirmed to herself, with a yearning to be sure. The declaration also came with the shadow of his betrayal and her greater transgression. She'd let herself be carried from the fight—from his side.

Sitting in the midst of the men he'd served with, Dárja understood what Marnej's life had been like before she'd taken his hand and pulled him into her world. He may have shared her Jápmemeahttun blood, but he was also one of these men, and she'd disregarded the struggle he must have faced when he came to the Pohjola. She'd belabored the fact his people had wronged him without giving any consideration to what he would face among her kind. He must have had his fears, his doubts. *And yet, he came*. He came and he stayed. When most would have wished him gone, he'd stayed. Even when she'd pushed him, just as she had with Irjan and Kalek and Okta. Perhaps if she'd stopped to think about what he wanted or bothered to ask what he needed, then they would not have ended as they did.

Dárja squeezed her eyes tight, trying not to see his face as they fought side by side in the onslaught of soldiers. She'd been so angry and hurt, she'd not been able to see, for even a moment, that Marnej had been willing to sacrifice himself for her, just as his father had been willing to sacrifice himself for Marnej. Dárja felt the lump in her throat welling. She pressed the palms of her hands into her eyes, determined to stay resolute in the company of these Olmmoš.

A *thump* on the door caused her to jump where she sat. Dárja roughly brushed her eyes. Through the blur she saw all the Piijkij stand with knives drawn. The door opened, letting in the dawning day, then a shadow blocked the sliver of sunlight. Dárja reached for her knife. The door swung wide, followed by an almost unrecognizable Válde, falling into their midst.

Dárja sat stunned as the hut erupted into a frenzy of bodies and voices.

"Was he followed?"

"Close the cursed door before we lose all the heat."

"I can't until we pull his feet in."

"Feles, Edo, Mures, set up a sentry," Gáral commanded, lost in the uproar.

"Careful."

"Well, move that big fish you call your foot."

"He smells like he's rolled in dung."

"Turn him onto his back and lay him out."

"There's no room."

Dárja jumped to her feet, shouting, "Then get out and leave me Edo to help."

~

Válde slowly blinked open his eyes. It was dark and warm. He smelled the sootiness of a fire. He gingerly rolled his head to one side and saw he was in the trapper's hut. He had made it somehow. Marveling at his luck, he sat up, then instantly fell back lightheaded. A fresh wave of searing pain blinded him. When he recovered, he slid his furs to the side. He was naked, save for the poultice strapped to his ribs and one wrapped around his thigh.

Válde explored the wounds and sucked air in sharply. The tenderness spread far beyond the bandages.

"They didn't think you would make it back from the dreams of the dark sky," a weary voice whispered.

Válde looked up from his wounds to see Dárja's pale face lit red by the embers of the low burning fire.

"You lost much blood," she added, scooting across the floor to sit adjacent. "Lie back down," she softly commanded.

Válde did as she said, his gaze wandering over her face as if seeing it for the first time. As she covered him again with the furs, he noted there were dark circles under her eyes and her face sagged despite its youth.

"What happened?" he croaked.

"Shh," she cautioned. "Let the others sleep. They are worn down with their worry for you. Even Herko." A corner of her mouth pulled back in a weak attempt to smile.

Válde slid his arm out from under the furs and touched Dárja's hand. He felt a tremor run through her. He pulled back, then felt the warm weight of her other hand covering his. He searched her face. Sharp angles had been carved even deeper into her features. She did not look away.

"Dárja." He spoke her name, his voice strange and tentative to his own ears.

"Close your eyes. Go back to sleep," she said, replacing his hand on his chest. "I'll stay with you until you do."

The warm exhale of Dárja's breath brushed Válde's cheek. He closed his eyes, feeling oddly at peace for the first time in many seasons of snow.

～

Válde woke to the low mutter of voices, gradually separating into recognizable words.

"How long do we let him sleep?"

"He will wake when he smells this rot you claim to be your cooking."

Válde coughed. Fresh pain washed over him. "I know I am alive when I hear Herko complaining," he said. "The gods would not be so cruel to me in the next world."

A round of laughter greeted his comment. Válde struggled to rise. Feles's helpful hand guided him to a seated position upon the floor. He looked around the tight room at the faces of men he'd known since his first days as a boy among the Piijkij.

Seated in a corner, Dárja had her head down upon her knees. Silently, Válde willed her to look up, needing to know if what had passed between them in the night had been real or a dream. When she did finally raise her head, her exhaustion was evident in her wavering gaze.

Válde shivered. "Where are my clothes?"

There was an awkward pause as the men looked at Dárja, seemingly waiting for her to speak. When she did not, Edo answered, "We had to cut them off." He hesitated before adding, "They were soaked in your blood."

"And your shit," Herko added, with distaste. "I'll give our healer-witch credit. She's got a strong stomach. She didn't once gag upon your foulness."

Feeling himself flush, Válde looked at Dárja. She had lowered her head to her knees again. "Is there nothing for me to put on my body?" he demanded, aware of his unreasonable embarrassment. "Or am I to survive my wounds only to die of cold?"

"Hardly cold," Herko said, as Mures rooted through a pile where he sat. He handed across a rough, woven tunic.

Válde snatched it with a curt nod of thanks. He slipped it over his head but when a hot flash of pain skewered his side, he failed to wrestle his arms into the sleeves.

"Gods curse the lot of you," he groaned.

Dárja pushed herself onto her feet. "Edo, give him a strap to bite on, then slide his arms in. I'll keep the wound from opening."

Edo held out the leather strap. Válde waved it off with a shake of his head. Dárja knelt beside him, her interest on his bandaged side. The others stirred uncomfortably. Válde clenched his teeth as Edo lifted first one arm into his sleeve and then the other.

Breathless from the pain, he said, "Help me to my feet." He held out his hand to Dárja. She stood and stepped back. "I should go and collect more uulo to freshen the poultices," she said, then slipped out the hut door before Válde could object.

Herko started to laugh. "I think we may have found the secret to fending off the Jápmea."

A couple of the men smirked. Edo looked uneasy. "Help me to my feet, Edo," Válde said.

The two wobbled to standing. Mures handed Válde a pair of worn leather breeches which took three men to pull into place. The door opened. Válde cinched the leather ties around his waist clumsily, expecting to see Dárja. Gáral's head peeked in under the low doorframe.

"The healer said you were alive and grousing in pain."

Válde shook off Edo's assistance. "What news of Oso?"

Gáral snorted, dropping onto bedraggled furs. "You ask us of news, when it is your tale we are anxious to hear. We'd given you up for dead, when you fell through the door, more a corpse than a man."

Válde stiffened. "I was pursued by soldiers when I left the garrison."

"At least the healer-witch returned," Herko said. "You've trained her well."

"I did not train her," Válde said, wanting more than ever to speak with Dárja.

"What happened at the garrison?" Gáral asked, echoing Válde's thoughts.

"I was careless," Válde said, reluctant to cast doubt on Dárja and her part in what he had envisioned. "A scouting party came upon me. They trailed me until I was able to shake free of them."

"For a week they trailed you?" Mures asked in disbelief.

Válde shook his head. "No, they tracked me for four days. Then I managed to elude them. I wound my way back to the cave, where I'd planned to hide out or hold them off if they discovered me.

"Did they attack the cave?" Feles asked.

Válde shook his head again.

"Then how is it you came to us as if you had waged a battle on your own?" Gáral asked, his question echoed by a rumble of interest from the others.

Válde held up one hand as a wave of dizziness clouded his eyes. When he was able to continue he said, "I led my horse over a trapper's claw. While I tried to free the animal, I encountered a soldier of the Vijns's personal regiment."

"In all the forest that surround," Herko grunted.

Válde disregarded the comment. "The soldier knew me. Although I could not distinguish him as one of the men I led into the Great Battle."

Gáral waved off the explanation. "This is too much to believe."

"Regardless of what you believe, the soldier knew me," Válde went on, undeterred by the disbelief he saw on Gáral's face. "He pleaded with me to choose the humble life over our current endeavors."

"So the man cut you with his words!" Herko jeered.

"His blade was sharper than his tongue," Válde said, recalling the man's reluctance. "He was a good man who was caught between hand and fist."

"You killed him?" Feles's question sounded more like a statement.

"We fought," Válde said. "We both drew blood, though I did not kill him."

A cry of outrage from Herko and Gáral drowned out Válde. He raised his voice and spoke over them. "I deposited him bound and gagged on the doorstep of some farmer in Hassa."

Gáral shook his head.

"I offered the soldier what he had offered me—a chance for a life," Válde said coolly.

"Gone soft I'd say," Herko said.

"He did what was right," Feles intoned with authority.

"Feles, you sound like our pious Edo," Herko teased.

"He had no choice," Válde said. "Just as we have no choice."

～

Dárja foraged among the thinning spruce. Usually, the quiet solitude of the forest acted as a balm for her nerves, made raw by the Piijkij scrutiny—her every act watched with suspicious eyes. Today she could find no reprieve in the cool green. Far to the north, the binna would be calving. She thought of the gangly legs of the newborn reindeer. So unsteady in the first moments, they'd become sure and swift. To forestall the desire to be elsewhere, Dárja reminded herself she was in the south, looking for uulo to make new poultices for Válde's injuries. As quick as a plummeting hawk, her thoughts shifted from remorse to outrage.

I didn't ask him to help me. She pushed past a stand of birch saplings. Her eyes scanned for the leaves she needed. *And I certainly didn't ask him to stay beyond what was safe.*

Then, just as abruptly, reason pierced her through and through. Válde acted not to save her. He acted to save his plan. Had he not said that without her the Piijkij's plan was at an end? *No. He'd said they were all at an end.* To stave off her growing misgivings, Dárja brushed her hands over the mounded shrubs on either side of her, looking for what might be hidden. Frustrated at not finding anything of use, she straightened and leaned momentarily against a birch tree nestled among its nascent offshoots. The wind held the scent of coming rain. She glanced up at the sky. The darkening horizon foretold the looming storm. She did not want to get caught in a downpour but she also needed to find the uulo. *If I were in the Song of All, it would reveal itself to me,* she thought. Not for the first time, she cursed the limitations of the Olmmoš realm.

Dárja pushed herself off the tree's curling bark. A petulance had taken hold of her. If she had to walk into the storm, then so be it. She would find the plant. Then the first crack of thunder boomed in the heavens and her resolve slackened. *I have no choice. I need the Song,* she told herself, taking shelter under a broad pine branch. She closed her eyes, bringing her song to the forefront of her mind. Each word seemed to echo in her as if she had become a vast canyon. She gave herself over to the building beauty of her song. Then the song of rain and wind and lightning interposed, bringing her back to her purpose. Uulo. She beckoned the All, asking for what she needed, presenting her gratitude and wish to heal.

The subtle voice was almost imperceptible in the larger chorus of the storm. White petals shook above green leaves, awaiting bird and bee. Dárja opened her eyes and began to follow the song as if in the wake of a beguiling scent. When she finally saw the white flowers she was so relieved she hurried through the honoring of the plant, making quick promises. Suddenly aware of a familiar chorus on the fringes of her refrain, she abruptly cut what she needed and let her song recede from her thoughts.

Breathless, her heart racing, Dárja came to herself, on her knees, hunched over the shrub. Her knife-hand shook. Her other hand clutched the leafy stems of the plant. Had it been Kalek? Had he heard her? *Oh gods, what have I done?*

"I saw how Válde looked at you," a voice said from behind her.

Startled, Dárja sprang up. Gáral stepped into view, leaving behind the cover of spruce trees. Dárja tensed, repositioning the knife in her hand for a fight.

Gáral remained aloof. "You may believe his fawning over you like some rutting moose means he is a changed man. But I can assure you, he is a Piijkij to his very core."

The force of the man's words was like a strike, made more stinging by his Olmmoš accent.

"As I am Jápmemeahttun," Dárja said, shaking with poorly disguised mortification.

"I have never forgotten that," Gáral said, then disappeared back into the trees from which he had emerged.

Dárja released her grip upon her knife. It dropped soundlessly to the forest floor as she doubled over. Her breath escaped her in short bursts, and her throat ached with a scream she held back. She picked up the knife and began to run as if she could elude the truth. The first heavy raindrop fell upon her head, dissolving her illusions. There would always be a clear divide between herself and the Piijkij.

Dárja ran on, her mind making plans. Her heart ached from effort and she recoiled from the disdain she'd seen in Gáral's expression as he'd described Válde as a rutting moose. A sickness rose from her stomach. *Is that what his touch had meant?* She shook her head to clear away the image, the feeling. She heard a burst of voices ahead. She veered away from them. She would wait until they slept and then take a horse. Fresh plans abruptly fell away as she came upon Válde, crossing the clearing to the south of the hut.

"Do not make me run after you and undo all of your healer's effort," he called, raising his voice.

Dárja froze as if she were a deer caught between wolf and hunter. He walked toward her painstakingly, his upper body cautiously stiff. She stood rooted, unable to move or take her eyes off of him. When he came close to her, she saw the sweat of his effort stained his tunic an earthy brown.

"They did not want to let me out of their sight," he said. "I assured them I would not piss in a pot in a corner while I could stand and walk."

"They were right to try and keep you in," Dárja said, aware of the hollowness within her.

"I choose one healer to the five nursemaids in there."

In the cool rain, Dárja's skin prickled with heat. "They had reason to worry."

"Dárja." Válde reached out a hand to her.

She dropped back. "Why did you stay?"

He took a step toward her. "You know why."

She shook her head, pivoting away. His hand caught her arm. He grimaced. "Dárja, what happened?"

"I did what you asked," she said, held there by his grip and her own need. "I took all the papers and maps upon the commander's desk, figuring your lot would decide what was of use and what was not."

Válde frowned and tightened his hold. "You know that's not what I mean."

"Haven't they told you?" She nodded her head in the direction of the hut. "I'm sure Gáral took pleasure in it."

Válde's mouth hardened into a bloodless line of disapproval.

She removed his hand from her arm. "And before you reprimand me for my actions, I want you to know I'd do it again. Without hesitation."

"Knowing what it might cost us?"

"Yes. It was worth it."

He swore under his breath.

She tensed. "If you have something to say to me, then say it out loud."

"It was irresponsible," he hissed.

"It was necessary."

"It was a selfish act."

"I am owed."

Válde grabbed her arm again, pulling her toward him. "I risked my life for you."

Dárja yanked her arm away and glared at him. "I didn't ask you to."

Válde rose to his full height. "Stop being childish."

"I'm not a child." Her voice shook.

He taunted, "No, you are an Immortal. Older than the trees and hills. But no wiser. You knew I would protect you."

It was her turn to scoff. "I know what you said to me before I left."

"That was then." He stopped abruptly.

"It doesn't matter now," she said, tired of the pretense.

"Of course it matters."

Dárja shook her head. "There's nothing we can say to each other to change the fact we are here together only until I manage to kill the Vijns. There'll come a time when you won't be able to save me or protect me. And it may come to it that you'll need to sacrifice me for what you want to achieve."

CHAPTER THIRTY-THREE

MY VIJNS, WE WILL give aid in any manner you see fit, but . . ." Siggur hedged.

Bávvál fixed his gaze on the upstart priest from Hemmela. "Counselor, your magnanimity would present a better face were it not marred by exceptions."

A snicker rippled through those gathered. For a brief moment, the High Priest considered letting the breach of decorum stand, then thought better of it. *They all need a lesson in respect.*

"Is there something amusing in what I have said?" Bávvál asked, his bearing icy.

A hastily voiced "no, my Vijns" followed a round of self-conscious coughing.

Bávvál kept his expression placid as he looked at the cowed men in front of him. "I thought not."

"Even so," a clear, chirpy voice rang out in the capacious hall.

Bávvál turned his eye to his counselor. Although Siggur had aged from his days as Rikkar's acolyte, he had not lost the hungry look in his eye, nor the honey-laced tinge to his challenge. He had thought the man malleable, given enough trappings of power. Now the High Priest saw he would have been better off to dispose of the presumptuous man in a bog.

"You have a vast army at your disposal. And a handful of Piijkij run rampant over the northern villages, pillaging and plundering," Siggur tutted. "Horses stolen from Oso. The commander of Mehjala killed." The man's pious expression deepened into pity. "How can it be that so few can create such havoc?" Siggur halted, his sly eyes downcast and his head slowly shaking in feigned sympathy. "Can you shed light upon this threat to our faithful, Áigin?"

Bávvál regarded his agent. He looked from his man to the usurper and back. His spy bowed to him, but before the gesture of allegiance, he caught the spark of interest in the man's eyes. To the room, Áigin stated, "My Vijns, you will find my answer distasteful."

"Be not concerned with my needs," Bávvál said with forbearance. "My concern is for the souls in my care."

Áigin acknowledge the statement with a bob of his head. His eyes were trained upon Bávvál. "My Vijns, they are better trained than any in our army."

"Better than you?" Siggur interposed. A murmur rose among the gathered counselors.

"My Vijns, I am not a soldier," Áigin answered, ignoring the man who had spoken.

"No, indeed," the High Priest allowed formally. "Let us hear your assessment."

"My Vijns, in heart and willingness to serve, there are none greater than our soldiers." The reedy agent paused. "But they have not trained since birth to hunt and kill Immortals.

"Bah," Siggur scoffed. "Immortals. They are nothing now."

"Perhaps," Áigin allowed, then turned to face the counselor. "They once had us at their mercy. It was the Brethren to whom we turned for our freedom."

"We do not need a lesson in history," Siggur said, piqued.

Bávvál stood, taking command of the room. "We do need an answer as to how these men will finally be stopped."

Áigin inclined his head again.

The High Priest turned to his counselors. "My agent tells us these rogues persist because of their skill. I believe they are receiving assistance from others."

"Others?" Siggur asked, sounding dubious.

Bávvál strode forward to stand before the irksome man. "Yes, others," he said with a touch of menace. "Where do they sleep? Where do they eat? Where do they hide?" He stepped back to scrutinize his other counselors. "They must be sheltered somewhere." Those gathered shied as if the High Priest's words were a personal accusation. Pleased with the impact, Bávvál continued, "Or do you believe that, like the Jápmea, they can just disappear?" He retook his seat. "They are harbored in some villager's hut or farmer's stable and their secret is being kept. But there must be whispers."

"My Vijns, we have heard no such whispers," the counselor Siggur answered primly.

"Then you are not listening well enough," Bávvál said, finally losing his temper. "Or you are not asking the right questions in the right manner." He narrowed his gaze on his agent. "I want every villager, every farmer, every travelers' hutkeeper to know the gods will show no mercy to those who protect the Brethren."

A stifled protest died upon the lips of all when Bávvál turned his imperious gaze to his counselors.

"I want these men brought before me before the next full moon, or I will have the heads of those who harbor them."

Bávvál straightened and smoothed the sleeves of his finely woven vestment. "Would any care to extend further counsel?"

The low rumble of "no, my Vijns" filled the quiet as the gathered men stirred uneasily.

~

Niilán pushed the plough through the boggy soil. Each step he took sucked and squelched. But even mud-soaked and tired, his physical discomfort was minor compared to the burden of doubt plaguing his thoughts. Niilán had cornered his former commander. The man had managed to best him. Válde owed him nothing. Yet he had spared Niilán's life and brought him to a place where he might receive care. *Was it pity? Or loyalty?* Whatever the reasons, Niilán considered himself fortunate.

Hale enough to plough fields, he should have long ago returned to his command. Nonetheless, he tarried on this miserable expanse of land. At first, he stayed because he was too weak to travel. He had been half-dead when the farmer found him. Later, he stayed because no horse could be spared for his return. Then, he stayed because he owed a debt to the farmer and his wife, who had many mouths to feed. Finally, there was the ignoble truth that Niilán welcomed the reprieve from what he had become—a commander with no hope for success.

Try as he might to convince himself he could disappear back into this obscurity, Niilán could not help revisiting his life before he been taken into the Believers' Army. He had been a poor excuse for a farmer then and his time as a soldier had not improved his skill or outlook on tilling. He was surer now than he had ever been that his wife and children were better off without him. Pushing a plough through earth not made for planting was no easy work. *Still, you farm what you have and hope it is enough.* He churned through the resistant lumps of soil, thinking it better for sealing chinks in a log hut than nurturing barley and turnips. His foot stuck in the thick mire. He swore, tugging his boot free.

A child's shrill cry for her mother caught Niilán's attention. He stopped his efforts to listen. Likely it was a fight between the children which would be set right by the farmer's wife, just as his own wife had done. When the screams did not stop, Niilán shadowed his eyes from the sun to see what was amiss. The middle girl, the one of nine or ten seasons of snow, the one named Álet, dashed out of the forest toward the hut. The farmer's wife appeared in the doorway, then rushed off in the direction the girl had pointed. A sense of foreboding took hold of Niilán. He dropped the plough and trudged across the length of the field, fighting against the muck. Gaining solid ground, he ran to the young girl seated on the ground, crying.

Niilán knelt before her. "Hey, now, little one. What brings these tears?"

She looked up. Red eyes swam in her muddy face. "The soldiers have taken Papa."

A cold shiver of familiarity ran down Niilán's spine. "Taken him?"

"They are making him tell the truth," she whimpered.

"The truth about what?" Niilán asked carefully.

"About you," the girl sobbed. Through her sniffles she asked, "Are you really a Piijkij?" Without waiting for an answer she went on, "Mama said you were a soldier. I saw your uniform. I touched it, even though Mama said to leave it alone. The other farmers say you are a Piijkij."

Niilán looked eye to eye with the girl. "I am not a Piijkij. I am a soldier as your mother said. Where did they take your father?"

"To the temple. Where the priest speaks." The girl wiped her eyes with the back of her hands.

"Do you know where my uniform is?" Niilán asked.

The girl nodded her sandy head.

"Show me."

Niilán followed the girl into the hut. He watched her crawl under the platform that served as the family's bed. Her little bottom wiggled as she backed out, pulling a tattered uniform behind her.

Her tears gone, Álet looked contrite. "I saw Mama hide it when she caught me touching it. I didn't do any harm. It was like this when I touched it."

Niilán smoothed the child's hair from her eyes, nodding. "I know you did no harm to my uniform. But I must put it on now. I need you to wait for me and show me where they have taken your papa." He held the girl's gaze. "Can you do this?"

Álet bobbed her head.

"Can you get me some water so I might clean my face?"

The girl trotted off to do what she was asked.

Niilán unfolded the uniform. The tunic, stained with blood where Válde had cut him and dirty from where he had lain upon the ground, would suffice for what must be done. He could not let the farmer suffer for his generosity. Niilán disrobed, shivering in the cold like a newly shorn sheep. His leather breeches were stiff and chilled. Sliding the tunic over his head and fastening the buckles, he was grateful for its warmth.

Niilán looked about for his breastplate. Then dropped to his knees and peered under the platform. Reaching into the dark recess, his hand came down upon the pommel of a blade. Niilán pulled it out into the light. It was his blade. He had thought it lost in his encounter with Válde. Perplexed by the man's choices, Niilán was nevertheless grateful to have his sword. He pressed his cheek to the earthen floor again, searching for his breastplate. His fingers brushed against a rolled leather hem, just as small feet appeared in front of his face.

Niilán dug out the last of his uniform and rose to his knees. The girl held a ewer of water in both hands.

"Hold this while I wash," Niilán said, trading his leather armor for the ewer. He walked outside and splashed water on his face and hands, rubbing off the worst of the mud.

"Did you fight in the Great Battle?" Álet asked.

Niilán looked down to see her staring up at him with eyes red-rimmed from tears and worry. Her scrutiny reminded him of his own children.

Niilán tugged on his mud-encrusted boots, unnerved by the regret he felt. "Yes, I fought in the battle," he said, taking up the ewer and pouring the water over his head.

"Did you kill many Immortals?" Álet asked, standing in the doorframe.

Niilán shook himself dry, running his hands through the tangle of his hair. "Yes," he admitted with sad reluctance.

The girl hesitated, then proffered his breastplate. "Were you scared?"

Niilán slipped the leather vest over his head and buckled it. He looked the girl in the eye. "Yes."

Álet raised her chin. "My papa wasn't," she said, her eyes challenging Niilán to contradict her.

"Your father is a brave man," he said. "And you are his brave daughter." He smiled at her. "Now show me where they've taken him."

~

Niilán remembered Hassa as a village that had no outpost. It was barely a village. *Still, there is a priest. There is always a priest.*

"There." The girl pointed to what looked more like a stable than a Believers' temple. And the more seasons of snow Niilán lived, the less difference he saw between men and animals.

He patted Álet's head. "Go home now."

"I want to go with you," she said. "I want to see Papa. I'm not afraid."

"I know you are not afraid," Niilán said. "I know you are very brave. That is why I need you to go home and care for your land while your father is away."

Álet looked unconvinced.

Niilán added, "I will send your mother home to you. Together you will safeguard the farm."

"What if Begá returns and insists he should be the one to protect the farm?" the girl argued.

"Tell your brother you have sworn an oath to the commander of the Vijns's personal regiment," he said.

"But I haven't," Álet insisted.

"Then repeat after me, I offer the oath . . ."

"I offer the oath . . ." she said, her expression serious.

"To the Vijns."

"To the Vijns." The girl's voice was strong and clear.

"To protect my family and lands."

"To protect my family and lands."

"And honor the gods."

"And honor the gods," she said solemnly.

"Now return home and keep your oath," Niilán said.

Álet turned on her heel and ran back the way they'd come, her braids bouncing as she went.

When he could no longer see the child, Niilán walked forward, hoping the worst had not befallen either the farmer or his wife. He had been foolish to think he would escape the Vijns's reach by hiding out on the farm. But he was clear on where his loyalty lay. He would return to whatever fate awaited him, and not because he had sworn fealty to the High Priest and the Believers. He would return because he had a duty to the men who served him and the people who had sheltered him.

His decision made, Niilán pushed open the door to the makeshift temple, his hand upon the hilt of his sword. A sallow-faced priest in his threadbare robes sat huddled in a corner. His eyes were transfixed on the soldiers, who held wide the farmer's arms. The man's head hung limp. His bare back was slick with sweat and blood. The farmer's wife knelt before her husband, her head pulled back, her braid wound tight around a soldier's fist.

"Please," she whimpered, looking directly at Niilán, who assessed his chances.

Four to my one. Odds he would take if further bloodshed could be avoided.

"Release the man and the woman," Niilán said, imperious anger swelling within him.

"By whose authority?" sneered the soldier who held his blade to the farmer's back.

"Niilán, commander of the Vijns's personal regiment."

"We don't serve you," said the other soldier, yanking back the woman's head.

"You serve the Vijns. My rank deserves the respect due."

One of the soldiers snickered.

Niilán drew his blade, advancing. "The Vijns will not begrudge me my honor when I tell him I was forced to put you under my blade."

He registered doubt in the face of the young soldier who restrained the farmer.

The other soldier kicked his comrade. "Hold him tight." To Niilán he said, "This man's harboring a Piijkij."

"You know this for a fact?" Niilán demanded.

"His neighbors say so," the soldier said.

"Then why do you not ride out to the farm and take the Piijkij prisoner?"

"This man deserves punishment," the soldier menaced.

Niilán stared him down. "Are you so weak that the idea of confronting one of the Brethren of Hunters makes your knees shake?" He let a smirk punctuate the insult.

"We'll take care of the Piijkij when we are done here."

"You are done here now," Niilán said evenly.

CHAPTER THIRTY-FOUR

ÁVRÁ LAY IN KALEK'S arms. She breathed in his scent—wood smoke, birch leaves, and sweet unknown herbs. She rolled onto her side to listen to his heartbeat. He pulled her in close to him.

"You are squeezing too tight," she murmured. "I am not leaving you."

Kalek eased the pressure of his embrace with a laugh that shook his chest. He nuzzled in close to her ear.

"You are all I need," he whispered.

Ávrá let his declaration go unanswered, sadness taking root in her heart. She had long known the depth of Kalek's need. She had wanted to banish that emptiness. But she was not Irjan or Okta or Dárja. She was one heart, one soul. She could not stretch herself to be more, and this fact filled her with apprehension. To know you are not enough for another does not make it any easier to let go of hope. She loved Kalek. Not in the way he needed but in the way she could.

Ávrá stirred to rest her chin upon his chest. The proud line of his profile pierced her heart. *He will do what is right*. Kalek turned his head to look at her. His pale eyes caught the candlelight. *Like deep pools of water*.

"You cannot put it off," Ávrá said, resolved to speak from her heart.

Kalek frowned. He closed his eyes, leaning his head back against the furs. "I am waiting for a suitable candidate," he said, with a sigh of annoyance.

"There are many suitable candidates," she said, letting Kalek's assumption momentarily distract her from her purpose. "You just do not want to replace Dárja."

Kalek tensed beneath her.

Ávrá sat up, looking down upon his reclining figure. "You are creating obstacles by believing there is a right individual." She softened her reproach. "Let it be like friendship. Let it be gradual and unacknowledged, until the feeling itself is undeniable." She smiled at him. "Let it grow and blossom. Then allow yourself to be surprised and grateful. Take on a herd of apprentices. Teach them. Let them learn from you. See who has a gift and then nurture the gift. It is time for you to stop being selfish."

Kalek opened his mouth to object. Ávrá placed her fingertips to his lips. "This was not my purpose in speaking with you," she said, sitting farther back from him.

He sat up straight. "Selfish? I am not being selfish."

Ávrá rolled off the pallet, picking up her shift. "Think before you speak," she warned.

Kalek continued to grumble under his breath, then stopped abruptly. A look of concern deepened the lines of his face. She slipped her shift over her head, then tied the smock at her waist.

"You cannot continue to ignore what happened in the Elders' Council."

Kalek turned away, pushing off the furs and linens that had so recently comforted them both.

"I have made my decision," she said.

"Selfish," he replied.

"You are right. I am selfish. I chose what was right for me, for my duty. I could not let Úlla be cast out from us."

Kalek jumped to his feet. "I would not have let that happen!"

"How would you have stopped it?" Ávrá asked, doubting he could answer.

"With reason."

"Reason is not enough," she said. "Action was required. Not by the Elders. Not by the almai. It is for the nieddaš to do. I choose not to give birth to stand with Úlla in solidarity, to let her know she will not be alone. I have been a biebmoeadni. I have loved a child. There may come a time when I will want to become almai. For now, I am content as I am."

Ávrá waited for Kalek to respond. When he did not, she added, "I hope you can love and honor me in equal measures."

❧

Úlla woke early. Her dreams had been dark and slippery, like eels in warm summer waters. She had been left with a profound sense of disquiet. Try as she might, she could not go back to sleep. Rather than thrash about in her restlessness and wake the others, she slid noiselessly from her bed. She dressed in a hurry, leaving behind the deep and sonorous sounds of those who slept.

With the door closed behind her, Úlla yawned and rubbed her face. She ran her hand through her short hair. Softening into subtle waves, she no longer felt like a shorn sheep. Nevertheless, it would be at least a season of snow before her hair would touch her shoulders, and many, many more after for it to reach her waist. *If we make it until then.* It was wiser not to plan that far into the future. Besides, her short locks were easy to comb and more suited to her work in the forge. Although she did miss the care with which the other nieddaš had stroked and braided her hair each evening before going to bed. The whispered secrets. The stories of the day. The easy laughter. Úlla had never realized how much comfort she had taken in those quiet moments among the other nieddaš until they were missing in her life.

It had been a full moon cycle since she had failed the dákti and started to walk an uncharted path. Unlike those rivgu who had come before and had been cast out to die, Úlla had been allowed to stay. For the first week, she had cried each day until exhaustion had claimed her. In the following fortnight, she had managed to gather enough courage to begin to work. Only then did she hear of Ávrá's action on her behalf. Stunned and humbled by Ávrá's sacrifice, Úlla avoided all common areas outside of the forge. She could not bear to see pity in the eyes of those around her or, even worse, scorn.

Even now, with the full moon above, Úlla's confidence balanced on shaky legs. Mercifully, the forge allowed her to find a connection with the part of herself that came before Marnej, before the birthing, before the dákti. Turning stone into metal gave her the strength to occasionally look upon her life in hopeful terms. Perhaps with effort and the right tools, her life might also be transformed into something else, something valued and respected.

Padding silently across the kitchen's threshold, Úlla's stomach gave a wishful growl. It was too early for a meal, but a piece of hard bread or cheese would be enough for her. She poked her head around the corner of the kitchen, surprised to see Birtá already lighting the fires. Úlla readied herself to step back, resigned to go hungry until her need for familiar company won out.

"Birtá," she called, thinking of the other times when she had been in the kitchen, awaiting the day ahead.

Birtá whirled around. "Gods save me, Úlla! You nearly scared my soul right out of me." She dropped her hand from her breast and brushed straight her apron. Taking in a couple of deep breaths, Birtá tucked a loose strand of hair back behind her ear.

Úlla stepped forward, picking up a cloth from the wooden table. "Here, you have soot on your forehead," she said. "Let me wipe it off."

Birtá's plump cheeks flushed. When Úlla finished, the nieddaš's eyes were trained on her. Her lips pursed with concern.

"What is the matter?" Úlla asked, instantly worried.

Birtá shook her head.

"Why are you lighting the fires?" Úlla inquired, feeling self-conscious. "Where is . . ."

"She's sick," Birtá interrupted, then stopped abruptly, her hands twisting her apron into knots. "We've been so worried. We've barely seen your shadow since . . . since . . . well, since the dákti," she burst forth in a torrent, then grimaced. "I'm sorry. I shouldn't have mentioned it."

Úlla momentarily regretted her decision to come into the kitchen, but she also knew she could not hide away for the rest of her life. *It is best to start here*. Aloud, she added, "Birtá, make us some tea. I will gather a little bread and cheese and we can sit together."

Birtá beamed. "Yes! That would be lovely." She turned with a swish of her apron to fill the hanging pot above the fire. "Don't forget the butter and pickles," she said, her voice light and happy as if a storm had cleared and the birds had returned.

Úlla rooted through the larder.

Birtá hurried over. "Here, let me do it," she said, taking over. "You sit down. I'll make us something to eat." The nieddaš hustled Úlla back to the fire and made her sit down. "It'll only take me a moment."

As absent-minded as Birtá sometimes was, she showed her authority in the kitchen. She emerged from the larder, humming softly to herself. In her capable arms, she held two crocks and something covered in leather. Birtá unsheathed her knife. She cut thick wedges of dark bread which she slathered with butter and then cut through the rind of hard cheese with effort. Úlla appreciated her skill, wondering why she had not seen it before.

"I can sharpen that for you. Or make you a new one if you need," Úlla said.

Birtá smiled, "I'd like that. I've been meaning to put a new edge to this knife. I've been so forgetful lately." She rested, looking to the fire. "Could you mind the tea? There's some muorji

Kalek gave me when I was feeling poorly. Oh. And honey too! Don't forget the honey." She started to come forward, leaving behind her preparations.

Úlla held up her hand. "I can find the honey," she said, with a knowing laugh. "And I know how to make tea."

Birtá blushed and returned to where she'd been working. She laughed. "It's silly. I know. I just can't help it."

Úlla placed large dollops of sticky honey into two wooden cups, then sniffed at the various dried herbs until she found what she was looking for. She stirred a scoop of dried muorji into the boiling water with her knife, then dried the blade and slid it back into its place at her belt.

When Birtá laid down the slabs of bread, heaped with butter, cheese, and pickles, Úlla's mouth began to water.

She met Birtá's gaze. The cook giggled. "Go on now! You're looking at the bread like a bear after winter. I'll finish the tea."

Úlla did not need to be told twice. She took a bite, groaning with pleasure which made both of them laugh.

Birtá placed a cup in front of Úlla, then sat down next to her. Úlla felt her friend staring at her over the rim of her cup.

"It's good to hear you laugh," Birtá said finally.

Úlla chewed and swallowed, nodding. "There has been little enough to laugh about."

Birtá frowned.

"I will not crumble like fresh cheese," Úlla reassured her. "I promise."

The cook took a bite of her food and chewed thoughtfully. Long minutes passed as the two ate in companionable silence.

When Úlla finished, she sipped her tea, fishing out errant leaves with her fingertips.

"We have known each other all our lives," she said. "You have always been the kind one and I, well, I have often been proud and prickly."

Birtá began to protest. Úlla stopped her with a quick shake of her head. "No. There is nothing wrong with my telling the truth.

They are traits I am not fond of acknowledging. I also know I balance them by being courageous and loyal." She fell silent as she thought about what she wanted to say. "Kálle's death hardened the part of me that held all the good." Úlla dropped her gaze to the cooling cup of tea in her hand. She watched a tiny leaf float on the surface.

"I did not mean for it to happen." Her voice came out as a whisper. "I also did not try to stop it. I wanted a hard shell to protect me, so I would never feel that kind of pain again."

Birtá put her hand on top of Úlla's and patted it. Úlla looked up to see her friend's dark eyes filled with love. Her words caught in her throat. She had to force herself to continue. "You have all stood by me. Ávrá has . . ." Úlla's voice cracked. She swallowed back the fear and guilty relief that chased each other like butterflies in her belly. "And the others," she said, feeling the warmth of Birtá's steady touch. "They have chosen to stay nieddaš. For me."

Úlla sniffed, struggling to explain herself. "It is not an easy or a simple matter to be different. To know you will never be like your friends. Never experience what they will. I know what it means now. I did not while Dárja lived." She lifted her gaze to look at Birtá, ready to see judgment in her friend's eyes. "I despised Dárja because she was different. Because her bieba was an Olmmoš Piijkij. Because she was taught to fight. In the end, we are not so different. And I will never be able to tell her this." Úlla hiccupped, making her way through a wilderness of pain. "I do not wish this for Ávrá or the other nieddaš."

～

The tallow candle in Ravna's hand sputtered as she watched Tuá sleep with Márgu tucked into the crook of her arm. The light would soon go out, plunging them all into darkness. Unlike her beloved, who would sleep through this peacefully unaware, Ravna was alert and filled with trepidation.

At first, she had thought it a dream that had woken her. Then the words continued to move through her as she had lain there with eyes open. It was Dárja's song. And it was no dream because the images continued to assault her in their detail and vibrancy. Ravna saw the images of the battle. She saw the red blood of Olmmoš and Jápmemeahttun dying in the black mud. She swallowed down the sickness, churning in the pit of her stomach, and murmured a prayer for these two she loved to continue their slumber. Ravna stared at Márgu, recalling the sensation of the child's song, coming through her as if it were her own.

There had been other songs since then that had surged through Ravna like lightning shattering a tree. She had been left shaken by them, furtively looking to see if the others had noticed. No one had remarked upon it to her. But the frequency of these occurrences had been steadily increasing, as had their duration. It was only a matter of time before someone noted her odd behavior. To forestall this, Ravna had begun to move with care, noting any changes in her body which might presage the bright flash in her mind just before a song possessed her body and soul. She could not discern a pattern. Nor could she tell Tuá. They had only just found comfort in each other. She did not want to complicate their tender embraces.

Ravna had considered confiding in Ávrá, then decided against it. Ávrá had her concerns, having chosen to remain nieddaš. Even though the immediate censure had died down, they all reeled from the impact of Ávrá's choice and her advocacy of Úlla. Ravna did not want Úlla to be cast out from them. Neither did she want to remain a nieddaš like Ávrá. She wanted a simple life. She was not a leader. She was the one who walked the middle path, aware of the need for balance. But more and more, the sense of harmony eluded her. In its place was the reoccurring dread of being pulled out of her body and plunged into another, to struggle like a mouse caught in a trap. So too had there been moments of sublime understanding, rare and intimate like a shared heartbeat.

If she were honest with herself, Ravna would admit to the eagerness they stirred in her.

~

The Elders sat in their chamber, seated in a circle, listening to the Song of All. Each had their duty to listen and interpret the signs and sounds they heard. Theirs was a practice developed over millennia, since the first Elders were chosen to guide.

Einár had always found it comforting to think upon the lineage to which he belonged, the traditions they upheld, and the responsibility he shared with all the other Elders to act with wisdom for the good of all.

Admittedly, there were instances where he believed he had failed. Thankfully they had been few and had not challenged his sense of what was needed. *Until now*, he thought. The future of the Jápmemeahttun appeared to him like a forest with the mist upon it. He knew a path existed. He just could not see it, nor could he assume it was safe.

Disheartened by this dawning realization, Einár brought his focus back to the Song of All. At times, the All was too much for him to take in immediately and he would begin with the individual parts, listening to how they built one upon another. He still took joy in receiving and returning each of these melodies into the All. He was as much a vessel as he was a guide. Even if it was becoming increasingly difficult for him to balance the two.

His awareness of this change had come in the days just after Okta had traveled out to his Origin. Einár had listened to the ancient healer's song with rapt concentration to the exclusion of all the others. He had justified this preference by telling himself it was the first time the life bringers would have escorts on their journey to their Origin. While the lives of Úlla, Dárja, Marnej, and Okta had all been in play, it was Okta's song Einár concentrated on. The song reminded him of what had transpired in their lives. It also presaged his time of ending. Filled with sadness, he had listened as Okta began to sing the song of ascension. When the last word disappeared from the All, he had mourned the loss of a soul he had called a friend.

In the days after, Einár thought he had heard the echoes of Okta's song, not the verse he had sung at the end, but the one he had sung in his life. Despite his duty to sing the songs of all the Jápmemeahttun, he allowed himself to be pulled into the past by flashes of the nieddaš Okta had once been and the almai he had become before the war. Einár had tried to hold on to this melody, his heart full of his friend's joy and confidence. When the refrain disappeared like a raindrop into a rushing stream, Einár once again felt the loss of the healer he had known.

As he sang the songs back into the All, Einár saw beauty and joy and hope, even if there was little of it in his heart. And there was some comfort in knowing the Song would continue after the Jápmemeahttun had joined the stars.

"Noaidi," a voice wavered in the circle. "Noaidi."

Einár opened his eyes. He blinked in surprise to see Ravna, standing before him. Her normally placid expression was twisted by anguish.

"Noaidi, I apologize for interrupting the Elders' circle without sanction . . . I believe I have heard something that cannot wait."

"No sanction is needed, Ravna. When you are compelled to speak, you must honor the spirit," Einár assured the trembling nieddaš before him.

A low murmuring of agreement rippled through the gathered Elders.

Ravna glanced around the room, then cleared her throat, saying softly, "I believe I heard the Song of Dárja."

Einár's breath caught. He had not been expecting to hear her name. He looked to the other Elders who reflected his shock. "And you are sure of this?" he asked, his doubt rebounding.

Ravna hesitated, then said with certainty, "Yes."

Einár suddenly felt uneasy.

"Noaidi?"

"Mmm," Einár answered, unsure what it meant that he had not heard Dárja's song.

"What are we to do?"

Einár's mind snapped back to the present. Looking at the other Elders, he said, "Leave me to a private counsel with Ravna."

"What about Kalek?" one of the Elders pressed.

"Kalek has suffered enough loss," Einár said.

"Now there is hope," another Elder added.

"And there is more pain if hope is crushed, because we have mistaken the signs and sounds we hear." The force of his admonition, surprised even Einár himself. He glanced at Ravna to see her chastened expression.

"Let me speak with Ravna," he said, moderating his tone. "Then we can discuss this matter further."

Much to Einár's relief, the other Elders stood and filed out of the chamber.

Alone with the nieddaš, Einár said, "Tell me what you heard."

The nieddaš swallowed, her hands clasped tightly in front of her.

"It is not what I heard," she began, then stopped, looking up at Einár. "I felt her song. I saw the battle."

Stunned by this declaration, Einár sat speechless.

"I am sorry, Noaidi," Ravna began to apologize.

"Do not be sorry for what you share with me," Einár said, regarding the nieddaš before him. *Was I ever this young?* Aloud he asked, "Is this the first time you felt a song this way?"

Ravna slowly shook her head. Einár felt as if the ground beneath his feet had given way. He wanted to demand that she tell him everything that had transpired. At the same time, he did not want to know. *Because it should not be possible.* The thought repeated again and again in his mind. Finally, he recovered enough of his composure to say, "Tell me what you have experienced, dear one."

As Einár listened to Ravna recount her story, he stared at her stupefied, his mind puzzling how it was possible. In his heart, however, he knew he looked upon the soul who would become the next Noaidi. This knowledge filled him with both wonder and apprehension. *So much change, too quickly. How will we survive?* It was a question he would need to leave for another time because Ravna's retelling of Dárja's song posed another, more pressing question.

If Dárja lived, then what was her purpose in not returning to them? Unless she was once again held against her will. This possibility chilled him to the bone. If she was a prisoner, there was nothing any of them could do for her. And if Kalek found this out, he would insist on attempting to rescue her. The healer had spent too many seasons of snow with Irjan to let such a quest go unanswered, particularly where love was concerned.

Child, what are you about? he silently demanded of the heavens, hoping for all their sakes Ravna had been mistaken and Dárja was truly dead.

CHAPTER THIRTY-FIVE

THE WARM GLOW OF the setting sun greeted Marnej when he emerged from the forge. He stretched his back, taking a deep breath of air in through his nose. He smelled the sweet spices he had come to love, together with the tang of metal that hung about him. His stomach grumbled and Marnej was grateful a good meal awaited him, coupled with a cup or two of mielakvu. He missed the warm spiced wine. Lávrrahaš had explained forrá was for the winter times and the fermented drink of lemons and honey was for the sun months.

"To prepare you for the heat of the day when the sun finally reaches the high point," his kinsman had said.

Lávrrahaš would also be awaiting him at the tavern, where, after his meal, Marnej would help serve the visitors and clean after they had gone. The work was not taxing, and the stories, filled the air with laughter and goodwill, made the time pass pleasantly. Marnej had gained enough skill with the language to piece together the premise of the stories told, even if he didn't understand everything said.

Walking with brisk steps back to the tavern, Marnej greeted those familiar to him, favoring them with a smile. Even after all his time in the south, Marnej was entranced by all the differences he saw around him. Often, he found himself speculating where certain people came from and what their lands might look like.

Standing at the door to the tavern, loud singing floated down from the open windows above. Lávrrahaš had taken down the leather coverings to allow the warming breezes to flow through. Garlands of bright colored cloth and bells hung from the windows in honor of the upcoming festival. Lávrrahaš had tried to explain it to him, but Marnej had failed to grasp the meaning of this event. He would just need to see for himself to truly understand. The garlands swayed in the wind, causing the bells to ting. Above him, the painted sea monster smiled, its teeth like white daggers.

The story of Marnej's sea crossing had become popular with visitors. They'd gasp as Lávrrahaš described how Marnej was tossed about by mountains of dark water. Then their eyes would narrow when they heard he'd awoken on their shore with no memory of how he'd found his way there. With sincere wariness, they'd asked to see his teeth. When he'd assured them they were not dagger-sharp, they'd asked him if he hid a tail. One woman, old enough to be his mother and beautiful in the way of the Aeopo, with honeyed skin and dark ringlets, had ask him to drop his leg coverings to prove he had no tail. The crowd had wailed with raucous laughter. Lávrrahaš had promptly translated when it was clear Marnej hadn't understood her intent. He'd flushed with the heat of embarrassment. Lávrrahaš had come to his aid, extending his services to the Aeopo woman, who, in turn, had waved him over, to the amusement of all gathered.

Marnej wondered about the truth of the sea monsters. He'd witnessed too much in his time with the Immortals to dismiss a legend. Just because he hadn't seen one with his eyes didn't mean sea monsters didn't exist. Perhaps he'd just been lucky, or perhaps he'd been protected by the gods—his gods, because the southern gods seemed very different than his.

His gods were in the heavens. They were in the stars and the sun and the moon. Here in Karvaluz, with its mix of peoples, they spoke of goddesses, who were the rumble of the earth, the bubbling of hot springs, and the roots of trees. "From the earth to the earth" was a common Irkati blessing when someone spoke of hardship or woe.

"From the earth to the earth," Marnej repeated to himself, climbing the worn stairs. While in the north, the heavens were only for the faithful, here in the south the ground upon which all walked was holy. There was no separation. Marnej stopped mid-step to stand lost in thought. A slow-dawning realization took hold of him as bits and pieces of conversation came back as precious recollections.

"The Olmmoš believe in their eminence," Okta had once said. "Just as we once did. Then the gods gifted us with the chance to see peace can exist when we do not hold ourselves apart."

Marnej had argued the Immortals did hold themselves apart. It was the whole purpose of the Song of All—keeping the Immortals hidden from the Olmmoš.

To which the ancient healer had asked, "Are we hiding if the Olmmoš simply cannot see us?"

Marnej'd had no answer for that. Now, standing on a step halfway between the southern earth below and the floor above, he believed he understood what the healer had been trying to say. It didn't matter how far he ran, he'd always be a part of the Song of All, whether he sang his chorus or not. Marnej swayed. He steadied himself with his hands outstretched to the walls on either side.

"Started early, did you?" a voice from below boomed in Bissmená.

Startled, Marnej looked behind him. A round Irkati man made his way up the stairs. Pushing past Marnej, the Irkati clapped him on the back and grinned. Marnej smiled back, letting the man go ahead. He needed a moment to gather himself before he entered and faced not only those there to drink and eat, but also Lávrrahaš. The man had a keen eye. And for the present, Marnej had no desire to discuss what he was feeling.

He took a couple of deep huffing breaths, then slapped his cheeks. The sting made him momentarily forget about the knot in his stomach. He took one last breath, then entered the tavern room to be hailed by his kinsman.

"About time, you laggard!" Lávrrahaš called out. "I have thirsty people here and only two hands with which to serve them their drinks."

Marnej hurried to the washing bowl, into which he poured a measure of clean water. He took the tallow soap to his hands and face and then rinsed off. Standing up straight, water dripped from his face.

"Tari! Dua urkreito ekaporis na boloj," someone cackled. The room burst with laughter.

Lávrrahaš tossed Marnej a piece of cloth. "Indeed, another sea monster has risen from the waters." Marnej dried his face and hands. "They are a lively bunch tonight," the tavernkeeper said, with a smile. "More coin for us if we can keep their cups filled."

∾

Marnej thumped down onto a stool to rest his head in his arms upon the table. A cool breeze came through the window at his back, chilling the sweat upon his neck and forearms.

"That was nothing," Lávrrahaš said without preamble.

Marnej raised his head to regard the man in disbelief.

The tavernkeeper laughed from his belly. "The festival of Pasatu will make you think this was a cold morning in a Believers' temple."

Marnej couldn't imagine anything could be more raucous than the crowd of men and women who'd crowded themselves into the tavern that night. They'd shoved and pushed and called for more mielakvu. All the while, they spilled what they already had in their cups onto the heads of others, who complained until their cups were filled. Then they all laughed and sang and joked with any who stood near.

"I don't know if I have the fortitude," Marnej said.

Lávrrahaš stopped sweeping. "Our sea monster can row across the treacherous waters, but he cannot brave the revelry of the wind goddess, bringing trade and fortune." He grabbed a sodden chamois and tossed it toward Marnej. The cloth landed in front of him with a juicy splat. "Wash the tables or they will attract every manner of crawling bug to feast."

"Doesn't the wind goddess bring fortune for bugs as well?" Marnej asked, his laughing joke cut short by earlier reflections. He began to wipe the tables with new vigor as if by working harder he could hold off the growing sense of urgency he felt.

"I said wash the tops, my friend, not plane them anew."

Marnej froze. He looked up at Lávrrahaš. The man rested the curved broom handle against his chest. He considered his kinsman with an appraising eye. Marnej wanted to crawl into a corner and hide. Instead, he stood up and wiped the sweat from his eyes with his tunic sleeve.

"Are you in need of a woman or a man?" Lávrrahaš asked, raising his eyebrows. "You are young and I have not inquired . . ."

"No," Marnej said, reddening. He'd been with women already. And among the Brethren, there had been no embarrassment to share the comfort of another man.

"Then it seems you are satisfied with your hand," Lávrrahaš said and began to sweep again.

"It's not that," Marnej said, suddenly needing to unburden himself.

The tavernkeeper stopped and straightened. "Then what?"

"Do you remember when I asked you if you ever thought of returning north?"

Lávrrahaš nodded, using his foot to slide a stool toward him. He leaned his broom against the wall, then sat down, resting his hands upon his knees. "I do."

Marnej remained standing, fearing if he sat, his courage would slip away. "Do you remember what you told me?"

Lávrrahaš's mouth slid back into a lopsided grin. "Something wise, I hope."

"You said coming here was the right choice, that you'd made peace with your family. You said you'd run from the war, not from yourself."

Lávrrahaš nodded.

"I know those last words were for me," Marnej continued, his mouth dry. "I did try to run away from myself. I can see now it was foolish. I don't regret coming here, because I don't think I would ever have understood what it truly means to belong, if I hadn't."

Lávrrahaš frowned.

Marnej shook his head at his earlier blindness. "It may not make sense to you. To me it's clear. I tried to leave something behind. But I'll always carry it with me. No time and no distance will change that."

"Well, if you have peace," Lávrrahaš said, "that is what is important. Though, I might ask, what do you intend to do with this knowledge?"

Without thinking, Marnej said, "I must go back."

The tavernkeeper laughed. "You should see your face, my young friend. All tight with concern." Containing his merriment, Lávrrahaš added, "Of course you must go back. It is something I have long known."

Marnej slumped down upon a stool. "If you knew, why didn't you say so?"

"What is the worth of advice when experience is what is truly needed?"

"What if I'd never figured it out?"

Lávrrahaš smiled. "Then it was never that important, hmm?" He ended on a questioning note.

Marnej had figured it out, and it was important to him. He needed to go back. He needed to face the Immortals and explain himself. They deserved to know the truth from him, just as much as he needed to speak it. Perhaps his failings had already been revealed within the Song of All. It didn't change his desire to tell the truth. Then, he'd live by any judgment they thought fitting.

Marnej looked at Lávrrahaš, who watched him thoughtfully. This man had showed him friendship and generosity, much like Kalek had when he'd first arrived among the Immortals. *He also deserves to hear the truth.*

"Lávrrahaš," Marnej said, then stopped, unsure of the right way to express his gratitude. "You've given me more than the opportunity of a new life here in Karvaluz. You've honored me with your friendship and wisdom. Without which, I would've searched beyond myself for answers." The tavernkeeper waved off the compliment.

"No," Marnej insisted. "It's important you hear me because you, like Aage, have given me too much not to be granted the truth in return."

Lávrrahaš's brows furrowed. Marnej pressed on. "I've told no lies. I've also not told you all of my story. The night I arrived here with Aage, I kept hidden one part of myself. Not because I feared your response, but because my guilt discredited me."

Marnej took a deep breath. "I shared that I was trained by the Brethren of Hunters to be a Piijkij. And I fought in the war against the Immortals, the last one—the Great Battle. What I didn't say was that I also share Immortal blood."

Lávrrahaš blinked in disbelief.

"I don't mean I shared in the bloodshed of the Immortals. Because I did. I don't know how many I killed. Their deaths are a regret I'll bear forever. What I mean is, the blood that flows through me is in part Jápmemeahttun."

The man's eyes widened. "You are an Immortal." The statement was a mix of reverence and incredulity. "Why would you hide this? I said I held no ill will toward them."

Marnej grimaced. "I know, Lávrrahaš. I know you spoke well of them. My reticence wasn't because of any fear of your reaction. It was because of my own dishonor."

"You are ashamed to be one of them?"

"No, no. I'm not. I was confused. Once. And angry, perhaps. Never ashamed."

Marnej looked down at the knife in his belt. He thought of the promise Úlla had made, to teach him the finer skills of inlay. "I betrayed someone very close to me and the guilt has settled into my soul."

"If you are an Immortal, why then were you trained to be a Piijkij?"

~

It was past dawn before Marnej finished telling the story of Irjan, the Avr, and the Vijns; about his escape with Dárja and his acceptance by the Immortals. He spoke about the Song of All and the attempt to protect Úlla and Okta at their Origin. Finally, he admitted to betraying Dárja's confidence and his subsequent heartbreak, watching her leave him behind. Through it all, Lávrrahaš had listened, asking questions only when Marnej had finished.

"Is she your sister then?"

Marnej shook his head. "No. We share no blood relation. My father was her bieba—her guide mother—when he came to live with the Immortals."

"To be both mother and father. Human and Immortal." Lávrrahaš shook his head, then frowned. "You say Dárja will not be like the others?"

Marnej nodded.

"You and your father before you were not like the others."

"True."

"And you were accepted."

"My father was a prisoner. Because, as a free man, he could lead the Olmmoš to the Immortals. As I eventually did."

"Were you not a prisoner?"

"No. I'd already been betrayed by my leader and the High Priest. I owed neither of them my allegiance and my Immortal blood gave me the chance to start again."

"All those seasons of snow I spent in the Pohjola, wondering about them. I could have been right next to the Immortals and never known it!" Lávrrahaš shook his head in disbelief. "Can you do it now?"

"What?"

"Disappear."

"No. There is no Song of All here. It's what I'd hoped for."

"And it turns out you miss it."

"Mmm." Marnej nodded.

Lávrrahaš slapped the table with both hands. "Well, we must get you back there."

"It's light out and I have work to do at the forge," Marnej protested with a groan.

Lávrrahaš stood and walked over to the counter by the wall. "If I were you, with the chance to be with this song of yours, then I would not be bellyaching about the time." He rummaged on the counter's cluttered surface, muttering as he looked for something.

His muffled voice emerged distracted as he continued to search. "How will you return?"

"The boat is gone," Marnej said, facing the enormity of his decision.

Lávrrahaš straightened. "By the goddesses below, you look like you have witnessed your last day."

"Didn't you hear me?" Marnej asked, crushed by the weight of his disappointment.

The tavernkeeper rolled out a piece of leather. "Here."

Marnej looked down at what appeared to be a map, with stars noted on the side. "What is this?"

Lávrrahaš leveled his eyes. "I will honor the possibility you are tired and not merely dense. If you are this thick, then you will never return home by the land route."

"Land route," Marnej repeated, then exclaimed, "You made a map!"

"Just because I do not regret my decision to leave does not mean there might not come a time when I need to return.

"You're coming with me?" Marnej asked, emboldened.

The tavernkeeper shook his head. "I am content where I am. But I believe we can convince Aage, upon his return, that a trip by this trade route might prove profitable."

"What if Aage doesn't agree or if he never comes this way?"

Lávrrahaš placed his hand upon Marnej's shoulder. The firm grip felt reassuring. In the man's pale gray eyes there was a strange sadness. "If Aage has not returned to us by the end of the festival, then I will take you to these mountains myself. From there, you will be able to make it back to the Pohjola and your kind."

CHAPTER THIRTY-SIX

VÁLDE'S WOUNDS ACHED AS he sat, hunched in the corner of a travelers' hut with Gáral. They had journeyed at least four leagues south of the trapper's hut, then had cut west, to the trade route. The western trade route was much less traveled than the eastern one, owing to the boggy tracks in the spring melt. Válde was heartened to see there were several others in the travelers' hut, biding their time with something to eat and drink before moving on.

For this foray, he and Gáral had forsaken disguise in favor of simple clothes: a rough linen tunic and thinning breeches. Still, they had their knives at their belts, even if they missed their swords, hidden in the woods.

For the moment, Gáral kept his head low. He watched with suspicious eyes the traders and travelers that kept them company. The talk, since their arrival, had been about the hardships of the preceding season of snow and the hopes they all held for good crops and healthy livestock. Gáral snorted as he listened to nearby conversations. Válde knew his comrade was eager to change the stagnant conditions they had shared for far too long. They were are all restless in the cramped quarters of the trapper's hut and aware that any day could bring the arrival of the true owner.

If their luck held, they would be gone before the close of the next moon-cycle and on their way to avenging their betrayal. Válde reviewed his calculations. He knew, to the day, when they had been set upon by the Vijns's soldiers at the fortress. But he could not pinpoint the moment his plan had come into being. *Had it been when Dárja first appeared? Or later?*

"Do you think she can do it?" Gáral muttered, breaking into Válde's musing.

"What?" he asked.

Gáral faced him directly. "Do you think she can do it?" Each word came out distinct and weighted.

When Válde did not answer immediately, Gáral added, "Too much rests upon her to not ask this question."

Since their last confrontation, Dárja had kept apart, which, considering their tight quarters, was just short of the work of the gods. She would find reason to be out when Válde was in or she would return after he had lain to sleep. He had been awake as she had come in, on tiptoe, careful to not wake the others. He had watched her sit with her head in her hands while the others slumbered. He had listened to her breathing change from restlessness to deep sleep.

In these unguarded moments, he had wanted to go to her, to reassure her it would all be for the best. Then again, nothing changed the fact that she was Jápmemeahttun and he Piijkij. She had been right to say they acted in concert only until she succeeded in killing the High Priest.

"She will do what needs to be done," Válde said.

Gáral's brows arched, his doubt palpable.

"And I will do what needs to be done," Válde assured him, recalling how Dárja had coolly accepted her role. *And yet.* How easy and dangerous to idle upon that phrase. There were larger forces at work, more compelling than his own feelings. He had pledged an oath to the Avr of the Brethren of Hunters. The others shared the same oath. *What of our honor? What of our duty to the people?* These questions battered him.

And yet.

Dárja had been the one to speak of sacrifice. She had looked him squarely in the eye and said she knew he would pledge her, body and soul, to the gods if it would serve his cause. She expected it. *Gods' mercy, she accepted it.*

"You look as if you have walked across your grave," Gáral said.

Válde drained his juhka with a shaky hand. "I may have."

"Well, put that ahead of you," Gáral said without feeling. "Listen."

"Drink up, my friend," a man encouraged, waving to the hut-keeper. "Before you know it, the soldiers'll be here to beat it out of you."

"Bah," another man said, taking a slurping draw upon his cup. "You speak like a winter minx afraid to get caught in the trap."

"Pass off my warning, if you will. I've heard it from others, the soldiers are out," the alarmist said.

"They're always about," the other scoffed.

From near the fire, a weathered man spoke up. "I hear they are putting to the blade any and all to find out where the Piijkij are hiding."

The naysayer laughed, "It's not like we keep their company."

"Doesn't matter," said the man opposite the fire.

"Hush," his woman said, stopping him from taking another swig from his cup.

Disregarding her hissed warning, the man went on, "A farmer from Hassa was cut within an inch of his life because he harbored one of them."

Válde watched the woman put a cautionary hand upon his arm. The man continued. "The farmer had cared for a wounded soldier, and look what he received for his efforts."

Dismay rumbled within the smoky space.

The hutkeeper tried to quell the growing agitation of her patrons by pouring the juhka liberally. "Come now," she said. "We cannot believe all the tales shared. Or next we will be believing the Jápmea are riding south upon us."

~

Dárja had left the Piijkij sound asleep save for Edo, who stood watch outside. He'd nodded to her, keeping any questions he might've had to himself. Dárja gave him a brief smile before pulling up the hood of her woolen tunic. There was a chill in the air before the sun topped the trees. She appreciated the cold upon her face and hands; it made her take greater strides to move the blood under her skin. She breathed in the damp morning air, rich and green. It tasted like mushrooms and seeds sprouting and water running swiftly in streams.

She held onto this feeling, wanting life to run through her, so she could believe in a tomorrow where the sun would shine higher in the sky. She needed some certainty to push back against the fears and doubts that occupied the void she'd created when she'd challenged Válde. *The truth is what it is. Stated or not.* And he hadn't denied it. She'd seen it in his eyes. The pressure of his grip on her arm had left a mark.

She'd held onto the vision of day's fading light, setting to flame his green eyes. *So like the forest around him.* The freckles on his skin had stood out against the flush of his anger. It was a moment's flurry of some deeper feeling which would be gone when she'd proved herself. *And he knows it too.* Dárja ranged across the spongy ground of moist, moldering leaves and refreshed moss until the sound of horses and men made her drop behind a trio of lichen-covered rocks. Wedged into the undergrowth that backed up against the rough granite stones, she listened to the voices grow louder. Her pulse quickened. She dared not peek out to see how many men came her way.

"This is a fool's errand," a high Olmmoš voice complained.

"Better scouting than stuck mucking stalls in the garrison," a deeper voice answered.

Someone laughed. "There's plenty of muck out here."

"I'll take mud over shit any time."

"Count yourself lucky," someone added.

Dárja closed her eyes and willed the soldiers to keep going.

The clatter of horses and the chatter of men continued, unhurried. *Had they been discovered?* she wondered, then dismissed the idea out of hand. If the hut were known to these men, they'd be riding at full gallop, with enough support to act with impunity. She'd heard maybe six and no more than ten riders, moving at a leisurely pace. But their meandering didn't mean these men weren't a threat to the Piijkij ensconced in the trapper's hut.

Dárja waited in agony until the voices finally subsided, then squirmed out from the undergrowth. Scanning the forest to the south, she saw uniformed riders, weaving in and out of larch trees.

~

Dárja approached the clearing around the Piijkij hut, out of breath. She had run at full speed and luck had been with her. She'd not encountered the soldiers on her way back. While no smoke rose from the chimney, she smelled the lingering scent of a fire in the air. A horse whinny from the lean-to stable heightened her awareness of the perimeter. There was no movement. Nothing amiss. Dárja unsheathed her sword. She walked out into the clearing. Feles came around the corner of the hut. He dropped the wood he carried to reach for his blade.

Dárja instantly pulled back and held up her hands. "I'm sorry, Feles."

The stoic Piijkij frowned and lowered his weapon.

"Where are the others?" Dárja asked, unable to keep the concern from her voice.

Feles stood straight, leaving behind the discarded firewood. "Mures and Edo are within, Herko is hunting. Gáral and Válde are scouting for a travelers' hut and information. Why?"

"Soldiers are riding south in the area," Dárja said.

"How many?"

"No more than ten. They rode to the west."

Feles gave a cursory glance in that direction. "Toward the trade route?"

"Perhaps," Dárja allowed. "They weren't riding for speed but they searched for something as they meandered."

Feles nodded, seeming to take her meaning. "One of us should stay to play the role of the trapper. The rest should scatter and hide until they've returned to where they came from."

He turned an appraising eye to the woods, then stooped to pick up the wood. Despite her sense of urgency, Dárja helped him. She knew Feles to be serious and able. If he thought the firewood important, then she'd honor his forethought. With arms full, Dárja followed him into the hut.

"There are soldiers in the area," Feles said to those within. The two Piijkij jumped to their feet, alert and ready for action.

"No more than ten. All mounted," Dárja added, while Feles stacked the wood adjacent to the meager hearth. She followed his lead.

"We should not be here if they happen this way," Edo said.

"Mures, you stay here and act the trapper," Feles said. "If we were to leave the hut unclaimed and recently occupied it would look suspicious."

Mures frowned. "What of Herko, Gáral, and Válde?"

"There is no way to warn Gáral and Válde. I do not know how far south they have gone," Feles admitted with his usual sobriety. "If the soldiers come upon them, we must assume they have the skill to overcome any difficulties."

"And Herko?" Edo asked.

"The same for him," Feles said. "Although he will have Mures here to warn him off when he returns."

Feles regarded the cramped space that had sheltered them. "For the moment, let us take all signs of our numbers and pack the horses." As an afterthought, he added, "Herko will be without a horse. He can make do."

"How long should we stay away?" Edo asked as he gathered his furs and weapons.

Feles looked to Dárja with an inquiring expression.

"They weren't provisioned for a protracted journey," she said, thinking back to what she'd seen of the soldiers. "The last of them hadn't a bedroll upon the saddle. That doesn't mean the first soldiers weren't better prepared."

"Give them two, maybe three days to pass northwards," Feles said, "then regroup."

~

Válde and Gáral rode in silence with a waning, last-quarter moon at their backs. There was little to discuss. Gáral had been right to press for immediate action. The days were lengthening and the Vijns continued to clamor for their heads. Válde's wounds had mostly healed. They were all back to their strength.

Gáral pulled his horse up short. "Wait."

Válde reacted in kind, leaving behind future plans for current danger.

"Listen," Gáral said.

Válde cocked an ear. He heard a distinct snap of a branch. Crisp and light. A branch on the ground, rather than one on the tree.

He drew out his sword. Gáral did the same. They urged their horses forward cautiously. The mounts took two steps, then reared as a man came charging, bellowing like a bear, his weapon glinting in the moonlight.

Válde regained control of his horse in time to spur the animal out of the way of a slicing sword.

Gáral whirled, shouting, "Gods be cursed, Herko! Have you gone mad?"

The man stopped in his tracks and lowered his sword. "You're lucky I didn't get you. You were slow."

"Slow?" Válde protested.

"Shh." Herko motioned with his hands for quiet.

"Do not tell us to quiet down when you are howling like some wounded beast," Gáral said.

"I didn't know if you were soldiers, did I?" Herko said, his spite at the surface. "The forest's crawling with them."

Válde looked around.

"What do you mean?" Gáral demanded.

"The healer-witch was foraging in the north. She saw maybe ten mounted soldiers, heading south and west. She brought back the warning. We scattered like birds," Herko reported, sheathing his sword. "Mures stayed at the hut. I was hunting when she returned. I knew nothing until I made it back and Mures told me. We were to stay away until the soldiers make their way back north." He spat upon the ground. "I thought the pair of you might have been what I'd been waiting for."

"Based on our clothes?" Gáral asked.

"Can't be too careful," Herko said, adding, "We took their garb. Maybe they've done the same."

"We have been gone three days," Válde said. Then asked, "How long have you been away?"

"Two," Herko said.

"If the hut has been discovered we will need to regroup swiftly," Gáral said, his voice made pensive by strategy. "We cannot be caught before we have had a chance to act."

Válde nodded, keeping his thoughts to himself.

"Well, I'm not walking back," Herko said, looking pointedly at Gáral.

"Why don't you have a horse?" Gáral asked.

"The others took them to avoid raising suspicion while I was hunting. They left one for Mures, in case it was needed."

❧

While the ride back to the hut proved uneventful, Válde could not shake a sense of unease. On the fringe of the clearing to the trapper's hut, Herko dismounted. He disappeared into the forest. Válde and Gáral waited in the shadows.

"If they have come through," Gáral began.

"Then it all might be over," Válde finished the man's sentence.

Herko appeared, startling the nervous horses. "No tracks leading into the clearing. There were some on the east side. They'd covered those well," he said. "I'll see if Mures remains alone. If he's got company, then I'll be his brother, returned to take my stint trapping."

Before Válde thought to object, Herko walked toward the hut with the air of a man who had a claim to stake. He did all but swagger.

At the door, he banged loudly. "Brother, are you in there? Mother sends me with word from our father."

The door to the hut creaked opened. At this range, Válde could not tell what was happening. Then he saw Mures emerge to embrace Herko.

~

Over the next day, the remaining two Piijkij returned, describing an uneventful foray in the woods.

"No soldiers," Feles said. "Only bears."

When another day passed and Dárja had not returned, Válde repeatedly questioned the men as to what she had told them.

"She said she'd been foraging less than three leagues north of here. She heard men and horses and hid. What she overheard made it clear to her they were soldiers," Mures recounted. "When they'd passed, she crawled out. She said they weren't provisioned for travel, at least the ones she saw."

"She suspected they would return north shortly and we decided it best to take no chance on being discovered here together," Feles added to the details.

"Maybe she finally got sick of Herko," Mures said.

"Maybe she has left," Gáral echoed Mures, but with none of his humor.

"She would not desert us of her own accord," Edo said.

"What did you expect. She's a Jápmea," Herko said. "They always disappear, then stab you in the back when you're not looking."

Válde paid no heed to the banter in order to give more thought to Feles's account. "There is no garrison north of us. Unless you go to Skaina. From there, soldiers would need provisions to travel. It is at least a three days' ride."

He tried to make sense of what he knew. "Did she take note of what they said?"

Feles shook his head. "She described their movement as meandering—searching. They wove their way south and west. I suggested they might be headed for the western trade route."

"It is time for us to move south," Gáral said.

"Not until Dárja returns," Válde said. "We need her for this plan to work."

CHAPTER THIRTY-SEVEN

H E SHOULD BE TOLD."

"No, Rássa, you are wrong."

"The nieddaš is alive."

"True, Ravna has heard Dárja's song. What we do not know is what keeps her from us. Kalek has finally taken on apprentices. He is going forward. To tell him now would be a cruelty to Kalek, to his students, and to Ávrá."

"Noaidi, the nieddaš has heard the song. She has seen the visions. How can we disregard them? No nieddaš has had this kind of insight."

"You are right about Ravna. I am aware of her skills and can only wonder what it means for us all. To sing the songs of all the Jápmemeahttun is as much a burden as it is a gift. I know from my experience it is an honor I would not have sought out were it not part of me."

The clatter of a dropping tray interrupted the conversation. The two Elders turned to a nieddaš who hunched over the jumble of wooden cups. They put their heads together, lowering their voices as they glided from the room.

Birtá's hands shook as she carried the basket of vegetables. She peered around the corner, watching the two Elders recede down a corridor. She couldn't hear them now. What she'd already heard was enough to make her heart race.

Ravna has heard Dárja's song. Dárja is alive!

The Elders knew this and had kept silent. Birtá couldn't understand why Ravna had heard Dárja's song and not the Elders. Or why Dárja would remain away from all of them. What mattered was she was alive. Birtá couldn't keep this a secret. She knew herself well enough to know that. She had to tell someone before it just burst forth from her. *But who? Who can I tell?* Then it occurred to her. Úlla. She would know what to do. Úlla still struggled with guilt over Dárja's death.

Birtá placed her basket upon the chopping block, then turned to leave.

"You'll not be leaving this here," one of the other cooks protested.

Birtá did not answer. Anger and blame would await her return. It was more important she go to the forge and find Úlla. Along the way, she waved off greetings by those who wished to talk, her mind intent on her goal. At the threshold to the forge, she hesitated. Úlla stood in the midst of the thunderous noise. Hammers clanged. The fire roared. An angry hiss came from a barrel, half-hidden by a thick post. Úlla brought her hammer down with heavy blows upon a glowing tip of iron.

Birtá looked to the four other smiths engrossed in their tasks, unsure of how to approach. She understood the harried chaos of the kitchen, not this world of stone, fire, and metal. The desire to shrink back pressed against her need to share her news. Birtá felt herself clamp her hand over her mouth to stop herself from shouting, "Dárja is alive."

An almai seated in front of the bellows gained Úlla's notice. Birtá waved, relief flooding through her. Úlla took off her gauntlets and wiped the sweat from her brow with her arm. Birtá took a couple of steps forward, then stopped, self-conscious as all eyes turned to her.

Coming to Birtá's side, Úlla wiped her face again, frowning. "You look like a blackbird with a raspberry in its beak."

Birtá reached out, taking Úlla's arm to lead her to a quiet corner. Birtá's eyes darted around, worried about who might be listening.

"I have something important to tell you."

"Really, Birtá. What is this all about?" Úlla demanded, with a hint of frustration. "I have work to do."

Over the clanging from the forge, Birtá spoke into Úlla's ear. "Dárja's alive!"

Úlla pulled back from her. "If this is a joke?"

"A joke?" Birtá's jaw dropped. "I'd never do that. I overheard the Elders. Ravna has heard Dárja's song. She's alive."

Úlla blinked once and then again. She frowned. "Why has she not come home?" She grasped Birtá hard about the shoulders. "Who else knows?"

Birtá squeaked. "Úlla! You're hurting me. Let me go." She prised herself free from the nieddaš's powerful grip. "No one knows. The Elders don't want to share the news. Once I heard, I couldn't keep it to myself. Not when you . . ." Birtá hesitated. Úlla released her hold.

"We both know I can't keep a secret," Birtá said, embarrassed.

Úlla nodded, her eyes centered on a distant point.

"What are you going to do?" Birtá asked, worried she'd just done something terribly wrong.

Úlla turned to her, a sad smile resting upon her lips. "I am going to do what I should have done from the start." She hugged Birtá tightly before walking away from the forge.

❧

Úlla had seen the concern in Birtá's eyes. She had wanted to reassure her friend it would all be okay, that she had done the right thing in coming to tell her that Dárja lived. Úlla could do neither. She could only think of her disgrace and her need to atone.

She had hugged Birtá, walking away with a semblance of strength when, in fact, her knees trembled. Úlla had left Birtá to return to her work in the kitchen. She did not want a witness nor an accomplice. Walking quickly through the corridors, she thought of Dárja, her own jealousy, and what it had cost them both.

At the door to the apothecary, Úlla wavered before knocking loudly. She was greeted by Ávrá unexpectedly appearing in the doorway. Her smile fell. "Úlla, are you well?"

Úlla nodded, at a loss for words. Ushered into the apothecary, she recovered herself enough to say, "I was hoping to speak to Kalek."

"He is with his apprentices," Ávrá said, guiding Úlla to sit. "He will be back soon if you wished to wait." She paused, concern flickering in her eyes. "I could wait with you, if you like."

Úlla shook her head again. "No. I will come back another time." She stood, readying herself to run.

Ávrá glanced sharply to the right. "I think they are already returning." She smiled sweetly. "You will get to speak to him after all. I must return to the weavers." Ávrá's exit took with her the last of Úlla's resolve. She turned to leave just as a welcoming voice hailed her from the shadows.

Úlla froze.

Kalek came forward into the apothecary, trailing a line of whispering apprentices.

"Are you quite well?" he asked. The whispers died out. Úlla tightened her arms about her, fearing her insides would tumble onto the floor.

She shook her head, unable to find her voice.

To the apprentices, Kalek said, "We will continue tomorrow with a review and then add more useful herbs."

The almai and nieddaš, six in all, drifted past Úlla, greeting her with muttered comfort. When the last "be well" echoed in the room, Kalek closed the door.

"Dárja is alive," Úlla blurted.

"Are you quite well?" Kalek repeated, stepping away to create a gap between the two of them.

Úlla shot out her hand to stop him. "I am neither fevered nor enfeebled. The Elders say Ravna has heard Dárja's song. She is alive."

Kalek retreated to the cold hearth. "Ravna? Why are you telling me that a nieddaš has had a dream?"

"It is not a dream. The Elders speak of Dárja within the Song of All."

He stared at her. Suspicion and hurt clouded his pale eyes. "How do you know this?"

"That is not important. What is important is that she is alive."

Kalek sagged into a chair. "Why did they not tell me?"

"I do not know," Úlla answered.

"Why has she not returned?" Kalek whispered, as much to himself as to her.

"I am the cause," Úlla said, looking down at her hands.

Kalek's attention snapped to her. "What do you mean?"

All at once, the guilt and sickness Úlla had carried in her heart came pouring out. "When Marnej worked in the forge, I said something unkind about Dárja. He defended her, saying she would never give birth to become an almai. He told me it was his fault. He said he was alive because of her and she would never be an almai." Úlla swallowed back her fear, knowing what it meant. "When we neared my Origin, I realized just how much Dárja had sacrificed. The pain she must have felt to be with me, knowing she would never experience birth herself." Úlla faltered, wanting to run from her shame. "I told her I knew it was not easy for her. I told her, in so many words, that I knew the truth." Úlla's voice dropped to a whisper. "I meant it from my heart—with gratitude." She wiped her eyes with her soot-stained hands. "Then the soldiers came and she bid me ride. I never had a chance to tell her I was sorry for what I said, for my seasons of jealousy. I am alive because of her."

~

"You have no need to apologize to me," Kalek said, the ache within him throbbing.

"I was so hurt. After Kálle," Úlla tried to explain.

He grasped her trembling hands. "Shh. I know." He leaned forward to lightly kiss her forehead. "We have all suffered."

She did not look up from her hands.

"You must not believe Dárja stays away because of you," he said.

When she finally met his gaze, her eyes were red-rimmed. "Then why?"

"I do not know, Úlla," he said with honest compassion. *But I intend to find out.*

Kalek guided the nieddaš back to the forge with the promise to revisit her later. He left her to the care of the other smiths, intent on confronting the Noaidi. Kalek found the Elder, finishing his evening meal.

"Kalek," the Elder greeted him with passing courtesy.

"Einár, we must speak," Kalek said, dispensing with pleasantries.

The Noaidi tensed momentarily, then inclined his head. "Then let us take a walk outside. I have a feeling the fresh air will do us both good."

The Elder stood, accepting the service of a boaris to take his bowl. Kalek stood impassive as the Noaidi walked ahead. All the while, he wanted to hurl accusations at this man who had kept from him the knowledge that Dárja lived. His daughter lived.

Well into the quaking forest, they finally stopped. Kalek's world wavered between abjection and wild anger. His voice, however, was icy and controlled. "Why did you not tell me?"

The Elder met his gaze unflinchingly. "At first, you were not told because I was not sure. Later, we withheld the news because we feared your reaction." The ancient leader sighed with resignation.

Kalek turned away, outrage burning within him. "My reaction is because I have learned from others and not from you of Dárja's song."

"It is regrettable the news came to light," the Noaidi said with a note of apology.

"Would I have ever learned this from you?" Kalek asked pointedly, not wanting to let go of his anger.

Einár smoothed his sleeve, snagged by a tall shrub. "That is not relevant. You know. The question is what you will do."

Kalek threw up his hands. "Find her, of course."

"And if she doesn't want to be found?" Einár arched his brows.

Kalek shook his head, denying the possibility. "There is no reason for her to stay away and every reason for her to return."

"Perhaps," the Elder allowed. "Why then does she not return?"

"I don't know," Kalek shouted, then added in a lower, but no less desperate manner, "You have heard her song. What is in it? What does it say?"

"Her song has changed in timbre. Gone is her fire and injustice. It is more the voice of her childhood. Wistful and determined," Einár said. "It gives no clear picture."

"Or it does and you will not tell me," Kalek accused.

The Elder's expression darkened. "What would be the purpose of the deceit?"

Kalek's inherent righteousness compelled him to risk angering the Noaidi, the Elders, even the gods. "For the same reason you did not tell me in the first place." He took a sobering breath. "Because you know I will go find her."

"Find her? How will you do that?" the Elder asked, sounding at once curious and skeptical.

"I did it once," Kalek said. "I will do it again."

～

For days after his encounter with the Noaidi, Kalek had done nothing except listen to the Song of All. He became like the old ones, shunning others, forgetting to eat, just waiting and listening. Ávrá had tried to persuade him to continue with his students. He had steadfastly refused, growing angry that she should even suggest he might divide his efforts when Dárja was alive somewhere in the Outside.

When his best efforts had gone unrewarded, doubt had crept in.

"You are where I left you this morning," Ávrá said, entering the apothecary with a tray of food in her hands. She placed the tray on the table, then crossed her arms in front of her. "It is nightfall now."

Kalek regarded the food with no appetite. *How can I eat when she is out there?*

"Hmm?"

Kalek realized Ávrá had asked him a question. "What?"

"I asked how long do you plan to go on like this?" she repeated.

He turned away from her. "As long as it takes."

"What if she does not want to be found?"

Kalek jumped to his feet, knocking over his stool, bumping the table hard enough to spill the contents of the tray.

"Why do you all keep saying this?" he shouted.

Ávrá wordlessly bent to pick up the bowl from the floor. Kalek had noted her stunned expression. Even so, his frustration clamored to be let free, to rampage across the room and out through the corridors.

"She would not do that to me! Not of her own will! She must be in danger or captured."

His sudden rage spent, Kalek righted the stool to sit back down. "I will find her." He closed his eyes and began to follow the melodies of the Song of All, aware that he had hurt Ávrá. He knew he risked her loyalty and her love. If he found Dárja, it would be worth it.

As if reading his mind, Ávrá said, "I know your bond to Dárja is strong." She halted. "You consider her your mánná. I have had my mánná, as have you. To be a guide mother is a wonderful blessing. Dárja is not your mánná. She was Irjan's."

Kalek shook his head. "You are Jápmemeahttun. You only see with those eyes."

"As are you," she said, with no sign of bitterness.

Behind him, the door closed. Kalek opened his eyes. The pottage and bread he had scattered lay upon the floor. His remorse welled in his chest. He had been unkind to Ávrá. She had tried to counsel, to guide. But she was wrong. Perhaps his body was Jápmemeahttun. His soul was not. He had been too much affected by Irjan, by Marnej, and most of all by Dárja.

He understood now Irjan's need to sacrifice all for the sake of a child. Dárja was no longer a mánná. She had fought in battle. She had killed men in defense. Those skills and her strength did not change Kalek's need to find her and protect her. He closed his eyes again, bringing her face into his mind's eye: her short cropped dark hair, the freckle upon her cheek, her reckless energy. He sank into the Song of All and followed the tendrils of voices that swirled around him, searching for one who held his heart unconditionally—his daughter.

CHAPTER THIRTY-EIGHT

MARNEJ LOOKED UP AT the new moon. He and Lávrrahaš had left behind Karvaluz, following the festival of Pasatu. The tavern man had traded his recent profits for two ekveduz. The slender, spirited horses were bred for fast travel. They were the horses of messengers. This time, they carried more than important news and documents. They carried Marnej's nascent hopes for what he might find in the north. They also represented Lávrrahaš's sacrifice. More than once, Marnej had caught his kinsman looking south to what he'd left behind.

Marnej had offered his thanks, aware it was meager reward. Lávrrahaš had shrugged it off with a good-natured joke. "Why should Aage have all the pleasure of your road company?" At the mention of the tinker's name, Marnej had felt a profound disappointment in the man's absence. He had not returned before the festival's end. Lávrrahaš, true to his word, had taken on the burden of this journey to the Elstora Crossing. He'd made it clear to Marnej he would guide him through the crossing and no farther. Marnej couldn't fault the man, for he had been generous in all ways.

Envisioning their future parting, the finality of it loomed large. Theirs would be akin to a farewell to family before a battle. Chances were, Marnej would never return once he made it back home to the north. *Back home*. He'd felt at home in Karvaluz and it was the furthest he'd ever been from the place of his birth. However, there was a part of him that yearned to hear his tongue spoken widely, eat the simple but rich food of his memory, and listen to the stories he knew by heart—of the bear with the broken claw or the owl who saved the first Olmmoš from the wolves. He was happy to know some of the tales of the south, and hoped they might be of interest to the Immortals. It was also possible that they were so content with the Song of All, they needed nothing new to contemplate. In all the millennia, they had not ventured beyond the Song's limit. It was the Olmmoš who had been restless and dissatisfied.

"If this weather holds, we shall make the crossing tomorrow," Lávrrahaš said.

Shaken, Marnej spoke from his heart. "So soon?"

"You look as if you expect me to toss you from the cliffs and not lead you across to the other side," Lávrrahaš said with a grin. The man's weathered face had taken on a deeper hue in the daily presence of the strong sun. Etched lines crinkled in the corners of his eyes. In that moment, Marnej knew it was not enough to hope he would once again see his kinsman. He wanted the comfort of this friendship to continue. He'd had so few friends in his life. None among the Piijkij. Kalek among the Immortals. His bond with Dárja had gone beyond friendship, although, at its core, there had been a companionship of equals.

"What of your family? Don't you miss them?" Marnej asked, measuring his hopes against an outcome where he'd soon leave behind a true friend.

"I have my memories of them to keep me company," Lávrrahaš said, slowing his horse in the rising heat of the day.

Marnej matched his pace. "My memories hold more pain than joy."

Lávrrahaš sniffed. "Were it any other, I would say you are too young to know such hardship. But you have walked a path few will travel."

"Aren't you curious to know what has become of your brothers and sisters? Your mother?" Marnej pressed.

As they began to climb the subtle slope out of the sparse cover of trees, Lávrrahaš said, "I have held only the best for them in my heart."

The lull in their conversation stretched out. The horses' shod hooves clattered against the rocky path, adding emphasis to Marnej's despondent conclusions. Tomorrow he would once again be alone. As he had been as a boy. As he had been when Dárja deserted him in the Great Valley. He was increasingly aware of a feeling of trepidation that hadn't existed when he'd left the northern shore to cross unknown waters. Then, he'd been wantonly reckless with his life, caring for little else than to escape his guilt and the Song of All. Now he worried less for his safety and more that another loss might prove too much for him.

While slow to admit it, Marnej understood Lávrrahaš was more than a friend. The man's guidance and his genuine care for Marnej's happiness and welfare made him more like the father Marnej had wished for. He didn't want to let this connection go. Briefly, he considered turning around and returning to Karvaluz. *With Aage and Lávrrahaš I'd have a family of sorts. I could be happy there.* But his sense of duty to the Immortals was bigger than his desire for happiness. Perhaps one day he'd return south again to the tavern where Lávrrahaš would greet him like a long-lost son come home.

"I have been giving your questions more thought," Lávrrahaš said.

Marnej looked to his friend. He couldn't trust his voice to respond.

Lávrrahaš kept his focus ahead. His energy suggested that he looked to the past. The light breeze from the east picked up, catching the man's pale hair.

He brushed the hair from his face. "My brothers and sisters must have many children by now. My mother may not be in this world." He turned to face Marnej. "There are moments when I fear my family holds my memory with bitterness. It is also possible I am kindred to the dead. Buried and forgotten."

"The dead are not forgotten," Marnej said, thinking of Irjan, Kálle, and Úlla. "They live in our bones until we join them."

Lávrrahaš shrugged. "Perhaps."

"Come with me," Marnej said, his impulse quicker than his reason.

The man shook his head. "I have built a life for myself in Karvaluz."

"You have a tavern and people who come to drink and eat at your table. It's not a family," Marnej said.

Lávrrahaš's stern expression met the outburst.

"I'm sorry," Marnej apologized.

"Not untrue, if roughly put." Lávrrahaš's voice sounded far-off, thoughtful.

Marnej hazarded a glance in his direction. "You have a family. I don't. There's no one in this world to call me kin."

"What of your Immortals?" the man asked. "Are they not your kin?"

Marnej shook his head. "They are neither mother nor father to me, nor brothers nor sisters."

"And yet you journey to return to them," Lávrrahaš said, not unkindly.

Marnej looked to the north where billowing white clouds dotted the stark blue sky. "After you, they are all I have left in this world."

~

As Lávrrahaš had predicted, the pair of them reached the Elstora Crossing the following day. Marnej dismounted from his horse and stretched. He became aware of a low moan, like a dying man upon the battlefield.

"What is that sound?" he asked.

"Josu's lament," Lávrrahaš said, sliding out of his saddle. "The goddess of the land cries because her heart has been broken in two."

Marnej walked to the edge of the cliff. Careful to stand back from the lip, he looked down the sheer white walls of the deep canyon. At the bottom was a thin strip of green water. Dizziness overtook him. Feeling his stomach lurch, Marnej stepped back. He returned to Lávrrahaš, who was removing the saddle from his horse.

"The rope bridge will not allow for the horses to cross," he said.

Marnej frowned. "You'll need the saddle to return to Karvaluz."

Lávrrahaš looked in the direction they'd come. "Perhaps one day. But not today."

Stunned, Marnej gaped at his friend, unwilling to believe what he'd heard.

"Remove the saddle," Lávrrahaš said, with a nod of his head to Marnej's horse. "We will let these beasts roam to find their way." The man rubbed the delicate, sleek neck of his horse. "Why do you stare at me like an owl upon a branch?"

"You are coming with me?" Marnej said, his statement more a question.

Lávrrahaš gave him a lopsided grin. "Did you not ask me to do so?"

"Yes, but," Marnej stuttered. "You said you had made your life in Karvaluz."

"And you pointed out it did not compare with family."

Marnej balked at the memory of his rash argument.

"Do not look as if a taste of truth is too much for me to swallow," Lávrrahaš teased. "The life I built for myself in the south is made of stone and wood. The life I had in the north is made of blood and bone."

~

Dárja stood before the Olmmoš outpost on the western border with the Pohjola. From the maps she'd taken from the other garrison, she knew it to be called Skaina. While the Piijkij had slept she had pored over the parchments and scrolls. For too long, she'd let Válde set their course, following like a good human soldier. At first, the maps had been so foreign to her she couldn't make sense of them. For the Jápmemeahttun, the Song of All guided them. They could listen within its sonorous choruses to find what they needed. The Olmmoš had no part in the Song. They'd flattened the splendor of the gods into inked lines and shapes. Despite her disdain for this shallow understanding, she traveled in their world and had to navigate by their means.

When Dárja had brought word back to the trapper's hut of the scouting soldiers, she'd not intended to travel to Skaina. She'd planned to do as Feles had suggested, scatter and return in a few days' time. But the farther she'd ridden from the hut, the more irritated she'd become by her complacency. She'd let her failure in Mehjala recede in memory. She'd brought back maps and parchments. She'd killed the Olmmoš commander. A worthy outcome in her mind, if not in Válde's. Still, she had not proven she could infiltrate the Olmmoš outposts undetected and unassisted. Nor was she confident she could do this.

Dárja had followed the western trade route north, keeping to the eastern forests. The journey there had taken more than the three days Feles had allotted for the safe return to the trapper's hut. Each day Dárja rode, she grew more determined this was the right course of action. She would use the power of the Song to walk through the middle of the unsuspecting outpost, gather what knowledge she could, without killing the commander, and leave with no help from Válde, no need of a soldier's disguise.

Standing in the forest's shadows, Dárja watched the ant-like meanderings of the Olmmoš soldiers. They looked to be a ragged lot as they kicked up dust along the cart path that led through the gate. Peaking over the sharp-pointed palisades was what

Válde had called a defense tower. In this case, it wasn't much of a tower. The trees which encircled her were taller.

Dárja inhaled, then exhaled, knowing she gained nothing by waiting. She closed her eyes, resolute in her heart the Song of All awaited her. She gave each word of her song the power of conviction. Again and again, she chanted her refrain, until the choruses of everything around swept her up. For one divine moment, she floated, carried by the pleasure of belonging, aware that this wasn't her purpose. She didn't belong. This truth brought a sharper note to her song.

> *I am daughter of the gods.*
> *I am sister among the Jápmemeahttun.*
> *I started my life at my Origin with sadness and joy as my companions.*
> *I have braved dangers and met enemies and can see the truth of friendship.*
> *I go into the world to meet my destiny, knowing that the stars watch*
>   *over me.*

She was no sister to the nieddaš nor would she return to her Origin. She opened her eyes to the destiny before her. An Olmmoš fortification. She stepped out of the shadows. The thrum of the earth beneath her feet sang of the slow turn of time and the deep layers of rock below. She called upon this strength. Behind her, she felt the pride of the pine trees, reaching for the sun. Ahead of her was the symbol of Olmmoš power.

By the time she reached the gate sentry, she felt as if bees had made a hive in her breast. She stood before the soldier, noticing the patchiness of his beard, the broken curve of his wide nose, and the dullness of his brown eyes. That this creature should lay claim to power in the world the Jápmemeahttun had nurtured made her want to scream at the injustice.

Dárja walked past him and through the gates unseen. She wrinkled her nose at the smell of unwashed bodies, horse dung, and Olmmoš piss. *No animal would live like this.* Emboldened by the power of the Song running through her, she crossed the ground toward the defense tower. She'd find the commander, take what she could, and leave him alive, none the wiser.

Near the defense tower, raised voices railed against each other. Dárja ran forward, eager to see and hear better. A red-faced man shouted at a puffed-up soldier with a colorful belt at his waist. He reminded Dárja of a bullfinch, preening for a mate. There was clearly no affinity between the two Olmmoš.

"If you take that many of my men, you will leave this garrison vulnerable to attack," the red-faced man protested.

"If I take that many of your men to flush these Piijkij from their hiding place, you'll have no reason to fear attack," the brightly dressed soldier said.

"I am the commander of this garrison," the red-faced man shouted. "I command these men."

"You are a soldier in the Believers' army. You answer to orders. The Vijns has demanded a southward march to corner these traitors. All garrisons will provide the required men." The puffed-up bird of a soldier turned smartly on his heel, leaving the commander muttering ugly curses and shouting orders at his men.

Dárja followed a trail of soldiers out through the gate as if she were one of them. She had what she needed. The commander was alive. And the Song of All pulsed all around her.

~

Dárja left her horse to forage in the birch grove while she approached the trapper's hut on foot. Nearing from the north, she couldn't see how many horses were stabled in the lean-to, nor could she see if they were those of the Piijkij or those of the Olmmoš soldiers. She was fairly certain she'd outpaced the southward march she'd heard mentioned. On the other hand, she didn't want to stumble into an ambush after everything she'd done to make it this far. She heard voices inside the hut. From where she stood, she couldn't clearly make them out. They could be soldiers or they could be the Piijkij. All she knew was they were Olmmoš. Dárja crossed to the corner of the hut, aware the door was open. Pressing her body against the sod and timber, she crept closer to listen.

"Maybe she finally got sick of Herko," she heard Mures say. She almost smiled at the familiarity of the man's heckling tone. She pushed away from the hut wall to turn to the door.

Gáral's acerbic voice stopped her. "Maybe she has finally left."

Dárja pressed herself back against the hut. Her pulse raced and her stomach had turned sour.

"She would not desert us of her own accord," Edo said, primly.

"What did you expect. She's a Jápmea," Herko said. "They always disappear, then stab you in the back when you're not looking."

Dárja waited for Válde to speak up as he'd done in the past. He'd brought her to the Piijkij. He'd argued with her to stay. The moments passed, each a lifetime filled with fragile hope. But he said nothing.

In an instant, she was running as fast as her aching legs could take her away from the hut, away from the ugliness of that name.

CHAPTER THIRTY-NINE

"SHE IS NOT COMING back," Gáral said. The man's matter-of-fact quality belied the censure Válde knew to underscore the comment.

Dárja had been gone long enough for the new moon to pass. He could no more appeal for delay. Even so, he held out hope she would return. In his mind's eye, he saw her appearing before him, her expression guarded and determined. That was how he thought of her. But there had been instances, quiet and exposed, which suggested a connection beyond a shared enemy. Perhaps he had dreamed it. Perhaps he had wished it to be true. He had been the one to make her see what was possible. Together they could defeat the High Priest. They could avenge those they each called kith and kin.

Through setbacks and challenges, he had held onto this idea, that with Dárja's skills as a Jápmea, he and the others might bring asunder the man who had rendered the Brethren's oath and sacrifice meaningless. The fact that she had not returned, either by choice or circumstance, altered neither the goal nor his commitment to it. Without Dárja, they stood less of a chance of success. Nevertheless, the Brethren of Hunters, the last of the Piijkij, would honor their Avr and take vengeance upon the truly faithless.

"We will not wait to act," Válde said to Gáral. The man gave him a questioning look. "Our skills are enough," he added, trying for a note of confidence. "Let us leave no sign here for others to follow."

"When the trapper returns, he will be more than a little surprised to find his stable made larger and his shelter with two additional bunks," Gáral said dryly.

"He may wonder at this boon," Válde allowed. "And perhaps he will talk of it to others over a cup of juhka at a travelers' hut. By then, our plan will have been put into action and either have succeeded or failed."

Either way, our lives will be forever changed, Válde thought.

He watched the others gather their supplies. His brooding nature led him to question whether this was necessary. Then again, perhaps there was a future for which they should plan. He, himself, needed only his blades.

When the flurry of activity subsided, Válde stepped forward. The onset of drizzle had acted like a burr in his breeches. His temper flared into irritation, but he refrained from letting it come to the fore. His men required a leader to inspire them.

"For the present," Válde said, raising his voice, "we should split into pairs to attract less notice as we ride. The muddy track will work to our advantage. We should establish a meeting point known to us all where we can regroup and finalize our attack."

"The Fortress of the Brethren," Edo said.

The suggestion hung in the air, too sacred to refute and too daunting to accept.

"I have no wish to see what has become of our legacy," Feles said with an intensity outside his stoic nature.

Herko spat upon the ground. "What good is it to smell the piss and shit of Believers in all our sacred corners?"

"Animals," Mures said with disgust.

"I do not oppose regaining claim to what is rightfully ours," Válde said, heartened by what he envisioned. "We are the Brethren of Hunters. Our history is founded in the darkest time of Olmmoš need. The people we have honored, the people we have served, do not know there is a greater evil than the Jápmea. They cannot see that a desire for unbridled power grows in their midst. The Piijkij are the only ones left to champion the will of all over the will of one."

"Fine words," Gáral said, his allegiance articulated in such a way to suggest a challenge.

The sky broke open with a loud crack of thunder. Válde looked up at the dark, heavy clouds in exasperation. Then the rain began to sheet down upon them. Válde ran to the denser forest to the east. He looked to see who followed as if this accounting gave him the investiture. The others had taken cover in the southern copse of pine, larch, and birch.

The tall stand of pines above Válde sagged under the weight of the cascading water. From nearby, he heard his men, making themselves comfortable as they groused about more setbacks. Gáral spoke up, bringing an end to the debate of the pairings. "Mures, you and Feles ride together. I will ride with Herko. I am used to his ill temper and complaints. Edo you will go with Válde." The man's directness drove away the last illusions that Dárja would return to accompany them, to act her part in their plan.

"I don't know about putting our pious Edo with our honorable leader," Herko objected. "They might get caught up on their principles."

The comment received a weak laugh from Mures.

"And if we were to leave you to your ways, we would find you taking to the travelers' huts like a pig to the trough," Feles said.

"I can wait for rest and reward until after we carve up that glorified village proselyte," Herko growled in satisfaction.

"It would have been easier with Dárja," Edo pointed out with a wistfulness Válde shared.

"You speak as if we were not the ones who put fear into the heart of that sniveling weasel who claims power," Gáral said, each one of his words cut spare by indignation. "The Brethren of Hunters led the Olmmoš soldiers to their victory over the Jápmea. Our honor was defiled by the Believers' basest betrayal."

"We do not need a history lesson," Feles said.

"And we do not need a Jápmea to act for us. We can act for ourselves and bring glory back to the title of Piijkij." Gáral's ardor continued untempered by Feles's usual dispassion.

"Look at Edo," Mures said with a note of merriment in his voice. "He's red with consternation. Or is it something else?" There was a brief pause before a bark of true laughter cut through the drowning rain. "I think our pious Edo is besotted by the unlikely charms of our healer-witch—isn't that what you called her, Herko?'

"She healed you, Herko. And you, Gáral. And Válde, as well. Yet you mock and chide her. I wonder who among us would go to the Jápmea to request an alliance?" Edo asked, his judgment evident to all listening.

"A traitor," Gáral said definitively.

~

Pissing drizzle soaked Niilán through as he rode at the head of his retinue of four soldiers. His sodden cloak dragged him down. His thoughts were dark and consumed by remorse. He had let an innocent man and his family suffer for his failings in dealing with the Piijkij. There was no excuse he could hold up. There was no travelers' hut where he could escape to find commiseration and solace. Who among those at that hearth had been put under the orders of the High Priest to bring an end to the Brethren of Hunters? He thought back to his encounter with Válde, looking for a different outcome, finding none. He could not condemn his former commander to death. As a result, he could not fulfill the Vijns's orders.

Niilán marched south, not so much a part of the campaign to flush from cover the Piijkij, rather as a man who had outrun his cursed fate for as long as he could with the result others had suffered for him. His wife. His children. The farmer and his family. Besides, he doubted the campaign would be effective, other than to turn neighbor upon neighbor and friend against friend. In the end, the Piijkij would slip through the advancing line. They would continue to plague the north or travel south, ahead of the converging soldiers, acting with impunity.

He wanted no part in the cruelty or the marching charade that would only come to an end when the soldiers reached the southern seas. What he did want was to save his men from the retribution of his failings. He cared what happened to Osku, Matti, Jonsá, and Joret. Two of them had served with him in the battle. The other two had joined their unit as they returned from the Great Valley.

He had sent Osku back to the Stronghold with the two slain Piijkij, hoping it would give the man the tribute he needed to protect himself. Then he had ordered Matti to travel west and south with his men in search of the Piijkij. Perhaps the giant of a soldier had already returned to the Stronghold. To what fate, he could only imagine. And five days ago, Niilán had given Jonsá and Joret the option of joining another regiment for the southern march. They had chosen to ride with the soldiers. He could not fault them. They were safer there than with him.

❧

Niilán sat upon his horse before the gates of the Stronghold of the Believers. The rain had not let up during his ride south. He was wet to the bone and no closer to a plan than when he had left the farmer and his wife to what he hoped was a quiet life without further persecution. The carved gates above him were designed to honor the gods and instill awe in all true Believers. He felt no awe, only dread. Once he rode through them, he resigned himself to whatever fate the Vijns had planned for him. With the hope that he could keep safe Osku and the others. He did not know how he would accomplish this. He only knew he had to try.

Niilán urged his horse forward, but the animal, like himself, seemed wary of what lay beyond the soaring gates. With a combination of whispered praise and gentle nudges, he coaxed the horse ahead only to be stopped by the guards on either side of the gate.

"Niilán, commander of the Vijns's personal regiment," he called out clearly, feeling resentment toward the dubious title.

The two men gave each other cautious glances before nodding and stepping out of his way. Beyond the palisades, few went about in the rain. Those who did, did so with a hurried step as if they could somehow avoid getting wet. Niilán felt like a toad with his belly against the mudbank. His one hope for himself was to have time before the fire before facing the Vijns. If he had to leave this world, then he would prefer to do so with dry breeches and boots.

At the stables, he slipped off his horse with a squelching plop. Fresh mud spattered up his legs to cover the old mud already coating him. He led the animal into the dank interior. A pungent scent of manure welcomed him, followed by a head popping out from the hayloft above.

"Put your horse to the end and take your saddle off. Leave the bit and reins," the man instructed. Then as an afterthought, he asked, "What regiment?"

"The Vijns's personal," Niilán answered as he walked under the hayloft.

"There's food in the trough," the hidden figure continued. "Go sparing. We've not brought in a spring harvest of fresh fodder."

Niilán nodded, though the man above could not see him. At the end of the line of horses, he tethered his beast. He removed his saddle and supplies. Finally, he placed food in front of the animal, who took to it with the gusto of the trail-weary.

"Enjoy, my friend," he whispered into the horse's ear. *Let us hope my homecoming is so welcoming.*

Niilán picked up his gear. He rested his saddle upon his hip. With measured steps, he walked back under the stableman. He called up to the hayloft, "Where is the quarterman?"

The man's head poked out over the straw forage. "Staying long, then?"

"Who can say," Niilán said with a shrug.

～

With his back to the fire, Niilán watched the other soldiers move about. He had reasoned that if he stayed in the dining hall, he would eventually see a face he knew and would perhaps gain information before he decided how best to proceed. He had been careful to step aside when needed and come back to his spot when it was open once again.

It was midday on his fourth day back when Niilán saw Osku enter the hall. If he had not known the man well, he would not have recognized him. Osku's normally meaty face was now almost skeletal. His nose stood out like a raven's beak, ready to peck at anything of interest. Unable to gain the man's attention from where he sat, Niilán stood and walked toward his old comrade.

"My apologies, friend," he said, purposefully bumping into him.

Osku's sharp eyes registered his face. The man grabbed him by the elbow. He led him to a quiet corner, away from the fire and the newly arrived sentries who sloughed off sodden layers to slump down on stools and call for something to eat.

"When did you arrive?" he asked, his voice a rasping whisper.

"Three days ago," Niilán said. "I wanted to learn as much as I could before I presented myself."

"Don't," Osku warned. "Leave if you can and never come back."

Niilán saw fear and wariness in Osku's face. "What has happened?"

"He took the whip to Matti," he said, his eyes darting around the room. "I was lucky. I brought back those two Piijkij. The High Priest was only just mollified."

346

Niilán was about to say something. Osku put a finger to his lips. He came closer, tipping his head toward Niilán while his eyes roved about the dining hall. "The Vijns's spy is everywhere," he whispered. "Some of the men say you can't piss without the High Priest knowing how much."

"But you and Matti," Niilán began to object.

Osku shook his head. "You saved us once, we cannot expect more. You are better served taking care of yourself."

Beside him, Osku tensed. Niilán cast a glance about the dining hall. *Áigin!* The Vijns's spy wove his way through those gathered like a snake in the grass. He recalled how the man had come upon him in the night to tempt him with this blighted bargain. His stealth and soft tenor had conveyed none of the peril to come. Although, if Niilán was honest with himself, he had known from that moment there would be no escape for him. He had been cornered and had trembled like a mouse.

The pair stood transfixed as they watched Áigin leave the hall to enter the kitchens.

"Who else knows you are here?" Osku asked.

"Only you," Niilán said.

"Good. Take your horse. Ride out of here. Hide. Before it's too late." Osku looked about the dining hall as if he expected a trap to be sprung at any moment. "I shouldn't be seen with you. I can't risk it. Nor should you." The man grimaced by way of an apology, then slipped away like an eel across a riverbed.

CHAPTER FORTY

D ÁRJA HAD A VAGUE sense of how far she'd need to travel to reach the Stronghold of the Believers. The word *Believers* made her mouth turn thick with disgust. They had nothing but lies and deceit to call their own. She'd committed to memory those Olmmoš documents she'd taken from their garrisons. One foray had been a failure. The other had been a success on her terms. Perhaps in Válde's understanding she'd proven herself as well. She'd made it out without sacrificing an Olmmoš life. They'd never know. They didn't even deserve her loyalty, as misplaced as it had been. She'd known they couldn't be trusted and had let herself believe in Válde's vision. In Edo's idealism. In Feles's stoicism. In Herko's heart.

Herko had no respect for her, even though she'd healed him. Miserable whiner that he'd been. His hatred of her kind would never be changed. Nor would Gáral's. Although Gáral's motives were less clear. There'd always been a tension between him and Válde. Her presence had, no doubt, been part of it. But she had the impression the conflict ran far deeper than her. Gáral had accepted her as a tool and he'd not let her forget it.

Dárja traveled on the border of the western trade route. She knew from conversations among the Piijkij this was the less heavily traveled path. When she'd seen the occasional trader with sparse goods upon their carts, she'd retreated behind the cover of trees. The traders, for their part, had interest only for the cart path. When they'd passed, she'd emerge to continue her solitary trek south. In the absence of Herko's grumbling and Mures's jokes, Dárja felt the silence of the Olmmoš world keenly. It was as if the Piijkij had become a chorus of voices during her time with them. They were each distinct within their greater story. It surprised her to realize she would, in some ways, miss them. Certainly not their use of *healer-witch* or, worse, *Jápmea* to refer to her. But there'd been moments of unlikely camaraderie: Edo helping her gather herbs, Feles lending her his whetstone, and Válde setting aside food for her return.

Dárja pulled herself back from the hazy vision of what might have been to the hard reality that was. She would be on her own among the Olmmoš. A rivgu—an outcast of her kind. She patted her horse's withers, then leaned forward to rest her forehead against the animal's shaggy neck. She smelled the tang of sweat behind the musk. The scent, so different than the binna, had become familiar and welcoming to her. She leaned into the animal, taking what little comfort the connection provided.

"It's just you and me now," she said into the horse's ear.

As if it understood, the beast nodded its head.

Dárja thought of the mount she'd taken north with Marnej. It was a bittersweet memory. The trust between her and Marnej had been fragile and overshadowed by suspicion and resentment. She'd been unable to bring the horse into the Song, though he'd been anxious for her to do so. *He knew nothing about what it means to be Jápmemeahttun*, she thought with regret. *And I knew nothing of him*. She'd fashioned an image of him from what she'd gleaned in overheard conversations and had let fear and jealousy fill in the details. It was true Irjan had shared her life force with Marnej. It was also true it had not been his choice.

Marnej had been more than the source of her pain. He'd helped her make it back to the Pohjola. He'd stood by her side when she'd argued to travel with the life bringers. He'd made her laugh. He'd also driven her mad with frustration. He'd been stubborn and vain and argumentative. He'd betrayed her trust. He was all this, and she'd also been happy. At least for a while. Both he and Irjan had given her that. She'd always have these memories. They weren't much. But if she was very careful, she might be able to make them last for her lifetime.

Dárja felt a wet drop upon her head. She looked up from her inner world to see the sky had clouded over. In the moment it took to realize what was about to come, the sky opened up. Dárja urged her horse forward to the closest shelter. She was drenched by the time she dismounted. The horse resisted her lead.

"Come now," she encouraged. "I don't have time to take off the saddle and I don't want to sit on soggy leather for leagues until it dries."

The horse took a step forward, then stopped, turning a dark, questioning eye toward her.

"We'll both feel better if we aren't soaked to the bone," she reasoned with the animal. It took another step forward. "I'll share my sour apples with you," she added, pulling one from the pouch at her belt.

The horse sniffed the offering, snorting warm breath across Dárja's outstretched palm. The tart apple disappeared with a lick of the animal's tongue. She couldn't help smiling. "You are a smart beast," she praised her mount, leading it deep under the arching branches of the dense pines.

～

Wedged under the spread of wide branches, Dárja sat with her eyes closed, listening to the sound of the pouring rain. It surrounded her, engulfing her in a torrent intent on stripping away her determination. If she listened closely, she could hear the drip, drip, drip of each individual drop that hung ready and waiting, much like herself.

To occupy her restless mind, Dárja tried to imagine herself in the future. What would she look like? Where would she be? Try as she might, she couldn't hold on to any detail. All she could see was the plan Válde had outlined. She saw the Stronghold as it had been when she'd escaped with Marnej: the unyielding door between the gathering hall and the courtyard, the open ground before the palisades and imposing gates, and the endless expanse between the pickets and the forest cover. She saw the Olmmoš High Priest in her mind's eye and Marnej's slack-jawed expression when he understood both the priest and his Brethren leader had betrayed him. Of the two Olmmoš men, only the priest survived. *But not for much longer*.

This thought emboldened her, holding at bay a deeper sadness. Her efforts might prove worthy of a Taistelijan. They wouldn't change the fact she was an outcast. She wondered if there'd come a time when the Song of All would be completely lost to her. Would it happen all at once? Or over time, like a memory fading? Suddenly, the urge to be within the Song was all Dárja could think about. She wanted to hear both the sound of raindrops and their song. She wanted to be awash in joy, not cultivating the Song as a ploy against the Olmmoš. Ignoring the note of caution in a remote part of her mind, Dárja searched within herself for the voices that had always been part of her. The Song of All was like her breath, her heartbeat. She couldn't live without it. She felt her chorus cocooned like a butterfly. It ached to be free. It struggled to open its wings. Then, in a flash, it flew out of her, powerful and resplendent.

I am daughter of the gods.
I am sister among the Jápmemeahttun.
I started my life at my Origin, with sadness and joy as my companions.
I have braved dangers and met enemies and can see the truth of friendship.
I go into the world to meet my destiny, knowing that I have honored my kin.

Around her, each raindrop had a voice as loud as the tree above and the ground below. Together, they swelled to encompass the moss where her head lay and the mushrooms somewhere close to her, bursting to life. On the verge of the growing chorus, the tentative refrain of her horse came through as heartbreaking as it was the first time she'd heard the Song of Horses.

We ran with the sun.
We ran with the stars.
Wind rushed.
Grasses bent.
Snow fell.

We are now tied.
We are now bound.
Back swayed.
Flesh cut.
Our path is not our own.

Dárja felt the prick of tears. She opened her eyes to see her stalwart horse, dripping water from its shaggy coat and tawny mane. She was no better than the Olmmoš for using this animal without giving it the gratitude it deserved. Dárja scrambled to her feet, breaking through the sodden branches of the tree above her, ignoring the soaking she received. She brushed the forelock from the horse's eye. The coarse hair ran with water. The animal looked at her with a yearning she understood.

I was once free.
I ran with the herd.
I was once free.
I ran with the herd.

Dárja felt the horse's heart beating in time as it galloped among its kin across great expanses.

She too had felt this as she'd ridden down the valley slopes to defeat the Olmmoš, one warrior among all the Taistelijan. She could still defeat them. She would. For herself. For Marnej. For the horses who once ran free.

Be free with me, she sang to the horse. *I will be your herd.*

Like a bolt of lightning, the horse's song joined with hers. Dárja didn't know where her song began and the horse's ended. She took hold of the reins, leading the animal from the cover. The horse followed. They were both in the Song of All. She'd done it. She'd brought the horse into the Song with her. Dárja laughed with abandon. The horse nudged her. She pulled a sour apple from her pouch.

"Have as many as you want!" she said, wanting to stay like this forever. Dárja rose up into the saddle, ignoring the squelch of wet leather. Her delight turned cold with dismay when she heard a recognizable refrain. It was at once everything she'd wanted and feared to hear:

I am the seeker
Who walks the path of warrior and healer.
I balance life and death.
I act with loyalty born of love.

⁓

Marnej and Lávrrahaš had walked long enough that, at present, the journey across the southern sea seemed the better option. For endless leagues, Marnej had quieted his anxious thoughts by observing the changes in the light. How the sun rose behind them pale pink and blushing on the eastern grassland. How at midday, the rays were like sharp knives, cutting through the wispy clouds. Ultimately, it was the sun's slow descent in the west that taxed the edges of his patience. Although Marnej knew they drew closer to the Pohjola with each step, he couldn't calculate how far they had to travel.

For his part, Lávrrahaš had been encouraging. "We have farther to go, but today's journey has been a hale effort."

Gone were the mild days of swishing through green grasses. Now, they climbed into the mountains where the tops of looming peaks lay hidden in clouds, presaging an ever-present rain. The easy conversation and shared stories accompanying the journey, thus far, fell away as each breath became more precious and hard earned. Lávrrahaš continued to lead. His steps were even and plodding. Marnej tried to match the beats, as much to occupy his mind as to pace himself. The slipping rocks and unstable ledges brought him back time and again to his current circumstances.

Tripping over his feet, Marnej wheezed, "Can't we stop to catch our breath?"

Ahead, he heard Lávrrahaš grunt which he took to mean "no." Marnej resigned his protesting body to keep moving, then his guide unexpectedly stopped. Lávrrahaš turned and slumped down to sit.

"It is no easier returning than it was departing," the man said. He wiped his brow. The pale hair on his forearm lay slicked with sweat. Freckles stood out against his weathered features and patches of dried skin flaked, revealing tender pink skin beneath. Marnej thankfully collapsed upon the rocky path. The sharp edges of the scree were a minor inconvenience compared to his greater relief. When the throbbing of his temples eased, Marnej realized the deeper meaning of his friend's seemingly casual statement.

"Do you fear your return?" he asked, his culpability making him flush.

Lávrrahaš stared back over the plain they'd crossed. "I wonder about the sadness I must confront."

Marnej winced, knowing his entreaty had brought his friend to this precipice.

"Do you wish to hold the responsibility of all of us upon your back?" Lávrrahaš asked. A crooked smile transformed his tired countenance into one of knowing kindness.

"I made you return with me," Marnej said.

The man barked out a laugh. "Made? You asked me to return. I am returning for reasons that are my own."

Marnej shaded his eyes. For as far as he could see, there was unbroken flatness, patched in greens and browns with hints of other colors—a flash of yellow or a swath of gray.

"Are we close?" he asked.

"A couple more days to traverse this mountain into the Pohjola. Then only you know how far you must go to reach your Immortals," Lávrrahaš said.

His friend's pronouncement renewed Marnej's worry about what he'd find when he reached the Northland. He'd left Karvaluz confident he was right to return and accept his part in what had come to pass, for better or for worse. Now he wasn't so sure. Would they even allow him within their walls? Or would they post a guard to keep him at bay? What would he say? More importantly, what would Kalek, Einár, and the others say? Then there was the other question Marnej couldn't give voice to: *What if I've traveled all this way for naught?* He shook his head, chiding himself for acting like a rabbit that sees a shadow and imagines an eagle overhead. *When did I become such a coward?* A needless question, he knew, because he could point to the exact moment it had happened. He'd been running the instant he woke upon the snow of the Great Valley to discover he was alive. He'd run for the cover of trees that night. Then he'd run the length of the land from the Song of All.

"It was easy to depart," he said, picking up on Lávrrahaš's earlier statement. "It's much harder to return."

"I suppose our reasons for leaving are not so different," Lávrrahaš said.

Marnej craned his neck to see the man on the path above him. "You left to avoid the war and bloodshed."

"And you left because of what happened after the war and bloodshed."

"It's not the same. You left in search of peace."

"As did you."

Marnej knew Lávrrahaš wished him well, unaware of the full extent of his disgrace. And, as a friend, Lávrrahaš had never pressed for the details of Marnej's actions.

"There's no hiding from dishonor when you see the world around you changed through your deeds," he said.

"Did you set forth with this outcome in your heart?" Lávrrahaš asked.

"No," Marnej said. "But I should've foreseen the outcome."

Lávrrahaš rose to his feet, taking up his satchel. "We cannot always see the ways in which heartfelt intentions come to fruition." He turned to resume the climb ahead of them. "Only the gods can do that."

❧

On their third day upon the jagged mountain, Lávrrahaš led them through a tight opening in the rock. Without his friend's guidance, Marnej would've never found his way. Boulders crowded down on top of the narrow fissure, turning it into a snaking, cavelike passage. Emerging from the shadowed interior, his breath caught, knowing he looked out upon the Pohjola. Recognizable trees dotted the landscape. Through their midst, large swaths of binna ambled. The same reindeer herds Lávrrahaš had once tended—that his father had also tended.

Marnej had been surprised by the yearning to descend the steep slope to the land of his home. His heart also harbored an equal amount of apprehension. He'd been gone long enough for much to have changed. Perhaps the Immortals didn't dwell in the Pohjola.

He'd dismissed his fear, saying aloud, "Where else would they go?"

❧

Marnej gathered what dried wood and grasses he could find. Lávrrahaš took his hatchet to the dead patches of scrub birch. The summer's twilight turned the sky a deep golden hue and fine, sparse clouds glowed red with the sun's just-setting rays. The air, cool and rich with a greenness, chilled the sweat upon Marnej's back.

Between the *thwack* of the hatchet and the snap of brittle branches, Marnej listened to the scurrying field voles and the far-away grunting of the binna. While the familiarity acted like a balm to his spirit, it did little for the ache in his knees and feet. Marnej tugged off his worn boots. They were of Bissmeni styling with low, slouching sides. He had worn a hole in the heel of his right boot. With his knife he cut a piece of leather from the hem of his jerkin. The leather had been softened by wear, but it would at least protect his heel. Unfortunately, he could do little for the blisters that pocked his feet. What was more, even in twilight, the black crescents upon his toenails told him he'd lose those nails somewhere in the coming days.

Marnej left his concerns for tomorrow. Tonight, they'd have a small fire and hot water in which to soak their dried meat. Layering his kindling into a welcoming nest, Marnej struck his fire steel. A bright spark took to the dry grasses. He blew upon the young flame. It flashed to life. Lávrrahaš crouched down beside him, feeding the fire. From his satchel, Marnej took out his waterskin and copper bowl, beaten fine in the manner of southern metalsmiths. He filled the bowl and set it next to the fire and pulled out two strips of kapralu. The dry, spiced goat meat had a sweet, slow burn which he'd grown to appreciate. He'd miss the flavor here in the north where fire berries didn't grow.

Lávrrahaš bit off a piece of meat. "Have you a sense of your people?"

Marnej shook his head. "I haven't tried to find the Song."

"Their joik?" Lávrrahaš asked, blowing across the hot water before taking a sip.

"Yes," Marnej agreed. The description was apt. "It is the joik of all things," he said. "Only they can hear it."

"And you can hear it," his friend surmised.

"Yes," Marnej said, chewing thoughtfully.

"Can you hear it now?" Lávrrahaš asked, his curiosity evident.

"No. I need to . . ." Marnej faltered, unsure of how to explain himself. "I need to . . . prepare." He thought of all the times he'd found himself within the Song of All. Once the dizziness had receded, the feeling of connection to everything around him would come to the fore, and he would feel whole.

"Then why do you sit there eating kapralu when you could be listening to their joik?" Lávrrahaš asked with good humor. "Unless sitting crossed-legged and holding a cup of hot water is how you prepare yourself."

Marnej choked on the water he'd just swallowed. "No. That's not how I prepare myself." He paused, thinking back to when the Avr of the Brethren of Hunters had asked him to use what he'd called Marnej's gift to find the Immortals.

"It's not something the Olmmoš understand," he said finally.

"Then it is good I am Bissmeni in my soul," Lávrrahaš said.

Marnej searched his friend's face for any sign of a jest. He found only patient encouragement.

He put down his food and drink. Doubts swirled in his mind. *What if I can't find the Song? What if they hear my song?* His uncertainty finally gave way to the desire to feel whole—to belong to the All.

"It may not be there," he said, giving voice to his fear.

Lávrrahaš smiled. "You will not know unless you try."

Heartened, Marnej closed his eyes. He took a deep breath, letting it fill him to the fullest. He listened to his heartbeat until he was no longer aware his breath entered and left his body. His heart slowed. For an instant, it stopped. When it started again, the steady beat brought with it the songs of everything around him. The voices joined together. They crushed him with their beauty and truth. His refrain rose up, parting the others with its unrestrained power.

I am the vessel of a father's soul.
I have journeyed into the realm of the dreams of the dark sky,
And traveled back in a blaze of light.
I enter into the world to meet my destiny,
knowing that I have been touched by the gods.
My journey is not complete until all are at peace.

The last line of his song was a revelation. He'd never before heard that part of the refrain. But he knew in his soul it was his truth. Until all are at peace. He let his voice recede into the background to take in the others, the grass, the earth, the wind, the stars in the heavens.

Then he heard a clear and unmistakable voice he'd believed to be lost to him forever.

I am daughter of the gods.
I am sister among the Jápmemeahttun.
I started my life at my Origin, with sadness and joy as my companions.
I have braved dangers and met enemies and can see the truth of
friendship.
I go into the world to meet my destiny, knowing that I have honored
my kin.

The name came to him like bringing forth a part of himself. *Dárja!*

CHAPTER FORTY-ONE

K ALEK CORNERED RAVNA IN the gathering hall. Her dark
eyes refused to meet his. She stepped around him, murmuring an apology.

Kalek blocked her way. "Have you heard her?"

He did not need to clarify who he meant. Ravna knew he
spoke of Dárja. She shrank back as if the gap would save her from
his hectoring.

"I know she is in danger," he pressed, stepping forward to
loom over the nieddaš.

When she stared at her feet without answering, Kalek
begged, "Can you not tell me something?"

Ravna looked up, her shoulders rising to her ears. He cared
little for her distress. He needed to know what was happening to
Dárja. He could not understand why he had not heard her song.
He should have. He loved her most. He was her father.

"Please, Ravna," Kalek entreated.

The nieddaš furtively glanced about the latnja, pausing to see
if any in the gathering hall listened. Under her breath she said,
"Dárja is determined. I do not know how she plans to act, but
she is resolute."

The nieddaš rushed around Kalek's imposing figure. He spun to catch her by the arm. She cowered in his grip. He did not loosen it. "You must tell me what you have seen, Ravna."

"I do not know what you want me to say," she pleaded.

"Tell me where she is. Tell me how I can find her. Surely you have seen something I can use," he said, hearing the desperation in his voice and not caring.

She shook her head, pulling against his hold. "I am sorry, Kalek. I do not know. There is this shadow around her. It moves and obscures. It is not part of her. I also do not know what else it could be."

"Is she held captive? Can you tell?" Kalek asked, the pit in his stomach cold with worry.

"I do not know," Ravna said, her voice trembling.

"That is enough," a deep voice intoned.

Kalek looked up to see the Noaidi, striding toward him with the energy of a warrior. The Elder's glower struck Kalek's conscience as hard as any physical blow.

"Step aside, Ravna," the Noaidi said.

"Why do you stand opposed to my search for Dárja? You must know she is in danger," Kalek said. His imploring swelled into defiance. "I will find her. You cannot stop me."

"Listen to me, Kalek," the Elder cut him off. "You are our best healer. If you are lost, what is to become of the rest of us who depend on your care?"

Kalek shook his head. "There are others here who can provide care and comfort."

"You would be taking all of Okta's knowledge with you," the Elder said, his voice rising, causing some in the gathering hall to scurry away and others to watch with interest.

Kalek stopped at the mention of his mentor's name. In his mind, he saw Okta, hunched under the weight of age and conscience, as they had taken their last walk through the snow-dusted forest. He had kept from Kalek the knowledge that he approached his end. Okta had kept much from him for unknown reasons. "No, Einár. I am due the chance to act for myself."

"You acted for yourself when you brought Irjan here instead of killing him," the Elder said.

Ravna dropped back, her arms wrapped about her middle.

"After what has happened, how can you say this?" Kalek demanded, spiraling through each loss. Aillun. Irjan. Okta. Dárja. If he could bring them all back, he would. But Dárja represented his only chance against the gods.

"It is because of what has happened I can say this," the Elder said.

The Noaidi's candor served to fuel Kalek's determination. "There is nothing you can say to dissuade me."

"It is a fool's errand."

"This is no fool's errand, Einár. This is Dárja we speak of. She has given more—sacrificed more—than many within these walls."

The Noaidi looked away. "You know my intent, however ill-formed my words might have been."

The struggle between Kalek and Einár continued into their silence. Ravna stepped forward. She placed a hand on Kalek's arm. The spell broken, he turned his gaze to her. He saw she too struggled.

"I will do what I can," she said.

Kalek's anger dissolved, allowing his doubt to come to the fore. *How will I find her? How will I save her?* He nodded numbly, unable to trust his voice.

Einár guided Ravna away, saying, "We are expected by the other Elders."

Kalek was struck by Einár's solicitude toward Ravna. It was more than the care of a Noaidi for one of his people. It was like the courtesy extended to an equal. He stared at their retreating figures, unsure of this insight and incapable of understanding what it might mean.

Before Kalek could settle his thoughts, he saw Ávrá approaching. She strode toward him with purpose. Her serious expression registered too late for Kalek to turn away without giving offense. He stood his ground, glancing about the gathering hall to see who watched. Mercifully, the latnja was nearly empty.

"Ávrá." He greeted her, then got no farther. He was about to say, "I know you have come to make me change my mind." It was the truth, petty and petulant. He just wanted to forestall another argument. He wanted her support. The kind he had granted to Irjan and Okta. Questioning, yes. But faithful to the end. Staring into Ávrá's knowing eyes, his heart silently implored, *Am I not deserving of support?*

"I have come from the kitchens," she said. "Birtá has cut herself."

"Again?" Kalek asked, his exasperation bubbling up. "Úlla should not sharpen her knives."

Ávrá raised her eyebrows. "You are needed."

Kalek heard her deeper plea. She too needed him. It should be enough. He closed his eyes, mindful that in some ways it would be easy to remain here with Ávrá, safe and wanted. The problem was he had been safe for too long. Kalek opened his eyes, remembering how he had saved Irjan's life, how blood pulsed through his body, and the power he had felt. Kalek understood now why Irjan had chosen to fight in the battle when he could have stayed out of it. His love for Irjan had not been enough to stop him, just as Ávrá's was not enough to prevent him from venturing Outside to find Dárja.

Ávrá stood in front of him. A look of resignation clouded her eyes. He reached out his hand and caressed her face. She tilted her head into his palm. The warmth of her cheek recalled to him all of their tender embraces and whispered hopes.

"I will see to Birtá's cut," he said, watching Ávrá's eyes flutter open. He traced the line of her cheek to her chin, then turned to go.

Walking through the gathering hall toward the kitchens, Kalek let himself acknowledge he had Ávrá's support, steadfast and resigned. It made him sad to think he was the source of pain in her life. She deserved more than he could give her. *Perhaps when I return it will be different.* He imagined a life with Ávrá and Dárja. He'd had a glimpse of its possibility before Dárja had come up with her plan. He shook his head at the thought. *Rash and ill-conceived.* Nevertheless, how could he fault her for it? She wanted to save the life bringers, like Ávrá wanted to save Úlla from being cast out. If he did return with Dárja, it would be different. But not in the way his heart wanted. There would come a time when the next life bringers would set out to give birth. If he knew anything about Dárja, she would want to protect them as well. He would not try to stop her. This time, he would be by her side.

"Kalek, you must take me with you." Úlla's powerful voice stopped Kalek in his tracks. The nieddaš ran up to him, her face streaked with soot. Her short hair stood wild upon her head.

"Úlla, this is not the best time," he began, then realized what she was saying. "What do you know of Dárja?" Kalek heard the anguish in his question.

"I owe Dárja my life."

Seeing Úlla transformed by raw emotions, Kalek's breath caught. "Why do you speak of this?"

Úlla's expression opened into disbelief. "It is all any can talk about. Your words with the Noaidi may have been private but your voices carried far beyond the gathering hall."

"It is not for you . . ." Kalek started to dissuade the nieddaš.

"I am a rivgu. What does it matter if I stay or go? I am only here by the forbearance of the Elders," she argued.

Kalek shook his head, thinking of Ávrá's sacrifice. "That is not true. You are our Forge Master."

"It means nothing when there is a debt I must pay," Úlla said, her bearing growing more forceful. "My going will allow us to return to the way we were."

"Your place is here, at the helm of the forge. You can honor Dárja by valuing the life she strove to protect."

The force of Kalek's appeal pushed Úlla back on her heels. He reached out to her, fearing she would fall back. His hand wrapped around the ropy muscle of her arm. "Stay and make this a place Dárja will be welcomed. As a rivgu. As one who has given much to our kind."

For an instant, Úlla looked as if she might crumble. Then she stood straight, her head held high. She nodded once, before turning on her heel in the direction of the forge.

～

Ravna sat at the Noaidi's side. She stole glances at the other gathered Elders. They were all so old. Her one thought was *I should not be here*. For all her curiosity, she knew the Elders in the circle stared at her. She should not be there. She could see it in their faces. Lined. Grim. Bearded. She was a nieddaš. She had yet to become a guide mother, let alone give birth and transition to almai.

It was the Noaidi who had insisted that she be included. Ravna had never been inside the Elders' chamber before. She had never needed to consult the Elders. Her life had been simple. Worthy, but simple. She cured the hides of the animals they ate. She dyed the wool and flax that the weavers made into cloth.

Ravna looked up to where she knew the roof to be. In its place were the heavens outside. Not those of Geassemánnu, the time of sun and twilight they were in. Rather, it was the heavens of Darkest Night. Deep. Black. Lit by the stars. The moon waned. Dizziness overtook her. She looked down at her hands clasped in front of her. The heavens above were too much to take in.

Without prelude, the Elders began to chant. Ravna did not know what to do. She sat listening, not daring more than a furtive peek. She had heard this song before in ceremony. She had always found it reassuring.

We are the Elders.
We are chosen to guide.
We listen to the voices of the gods.
We seek to avoid the mistakes of the past.

As the chanting continued, Ravna felt increasingly uncomfortable. She listened to the Elders but there was a sound beyond their chant. It felt dark and unfamiliar. Ravna wondered if this was Dárja entering the Song. The last time she had heard her refrain, it had filled her with fear. *I go into the world to meet my destiny, knowing that I have honored my kin.* Dárja's words had filled her with foreboding. She could not tell this to Kalek. Not with the Noaidi alongside her. She had felt Dárja's despair, along with a moment of joy she could not reconcile.

Ravna sifted through the darkness within the Song of All. It swirled around her, wordless and undefined. The more she tried to grasp the presence the farther it retreated. After a while, she gave up on bringing the unknown song within her and chose to follow it. She became like the eagle flying over the Pohjola, her eyes trained upon the ground, searching. The wide vista changed to deep forests. The tips of her wings feathered over the tops of pine, spruce, and larch. Her keen eyes pierced through the dark forest. There was something down there, moving.

Ravna swooped down to slip through the branches. In the back of her mind, she held onto the hope she would see Dárja. In an instant, the forest opened onto a winding trail of Olmmoš. Some of the men were on tall beasts she had never before seen. Most walked eight abreast down a muddy path. Ravna pulled back immediately, fearing they had seen her. Her wings beat furiously, trying to reach the forest cover. Behind her, she heard a screech of anger. *Fly faster*, she told herself.

Ravna came back to her body, rocking back and forth. She chanted the song of the Elders as if it were her own. Her voice seemed outside herself.

We are the Elders.
We are chosen to guide.
We listen to the voices of the gods.
We seek to avoid the mistakes of the past.
Our undoing walks toward us.

As the Song of All continued in the back of Ravna's thoughts, she became aware of the quiet all around her. She prised open her eyes. Her vision swam. She turned to face the Noaidi, blinking. His mouth hung open as if he gasped for air. A chill ran through Ravna. She looked to the other Elders. In their expressions she saw unmasked fear.

"What has happened?" she asked, afraid to hear the answer.

Her tremulous question opened a floodgate among the Elders.

"How is this possible?"

"What does she mean?"

"Is this some kind of jest?"

The Noaidi held up his hand. "This means what I have long believed. Ravna is the Singer of All Songs." Ignoring the protests among the other Elders, he turned to her. "Can you tell me what you saw?"

〜

Marnej let the Song of All slip from his mind, disappointed he hadn't heard Dárja's chorus. He had tried daily since he'd heard it, always waiting for Lávrrahaš to go to sleep first. The power of the Song of All had grown in strength over the last few days. He was close to the Immortals' sanctuary. His thoughts buzzed with concern for Dárja. Had she managed to return north? If so, he would tell her everything he'd realized on his sojourn. Most of all, he wanted to return them to the way they'd been before they'd set out with the life bringers. He'd lost more than love on the battlefield. He'd lost a part of himself. He'd thought he could find it elsewhere. And, for a time, he had.

The ease of his life in the south had let him believe he'd been accepted. Really, he was just one of many travelers, traversing the Southern Lands. He'd been welcomed, but he'd always be a Northern One. Half-Olmmoš and half-Jápmemeahttun, he'd been too different for the humans and too human for the Immortals. He knew he wouldn't find welcome among the Olmmoš as he truly was. With the Immortals he *had* found a place. It had been hard fought and contentious. He'd gained the trust of a few, found friendship in unlikely ways, and saw that all of it was worth fighting for.

"You are spending more and more time on the other side," Lávrrahaš said.

Startled, Marnej looked up to see his friend's frank appraisal.

"I think our ways will soon part," the man said.

Marnej started to protest. Lávrrahaš put a hand up to stop him. "I cannot go where you are heading," he said, a knowing smile upon his lips. "And you have no desire to go where I am going."

Marnej found himself nodding. His friend had done what he could not, had seen that their time together had ended.

"I cannot take you into the Song of All," he said, downcast by the fact. "I don't know why the Olmmoš do not have a part in the chorus. All I know is the Song keeps the Immortals safe."

"A gift of wise gods," Lávrrahaš said, then looked to the eastern mountains.

Marnej followed his gaze. The treacherous peaks looked unimposing from where they sat.

"The sun rises," Lávrrahaš said, then seemed to consider his next words. He gave Marnej a wide, toothy grin. He rose to his feet.

"Sea Monster, you have helped me return home. I had not thought it possible or needed and find that it is both," he said.

Lávrrahaš held out his palms in the southern tradition, Marnej placed his hands on top.

"May we meet again," Lávrrahaš said.

"May we remain in each other's hearts," Marnej replied in Bissmená.

CHAPTER FORTY-TWO

ARNEJ LOOKED UP AT the beautiful carved wooden spires of the Immortals' sanctuary. The yellow lichen bloom of his recollection had spread like flowers across its dark wood. He touched the splintered and deeply grooved surface. He felt the hum of life within. He recalled the first time he'd seen this structure. It had been a vision and he'd been elated. He'd discovered where the Immortals hid themselves away. No other Piijkij could do what he'd done. He'd believed he'd acted out of loyalty to the Brethren and to the Avr.

When he'd come with Dárja to this exact spot, the one of his vision, he'd been betrayed by his kind. He'd craved his father's love, and he'd hoped he had a place to belong. Marnej had worked to fit in with the Immortals, never letting himself ask aloud, "Where will I go, if they reject me?" This question had been in the back of his mind each day he awoke among the Immortals. After all that had transpired, he wasn't sure they would welcome him back. But he deserved to be heard. He was Jápmemeahttun.

He walked along the low stone wall bordering Okta's herb garden. *Kalek's garden now.* He thought of Kalek inside the apothecary, standing before the scarred and bowed table. Perhaps Dárja worked at his side. The thought of seeing her made his heart race. He jumped the stone wall and ran to the door, then hesitated before lifting up the iron latch.

The smell of herbs, bitter and sweet alike, assailed him. The scents took him back to the moment he'd entered the apothecary, wary and ready for a fight. He came forward, his heart pounding in his ears. Candles burned low in their holders. The apothecary was empty except for shadows. He passed the work table. His gaze rose to the script upon the numerous jars. Dárja's script. It was a sign there'd once been a future for them here.

Disappointment drove Marnej through the inner door, recalling his first steps into what would become his life among the Jápmemeahttun. At that time, he'd been aswirl with arrogance and anguish. Now, he walked the path of honest humility. He knew what he wanted. He knew the perils. He also knew he would not run again.

Standing at the edge of the gathering hall, he regarded the carved trees, supporting the roof above. Though their intricate beauty remained unsurpassed, they no longer towered above him as they did in his memory. Marnej released the breath he'd been holding. He stepped out into the open. The voices in the latnja died away. They were replaced by stultifying quiet. Marnej looked about the gathering hall with eyes of recognition. Familiar faces dotted the communal space. Their startled expressions revealed little about deeper sentiments.

From the direction of the kitchens and the forge beyond, Marnej saw Úlla striding into the latnja. With her hair short and wild about her head, she looked to be haloed by the sun's glow. Seeing her lifted a weight from his spirit. His gratitude drove him to his knees. Úlla ran across the gathering hall. Her powerful arms embraced him, crushing him to her as she pulled him to his feet.

At first, his shame so overpowered him all he could say was her name. Finally, held against her powerful frame, he whispered, "I'm so sorry." Úlla's arms tightened around him further. Marnej struggled to breathe.

"I should've fought my way through every one of those soldiers to reach you," he said, hearing the screams again in his mind.

Gripped by a new surge of fear, Marnej pulled away from Úlla. "The baby?" he asked, preparing himself for the worst.

"She is fine, Marnej," Úlla said, placing her hand on his cheek. "She is with Tuá, her bieba."

Marnej took Úlla into his arms, spinning her around and lifting her off the ground. He heard her full throaty laugh, and realized he'd missed her exacting orders and her begrudging praise.

"Úlla, I've been to the south. There's a place where no life bringer must fear the Outside!" he said in a rush.

Úlla's happy expression transformed to suspicion. "The south? There is nothing but Olmmoš in the south. How can you say the nieddaš have nothing to fear?"

"No, not here," he said, feeling the surge of possibility within him. "Across the southern sea. There are lands where we can go. Where we can be safe, accepted."

Úlla shook her head. "You have lost your wits."

"I have been there," he said, gripping her hands. "There are people who will welcome us. People who are different, beautiful, kind."

She glared at him. "They are Olmmoš."

"No, Úlla. They are Bissmeni, Aeopo, Irkati, and others whose names I don't know!"

"Humans."

"Yes. Humans. I don't know if there is a place without humans. A place like this." Marnej spread his arms wide to encompass the sanctuary. "Even here there are humans."

Úlla looked ready to protest. Marnej cut her off. "And don't say the Song will protect you, because you of all Jápmemeahttun know it can't."

"Will the Song protect us there any better than here?" she demanded.

"There is no Song there. There is no need for it. We'd be safe in the south."

Úlla gaped at him. "No Song. It is silent like the Olmmoš world?"

"Yes. But we'd be safe."

"No. It is no life for a Jápmemeahttun."

"So you would choose death over a life outside the Song of All."

"Yes!"

"You can't . . ." Marnej's response was cut short by Árvá rushing between him and Úlla.

"Kalek has gone!" she gasped, out of breath.

Confused, Marnej looked from Ávrá to Úlla. "Gone where?"

"To find Dárja," Ávrá said, her face pale and drawn.

"Dárja." Marnej breathed in her name, realizing that in his joy at seeing Úlla and his attempts to make her see reason, he'd let Dárja slip from his thoughts.

"She's not here," Úlla said.

All his hopes dashed, Marnej reeled. He barely took in Ávrá's wary regard. He'd wanted Dárja to be here. He'd hoped it might be true. "I must go after him," he said, regaining his resolve.

"I am coming with you," Úlla said.

Both Marnej and Ávrá turned to her in shock.

"I owe Dárja my life," she added. "I am coming with you."

"No, Úlla. You cannot."

"You"—she pointed her finger into Marnej's chest—"cannot tell me what I can do."

"Úlla." Ávrá put a hand on her arm. "You are needed here."

"I am rivgu," Úlla said, her venom turned upon the other nieddaš.

Ávrá's expression darkened. "You are our Forge Master."

Marnej turned Úlla toward him, making her meet his eyes. "You must lead them south. You must convince the Elders. There's a safe place for us."

Úlla's green eyes widened. "I cannot lead our kind south through the Olmmoš. We cannot cross the sea like fish."

Marnej tore at the leather ties of his faded jerkin, struggling to reach inside of it. He pulled out a folded piece of parchment. "Here, take this." He pushed it into Úlla's hands, closing her fingers around it. "It's a land map. A map of the way I returned. If I don't come back. Take our kind east through the mountains and then south to the Elstora Crossing. From there continue south to Karvaluz. They know our kind there. We are the Northern Ones to them."

"We are Jápmemeahttun," Úlla said. "We belong here."

"We deserve to live in peace," Marnej said, his voice an urgent whisper. "You can do this, Úlla. You must do this."

"And you believe the Elders will take me at my word, take you at yours, when they listen to the gods?"

"I hope so," Marnej said. "For all of our sakes."

～

Marnej entered the stables, carrying what supplies he could quickly gather. He didn't know how far ahead Kalek had gotten, but each moment he delayed the distance would grow. The binna snorted, sidestepping his first attempt to place the saddle upon its back. He thought of Okta scolding him for his lack of skill as they'd rode toward his Origin. Marnej hoped what little proficiency he'd garnered had stayed with him.

He shushed and whispered to the reindeer, promising his best and asking for the right to ride. The animal turned an eye to him, then calmed. When he was reasonably sure his entreaty had been accepted, Marnej gently placed the saddle on the binna's back. He tightened the straps, then brought the harness up and over the animal's muzzle. The binna shook its head.

"This is only so I won't fall off," he said to appease the reindeer's pride. "Be gentle with me. I'm only just learning your song."

The beast snuffled, then resumed its patient stance.

"Still talking to yourself, I see," Úlla's voice cut across the stables.

Marnej turned, nearly dropping his supply bag. With her face in the shadows, he couldn't tell her intent. Coming into the light that streamed through the open stable door, he saw her tight smile.

"I find I like my own answers," he said, hoping he'd managed to sound lighthearted.

Her smile broadened into a lopsided grin. "You may be the only one who does."

The sense of deeper meaning to her words put Marnej on guard. He returned to his tasks. "I've seen what's possible."

"And know it all," she said, with a shake of her head.

Gathering up the reins, he turned to face her. "I've learned so much more since then."

Úlla stared at him, then pulled from behind her a sword, unlike any he'd seen before. The detail work of the hilt and pommel looked like woven threads. "It is Kálle's work," she said. "I want you to take it." She held it out to him.

Marnej hesitated, taking in the sword, the gesture, and what it all meant. He accepted the blade with reverence. He marveled at its beauty. Even among the lauded blades of the Piijkij, they'd not had anything to compare with this.

"You can return it to me when you come back," Úlla said, breaking the spell.

Marnej lowered the sword. "I may not return," he interrupted, then added, "You must convince the Elders."

Úlla looked away. "How can I convince them when I am an outcast? I have no standing. I am allowed to stay through pity and charity."

"You once said the forge is the heart of us," he said, stepping closer to her. Marnej cupped her face in his hands. "And you are the heart of the forge."

～

The moment Kalek had heard Dárja's song, nothing and no one could have stopped him. He had finally heard her chorus and knew from it she was in danger. What kind, he did not know. It did not matter. All that mattered was to find her. He'd had a hard day's ride with rain falling upon him the entire time. The binna did not seem to mind the wet conditions and he was resigned to being soaked through. But league upon league, Kalek's tension built. While he trained his eyes on his surroundings, his mind stayed in the Song. He listened for Dárja and in return sent his song out in the hopes it might reach her.

I am the seeker
Who walks the path of warrior and healer.
I balance life and death.
I act with loyalty born of love.

Kalek noted the change in the timbre of his song. Gone was the remorse and the sadness. They had been replaced by fierce and unconditional love. Irjan had made Dárja into an image of himself—a warrior. As her guide mother, he had done his best. It was not what Kalek would have chosen for her. He had tried to keep her safe. He had tried to stop her through reason and anger. He could not change what had happened. He could not change who she had become. He could, however, be with her and let her know she was not alone. *Let her know that whatever has happened means nothing to me compared to the fact she is my daughter.*

Kalek brought himself back from the past. Only the present moment held the promise of hearing her song again. He listened anew, searching deep within the strands of the All for some sign of where he should go. He cast his song into the chorus with the full strength and power of his soul. *Let it be a beacon for her*, he begged the gods.

In a distant part of his thoughts, he recognized a voice he had not heard since the life bringers had journeyed out. He thought of Okta. He thought of Irjan. Then the full intensity of the song hit him.

> *I am the vessel of a father's soul.*
> *I have journeyed into the realm of the dreams of the dark sky,*
> *And traveled back in a blaze of light.*
> *I enter into the world to meet my destiny,*
> *knowing that I have been touched by the gods.*
> *My journey is not complete until all are at peace.*

Kalek whirled around in his saddle, looking for Marnej, even as he thought, *He is dead.* Like his father before him. Emotions fought against reason within Kalek, his anger coming to the fore. *I befriended him when he was not wanted. I stood by his side when no one else did. He should have protected her. He said he would.* Kalek did not know whether he spoke of the father or the son. It did not matter. They had both let Dárja down.

Kalek unsheathed his sword. The weapon felt unwieldy in his hand. He tightened his grip on the hilt, holding the blade out in front of him. Rain dripped from its tip, unscathed by the sharp edge. Before Irjan had come into his life, Kalek had considered becoming a warrior. He had trained with the Taistelijan. Okta had forgiven him his divided loyalties, knowing that he had also manipulated Kalek for his own ends.

Kalek turned his binna in a slow circle. The crush of forest undergrowth grew louder. He faced his mount north to meet what came. Marnej's figure, astride a reindeer, teetered into view. He rode hard and reckless. Kalek held onto his weapon, part of him listening to the Song of All. Listening for Dárja. Marnej skittered to a halt. His expectant expression fell as his gaze shifted from the blade in Kalek's hand to meet the healer's eyes.

"Dárja's in danger," he said. "We must find her."

A fury fueled by fear took hold of Kalek. "You were supposed to protect her. You said you would be with her, that she would not be alone. You are here and she is not."

The blade in Kalek's hand shook but he did not withdraw it. He stared at Marnej's soggy figure above the bedraggled binna. He saw Irjan in the slump of the boy's shoulders. Irjan had looked the same, seated in his cell, after they had failed to rescue Marnej from the Piijkij. It had taken Kalek the better part of the long summer to recover from the wounds he had received defending Irjan.

"Do you mean to use that against me?" Marnej asked.

Kalek sheathed his blade, unable to answer the question.

～

Since their initial encounter, Marnej and Kalek had ridden in silence, keeping within the Song. Their exchanges were limited to spare courtesy. On the first dry morning of their trek, Kalek wordlessly held out a cup of tea and dried meat to Marnej.

Marnej accepted it with a grateful look. Kalek observed him thoughtfully chewing. The boy's methodical movements irritated him, anxious to be moving again. The healer downed his tea, scalding his mouth. He was about to push himself to his feet when Marnej's words stopped him.

"When I last saw her," the boy began, then faltered as if he could not bear to share what came next.

Kalek said nothing. His heartbeat pulsed in his ears.

"She rode off with a Piijkij," he said finally. "I knew him."

Kalek could not speak.

Marnej glanced up at him, challenge in his eyes. "You know she's about to do something reckless."

It was as if the boy deliberately wanted to provoke him. "I do not know that. She may be hurt. She may be a prisoner," Kalek growled. "What I do know is you have cost me a day of traveling."

Marnej shook his head, paying no heed to the censure. "I think she's going to the Stronghold. The words in her song sound . . ."

Kalek thought of what Ravna had said. "She is determined, resolute."

"Yes," Marnej readily agreed, jumping to his feet. "She has planned some action."

"Maybe against your Piijkij," Kalek said.

"They're not my Piijkij. They betrayed me. They betrayed my father."

Kalek wanted to point out that Irjan had betrayed them first. He let the taunt die upon his tongue, saying, "Perhaps they keep her for their purposes."

"If she's with them, they act in consort," Marnej said, seeing Dárja's hand take hold of Válde's on the battlefield.

"How can you say that?" Kalek demanded.

The boy wheeled on him. "You weren't there!"

Kalek felt the sting of truth. His regret bloomed hot and inescapable. *I should have been there. I should have been the one to go. Not this boy.*

"Otherwise, she would've escaped," Marnej said.

The implication behind the boy's reasoning took hold in the dark corners of Kalek's mind. He fought back, saying, "Then they have kept her for their purposes. They must be using her to bait a trap of some sort." He clutched at the only possibilities that made sense to him. If she had escaped, then why had she not returned to the Pohjola, to him, as she had promised?

"If she is meant as bait," Marnej began carefully, "then we'll have to reach her before the trap is set." He paused, meeting Kalek's eyes. "I may have cost you a day to start, but I'll save you time wondering and wandering. They're going for the Stronghold."

CHAPTER FORTY-THREE

DÁRJA SAT UPON HER horse, looking out through the thinning treeline to the Stronghold beyond. She smiled at the recollection of how she and Marnej had cut a swath through all those unsuspecting soldiers. What had they seen? A nieddaš and a boy, running together. Those soldiers may not have believed their eyes, but they'd felt the sting of her and Marnej's swords. *No question of that.* Somehow, through a rain of arrows, they'd made it to these woods where she stood. She'd prayed for and found the Song of All, her hands holding tight to Marnej. The Song of All had embraced them and the soldiers had gaped in wonder as they disappeared.

In their last skirmish she'd taken Válde's hand and not Marnej's. She didn't regret that because she now readied herself to strike a blow at the heart of the Olmmoš. She did wish that she'd been able to set matters straight with Marnej. She wanted him to know she didn't blame him. The fact she would never return to her Origin to give birth and become almai didn't matter. She'd guarded this secret as if by doing so she could change who she was. The self-deceit had cost her the love she'd been given by Irjan, by Marnej, and by Kalek.

Dárja thought of the Piijkij, who had seen her as a healer, a witch, and a Jápmea. And Válde, who saw in her the key to revenge against the Olmmoš High Priest. *Because the enemy of my enemy is supposedly my friend*, she thought, repeating Válde's reasoning for saving her life. He wouldn't be there to do so again. *After today, it will be over.* For a while, she allowed doubt to seep in around her decision to act alone, feeling guilty about abandoning Válde. The truth was, after today, he'd be a man without a future and she understood what this meant. Briefly, she reconsidered her decision to enact his plan on her own. *No. It is better this way.* This was what Irjan had trained her to do. She'd honor her bieba and his sacrifice. She'd also clear the debt she owed Marnej.

To the sky above, she whispered, "We are the Taistelijan. We are the warriors of the Jápmemeahttun."

From under her leather jerkin, Dárja pulled out a map of the Stronghold she'd taken from the Piijkij. She reviewed the twists and turns and the possible ways out. If it all went according to plan, she wouldn't need this anymore. Válde had said the Vijns would likely be in his chambers or with his counselors in the great hall. She remembered the details of the place as if they'd been burned into her mind. The dais. The crudely carved bears that, to her, mocked the beast itself. The Olmmoš priest, with his ornate robes, sitting in his black-and-white chair, smirking.

Turning to walk back to her grazing horse, she tucked the map away. At her approach, the horse lifted its head. Its ears twitched with interest and its tawny tail flicked against the midges, warmed by the sun. She looked at the soldier's uniform rolled at the back of the saddle. It had served its purpose in Mehjala and Skaina. Here she would have no use for it. Her last actions in this world would not be in the guise of an Olmmoš. She'd enter the Stronghold within the Song of All. She'd fight like the Taistelijan. If she couldn't find the Song again, then she'd die in the Olmmoš realm. But she would die as a Jápmemeahttun.

Dárja stroked the horse's mane. The muscles in its neck shivered and the animal turned its head to her, its nose nuzzling her belt.

"The last of the sour apples," she said, pulling them from her pouch. "I won't need them in there."

While the horse crunched upon the fruit, Dárja unfastened the saddle. She slid it from the horse's back, taking with it the saddle blanket. Fresh sweat attracted the midges. She brushed them away, then removed the bridle. The horse shook its head, its coarse mane stinging her eyes. She stepped back, wiping them. Watching the animal go back to foraging, she thought, *The time has come.* She turned her back on the horse and walked to the forest's edge.

Dárja swallowed hard. *After today it will be over.* She released a slow breath. She let her song rise within her.

> *I am daughter of the gods.*
> *I am sister among the Jápmemeahttun.*
> *I started my life at my Origin, with sadness and joy as my companions.*
> *I have braved dangers and met enemies and can see the truth of friendship.*
> *I go into the world to meet my destiny, knowing that I have honored my kin.*

A push from behind broke her concentration. Her hand immediately went to the knife at her waist. She spun around, ready to fight, finding herself facing the horse. She laughed, dispelling her tension. She sheathed her knife. The horse nudged her arm again.

"They're all gone," she said, wishing she had more apples to give as thanks. "It's time for us to part ways. You're free to go."

The animal didn't stir.

"Go," Dárja encouraged. When the horse didn't move, she gave up trying to get it to see reason. She faced the looming outline of the Believers' Stronghold. She closed her eyes again to search for the song. When she found its thread, she held on, pulling the refrain up from the deepest parts of her soul. The melody swelled within until she couldn't contain it. Dárja's song burst from her. She felt its power as she never had before.

Emboldened by the connection surging through her, she reveled in the sensation of life quickening all around. The air, brushing her face, hummed. It spoke to her of the far-off places it had visited. Behind her came the song of the horse. She felt its joy, running free in the herd. Dárja opened her eyes to see the animal step toward her within the Song of All. She hadn't thought it possible to bring it into the Song while standing apart from it. She stepped farther away, thinking she would break the link. The horse followed.

"You must stay here," she said to the animal. "This isn't your fight."

The beast followed her again. Dárja retraced her steps to the horse. She rubbed its muzzle. It was soft like the furred antlers of the binna before mating season. She placed her forehead to the animal's.

"Thank you. You are loyal and faithful," she said. "You can't come with me. This is something I must do alone."

~

Válde looked around at the ruins of the Fortress of the Brethren of Hunters. From the outside, it had appeared derelict but intact. Inside, the wooden roof had been burned, the stone wall scorched black by flames. What comfort the Brethren had in their noble home had been scavenged or destroyed. There was no sign of the Piijkij swords that had hung from the rafters in the Hall of the Fallen. What was left of the Brethren stood in front of him, wearing the ragged uniforms of Believers' soldiers.

"You look concerned," Gáral said, sliding on his chest piece.

Válde exhaled. "No. Not concerned. Expectant."

Edo threaded his lanky arms through the patched soldier's tunic, then slipped it over his head. His shorn crown emerged from the neck like a turtle, taking interest in the world. Cinching the belt at his waist, he said, "I do not know what I thought I would see coming back here." He sheathed his sword and dagger. "Maybe the bones of the soldiers we killed."

"The wolves and the foxes probably carried them off," Feles said, adjusting his saddle.

"It's as if nothing has changed," Mures joked.

"Of course it has," Herko barked. "Back then there were nine of us, fighting for our lives. Now Beartu, Redde, and Daigu are gone. We are six. And this time, we aren't running. We're bringing the fight to their gates."

Edo sniffed. "I remember when you were more interested in saving your skin and going through the pockets of the dead."

"We can't all have your piety, Edo," Herko said.

"Herko's right." Válde spoke up to forestall a quarrel. "Each of us carries something important within us that gives us an advantage. Where one is weak, another is skilled. Where one is rash"—Válde looked at Herko—"another is calm and clear of thought."

"After today, it will be all over," Gáral said.

Válde nodded, appreciating the solemnity of his men. He cleared his throat.

"I am honored to be with you once again in battle. After today, the world will be changed by our actions. The Brethren of Hunters may cease to exist. But our legacy will live on. When our people speak of us, it will be with hallowed voices."

Válde began to recite the Oath of the Brethren of Hunters.

To the mothers, who gave us life.
To the fathers, who gave up theirs.
We are brothers sworn to serve.
To the Olmmoš, to the Avr, and to the Brethren of Hunters
We swear our oath to those deserved.

As the voices of the others joined in, Válde felt the enormity of what they were about to undertake.

"If the Avr could see this," Gáral said with feeling, then stopped.

"If the Avr could see this," Válde repeated, "he would be proud we are about to avenge the lives and honor of the Brethren of Hunters."

"Those Believers will shit themselves when they realize we've come for them in their Stronghold!" Herko said with glee.

CHAPTER FORTY-FOUR

DÁRJA WALKED OUT ACROSS the marshy ground between her and what the Olmmoš brazenly called their Stronghold. She felt her strength welling with each step, and laughed at the notion of a Stronghold. Their walls couldn't keep her out, just as they couldn't contain her. Beneath her feet, the earth was ready to lend her its deep slumbering power. In return, she gave the earth her grateful thanks, striding toward the bridge, joining earth and the Olmmoš structure.

Nearing the arched battlement, Dárja was struck by the fact she'd not noticed the carvings upon the gates the last time she'd passed through them. They were so primitive and garish, perhaps she had overlooked them on purpose. Now, they served to remind her she acted to cut away a blight from the world.

Before her, one sentry guard stood staring ahead, the other looked to the sky as if doubting the sun overhead. Passing by them, her disdain swelled, amplified by their crude posturing.

"Did you see that?" one of the sentries asked, his voice excited.

Dárja froze. She looked over to see the short, bowlegged sentry pointing to the west.

"There's nothing there," his friend said, as though this was a common conversation between the two.

I've been among the Olmmoš too long, Dárja chided herself for hesitating. The Song was strong within her. The gods knew her intent. They understood. She only needed to act and it would all be made right. Dárja resumed her sure steps through the keep. She looked at the faces of the Olmmoš soldiers around her. Some were young. Some old. Some almost pleasing looking. Most were a sight to pity, with scar-marred faces and limbs. Perhaps these were the survivors of the last battle or maybe the result of a cruel Olmmoš society. Marnej had told her such harrowing stories of his time with the Brethren she could easily believe brutishness to be at the heart of all Olmmoš. Even Válde's parents had sold him to the Brethren to feed the rest of the family.

Mánáid should be loved and cared for. As she had been cared for. Only the vilest of creatures would rid themselves of their young. *Even in times of famine, the wolves and bears care for their offspring as best they can.*

Dárja wound her way through the unaware Olmmoš soldiers, finding direction for her loathing and her anguish until she stopped before an imposing door. It was cracked in places and repaired with iron cleats. It looked to be the one that had loomed hated and impassive in her escape with Marnej. Now, it stood in the way of her entry to the inner reaches of the Olmmoš Believers and was no less formidable because she was power-less to move it while in the Song. Her choices were to wait until the inner doors were opened by an exiting soldier or enter the Olmmoš realm. Neither appealed to her.

She had no sooner cursed her situation than the doors opened with a mournful groan, disgorging a trio of finely dressed soldiers. They wore colorful, braided belts around the waists of their crisp linen tunics. Dárja slipped through them like a salmon through a bear's claws to make her way inside before the doors closed. She left behind the bright glare of the world outside for the dark, shadowed interior. Momentarily blind, she panicked, convinced she'd find herself in a hall rife with soldiers and servants.

❧

Bávvál raised his hand to Áigin to come forward from the gathered counselors. "I assume you bring me news."

The lanky spy approached the dais, his expression unreadable. "Your orders are being carried out as we speak."

Sensing doubt behind his agent's cool gaze, Bávvál said, "You think my decision unwise."

"My Vijns, I would never suggest such an opinion," the man said.

Bávvál sniffed. He knew his agent's game. "No, you would not suggest that opinion. But you would think it."

The spy inclined his head in deference. "I am paid to think many things, my Vijns."

"Enough with the sly tongue, Áigin," Bávvál said, returning to his seat with a flourish of his heavy robes. "What of success?"

The man followed, a pace behind. "The soldiers are duly questioning everyone," he said, then waited as if choosing carefully what he would next say. "There have been many who have come forward to supply information . . ." He trailed off.

"And?" Bávvál dragged out the word, his ire growing.

"No Piijkij have been found so far."

Bávvál hit the arms of his chair with such force his palms stung. "No Piijkij."

"No, my Vijns, just farmers and wayward handmates," Áigin said, seemingly unmoved by Bávvál's display of anger.

"And what of the man who leads my regiment?" Bávvál asked. "The one you chose to lead. Have you found him?"

Here, the spy twitched.

Bávvál took satisfaction in that he had hit upon a tender subject. *Apparently, the man is not bloodless.*

"He traveled south and is rumored to have entered the Stronghold," Áigin answered.

"Rumored to have entered the Stronghold!" Bávvál sprang out of his seat, charging at his spy, "Worthless, the lot of you. My spy. My counselors. My personal regiment." He pushed past his agent, who took the blow, folding into an easy bow. "None of you can put an end to these upstarts. You are only good for excuses and mewling."

"Yes, my Vijns," the spy said in his wake.

Niilán wiggled in the too-short saddle. He had wanted to give his horse time to accept the stolen saddle which sat high up on the beast's withers. He was also conscious that his opportunity to escape dwindled with each moment he hesitated. *It will have to do*, he thought miserably. He had already waited too long. He had not seen Osku since his friend had warned him off. He did not know if this was by chance or of the man's making. In his place, he had seen Áigin at every turn. It was as if the spy knew where he was and enjoyed playing with him.

He had hidden in barracks and grain stores. When he made his way back to retrieve his horse, Áigin had been speaking with the stable man. Niilán could have left on foot then, but he feared he would need the animal if he was to make it out of the spy's reach.

Niilán nudged his horse forward with his knees. Keeping to a plodding pace, he let his gaze wander to see if any took note of him. Soldiers ambled about, some with purpose, others without. None seemed to give him a second glance. He guided the horse to the outer gates, feeling something akin to loss. By the gods' strange will, he had been a good soldier and a mostly fair commander. Now he would need to find a new path, one which would take him beyond the bounds of the Vijns's power. He thought of the farmer and his family who had sheltered him and paid the price for it. Perhaps he could travel to the Pohjola and become a badjeolmmoš. *There are worse things than being a reindeer herder.*

Niilán rode under the arched battlement, his plan forming. On the wooden bridge that spanned the defensive ditch, he passed a line of six mounted soldiers, returning to the Stronghold. They were a ragtag lot, muddied and bloodied. Coming upon the last in the line, he nodded to the man. For an instant, they locked eyes. Niilán's mind reeled. He could utter no word. Válde nodded back to him as he continued on ahead.

The guard's challenge boomed, "Who approaches?"

Niilán fought the temptation to turn and stare at the men who had just passed him.

Another voice answered. "Oso garrison men returning, with news for the Vijns."

Niilán's horse sauntered forward while he listened. There was no hue and cry, nor sounds of fighting. It seemed Válde and his men had made it through the gates unchallenged. To what end, Niilán did not want to know.

He crossed the barren marsh separating the Stronghold from the dense forests beyond. In a stand of welcoming birch trees, he turned to look at the Stronghold, its hulking structure and its pike-lined palisades. He revisited everything that had happened to him since he had become a soldier. Osku had told him he owed his men no more than he had already given them. But there was someone he still owed a debt to—Válde. To act for the Piijkij would be the end of his hope for a quiet life. Then again, Niilán had not wanted a quiet life. He had wanted to remain a common soldier. With one last look toward the forest, to see if it held any sway with him, Niilán turned his horse around and headed back to the Stronghold. He would remain a soldier. A soldier in Válde's ranks, as he had been upon the battlefield of the Great Valley.

&

Niilán approached the bridge to the sound of men shouting. He spurred his horse forward, prepared to run over the sentry and any who got in his way. His horse's hooves echoed on the wide wooden planks, matching his heartbeat. The guards dove out of the way.

Inside the keep, Niilán pulled hard on the reins to bring his horse to a stop. The beast reared, nearly toppling him from the saddle. Regaining control, he spurred his mount forward to join the Piijkij. Niilán drew his sword. Coming alongside Válde, the man swung at him. Niilán blocked the blow, then parried the thrust of a soldier's sword aimed at Válde.

Confusion flashed across the Piijkij's face. Swarmed by foot soldiers, there was no time to explain. Niilán acted as a shield to Válde, who swung and thrust to kill. The shouts and cries around them became deafening. It was as if he were back on the battlefield.

More men came running from the armory, ready with pikes and bows. Niilán ducked, then deflected the jab of a pikeman. His horse whinnied, then screamed and reared, throwing Niilán back against the sharp rise of the saddle's wooden stays. He clutched at the horse's neck with both hands. The animal came down on two soldiers, crushing them with its flailing hooves. Niilán tried to turn the horse. It bolted ahead, trampling any in its way. Above, the air hissed with arrows. Then on all sides came the cries of men and beasts as the arrows found flesh.

Niilán gained control of the horse in time to see Válde pulled from his saddle. This time it was Niilán who led the charge. He cleared the men between himself and Válde with brutal, hacking cuts. Circling the Piijkij, he saw the man was blood-spattered but alive. Niilán held out a hand and Válde took it, pulling himself up onto the horse's rump.

"Get me inside," Válde shouted.

CHAPTER FORTY-FIVE

WITH EACH STEP DÁRJA took, her confidence in her recollection ebbed. She'd been sure she and Marnej had only gone through the one door. But they'd been engaged almost immediately by soldiers. Perhaps she'd fought her way through others. If this wasn't the great hall of her memory, then she wasn't sure where she was headed. She followed indistinct, guttural sounds that gradually coalesced into something meaningful.

"My Vijns," a high, thin voice rang out. "If you will consider the proposal before you."

"Who does it serve?" asked another.

This voice sounded familiar to Dárja.

"I do not understand, my Vijns," the first said.

Dárja's heart skipped a beat. She picked up her pace, striding toward the voices. She foresaw the last moments of the High Priest's life. The shock upon his face. His dead eyes, staring into the eternal darkness of a cursed spirit. This vision swept her forward as if only she and he existed in the world. Movement across an open doorway presaged the servants she'd anticipated. Drawing closer, she heard the soft undercurrent of whispers and coughs while the Olmmoš priest hurled insults at the present speaker.

Dárja slipped around the door to find herself in the room she remembered. The Olmmoš stood in clusters. Some wore robes as bright as berries. Others wore simple shifts the color of pine cones. They masked their faces with their hands as they whispered one to the other. Several Olmmoš ran at the whim of the Vijns, who sat flanked by the carved bears, sneering as his people fawned over him. He waved away platters piled high with enough food to feed all in the hall. She tightened her grip on her sword. Walking toward the dais, her eyes bore into the High Priest.

From behind her, a terror-stricken voice cut through all the others. "My Vijns! We are under attack!"

Dárja turned around to see who or what approached. A breathless soldier ran past her to kneel before the High Priest.

"We are under attack," he cried again, as if it was all he could utter. "By our own soldiers," he added with a gasp.

A chill ran down Dárja's spine. *They can't take this from me.* Not after all she'd done for the Piijkij. *Not after everything they called me.* She broke into a run, springing up onto the dais as she released the Song of All from her mind.

The cold, leaden feeling of the Olmmoš realm gripped her as if it meant to squeeze the life from her. Screams echoed all around. Her feet felt as if they'd grown roots and she struggled to move. The priest leapt up. The Olmmoš soldiers on either side of him gaped in open-mouthed shock. Dárja stumbled forward. Instinctively, she rolled to come up on her feet to face the two soldiers, who'd closed rank.

"You!" the Vijns shouted at her, taken aback.

She thrust at one of the soldiers, then blocked the attack of the other. She sensed someone behind her and dropped to a crouch to roll sideways, finding herself facing three armed men—two soldiers and a gaunt man with a slit for a mouth. Dárja ran at the two soldiers, releasing a cry that shook her to the bones. She kicked hard to the right as she cut left. Blood sprayed upward in lurid fountain. Beyond, she saw the Vijns. His beady, ferret-like eyes were wide with terror. He pushed a soldier into her way, trying to run. His foot caught on his robes, sending him sprawling onto the dais. He scrambled on his knees to get away. Dárja kicked him over onto his back. "Please," he sputtered through spittle-flecked lips. She ran her blade through the man's soft, meaty middle, watching his life slip away with a smile.

It's done. Dárja searched within herself to find the Song. Somewhere to her left she heard the sounds of boots running. The rush of other choruses came in a flash. She felt the vibration of the earth below her, the hum of the soil pressed hard by the feet of men, then she felt a biting sting at her side. Dárja grabbed at her ribs with her free hand. In an instant, the Song was replaced by throbbing blood, leaking through her fingers. She turned on the gaunt man. The tip of his blade dripped red with her blood.

Dárja feinted as if to attack, then called upon her Song again. He stepped toward her with the intensity of a wolf stalking its prey. She blocked his thrust, deflecting the tip into the meat of her arm, her breath coming fast and thin. Dárja again reached for her song. It was there, soft and weak. A haze she couldn't clear with the back of her hand covered her eyes. Blocking another thrust, she knew this time there'd be no escape.

～

Válde entered the hall upon Niilán's heels. He looked behind to see if Gáral and the others followed. He heard the shouting and then a collective gasp. Válde turned back around in time to see Dárja appear upon the dais, running toward the Vijns, who had jumped to his feet. Válde dodged the strike of a soldier's blade, cutting through the man's middle as he tried to keep his eyes upon Dárja. He shoved a frightened servant out of his way. Dárja fought off two soldiers, while three more men approached from behind. Before Válde could reach the dais, two men, locked in each other's grasp, barreled into him, knocking him to the ground. He got to his feet in time to see Dárja plunge her sword into the center of the Vijns's chest. For an instant, he felt the pure satisfaction of vindication. Then he saw a lithe man with lank gray hair appear between two soldiers to pierce Dárja's side with his blade. She turned and swayed, one hand at her side and the other holding her blade to parry.

He ran in her direction straight into the glancing blow of a soldier's sword. The full measure of impact landed on Niilán, who had appeared at his side. The man doubled over in pain. Válde exploded with anger. He lashed out at the soldier as Niilán fell to the floor. Válde dropped to give aid, only to be forced to leave him when the downward arc of another blade threatened to cut him in two.

Válde just managed to block the blow. He jumped back, swinging upward, catching the attacking soldier under his arm. As the soldier began to crumple, Válde cut across the air, separating the man's head from his body. He kicked the bloody stump aside, catching sight of Herko's bald head, crowned with blood and gore. Two uncertain soldiers, more boys than men, confronted Válde. They held their swords at the ready, fear clouding their eyes. For a moment, he pitied them, then lunged at them, growling like a beast with bared teeth. The youth wavered but did not run.

"You had your chance," Válde yelled at them as he charged, hacking left and right until the two slumped together in death.

Making his way to where he had last seen Dárja, Válde cut and swung and pushed his way through soldiers, who fell around him, some by his hand, others by their comrades. The confusion was so great the Vijns's men no longer knew who their enemy was.

Válde saw the body of the Vijns. Men stepped on and around him in their attempt to fight off their attackers. Blood-soaked in his rent and tattered robes, his body suffered a rush of indignities. *No honor in death.* He spat on the corpse, then scanned the bodies close at hand, finding Mures among the dead. Válde looked away from his lifeless eyes.

Above the din, he heard, "Válde! Here!"

He turned in all directions, then crouched to avoid a high slice. He sprang forward to gut a man before he ever realized his life was over.

"Válde! Here!" the voice repeated, filled with urgency.

Válde scrambled up, pulling free his sword. He whirled in time to see Edo, fighting off a soldier with one hand as he pulled Dárja's limp body with his other. Válde ran in his direction, heedless of the men in his way.

Upon reaching Edo, it was clear the young Piijkij could barely stand upon his feet. He bled from his head and his arms and the gods only knew where else.

"Take her," Edo implored. "Take her and go!"

Válde scooped up Dárja's battered body in his arms. Her head rolled back like the dead.

"Go," Edo yelled at him, and hacked at a looming soldier.

Everywhere men blocked Válde's way.

"Come," a voice commanded.

Válde whirled to see Gáral.

"I will fight them off until you are free of this place or we are all dead," he said.

Válde did not need to be told twice. He heaved Dárja up and pulled out his dagger. He followed Gáral at a side step, making sure they were not attacked from behind. With the gods' help and their ferocious skill, they charged out of the hall and into the corridor where more soldiers approached.

Gáral waved his arms as if to clear the way. "One dead. The rest escaped," he said. "There are only soldiers attacking other soldiers in there."

The converging men stopped, looking from Gáral to Válde with a body slung over his shoulder. Gáral took advantage of the hesitation and jumped at the six soldiers; two died immediately, another two were wounded. The last two ran.

"Quickly!" Gáral said, unwrapping the cloak he had swaddled about his arm for a shield. "Put this on her."

"We don't have time," Válde said.

"Just do it! I will fend off any who come."

Válde dropped Dárja to the ground, rolled her in a soldier's cloak, and then hoisted her back up.

"Ready."

Gáral looked them over and nodded. "There is no fighting your way out of here."

Válde shadowed Gáral as they wound their way through the Stronghold to the kitchens and from there to the stables.

At the sound of their footfalls, a soldier appeared within the stable entrance. "What are you doing here?"

The soldier got no further. Gáral slit open his thigh, then took his hilt to the man's chin. "Take the horse there. Put her over its back."

"The gates are closed," Válde pointed out.

"The gates, yes. Not the walls." Gáral searched until he found two coils of sturdy rope. He slung the coils around his arm. "Come."

Gáral went first, his sword out. Válde followed, leading the horse with Dárja draped across its back. They crossed the kitchen gardens to the rear fortified wall.

"This place was never designed to keep enemies out," Gáral said. He flashed a wry grin at Válde. "I suppose they believed the gods would protect them."

"Here." Gáral handed Válde the end of a rope. "Tie this around your waist, then climb onto the horse. From there you can go up and over the top. I will hold on to the slack so you can make it down without falling. Between the two of us, we can raise her over, without dropping her on your side." Gáral glanced at Dárja. "She looks bad enough already."

"What about you?" Válde asked, tying the rope about his waist, then testing the knot.

"I'll hide and then sneak out when they open the gate," Gáral said. He unwound the rope, then slid it behind his back and around his arm. "I may even dispatch a few more while I wait."

Válde lowered Dárja from the horse to the ground, then climbed up on the animal's back. Gáral held on to the beast until Válde gained a handhold on the wall. Using the friction of his feet, he managed to push and pull himself up to the top of the rough-edged palisade. At the top, he carefully swung a leg over, then gave Gáral one last look before sliding down the outside.

True to his word, Gáral eased Válde down until his feet hit the ground. He undid the knot at his waist, looking around to see there was no one near. He tugged twice on the rope, then positioned himself as he had seen Gáral do.

In turn, when Válde felt the twice tug, he began to pull upon the rope, easing backward as he did so. It seemed an eternity before Dárja's body crested the palisade. He cringed, watching the sharp edges cut into her slack body. Once on the ground, Válde loosened the knots at Dárja's waist and tugged upon the ropes. The dark, rough coils disappeared over the top like a snake sliding back into its hiding place.

Válde lifted her into his arms, rising with effort to his feet. He needed to get her a horse, but he was not willing to leave her behind. They would go by foot for now. If they were caught it would be together. And if they died, then it would also be together.

～

Áigin stepped across the bodies littering the room. At times, he could not tell where one began and another ended. The blood and offal of all the dead and dying mixed together into one sticky, foul-smelling mess. He held his nose to guard against the stench.

The room was quiet except for the occasional groans of the dying. Áigin looked down at the Vijns, lying wide-eyed in death.

"The gods have saved us," a voice pronounced somewhere behind him. Áigin straightened to see who spoke.

The Vijns's counselors stood, peering over each other's heads, whispering among themselves.

"Let us thank the gods," the voice added.

This time, Áigin saw it was Rikkar who spoke. The old priest came forward, hesitantly, only to stop when the stench overwhelmed him.

"Perhaps it would be best if we honor the dead by waiting for their bodies to be readied for prayers," another, stronger voice spoke from the back. The crowd parted, revealing Siggur, the youngest of the counselors.

Always the sly one, Áigin thought, curious to see what his game might be.

"Áigin," Siggur called to him. "Have the soldiers clear these bodies. Leave the Vijns for the priests to give proper honor."

Rikkar stood before the young counselor, bristling with anger. "Who are you to give commands within these halls?"

Siggur gave the old priest a faint smile that did not reach his eyes. "I am the only one among us ready to do what needs to be done."

Rikkar sputtered. He was cut short when Siggur added, "The Vijns was lax and forgiving. Look what became of him. We have been attacked by those creatures of the Northland." He stopped, surveying those around him. "Did you not see how the Jápmea appeared before us, to stand in our midst, and take our Vijns from us? We are vulnerable. We will always be vulnerable while even one of them continues to live."

A murmuring of agreement spread. Áigin looked over to Rikkar, who to his eye had already lost the contest of power. Rikkar countered Siggur with weak words that were easily pushed aside. He was called timid and mild by the others, who saw a chance to forget their own cowardliness when the moment of fighting had begun.

"Burn the Pohjola! Burn the Northlands!" Siggur exhorted. "They might hide from us, but they cannot hide from the righteous flames of the gods. Let us not wait for them to come once again like vipers into the heart of our nest. Let us take our soldiers north and set to blaze every bush, weed, and blade of grass."

The counselors gained momentum, chanting, "Burn the Pohjola!"

Siggur held up his hands to accept their voices of support.

Áigin transferred his gaze from Siggur to Rikkar and back again. He stepped forward to stand before Siggur. He bent his tall, spare frame into a deep bow. When he stood he said loud enough for the others to hear, "Yes, my Vijns."

CHAPTER FORTY-SIX

W E ARE TOO LATE," Marnej muttered to himself, pushing his mount to go faster.

"Perhaps not," Kalek said.

Marnej could see in the healer's taut expression he didn't believe his answer.

"We can find her," Kalek said.

Her voice had been so strong. It was as if she'd been next to him. Then it went silent. "Can she hide within the song?" Marnej asked, looking to find a reason other than what he feared.

While Kalek considered this question, Marnej wondered if the healer had become embroiled in his own dark thoughts. In the absence of a response, he renewed his private entreaties that Dárja should live, promising sacrifices he'd pay if the gods would spare her.

"It is hard to know," Kalek said, breaking into Marnej's imagined atonement. "The constants in our lives are changing faster than the seasons." He faltered, his eyes lifted in supplication. "Who can say what is possible now."

The faint sound of voices lured Marnej's interest away from the healer. He sat straight in his saddle, craning his head in all directions for any signs of someone approaching.

Kalek seemed not to have heard because he continued to speak. "Perhaps the song is too weak in the south."

Marnej shushed him. "Someone's coming. Listen."

The two stopped.

"Do you hear that?" Marnej asked.

"Horses," Kalek said. "Too many to count."

"Soldiers," Marnej said. "We should get well off this path. Just in case."

Kalek guided his binna toward a dense thicket of pines. They did not have long to wait for the first bannerman to come into view, heading north on the cart path to the trade route. Behind the bannermen, mounted soldiers road three abreast, talking and laughing among themselves.

"Where are they going?" Kalek asked in a whisper, as though he didn't trust the Song to veil them.

"I don't know," Marnej said. "But I intend to find out."

"No, Marnej," Kalek hissed. "We must find Dárja."

"They may tell us that," Marnej said, dismounting. "I'll wait for the foot soldiers, then make my way to the path like a trapper come out to see what all the noise is."

In response to Kalek's frown, he said, "I am just another Olmmoš, remember?" Unfastening his sword and sheath, he gave the healer a reassuring smile. "A trapper doesn't need these," he said, handing them up to Kalek.

"You are unarmed," the healer said, his concern showing.

Marnej picked a thick, tapered branch from the ground. He trimmed the twigs with his knife, then carved smooth the top for a grip. "I'll work my way north before leaving the Song."

He squinted up at the sky. "Give me until the sun tops the tree over there. If I haven't returned by then, go on without me. I'll get to you somehow."

Whatever doubts or plans Kalek had, he kept them to himself.

Marnej padded through the woods within the Song of All. With each step, he felt the pulsing thrum of the earth. Above, the birds sang their songs. They spoke of fledglings in the nest, calling out in hunger. He'd run from all this: his past, his life with the Jápmemeahttun, and his place within the Song. And yet, here it was for him, just waiting as if he'd never run away, as if he'd never rejected it. The Song of All held no grudge against him. It held no judgment of his action. It just continued to flow, taking him along when he chose. What the Song of All did not contain was Dárja. This frightened him. And Kalek's hedging had done nothing for his spirits either. Her last words had been, *I honored my kin.*

The sound of men and horses grew louder, crowding into the sounds and sensations of the Song. Marnej stopped and listened one more time for Dárja, then released his song from his thoughts. A sudden thickness blanketed his mind. He shook his head, trying to clear it. As he did, the connection he'd come to expect had vanished. A profound sense of unease filled the new void around him.

Marnej took a wobbly step forward. He steadied himself with his walking staff. After a couple more coltish steps, he regained his normal gait. Peering ahead through the trees, he saw the trail of foot soldiers. He stopped in feigned surprise at the border of the cart path. The nearest foot soldiers gave him a quick appraisal, then fell back into their conversations. Marnej let several rows pass, nodding to those who looked his way. Finally, he fell in with a soldier about his age.

"Where are you headed?" he asked.

The young soldier, eager in his appearance, grinned. "We're going to burn out the Jápmea!"

This time, Marnej didn't need to feign his surprise. "Burn them out?"

"They attacked the Stronghold and killed the old Vijns!" the boy said. "And they'll pay for it! There won't be an inch of the Pohjola left for them to hide in when we've finished."

The young soldier then turned a critical eye on Marnej, and he realized he'd been walking slack-jawed. Marnej recovered himself, patting the soldier on his back. "By the gods! You have a march ahead of you."

The young soldier nodded. "I was too young to be on the battlefield the last season of snow. Now I'll be among the first to put an end to all Immortals."

"A task I'm sure you are ready for," Marnej said, stepping off the track with a nod, his pretense of good cheer forgotten.

～

The moment Kalek saw Marnej, sprinting toward him, he knew something was terribly wrong. Kalek jumped to his feet, startling the reindeer who grazed nearby. "What has happened?"

"They are riding north," Marnej said, coming to a breathless stop. "They mean to burn the Pohjola."

Kalek stood rooted, unable to break through the terror that gripped him.

"An Immortal killed their High Priest," Marnej panted. "They're set to scorch the north. To kill all the Jápmemeahttun."

Kalek met Marnej's eyes. He saw they had come to the same conclusion. It had to have been Dárja. "Fool," he swore.

"How long will it take them to make it north?" Kalek asked, his mind beginning to work after the shock of the news.

"Two weeks, maybe a full moon cycle," Marnej said. "It will depend on the number of men and the supply train they'll need. Did you see wagons at the end of the foot soldiers?"

"Yes," Kalek answered. "There were ten or more."

Marnej nodded. "They mean for this to be the last campaign against us."

"They do not know," Kalek said, his voice shaky. "You must ride north," he added, coming back to himself. "Warn the others to prepare for war or . . ."

Marnej shook his head. "No. I will ride south and find Dárja."

"If she killed their High Priest, she must have been within their Stronghold. How would she have made it out on her own? Look at what happened when Irjan and I came for you. We both barely made it out with our lives."

"No. I've seen her fight her way through more men than you can imagine," Marnej argued. "She could've found the Song. She could've made it out."

Kalek shook his head. "I will ride south. If she survived, I will find her. You must go north, warn the Elders. Help them figure out a way." He wanted to say, *to save us*. But he was not sure it was possible.

"If you ride south, then I do as well," Marnej countered. "Besides, Úlla knows what to do."

"Úlla? What has she to do with this?" Kalek asked, his suspicion of the boy growing.

"There is a way," Marnej said.

"To find Dárja?" Kalek asked.

"No. For us to escape the soldiers heading to the north."

Kalek narrowed his eyes. "What do you mean?"

"We can go south."

"The south is filled with Olmmoš!"

"I mean beyond our borders. Beyond the Pohjola. Beyond the mountains and great plains, into the south. To Morallom or Karvaluz."

Kalek picked up his binna's reins. "You delay me with fanciful dreams."

"It's no dream. I've been there. To the south. When Dárja left me behind." Marnej stopped short.

Kalek studied the boy to see if he lied. He had not thought it in his nature. Then again, much had changed since he had seen him ride off with Okta. "To the south?" Kalek scoffed. "How is that possible?"

"There's no time to explain," Marnej said, coming forward to block Kalek from mounting. "Believe me. I've been beyond our borders. There's a world out there to welcome us, not as one of their own, but as one of many."

Kalek hesitated. The boy's fervor felt deep and true.

"I left Úlla the map to guide all to safety," Marnej said as if it would make everything clear. "I told her she must convince the Elders to travel. She can do it."

"It is our home," Kalek argued.

"There'll be no home after they burn the Pohjola."

Kalek stopped himself from saying out loud, "The Song will protect us." He said, "You must go back now. If you have been to the south, then you should guide our kind there. Not Úlla."

"Not without trying to find Dárja."

Kalek threw up his hands. "You can save the rest!"

"I want to be able to save all of us.

"I will not leave her behind."

"I know, Kalek," Marnej said softly, adding, "And I won't leave you behind. The Stronghold is ahead. I can go in and see if there's anything to be learned."

"No," Kalek said, his resolve firm. "You are not as skilled with the Song as I." He broke off, reflecting upon what he had just said. "If I do not make it back, then you can find Dárja and take her to the south."

~

Kalek approached the gates of the Olmmoš fortress within the Song of All. He had more than Dárja on his mind. Marnej's story swirled in his thoughts. It seemed impossible, but the boy's claims carried the weight of truth. Standing in the midst of swarming soldiers, it was impossible to think upon a future for all Jápmemeahttun when he needed to find just one—Dárja.

Kalek followed the stream of soldiers into the less-than-imposing structure before him. It paled in comparison to the Brethren's Fortress he had once helped Irjan attack.

"It's foul in there," one Olmmoš soldier said to another. "Blood everywhere. There hasn't been time to mop it all up, what with all the preparations to ride."

"I wish I was going north," the other soldier said, "and not staying here to clean up the muck."

The first shook his head, striding across the open hall. "It's all bits and pieces. You can't tell who was who with everyone in uniforms."

"I heard they got away," said the soldier who wished to ride north.

"Well, of course they got away," the first chided. "They are Jápmea, aren't they? Still, they stayed to kill us in our beds."

Kalek's heart leapt at the possibility Dárja had escaped. Then he smelled the rank odor of a battlefield. He held his nose in the crook of his arm. The fetor would not be fended off. Entering through another pair of doors, he first saw two columns that looked to be carved bears. They flanked a garish chair of black and white as if snow and soot had mixed. Then Kalek let his eyes fall to the floor. The whole surface was smeared with the aftermath of a brutal slaughter. *Dárja could not have done this by herself.* Then he recalled Marnej saying he had seen her kill more men than Kalek could imagine. Looking around, it was hard to believe anyone survived.

"Sir, she's not among the dead and wounded," a soldier reported to a tall, gaunt man with a shrewd look to him. "About the others we can't be sure."

Kalek's ears pricked up at the mention of *she*. It had to be Dárja of whom they spoke.

The gaunt man regarded the carnage.

The soldier mirrored him, saying, "Wearing Believers' uniforms is a cowardly act. Those Immortals'll pay for it in blood."

"We may well avenge ourselves against the wrong enemy," the man said, with no hint of feeling.

The soldier looked to protest. The man cut him off. "Rejoin the others to clean up this mess."

"My Vijns," the soldier said, abruptly bowing.

Confused, Kalek looked to the gaunt man who, though of a wise age, wore no beard as an Elder. In response, the man turned on his heel, then inclined his head in deference, echoing "My Vijns."

Kalek gawked at the arrival of a man in ornate robes. A line of Olmmoš trailed him like tottering ducklings. The soldiers all bowed deeply to this figure who appeared to be barely older than a youth. Marnej had told him a Jápmemeahttun had killed their High Priest in the Stronghold. Yet, it seemed their High Priest stood before him. Baffled, Kalek wondered what Dárja's role in all this had been. She and Marnej were the only of their kind brazen enough to attempt such a desperate action. *The kind of action Irjan would have undertaken.* Both Dárja and Marnej were so much like him. Then again, he too stood as party to another foray among the Olmmoš.

"The Jápmea female is not among the dead and wounded," the gaunt man said upon straightening.

A murmur of dismay spread through the Olmmoš.

"We have given all our men to ride north," a voice from the crowd said. "Who will protect us, if they should attack again?"

"They will not attack us now," the boy-man they called their Vijns said forcefully.

"We've heard rumors more soldiers were killed in the night," said another Olmmoš hidden within the group.

"Rumors are for men who fear their shadow," the High Priest said, a sneer upon his petulant lips. "Let the Jápmea run away. Unlike our last Vijns, I will not be satisfied until I see every last one of the Immortals dead upon the fields of the Northlands."

Kalek felt his fear coalesce into clarity. In the aftermath of the last battle, Kalek had been overwhelmed by his loss. In this moment, he understood the sacrifice Irjan had made countless times for what he held dear to his heart: his son, Dárja, and the Jápmemeahttun. He had sacrificed himself for the chance those he loved could live. *Just as I must do for those that I love.*

Ravna sat with the Elders, listening deep within the All. Song after song came through her as if she were the only one who could understand or answer. While her body was exhausted, her mind hummed with energy, excited to see new connections at each turn. With a twinge of guilt, she found herself engrossed in Tuá's song. She realized with regret she'd only had a glimpse of her beloved's world. Within Tuá, there was a deep fear Ravna had not known. A fear for the future. A fear for her mánná. She felt Tuá's love for Márgu. It was vast like the night sky and almost too much for her to contain. She was at once heartened and wounded by this love that existed beyond her.

Ravna understood her time with Tuá had come to an end. Her world was with the Elders and the songs of all Jápmemeahttun. She could not share this with Tuá, like the secrets of their childhood. She could barely accept it herself. All around her, she heard the Elders chanting the same words she chanted. It did not seem possible. But neither was it a dream.

Next to her, the Noaidi sighed. Ravna peeked at him through lowered lashes. His calm expression gave no indication of the tension beneath his song. She felt his doubt, his dejection. Despite all his years and wisdom, he could not see a way forward. This awareness hollowed a pit in Ravna's stomach. *How am I to lead when I have none of his experience?* she wondered, fear rising within.

An image flashed in her mind's eye. A raven. Its wings unfurled across a blue sky. She saw through its sharp eyes a landscape unlike any she had ever seen before. Earth the color of iron. Trees with great, arching branches. A wind came from the east. It sounded like the broken-hearted. The more she listened to the wind, the more beguiling it became. It spoke to her like an old friend, welcoming her home.

Ravna then saw herself as a spider, spinning a large web in an open window. Resting in the center, she felt a wind from the south ripple across the strands she had woven. The wind was as hot as flames. As the spider who holds the world together, Ravna heard the cries of all living things. They spoke as one. They spoke one word. *Run*. Flames raced across the Pohjola, burning all in their way. Behind the flames came the relentless, plodding steps of men and their beasts.

"The Olmmoš come!" Ravna cried, her eyes flying open.

CHAPTER FORTY-SEVEN

THE STUNNED SOLDIER GRASPED his middle. He stared at Válde in open-mouthed disbelief. Válde pulled his blade out of the soldier's gut a moment before the man toppled from his saddle. Before the horse could bolt, Válde grabbed for the reins. The man, a heap upon the forest path, groaned, then went silent. Válde listened for sounds of other soldiers. He heard only the reassuring buzz of a quiet forest. He took hold of the soldier's collar and dragged him into the undergrowth.

Though Válde had been reluctant to leave Dárja, he had soon understood the impossibility of escape on foot. He had stanched her wounds as best he could, but he needed a safe place to care for her. This close to the Stronghold, they risked capture. If they could make it to the Brethren's Fortress, perhaps he would find the others there and they could make shelter as they had done in the north. *Why had she gone off on her own? If we had acted together* . . . Válde let the thought trail off. He could not say the outcome would have been any different. The High Priest was dead. His plan had been executed. He had lost his men. And if Dárja died, her blood would be on his hands as well.

Válde heard a low moan, followed by a thick, wet cough. He ran to where he had left Dárja, leading the horse behind him. In the cool shade, Dárja lay upon a soldier's cloak. She attempted to sit up. Her arms shook with the effort. Before Válde could caution her, she slumped back down with a painful grunt. He tethered the horse, then kneeled at her side. Fresh blood seeped through his makeshift binding.

"Gods curse me," he muttered, shifting one of Dárja's arms around his neck.

"I'm so thirsty," she whispered through cracked lips.

Válde laid her back down. He jumped to his feet, covering the distance to the horse in two strides. The waterskin was barely half-full. Returning to Dárja's side, he knelt and gently lifted her head to tip the water into her mouth. She gagged, sputtering water down the front of her ripped, leather jerkin. Válde swore under his breath, saying aloud, "I am sorry." In his second attempt, he dribbled water into Dárja's mouth and she swallowed.

A weak smile parted her lips. "Better."

Válde placed the waterskin on the ground, mindful of not losing a drop.

"I need to get you to somewhere safe. Somewhere where I can care for your wounds," he said, watching Dárja's eyes flutter. "Do you understand? Can you ride?"

"I've been riding longer than you have been alive," she rasped, her smile returning briefly.

Válde could not help himself. He laughed, hearing his words echoed back to him. Dárja had once warned him if he could not stay up in the saddle, she would tie him to it. "I will not repeat the warning you gave me," he said. Drawing another weak smile from her, he added, "I will not let you fall."

Dárja mouthed something he could not hear, but Válde did not miss the tear, sliding from the corner of her eye to lose its shape in the curve of her ear.

～

The horse shifted. Válde tightened his arms instinctively around Dárja. For an instant, it seemed she wavered in substance, then she was solid in his arms again. Válde shook his head, berating himself for drifting off to sleep when he needed to stay alert. Ahead, he saw the first of the farms that had once supplied the Brethren with food. No smoke rose from the chimney.

Válde guided the horse to the start of a fallow field. "The Vijns's soldiers require your assistance," he called out, his voice trailing off.

He tried again, "The Vijns's soldiers require your assistance."

Again, the quiet crept back as soon as his voice faded.

Válde slid off the horse, holding Dárja upright. With his feet on the ground, he let her slip down into his arms. If the hut housed someone armed, they would have the advantage. He tucked the horse's reins into his belt, then adjusted Dárja in his arms. Her mouth fell open as her head rolled back, reminding Válde of a corpse. He closed his mind to the image.

The low door to the farm hut hung open. He kicked it wider with his foot. Peering inside, he called out, "We offer no harm." When no response came, he pulled free the reins from his belt and entered the dark interior.

The hut smelled of ancient smoke and the fresh growth of mushrooms. Chairs were knocked over, broken. In a corner, a wooden pallet remained intact. Válde laid Dárja upon it, easing her into what was hopefully a comfortable position. He went back outside, shielding his eyes from the sun's glare. The horse grazed upon the grasses grown tall in the absence of anyone to tend the farm. He led the horse to the shed attached to the hut. By the smell, it had probably housed goats and was barely big enough for the horse. It would have to do for shelter against prying eyes. *For tonight at least.*

Válde returned to the hut with the supplies from the saddle. Dárja lay in the deep shadows as he'd left her. He sat at her side and felt her face. Her cheeks were hot and damp to the touch. *It could be from the sun's heat*, he thought, holding on to hope. Reason told him it was a sign the wound had turned. He needed to clean it before it was too late. Wood lay tumbled by the hearth. A rusted pot sat on its side.

Válde picked up the pot and blew the dust from its interior. He did not have enough water to waste on washing it. He went outside and cut a handful of young, leafy birch branches. Returning to the hearth, he brushed clean the pot with the leaves. Dárja lay quiet and unmoving. Válde stomped the wooden chairs as if he could, by his action, ward off death. He laid the splintered bits upon what kindling he'd gathered. When he struck his fire steel with his flint, the spark died. He tried again and again. Doubt began to cloud out his confidence in his skills. When the spark finally caught, Válde thanked his fickle gods.

As he sat, waiting for the water to boil, exhaustion edged in all around him. He shook it off. He needed to check Dárja's wound before he could let himself rest. A shattered breath escaped him, filled with more than fatigue. Exhausted, he could do nothing but worry. *What will the next day bring? Will we even make to the next day? What if I manage, with the gods' help, to save Dárja? What will become of us, of me?*

Dárja could return to the north, to her kind. His kind was gone, save Gáral, perhaps. What was he to do? Wander into some village to work upon a farm. Take a wife. Live out his life like any other. He watched the slow rise of Dárja's chest. His breath caught. How could he? With everything that had happened? There could be no wife while he desired another. There could be no other life.

~

Dárja stirred. The threads of the Song of All frayed around her. She tried to hold on to them, to her song, to the connection. It was gone. A remote part of her mind cried out, *I don't want to be alone.* She blinked open her eyes, aware of the hard surface on which she lay. She didn't recall lying down. Light flickered at the edge of her vision. She turned her head. Someone sat by the hearth, head bowed to their knees, arms wrapped around their bent legs. As her eyes focused, Dárja saw the soldier's uniform.

Fear spiked within her chest. She had to get up. Only her body wouldn't respond.

It took all her effort to roll onto her side. Panting with the strain, Dárja managed to push herself to sitting. The world around her spun and she closed her eyes, hoping to make it stop. When she opened them, the soldier still sat near the fire, a deep, rumbling snore rose from him. Dárja tried to stand. A sharp pain stopped her. Her hand went to her side. She cried out at the agonizing touch, her hand coming away wet and sticky.

"Dárja!"

At the sound of her name, she looked up from her bloody hand to see Válde scrambling to his feet.

Then, he was before her, taking her hand in his, his eyes wide. "Gods! The water!" He shot to his feet again, returning to the hearth. "No!"

Dárja could not see beyond his hunched back.

Válde shouted a string of invectives, kicking aside the embers. "I was boiling the water, and I fell asleep."

His anger and contrition confused her. She touched her ribs again and her vision turned black with a fresh wave of pain. Dárja sucked in air through clenched teeth, an inner keening muddling her thoughts.

"Tell me what to do!"

Dárja opened her eyes. Once again, Válde kneeled before her. "The Vijns," she slurred.

Válde took her hand in his. "He is dead. You killed him."

Dárja tried to remember. "The Vijns," she repeated.

"You did it. You killed him," Válde said. His hopeful smile wavered, at odds with the pain in his eyes.

Dárja looked down at her hand in Válde's. His thumb rubbed the calluses crossing her palm. Images flashed in her mind. The man seated in his chair, sneering. The platters piled high with food. His spittle-flecked mouth, begging, "Please."

Válde wiped away the tear that rolled down her cheek. "It is all over now."

"It was over so quickly," she whispered, seeing her blade slide into his soft middle.

Válde squeezed her hand. "You fought like a warrior."

"I am a Taistelijan," she said, closing her eyes, reliving the throbbing terror of fighting off Olmmoš soldiers. *Please, let this be enough*, she prayed to the gods, the Song, and the memories of all those she'd loved.

"I'm so tired," she said, her eyes fluttering open.

"I know," Válde said, his voice thick and low. "I need you to tell me how to care for your wound."

"Is it bad?" she asked, hearing a willing resignation in her question.

"Nothing you cannot heal," he said, sounding too confident for it to be the truth.

"You lie like an Olmmoš," she said, with a weak snort.

He shook his head. "I lie like a Piijkij."

Dárja felt her energy ebbing.

Válde shook her. "Tell me what to do, Dárja."

She roused herself from the whisper of a restful dream, listing off, by rote, what Válde needed to do.

She heard him say, "If I am to clean the wound, I must be able to see it."

Dárja nodded, her fingers fumbling with the ties of her jerkin. She felt Válde's hands cover hers, gently pushing them aside. She didn't protest. In his tender and attentive motions, she recalled a time when she'd lived in a world of certainty. Where she'd expected love and protection with the same thoughtlessness she gave to her heartbeat and her breath. A time before she learned what it meant to question herself.

"You saved me," she said.

Válde paused. Her jerkin hung from one shoulder. "This may hurt," he said. He lifted her left arm.

She winced. "Why did you do it?"

On his knees before her he said, "Edo found you. Gáral helped me to get you out of the Stronghold."

Dárja saw them both in her mind's eye. Edo's bashful concern. Gáral's cold scrutiny. "Where are they now?"

"Can you raise your arms or should I cut the tunic?" he asked, not meeting her eyes.

She unbuckled her belt, her gaze wavering on Válde's features. Even in the shadows of the hut, the freckles on his face drifted like the stars at night. She gritted her teeth as she used her right hand to raise her left arm. Válde's eyes did not leave hers. In the gloom, she could not see their green color so like the springy moss of cool places.

"Why did you do it?" he asked.

To Dárja's ear, his question yearned for an uncomplicated answer. She didn't have one. "I had something to prove," she said, speaking her deepest truth.

The cloth of her soiled tunic passed before her eyes. The fabric, worn thin by use and wash, couldn't shield her from Válde's penetrating gaze. She held her breath to stave off the pain—the pain of her wound and that of her heart. *I didn't want this*, she thought. But this was who she was. Released from the tunic, Dárja sat before Válde, unable to hide.

"I saved you because your fate does not lie upon that field," he said.

Dárja's skin prickled with the twilight's chill. This time, it was she who couldn't meet Válde's directness. She lay back down, her bare skin finding all the rough edges of the pallet.

"Pour as much boiled water over the wound as you can spare," she said.

Válde hesitated, caught between action and staying by her side.

"Let it dry with the air. There's nothing upon either of us clean enough to cover a wound," she said.

He squeezed her hand and looked away as if he were to blame. The warmth was like the promise of the sun. She pulled his hand to her lips. She tasted the salt of sweat and the iron of blood.

"I have nothing left to prove," she said, her voice wavering. "To myself. To anyone."

CHAPTER FORTY-EIGHT

ARNEJ PACED AT THE edge of the clearing. His eyes ranged back and forth across the open ground. It was the same piece of land he and Dárja had crossed when they had fled the Stronghold. She'd waited for him just as he waited for Kalek. *It's been too long*, he thought. *I should've gone.* Even if Kalek was more skilled in the Song of All. *What if it had failed him?* Marnej instinctively sent his song out into the All as if testing its presence. He felt the thrum all around him. The beauty of the intertwined choruses did little to stave off his lurking doubts.

Part of him feared Kalek would find Dárja. Another part worried he would find nothing. Even if they did locate Dárja, could he bring them safely to Karvaluz, as he'd promised? This far south it made more sense to go by sea. The problem was, Marnej wasn't sure he could repeat his original journey. *No, we must go north, on the land route*, he reasoned, praying Úlla had managed to convince the Elders. *Otherwise*, he thought, then couldn't face what it would mean.

"Úlla can do it," he said aloud, as if by giving voice to this assertion, he could make it true. If any could, it would be her. He conjured an image of Úlla as he'd last seen her. The determination to honor her debt to Dárja had made her eyes flash with the fire that lit her forge. She'd made it clear to him he wouldn't tell her what to do. The fierceness of her ways made him smile.

As this wave of confidence ebbed, Marnej heard the words he'd wanted to hear.

I am daughter of the gods.
I am sister among the Jápmemeahttun.
I started my life at my Origin with sadness and joy as my companions.

Dárja's song didn't finish. He didn't know what to make of it. Maybe it had trailed off to where he couldn't hear it. But he'd heard her. He hadn't imagined it. It was Dárja. She was alive. He scoured his memory of her song, trying to find any clue within it. There was nothing. No image. No sense of where she was or if she was in danger.

Marnej began to pace again. *How long should I wait?* he agonized. He needed to take action. What kind of action he didn't know.

∽

When Kalek finally came into view, he was at a run across the boggy fen. Marnej waved to him. His elation at having heard Dárja's song had turned to a cold pit in his stomach. *She's alive*, he reminded himself over and over again until Kalek stood before him, doubled over, panting.

"I heard her," Marnej said.

Kalek sprang up. "When?"

"Just before you appeared. I thought you might have found her. Did you hear her?"

"No." Kalek swore. "Did you get anything from her song?"

Marnej shook his head. "It didn't finish."

"If she is injured, she cannot travel far," the healer reasoned, looking about him as if his sight could penetrate the forest. He swore again, gathering up his binna's reins. "She could be any-where within these woods. Dying."

"What did you see inside?" Marnej asked, fighting against his instinct to act.

"What does it matter?"

"Tell me."

"They are cleaning up the aftermath," Kalek said with a visi-ble shiver. He met Marnej's gaze. "She could not have done it all by herself."

"The Piijkij," Marnej said. "She could've been with them."

Kalek's eyes glazed. "They were burying the bodies out back," he said. "I overheard the soldiers. They said the Jápmemeahttun, who had attacked, had escaped."

"If Dárja got away with the Piijkij?" Marnej wondered out loud.

Kalek came back to himself. "Where would they go?" he demanded.

Marnej thought about the area. "Hemmela is too far," he said. His eyes flashed up to meet Kalek's. "The Brethren's Fortress. They'd lay claim to it."

∽

"Are you sure they would head for the fortress?" Kalek asked, scanning the forest as they rode.

"I'm not sure of anything," Marnej said, his frustration growing.

"How much farther?" Kalek pressed.

These woods were familiar to Marnej, having grown up in them. "Beyond the rocky outcrop there and the stand of trees behind, there's a farm. From the farm it's maybe two leagues to the fortress."

The healer nodded, urging his binna ahead.

"Wait, Kalek," Marnej called after him. "We can't just go storming in there."

"I've done it before," Kalek said.

"I have no idea how many of the Brethren remain or how many will be awaiting us," Marnej said, spurring his reindeer forward. Coming alongside Kalek, the healer's proud profile suggested he wouldn't be swayed. Marnej tried once again. "All I know is there were Piijkij in soldiers' uniforms, fighting against the Vijns's soldiers, and Válde carried Dárja out of the Great Valley."

"It does not matter how many of them there are," Kalek said.

"Because you think we will walk into the fortress within the Song of All and take Dárja out with us?" Marnej asked, unable to keep the bite of skepticism from his question.

"With or without the Song, it does not matter. If she is there, then I will be by her side."

"I didn't travel all this way to let you get yourself killed."

"I did not ask you to come."

Marnej fell silent, letting his rancor settle.

As they wound their way through a stand of birch, Marnej saw the beginning of the farm fields. They were fallow. No smoke rose from the hut.

"It looks like they've left or have been run off," he said aloud, glad to have something to say that wouldn't lead to further argument. "Perhaps it's the Vijns's work. Or they may've left of their own accord."

"Look at the ground." Kalek pointed, his body tense as he gestured ahead of them.

Deep hoof-prints marred the untilled soil. The crushed grasses had not sprung back yet.

"They are recent," Marnej said, looking ahead to the hut. "Only one horse."

Their eyes met. Kalek's hope sprung to life, unspoken.

After a moment's pause, Marnej said, "We should approach cautiously, even within the Song."

Kalek gave his binna's reins a light snap. The reindeer rambled forward in a slow rolling gait. Marnej followed, listening for anything to suggest a trap. The Song could veil them from detection; his training told him not to rely on any one weapon.

They circled the hut on their mounts. Kalek pointed to the shed. With the noonday's glare, Marnej couldn't see into the darkened interior.

Kalek went around the corner of the hut. When Marnej reached him, the almai had already dismounted.

The scent of smoke hung about the air, putting Marnej on guard. "Kalek," he hissed, "the door of the hut is closed." The almai ignored him.

Marnej dismounted, bringing his binna over to Kalek. "I'll go. It's better if an Olmmoš comes through the door and not an Immortal."

Kalek frowned, then took the proffered reins. Marnej rested his hand on the blade at his side, then released the hold on his song. The silence of the Olmmoš world, his world, stunned him. He staggered, shaking himself free of the immediate desire to reclaim the Song of All. He worried he might miss Dárja's song while he followed ghosts and false tracks in the human realm. The sharp crack of his pommel against the door fractured the air. Inside, a muffled sound rose, then fell away.

Marnej pushed open the door, his weapon ready. Sunlight flooded in through the threshold. His eye followed the beam of light to a pallet in the far corner where a prone figure lay. He entered, his heart pounding in his ears. The sound of metal against metal shattered the hush. Marnej's arm quaked in the aftermath of a brutal blow. He pivoted out of the way in time to save himself being cleaved in two. Even so, his eyes couldn't make out the shape in the shadow.

"Kalek!" he screamed, his eyes as useless as if he were blind. "Soldiers!" he shouted, catching a glimpse of a blade and the yellow, blood-spattered sleeve of a Believer's uniform. Marnej spun, lashing out with his sword. He felt the blade catch on something solid. The soldier grunted. Marnej raised his weapon, the outline of the man sharpened. He stepped forward to attack.

"No! Marnej!" the unmistakable voice of Dárja called out.

He looked to the pallet. In the shaft of light, Dárja lay on her side, her arm reaching out. But not to him.

Kalek came charging through the open door, his sword drawn, ready to cut down the soldier that Marnej saw was Válde.

"Kalek!" Dárja called out, the name made shaky by surprise.

The healer pushed past both Marnej and Válde. Falling on his knees before Dárja, he brought her into his arms. She cried out in pain. Válde lunged in her direction, then stopped short when Marnej's sword crossed his path.

Kalek murmured soft reassurances to Dárja as he brushed the hair from her face. *She's kept it short*, Marnej noted. It suited her. He recalled her sad expression when he'd laid her beautiful, dark braid in her hand. Kalek shifted back. The sun lit her chiseled profile. Marnej's eyes followed the sharp angle of her nose down to her squared chin. Her once-soft lips were stretched taut in agony. These lips had once kissed him and he'd felt as if the gods had taken him body and soul. But that moment had passed. And while sadness shrouded his heart, a greater hope filled him. They'd gotten past enmity and mistrust before. Perhaps they would both be able to find forgiveness.

Kalek whirled on Válde, shattering the stillness in the room. "Are you the one who cared for her wounds?"

The man raised his chin. "Yes."

Marnej stared at Válde, thinking of how he'd once called him brother in the Brethren of Hunters. He'd heard in the man's answer not the fear of failure, but rather the desperation of needing to prevail. He followed Válde's gaze to where Kalek had exposed Dárja's wound. Marnej steeled himself, expecting to see the rot of flesh turned foul. What he saw was a swath of birch bark bound to her exposed ribs.

Kalek's booming voice shook Marnej out of his stupor. "Do not stand like useless rocks. Get me more wood for the fire. And water from the well." To Válde he said, "I need more birch bark and fresh moss to replace what is here."

~

Válde looked from Marnej to the one called Kalek. "You are the healer."

The man nodded. His pale hair shimmered in the light.

"She spoke of you," Válde said. He untied the pouch at his belt and handed it to Kalek. "I foraged these for her. It is not much."

Válde's arm fell back to his side. *It is finally over.* Suddenly, he was done with it all. Done with fighting for a past which no longer existed and of hoping for a future he would not live to see.

The healer glanced inside the pouch. "It will help."

Válde turned on his heel.

"Wait," Marnej called after him.

He could not make himself turn back. He stooped under the doorframe, taking a step out into the waning light of day.

"You can't leave," Marnej said.

Válde continued, walking to the shed.

"You saved her so she must mean something to you."

"It is for the best."

"And when she wakes up and asks for you. What then?"

"Tell her I am gone. Tell her I am dead."

"She deserves more than that. She nearly died for you."

Válde whirled around to confront Marnej's arrogant challenge. He wanted to yell at him, push him, and make him take back his words. But Marnej had spoken the truth and this dug under Válde's skin.

"She deserves more than I can ever give her," he said finally.

Marnej shook his head, denying Válde the end he wanted. "If you're what she wants, then that's enough."

"No!" Válde said, immediately regretting his forceful tone. "There is no place for me." A creeping sadness threatened his resolve. He sounded weak and desperate to his own ears.

"Believe what you will," Marnej said, his expression hard beyond his years. "The Vijns has ordered his soldiers north to burn the Pohjola. If you can't stay for love, then stay and honor your debt to Dárja. See us safely north, so we can save all the Jápmemeahttun."

Válde shook his head. "The Vijns is dead."

The boy snorted. "Where one man died, another took his place."

Válde staggered back. *Everything we did. Everything we hoped for. Wasted.* He thought of Dárja, lying on the pallet. He owed her more than anyone could ever know.

He raised his gaze to meet Marnej's intent stare. The setting rays glinted off the cold determination in his eyes. *So much like Irjan.* Aloud, he asked, "How do you plan to save the Jápmea?"

"We will leave. Disappear, once and for all," Marnej said

～

Kalek held Dárja's hand in his. She was cool to the touch. "I must clean your wound," he said, holding back the fear he was too late.

"The Olmmoš High Priest," she said in a far-off voice.

"He's dead," Kalek said, carefully removing the leather binding.

"I killed him," she said. "I had to do it."

Kalek stripped back the bark and moss. Deep and angry, at least the wound had not festered. He thanked the gods for their mercy. "I know," he said, going to the fire to retrieve the water he had set to boil.

"I couldn't come home. I had to set things right," she said.

Kalek felt as if the weight of a mountain had crashed down upon him. He struggled to get enough air. Holding the pot of water, he turned to face her. His healer's mind told him he must treat the wound. His father's heart wanted to wrap Dárja in his arms and never let her go again.

Her rasping voice shook as she said, "I am so sorry."

Kalek rushed to her side. His throat tightened against sound and breath. He saw tears welling in her squeezed-shut eyes. "You have done nothing for which you must apologize," he said.

"I thought I could protect them." Her whisper caught. "I was so sure." She began to shake. Her eyes flew open, her fingers digging into Kalek's arm. "I heard Úlla screaming. And I could do nothing. I did nothing. I had no weapon."

Grief poured out of her in a deluge. Kalek pulled her into his arms, shushing her, feeling how fragile she was beneath her taut muscles. *Like a wounded bird.*

"Úlla lives," he said. "Her mánná lives." He repeated this until Dárja's sobs subsided into hiccups. He held her away from him to look at her. Red-eyed and gaunt, she was precious to him.

"Úlla is Forge Master. Tuá is Márgu's guide mother. You protected them. You gave them more than the chance to live. You gave us all hope."

Dárja began to shake her head. Kalek cradled her gaunt cheeks in his hands. "I cannot say what tomorrow will bring or what any day in the future might bring. I can say that I will always stand with you. I am your father. You are my daughter. Nothing will ever change that."

EPILOGUE

ÚLLA LOOKED UP AT the imposing mountains before her. A trail of brown earth cut its way through rocks as black and endless as night in the season of snow. They would need to leave their carts behind here. The youngest and oldest would ride. The rest would walk. Their reindeer would carry all that belonged to them of their world.

She shaded her eyes to watch a lone hawk circling. She listened to its song, curious about what it saw from on high. Could it see their future? She could not. Ravna could and this was good enough for her.

Marnej's map lay next to Úlla's chest. Her heart beat against it, sometimes hopeful, other times fearful. When doubt claimed her, she held on to the feeling of her song.

I am the daughter of the gods, made of flesh and fire.
I carry the heart of all my kind within.
My will is strong.
My guide is ready.
My journey stretches beyond the heavens.

It was the song of Úlla, neither nieddaš nor almai nor rivgu. She did not know how much longer her song would remain within the All. But she had been Outside. She knew what it was like. She had thought Marnej a fool for tasking her to lead their kind so far from home. Now she understood she was the only one among the Jápmemeahttun who could. There would come a time when there would be no Song of All. She knew what it felt like. When the others faltered, lost without the connection they had always known, she could be by their side. She would tender the comfort Dárja had given to her. *To be outside one's understanding is terrifying. To have someone beside you to help you go on is the difference between madness and possibility.*

Úlla looked back at the trailing line of Jápmemeahttun. She saw Birtá's round outline, leading the kitchen wagon. From here, she could imagine the nieddaš devising a plan to feed all as they journeyed. Behind her, Tuá walked with the livestock, a switch in her hand for errant wanderers. Márgu's dark head peeked over Tuá's shoulder, the babe's growing body swaddled in a sling. Ravna rode with the Elders near the front. As Noaidi, she could have had the comfort of a cart. Instead, she had let the boaris rest while they could. Úlla could not see Ello. Doubtless, wherever Ello was she would have a joke and smile for whomever rode with her.

Had anyone told Úlla she would guide the Jápmemeahttun beyond all their imagined borders, she would have laughed in their face. But in the time it had taken the sun to reach its apex, she had come to understand that their destinies were made of more than the songs which had defined their lives. She could not imagine what their future would look like but she hoped they would all live to see what might be possible.

CAST OF CHARACTERS

Jápmemeahttun

Aillun	nieddaš	oktoeadni to Dárja
Ávrá	nieddaš	weaver/Kalek's love interest
Birtá	nieddaš	cook
Dárja	nieddaš	Aillun's daughter
Ello	nieddaš	farmer
Einár	boaris	leader/Noaidi
Gáre	nieddaš	Ávrá's guide daughter
Kalek	Healer	Aillun's mate/Okta's assistant
Kálle	almai	blacksmith/Úlla's lover
Kearte	nieddaš	Kalek's guide child
Lejá	nieddaš	traveling to her Origin to give birth
Márgu	mánáid	Úlla's birth child
Okta	Healer	former Taistelijan
Rássa	boaris	Elder
Ravna	nieddaš	tanner
Tuá	nieddaš	butcher
Úlla	nieddaš	blacksmith

Aeopo

Aage	from Halakzan	traveling tradesman

Irkạti

Georyus	from Karkut	Forge Master

Olmmoš

Áigin	Order of Believers	spy/agent for the Vijns
Álet	female child	Hassa villager
Bávvál	Order of Believers	High Priest/Vijns
Beartu	Brethren of Hunters	Piijkij/rogue
Begá	Árvet's older brother	Hassa villager
Daigu	Brethren of Hunters	Piijkij/rogue/deserter
Dávgon	Brethren of Hunterss	leader/Avr
Edo	Brethren of Hunters	Piijkij/rogue
Feles	Brethren of Hunters	Piijkij/rogue
Gáral	Brethren of Hunters	Piijkij/rogue
Hárri	Order of Believers	soldier
Herko	Brethren of Hunters	Piijkij /rogue
Irjan	Brethren of Hunters	Piijkij
Jonsá	Order of Believers	soldier
Joret	Order of Believers	soldier
Jusse	from the southern sea	fisherman

Olmmoš (cont.)

Lávrrahaš	from Karvaluz	tavernkeeper
Marnej	Brethren of Hunters	Irjan's son
Matti	Order of Believers	soldier
Mures	Brethren of Hunters	Piijkij/rogue
Niilán	Order of Believers	soldier/commander
Osku	Order of Believers	soldier
Redde	Brethren of Hunters	Piijkij/rogue
Rikkar	Order of Believers	Apotti/Priest of Hemmela
Siggur	Order of Believers	Current Priest of Hemmela
Válde	Brethren of Hunters	Piijkij/rogue

GLOSSARY OF ENGLISH TERMS

Breath of Gods: strong westerly winds.

Brethren of Hunters: group whose original function was to hunt and kill the Jápmemeahttun.

Chamber of Passings: ceremonial group charged with overseeing the Jápmemeahttun life bringers.

clasp arms/clasped arms: greeting and parting gesture.

Council of Elders: the guiding group of Jápmemeahttun.

Court of Counselors: advisors to the High Priest of the Believers.

end time: the period of time when the Jápmemeahttun boaris experience the change in their body that signals their end.

fire berries: peppercorns.

Fortress of the Brethren of Hunters/Brethren's Fortress: fortified encampment of the Brethren of Hunters.

handmate: spouse for the Olmmoš.

heart-pledge: to be "in love/monogamous/together as an understood partnership" for the Jápmemeahttun.

High Priest of the Believers: leader of the Order of Believers; theocratic/military leader of the Olmmoš.

Hunter: English term for a Piijkij; capitalized to distinguish from an ordinary hunter.

hutkeeper: wayside Olmmoš tavernkeeper.

league: measurement approximately equal to three miles.

life bringer: term used by Jápmemeahttun to refer to the individuals involved in the birthing process.

moon cycles: how the Jápmemeahttun and Olmmoš mark the passing of a month.

Northland: geographical term associated with the Pohjola and the Jápmemeahttun.

Order of Believers: religious hierarchy developed by the Olmmoš after their rebellion against the Jápmemeahttun; became a theocracy.

Origin: birthing area for individual Jápmemeahttun.

Outside: Jápmemeahttun concept of everything "outside" the Song of All; the Olmmoš world.

quickening: Jápmemeahttun concept of pregnancy.

season of snow: how Olmmoš and Jápmemeahttun mark the passing of one year.

Southern Teeth: the reef shoals in the southern sea protecting the fishing waters of Davvieana.

spirit stream: the energetic force released at the death of a Jápmemeahttun boaris as part of the birth process.

Stronghold of the Believers: fortified temple for the religious seat of power.

travelers' hut: wayside tavern.

JÁPMEMEAHTTUN/OLMMOŠ GLOSSARY

Many of the words used in the Legacy of the Heavens trilogy are derived from various Saami dialects spoken in northern Finland, Norway, Sweden, and extreme northwestern Russia. The definitions in this glossary reflect the meanings as related to the books and are not intended to be a dictionary of Saami dialects.

áddjá: grandfather and honorific for an elderly Olmmoš male
almai: male Jápmemeahttun
Avr: leader of the Brethren of Hunters
badjeolmmoš: reindeer herder
bieba: short form of biebmoeadni; term of endearment like "mom"
biebmoeadni: guide mother
binna: herd of reindeer; used as singular and plural for the animal
boaris: the old ones among the Jápmemeahttun males
chuoika: mosquito
Cuoŋománnu: snow crust month (April)
dákti: three-day ritual of contemplation for a nieddaš to become an almai
Davvieana: Olmmoš name for their land
Geassemánnu: summer month (June/July)
Guovassonásti: Life Star; its cycle marks the ages of Jápmemeahttun individuals
Hassa: name of a village
Hemmela: name of a village
Jápmea: Olmmoš name for the Jápmemeahttun (slang pejorative)
Jápmemeahttun: tribal name for the original inhabitants of the area

joik: personal song (chant); story of an Olmmoš individual (plural: joiken)

juhka: alcoholic drink

latnja: gathering hall

lavvu: leather tent

máksu: tithe/tax

mánáid: children

mánná: child

Mehjala: name of a village

miehkki: sword

niibi: knife

muorji: berry

nieddaš: female Jápmemeahttun

Noaidi: head of the Jápmemeahttun Council of Elders

oktoeadni: birth mother

oarri: squirrel

Olmmoš: name for the "human" tribe; man or men

Oso: name of a village

Piijkij: title for a member of the Brethren of Hunters

Pohjola: Northland; literally "north" in Finnish

rivgu: name for an outcast Jápmemeahttun

Skaina: name of a village

spiidni: pig

sávdni: steam bath

Taistelijan: title for Jápmemeahttun warrior

Ullmea: name of a village

uulo: plant tea used for medicinal purposes

Vijns: High Priest of the Order of Believers

GLOSSARY OF
SOUTHERN LANDS TERMS

Aeopo: people from Halakzan
amiku: friend
amikuz: friends
arbu: tree
Bissmená: language of the Bissmeni people of Morallom
Bissmeni: the people of Morallom
dua: other/another
boné: thank you
boloj: fresh water/clean water
egrada: small
ekapori: to rise
ekveduz: messenger horses
evalu: draft horse
Estora Crossing: the bridge crossing from Morallom to Nossalmi
Falkuj: the Hawk Peoples to the far east of Karkut
forrá: sweet, mulled red wine
fremdu: foreigner
fuelluz: bellows
Glaciuvortoz: "frozen words": Bissmená word for the language spoken in the Northlands
grada: big
Halakzan: lands to the south of Morallom and southwest of Karkut
hazz: whoa
Irkat: language of Irkati people of Karkut; a variation on Bissmená with an emphasis on hard sounds
Irkati: the people of Karkut

Josu's lament: the wind that comes from the east through the gorge that separates Nossalmi in the north from Morallom in the south

kapralu: spiced, dried goat meat

Karkut: landlocked region to the southeast of Morallom

Karvaluz: name of the biggest settlement in Karkut

kreito: creature/monster

martelu: hammer

mielakvu: alcoholic drink made from fermented lemon and honey

Morallom: region bordering the northern sea

na: from

nesdané: you are welcome

or: to be

Pasatu: Late spring festival in Karvaluz to celebrate the winds that bring traders

taƙi: look/observe

ur: sea

urkreito: sea monster

urbej: city

urĝu: hurry

virta: honorable

virulu: man

vojetu: alley

ACKNOWLEDGMENTS:

I am blessedly indebted to the vision of my agent, Mark Gottlieb, and the editorial team at Night Shade Books/Skyhorse Publishing, past and present: Jeremy Lassen, Cory Allyn, Oren Eades, and Paula Guran. I am wholeheartedly beholden to the following, for gifts too numerous to list: my husband, Benjamin Thompson, my parents, Kay and Don Myers, the Castro Writers' Cooperative, Shana Mahaffey, Sage Lee, and Melina Selverston-Scher. I am also indebted to Artemis Grey and Jennifer Adam for their equine knowledge. Any shortcoming is my own and not that of his noble animal.

For the past ten years, I have lived with the characters of The Legacy of the Heavens. We have found our way forward through both life and plot challenges. In essence, we have grown together. I am eternally grateful for what each of these characters has taught me, not only about themselves, but also about myself. Each book in the series gifted me a greater understanding of this story. Originally, I thought I was writing a story about elves—without using the word "elf." It turned out that I was actually writing about the parent/child relationships of individuals who just happened to be elves. I began writing what would become

The Song of All in 2009, a year after my father died. It would take another eight years before I realized that I was, in many ways, writing about him: who he was and who he wanted to be. I hope I have done him justice in honoring his journey, as well as those of all the characters in this series. They have rich lives beyond the last page of this book.

TINA LeCOUNT MYERS is a writer, artist, independent historian, and surfer. Born in Mexico to expat-bohemian parents, she grew up on Southern California tennis courts with a prophecy hanging over her head: her parents hoped she'd one day be an author. Tina has a Master of Arts degree in history from the University of California, Santa Cruz. She lives in San Francisco with her adventurer husband and two loud Siamese cats.